I0596313

Pretty Lies

Book 1

A New Adult Dystopian Novel
by Jessica Scurlock

Cover design by Martin Scurlock
Edited by Emma O'Connell
First Edition
ISBN 978-1-7348368-9-9 (hardback)
ISBN 978-1-7348368-8-2 (paperback)
Printed in the United States of America
Visit my website at jessicascurlockbooks.com
Instagram: @jess_scurlockauthor

For everyone who said I couldn't do it.

"Don't stand out or they'll destroy you
Words are sharp and filled with poison
Every step that you take forward
They'll pull you back a thousand more
So give up your imagination
Take the pill, it's just sedation
Be a member of society"
                        - *Written by Wolves*

1. Bleed

I mash my palms against my ears as one final blood-curdling scream erupts from his victim. The cracking of bone splits the night, the echoes burrowing into my skull.

The entrance to the alley is diagonal from my spot behind the dumpster. Tears burn my eyes, and I hold my breath as the heavy footsteps return, accompanied by the sickening sound of flesh scraping against asphalt. My legs ache from crouching for so long, and the wind nips at my exposed face.

It's three hours past curfew, and everyone else is tucked safely away in their homes.

The footsteps pause at the other side of the dumpster, and my blood turns as cold as the brutal December air. The stench of blood and cigarettes lingers so heavily even the wind can't carry it away. My pulse thunders in my ears. He starts toward the street again, and I retreat deeper into the shadows. Falling back on my bottom, I pull my knees to my chest, trying to make myself as small as possible. He crosses my line of vision, his back to me, dragging his lifeless victim with him. His fingers are tangled in her long hair, and a dark trail follows her body. Bile rises in my throat as he jerks her out into the street. With a grunt, he hoists her over his shoulder and disappears into the night.

It's a good five minutes before I can convince myself to stand. My stomach is still churning and my legs feel too weak to hold me. Frantically, I check my surroundings, expecting him to come back any second, but the city is still. Pulling my hood over my head, I abandon my shelter. The ground is slick with the woman's blood. My panic grows. There has to be an officer out here somewhere; they're always patrolling the streets after curfew. Someone has to have heard the screams. If not an officer, then someone nearby in their home—not that they would come out. I have half a mind to track down an officer myself and report what I witnessed, but that would lead to questions as to why I was out past curfew—an offense punishable by two weeks of re-education.

I make my way out of the alley, cautious not to step in the blood. Not a single officer or curious citizen is in sight. Streetlights cast their eerie orange glow over the city, and the surrounding buildings are locked up until dawn. Snow begins to fall again, which means the plows will be sent out within the next couple of hours. Keeping my head low, I run home, unable to shake the prickling sensation creeping up my neck.

After tiptoeing into the dark apartment, I slip off my snow-covered boots and coat. Our small three-bedroom home is quiet, just as I expected—I've mastered sneaking out without my mom or brother ever knowing—but the familiar aroma of pumpkin and vanilla fills my nostrils.

Someone's awake.

A strip of dim light comes from the kitchen above the sink, and once my stockinged feet meet the linoleum, I flick on the main light. Mom stands before me, arms crossed over her chest, her pale pink lips twisted into a frown.

"Where the hell were you?" she demands. Her tone is harsh, but her vibrant hazel eyes—identical to mine—betray her. She's more worried than angry.

Part of my brain doesn't yet understand that I am home and safe. My fight-or-flight instincts are still in full swing, and adrenaline courses through my veins. Every beat of my heart echoes in my ears. All I can do is stare at her and focus on the sweet smell wafting through the apartment until I calm down. Mom taps a bare foot against the linoleum.

I attempt to shrug off her question, but it comes out more like a shiver. "Out."

She arches a perfectly plucked eyebrow, awaiting a better explanation.

"I was just taking a walk. I'm fine."

Her face softens, and she draws in a deep breath. "Ivy, you know the rules. If you're caught outside you'll be taken to—"

"I know. Re-education." I roll my eyes. The consequence has been drilled into my head every day since infancy, and my father having been a police officer makes it harder to forget.

"I worry about you. You and Liam." She closes her eyes and massages her temples. "You know just as well as I do how hard it's been these past couple of years, and we're finally getting back on track."

I drop my gaze to the floor. No matter how hard we try, we'll never go back to being normal. The three-year anniversary of my father's disappearance is just four months away, and every day that passes is a painful reminder to all three of us. Our world fell apart when he left; Mom had to work longer hours—seven to eight days in a row—at her flower shop, and Liam picked up more shifts at his job. He even delayed his plans to move out so he could help us, both financially and emotionally. And while he spends less and less time at home, at twenty-one, he hasn't mentioned leaving any time soon. I've been a legal adult myself for a year now, but I can't bear the thought of leaving Mom behind either. Family always sticks together.

"I thought you could use this after being out in the cold," Mom says.

I look up, and she passes me a mug of her homemade vanilla pumpkin spice tea. Offering me a sad smile, she brushes a strand of blonde hair behind my ear.

"Thanks, Mom," I say, taking a sip. The familiar wave of warm liquid grounds me. *I'm home. I'm safe.*

She kisses the top of my head and whispers "I love you" before shuffling off to bed.

I finish half of the tea and dump the rest in the sink, my stomach protesting at the thought of consuming any more. Shutting off the light, I make my way to my room. Down the hall, Liam's obnoxious snoring rattles his door. As annoying as it is, I've grown accustomed to it and can't imagine drifting to sleep accompanied by any other sound.

I slip into my room, across from his, and dig through my dresser, desperate to escape my current clothing and the filth I feel it's absorbed. Tossing it into a corner, I change into fresh clothes. As I move toward my bed, I catch my reflection in the full-length mirror standing next to it. My gaze falls to the faded white scar across my right collarbone, and my fingertips find their way to it, caressing the permanent mark as my mind is invaded with the memory. It was the night after Dad left.

I jerk my hand and shake my head, pushing the memory to the back of my mind where it belongs.

The tremor in my hands has subsided, but I can't shake the fear and paranoia still worming itself through me. I turn off the lights and crawl into bed, hoping for some sort of comfort to present itself in my dreams. But images continue to flash before my eyes like a movie skipping scenes: The woman running into the alley behind me, screaming, begging me to help her. I'm frozen, useless. Out of nowhere, he appears, completely focused on her. And I dive behind the dumpster.

Those last few seconds before I was fully concealed, I swear I felt his eyes on me. A shiver creeps up my spine as the image of her lifeless body fills my mind. Nausea overcomes me again, and I swallow the bile and tea back down.

Hours pass; my nerves are shot. I focus on Liam's snoring and my own breathing.

I'm safe, I remind myself. *I'm safe.*

2. Roots

The blaring alarm startles me from an all-too-real nightmare. Groggily, I sit up and turn it off. Four hours of sleep is nowhere near enough time to recover. The early morning sun pours in through the window across the room, and recollections of last night flow in with it. The stench of blood and cigarettes faintly lingers, mixed with the smell of freshly brewed coffee.

Footsteps briskly make their way around the apartment, along with melodic humming. My aunt is coming over today, and knowing Mom, she's cleaning our already-spotless apartment. With a groan, I push my blankets off and leave the warmth of my cocoon. I rummage through my closet, not yet fully awake, in hopes of finding an outfit that will deflect snarky comments from my mother's overly opinionated sister.

Once dressed, I reluctantly abandon my safe haven. Mom is scrubbing the counters in the kitchen while humming her made-up tune. Candles flicker in the unblemished living room, filling our home with a sweetness that mixes with the bitter scent of coffee. The two sofas hold freshly fluffed pillows, and the glass coffee table between them is free of streaks and clutter. As I venture farther into the living room, the floor creaks, announcing my presence.

Mom glances over her shoulder. "Coffee's ready for you, V."

I smile at the childhood nickname my father always used. She pulls a mug from the cupboard above her and hands it to me as I pass by. I prepare my drink and lean against the counter, watching as Mom gives the white countertop another spray of all-purpose cleaner and continues to scrub. Her dark brown curls are pulled up into a high ponytail with a frayed elastic band. She's already changed into a deep purple long-sleeved dress, and I can tell she took extra time on her makeup this morning. Despite our financial status, she's always masqueraded as one of the Elite. We're not exactly poor—no one is anymore—but Mom has always had a taste for a more luxurious lifestyle.

"Don't you think you're going a little overboard?" I half-joke as I sip on my piping hot drink.

Mom chuckles. "Maybe a little, but a clean home puts my mind at ease. And besides…" She pauses, attempting to eradicate an imaginary stain. "Since Kyle… passed away, I want to make sure Naomi is as comfortable as possible."

"I'm sure the cleanliness of our apartment is the least of her worries."

She trades her sponge and spray bottle for a broom and dustpan. "Why don't you get your brother up? It's late."

The green digital numbers above the stove show that it's only five minutes past nine, but Mom is all about punctuality.

"I'm up," a sleepy voice calls from the hallway.

Liam pushes past me to pour himself some coffee, and I wrinkle my nose as he drinks it black.

"You look like shit," he tells me.

"Thanks, asshole. You too, but that's a regular occurrence."

Squeezing past him, I grab a basket of clothes from the tiny, closet-like laundry room at the back of the narrow kitchen. He moves out of the way for me to pass through again.

"I can't believe you're actually letting her over here," Liam says.

I'm barely in the living room. Despite my mind telling me to ignore him and continue to my room, I turn around.

Mom stops sweeping and narrows her eyes at him. "What's that supposed to mean?"

The atmosphere is suddenly electrified with tension. Taking another sip of coffee, Liam glares at her, and Mom's demeanor hardens.

He shrugs as if it's nothing, but his eyes remain fierce. "Just after hearing what people say about her, I'm surprised you're still even in contact. You wouldn't want to ruin your reputation, would you?"

I suppress the urge to groan. Not this again.

Liam changed when our dad left. He closed himself off for a while, and when he finally emerged from the dark place he was in, he wasn't the same. He became colder, more distant, mostly toward our mother. I know he blames Mom for Dad's leaving. Maybe part of me does, too, but I don't care to pick fights with her like he does.

The government got involved when Dad didn't show up for work. Their grueling interrogations consumed our lives for weeks. Investigators scoured every zone of the Northern Unity, and the Enlightened Society kept a close eye on us and everyone we came in contact with for the first year. Their all-seeing eye has let up since then, but we're well aware that they're still lurking, waiting for his return. Nearly three years later, there's still no sign of him. It's like he vanished from the world.

But Liam's smart-ass comment isn't about the mystery of our missing father. Two months ago to date, Naomi's husband died. Now, our city is buzzing with theories of his death. An investigation was launched, but the case was closed fairly quickly. Police agreed there was foul play, but they were unable to pin a suspect. Whoever did it covered their tracks well. No funeral was held—those are only for the rich. Naomi is said to be the only one who saw the body, aside from the officials who took the case. Allegedly, she came home from work and found their house had been broken into. Valuables were missing, and Kyle was found dead from a gunshot wound to his head.

The public was furious. Some people accused the police of being lazy and not wanting to thoroughly investigate. Then came the rumors that Naomi did it herself. They gained traction, and people began to question Mom, assuming she knew something about it. She didn't indulge in the gossip, but she didn't defend her sister either. In fact, this is the first time to my knowledge that she's attempted to communicate with Naomi since that night.

Mom takes a deep breath. "I know the terrible things people are saying." She's surprisingly calm, but there's an edge to her voice. "People can think whatever they want, but she's my sister, and I want to help her."

"How very noble of you," Liam says sarcastically, grabbing his own laundry basket and storming to his room.

The door shuts and I exhale. Mom returns to her chores without another word, her face displaying hurt and something else I can't pin down. It's hard to believe Liam was once Mom's golden child; they were inseparable. I want to say something to comfort her, but I can't find the words. I settle for, "I love you, Mom."

"I love you, too," she replies without looking at me.

I escape to my own room, pushing the door closed with my foot. Thoughts race through my cluttered mind while I fold and store my clothes. When the basket is empty, I throw last night's clothes in it and push it into my closet. The sight of them makes me sick. Trying to forget it all, I straighten up my mostly empty room. No matter how much I try to distract myself, though, the murder creeps its way back to the front of my mind. I need to tell someone. Anyone. Mom seems to have a lot going on right now, so I don't want to add to her plate. Authorities are out of the question, unless I want to face the consequences of being out so late.

I've never been re-educated, but I've seen people who have. They're few and far between, but they're out there. One man in particular comes to mind. I met him when I was maybe fourteen, while I was helping Mom at her shop. He was a regular who came in every Monday and Friday and purchased a single pink carnation for his wife. He was soft-spoken yet so full of life and told the most fascinating stories about the Old World. All of a sudden, he stopped coming in, and we didn't see him for three weeks.

When he came back, he was different. The life was drained from his eyes. He no longer told his tales, and I can't recall seeing him smile after that. At most, he would offer a nod and quiet thank you when his transaction was complete. Mom later found out through his wife that he'd been sent to re-education for unknown reasons, and we never spoke of it again. I have no idea what the process is, and I decided then that I never want to know.

"Hey."

I spin around, panic washing over me again. "Jesus, you scared me! Learn to knock."

Liam closes the door. "I did. You didn't answer."

How did I not hear him? His wavy brown hair is styled with gel that glistens under the light. Instead of his usual T-shirt and gym shorts, he's put on a semi-casual button-up shirt and dark jeans. I guess he's trying to avoid our aunt's criticism as well. He doesn't say anything for a few moments. His eyes find their way to different objects in the room, not once meeting mine. Pulling at each individual finger, he pops almost every knuckle and then repeats the action twice.

"You okay?" I ask. Although Liam hasn't exactly been himself the past couple years, I can still tell when something is bothering him. We've always been close, and reading each other is an art we've perfected.

He clears his throat, and his eyes finally meet mine. "Yeah. I just came to check on you."

"Me?"

Crossing the room, he plops onto my bed, folding his arms behind his head. "When I said you look like shit, I meant it. Late night?"

Unconsciously, I cross my arms over my chest. "Couldn't sleep."

"Is that it? Because you seem on edge about something."

"Like what?"

"I don't know. You tell me."

"I'm fine. What's with the interrogation?"

He doesn't say anything. No sarcastic remark or defensiveness. He's just quiet, his eyes locked on the ceiling, chewing on the inside of his bottom lip.

"Okay, fine," I finally say. Maybe if I open up a bit he'll do the same. "There is something, but you have to promise not to tell *anyone*. I'm serious."

Sitting up, he nods. "I won't tell anyone. I promise."

I sit beside him, legs shaking and heart racing, and tell him everything, keeping my eyes on the floor. He listens intently, doesn't interrupt, and is patient when I need to collect myself. As I let everything out, a weight lifts off my chest and my mind momentarily becomes clear. But when I finish and look at Liam, his face is pale and he's as still as a statue.

"What is it?" I ask. "What's wrong?"

"The woman... What did she look like?"

I wipe tears from my face that I didn't realize had spilled over. "I don't remember."

"Think!"

"I don't know! It was dark, and—and I was scared."

He abruptly stands and starts pacing back and forth, running his hands through his hair. "Please, I need you to try. This is important."

"You think I don't know that? I was there when she was *murdered*. This is the type of stuff that happened in the Old World. It shouldn't be happening now." I close my eyes and remember the moments before seeking shelter. A face pops into my mind, but it's blurred and distorted. She was hysterical and my adrenaline immediately kicked in. "I think she had black hair. Maybe dark brown. It was too dark to make out any defining features, but she looked young. I don't know—your age, maybe a couple years older."

"What else?"

Reluctantly, I dig deeper. Although it's fresh in my mind, I don't want to continue reliving it. There was something about her that freaked me out, aside from her obvious terror. "She was hurt. She was already bleeding when I first saw her."

Blood oozing from the right side of her abdomen, soaking her torn shirt. When she came half-running, half-limping toward me, her palm was pressed against the wound. The blood seeped between her fingers and glistened under the dim streetlight.

"Why?" I ask. "Why would someone do that?"

Liam lets out a long breath and stops pacing. "I don't know." He's quiet and then says, "You didn't tell anyone, did you? Police, Mom…?"

"No. No one knows except you."

"Good. Keep it that way."

"Did you know her?"

"If she's the person I think she is, yes. Sort of."

"What do you mean, 'sort of'?"

He shrugs. "We have mutual friends. I don't know her too well."

Before I can pry any more out of him, Mom calls for us. Liam makes his escape almost immediately, but I take my time. I'm not exactly in the mood to be social today. When I do make my appearance, Mom and Naomi are already perched on one of the sofas and Liam is seated across from them. The coffee table now holds a tray of assorted sliced fruits and four glasses of water. In the center is a black, narrow vase holding a bouquet of deep burgundy flowers.

Naomi smiles at me as I take a seat next to Liam, but it looks forced. Her face is worn and her eyes are puffy. The last time I saw her was maybe four or five months ago—not long before Kyle died. Now she looks a decade older, despite the makeup caked on her face. She's pressed into the corner of the sofa, putting as much distance as possible between her and Mom.

"It's nice to see you, Olivia," she says.

"You, too," I reply.

No rude comments or backhanded compliments like her usual greetings. Maybe she's turned a new leaf since losing her husband.

"How have you been, Naomi?" Liam asks.

"Not great," she says, staring at the bouquet. "It's been hard without him, and I've been completely alone." Tears well up in her eyes and she shakes her head. "And I can't believe what people are saying about me. They actually think I could *kill* my husband?"

Mom scoots closer to Naomi and rests a hand on her shoulder. "No one really knows what happened, Naomi. They're confused, but that's no excuse for their accusations."

"We know you didn't do it," I offer. And I mean it. Regardless of how Naomi usually acts, she's not a killer. Her husband was the light of her life. He and my father were close, and Kyle always gushed about his wife to all of us.

There have only ever been two murders that I know of in the Green Zone—specifically our city—and those have been in the past two months. Crime was mostly eradicated after the Enlightened Society took over. An assault is reported every now and then, but it's extremely rare. Our reformed country is much safer than the Old World, where crime and corruption were rampant.

The Second Civil War is what finally made the United States of America crumble. Citizens were sick of being kept in the dark when it came to so-called classified information. The military claimed everything was on a need-to-know basis—if we truly needed to know, we would. But even when top-secret documents were released for the general public's consumption, they were so heavily redacted no one could draw an actual conclusion from them—they were just words on paper that didn't actually say anything. That had been a normal occurrence for centuries, but no one seemed to notice or care. It only became an issue in the last two decades before the country's downfall.

Presidents started being assassinated at an alarming rate, and the government refused to release any information to the public, assuring everyone they had it all under control. After the seventh assassination in a row, the war broke out. People were terrified and tired of the empty promises. The public became split into two groups: Those who still trusted and defended the government, and those who sought to overthrow it and get actual answers. Six years of bloodshed later, the Enlightened Society took over, exterminating nearly every member of the old government. They implemented new laws and punishments to ensure our safety, and they split the northeastern portion of the country into four zones—Green Zone, Blue Zone, Yellow Zone, and Red

Zone—which work together for the good of the people. While we still don't know everything that goes on behind the scenes, our current government shares enough to keep us informed.

Tears well up in Naomi's eyes, and Liam shifts awkwardly beside me. He's always hated seeing people cry. Mom attempts to pull Naomi into a hug, but Naomi shakes her off.

"It's not fair!" she sobs. "How could they do this? How could they take him from me?"

A confused expression crosses Mom's face. "What do you mean?"

Naomi lets out a couple of shuddering breaths and wipes the tears from beneath her eyes. Liam sits up straight, suddenly interested.

"You know who did it?" he asks.

Naomi crosses her arms over her chest and sinks deeper into her little corner. She doesn't say anything, but tears silently streak her face again. Mom launches into a speech that sounds a little too rehearsed about how things will get better. While they're distracted, I quietly excuse myself, pulling on my boots and grabbing my coat before slipping outside.

3. *Puzzle Pieces*

The snow has stopped and the heavy clouds have dispersed, allowing golden beams of light to cast a dazzling glare on the city. Remaining patches of ice on the ground sparkle, and the buildings gleam with confidence as they touch the sky. Schools are out for winter break, and businesses are preparing for this high-traffic time of the year; wreaths and strings of lights brighten up the otherwise dull community, cars speed past, and the chatter and laughter of numerous passersby bring the downtown area to life. Strangers' shoulders bump mine as I navigate the crowded sidewalk, but I don't mind. Seeing everyone so full of life brings me enough joy to temporarily forget the two who lost their lives.

I've been walking aimlessly for at least a couple of hours, and I'm half surprised that no one has come looking for me. When I look up, I realize that my legs have carried me to the same location I was at last night. Breaking away from the crowd, I take a few steps into the alley and freeze. Considering the atrocity that took place, the little road between the buildings should be blocked off and police should be swarming the area. But there isn't a single trace of the law enforcement's presence. Four more steps and I'm standing beside the dumpster I used as a shelter. Not even a drop of blood remains on the asphalt.

It doesn't make sense that investigators aren't tearing this place apart, unless the killer was smart enough to come back and cover his tracks. That's a possibility, but with police being on the lookout every night past curfew, the chances of him being able to do that without caught are slim. I glance back at the wave of people in the streets behind me and wonder if anyone else knows the dark secret of last night. Maybe the police were here after I left and cleaned up before the city awoke. Our zone erupted with panic when Kyle was killed. It would make sense for this to be kept a secret for now.

I venture farther and am almost at the other end of the alley when something catches my eye. On the brick wall to my left is a poster of our current president, Lena Hoffman, complete with an array of graffitied slurs and devil horns jutting from her head. The sight of it angers me. While our country isn't perfect, it's a lot better than it used to be. It's normal for every government to have people who dislike some of their policies—and we definitely have those—but there are some who take it too far. They form groups with violent intentions and work against the greater good of our country. The Society assures us that any members, confirmed or suspected, are taken into custody and dealt with accordingly; as a precaution to prevent domestic terrorism, anyone speaking or acting in a way that could be interpreted as threatening should be reported. The groups have dwindled over the years, but it's clear that there are still a few out there. Without a doubt, this is the work of one of them, and it's not the first poster I've seen like this.

It dawns on me that what I saw last night could have been an act of one of those groups or someone aspiring to be in one, and I suddenly have the urge to tell someone, anyone. Re-education would be my fate, but I'd rather face that than watch more people die.

"Did you do that?"

I turn to see Liam heading toward me with a hint of excitement in his eyes.

"Of course not," I say. "I would never."

"Too bad." He studies the vulgar poster with a trace of a smile. "We should probably get back home. Mom sent me out to find you."

"Did Naomi finally calm down?"

"Actually…"

"What did you do this time?"

"For once, it wasn't my fault. Mom tried to pry information about Kyle's death out of her and kinda hinted that she thinks Naomi had something to do with it. They ended up fighting, and Naomi left."

As much as I hate to admit it, Liam was right earlier about Mom not wanting to ruin her reputation, but I never suspected she'd hurt her own sister in order to protect it.

"You go home," I say with a sigh. "Tell Mom I'll be back soon."

His eyes shift to me. "Where are you going?"

"Going to play peacemaker as usual," I say, already starting back toward the street.

"Wait!"

I glance back at him. "What?"

He has his phone out, and his fingers are flying across the touchscreen. "I'm coming with you. Just wait a minute."

"I don't need your help. I'm used to this stuff."

His phone dings and he catches up to me, grabbing hold of my arm and stopping me beside the dumpster. "I have a friend who's in the area and can give us a ride. You know how far Naomi lives from here. Besides, I can't let you take all the credit and be the only one to get on Naomi's good side."

I roll my eyes. "How long do we have to wait?"

"He'll be here in a few minutes."

Usually, I'd insist I go alone, but I'm freezing and not having to walk all that way is a plus. As long as Liam stays quiet, there shouldn't be any issues. Neither of us have ever really been close to Naomi, but our dad always said I had a way of talking to people. I'm a good listener and hardly raise my voice. Since Dad left, I've become the moderator any time Mom and Liam get into their arguments, and I've always been the peacekeeper among my friends. Liam shares the same talent if he tries, but he's more blunt and doesn't usually take people's feelings into consideration until later on.

A black, compact car pulls into the parking spot on the side of the road closest to us.

"That's him," Liam says, and I follow him to the vehicle. He gets in the front passenger seat, and I slide into the back seat behind him.

"Thanks, man," Liam says to the man in the driver's seat. "This is my sister, Ivy. Ivy, this is Nixon."

Nixon turns to look at me and offers a half-smile. "Nice to meet you."

His radiant blue eyes lock with mine, and I shift uncomfortably under his gaze. His dirty-blond dreadlocks are loosely tied on top of his head, exposing a jagged, diagonal scar that starts beside his right earlobe and ends just below his jaw. He looks to be around Liam's age, but I've never seen him before.

"You too," I say.

Nixon pulls out into the road, and Liam brings up the directions to Naomi's on his phone. They talk to each other and I try my best to ignore them, feeling out of place and wishing I'd insisted on walking by myself. I catch Nixon glancing at me in the rearview mirror, making me feel even more uncomfortable. Although he seems young, there's something intimidating about him.

Faded signs and abandoned buildings that once belonged to companies come into view, signaling that we've left the lively city behind and are nearing our destination. The roads out here are bumpy and littered with potholes. This part of town is a wasteland, though it was once a thriving suburban area of the Old World. The only ones who still reside here are those who refused to leave family homes that had been passed down for generations, and Naomi is no exception. While Mom was eager to break away and start her own new life, Naomi wanted to hang on to the memories that their childhood house holds.

My thoughts backtrack to the slander of President Hoffman. It's the fourth one I've seen in the past month. Whenever they pop up, they're almost immediately taken down by law enforcement or dedicated citizens. I can't fathom why someone would risk re-education to rebel against the Society and publicly dishonor the President. Seeing an influx in negative propaganda worries me. Maybe my home isn't as safe as I always thought it was.

Nixon pulls a buzzing phone out of his pocket and hesitates before answering. He hardly has time to say "hello" before the person on the other end interrupts. I can't hear what's being said, but I can tell from the distressed voice that it's a woman.

"Okay, okay. Calm down," Nixon says, but she continues and her voice gets louder. "Stop!" The authority in his voice makes me want to sink deeper into the seat and disappear. "Listen to me. I'm with Liam right now. I'll be there as soon as I can, but until then, I need you to get yourself under control. Okay?"

The lady says something, and Nixon hangs up, tossing the phone into the center console. I lean my head against the window and lock my eyes on the world outside, pretending to not have paid attention.

"Do you want me to go with you?" Liam asks.

"I can handle it," Nixon says, just as calm as he was before. "You need to stay with your sister."

"I don't need a babysitter," I interject. "I originally planned to go alone anyway."

"If it's about what we discussed this morning," Liam says, "I can help. I have new information."

"Good," Nixon says. "And you can gather some more information when I drop you off, and we'll talk about it later."

I finally look back to them. "Information about what?"

Neither of them says anything. Nixon's phone buzzes once in the console, but he ignores it.

"Liam, what information?"

"It's none of your business, Ivy," he says.

"Are you spying on Naomi or something? We're supposed to be helping her!"

"And we are."

"So why do you need to 'gather information'? And why the hell is it any business of *his*?"

"It's nothing, okay?"

I lean as far forward as I can to look at Liam before the seatbelt locks up. "What, are you guys trying to play detective or something? Kyle is already dead, and the police have closed the case. Leave it alone."

"Can't always trust everything they tell you," Nixon says as he turns onto Naomi's road.

"Our father was a police officer," I say, redirecting my glare to him.

"I'm aware, but a lot of people think the investigation was bullshit."

"So *you* think she killed him, too?"

"I never said that." The way he's remaining so calm irritates me. His entire existence is irritating me.

"You're the one who brought up Naomi," Liam tells me. "Since you obviously don't know what you're talking about, just be quiet."

"Please take him with you, Nixon," I say, sitting back in my seat, "or there might be another mysterious murder in our family."

He smiles at that.

"Are you sure I can't help?" Liam asks.

Nixon pulls up to Naomi's house and stops beside the driveway.

"I'll update you later," he says.

Liam agrees and they exchange goodbyes before he exits the car. I unbuckle my seatbelt and open the door, pausing before getting out.

"Thanks for the ride," I say to Nixon.

"No problem," he replies.

He drives off once I'm out, and I begin the walk up the winding driveway with Liam behind me. The battered two-story house looms over us. Decaying trees surround it, and the windows are boarded up. It feels like we've walked right into a horror movie. While the rest of the city has been graced with sunlight, the gray clouds linger here. We climb the rotting, wooden stairs, and I knock lightly on the weathered door. A couple of minutes pass, and I try again. The door swings open, exposing my aunt, who seems to be unbalanced and reeks of an unfamiliar odor. Mascara streaks her face, and she has changed into a pair of sweatpants and one of Kyle's old T-shirts.

"What do *you* want?" she slurs, narrowing her glassy eyes at us.

"We just came to make sure you're okay," I say. "Can we come in?"

She rolls her eyes but steps aside, allowing us in. The bright living room opens up in front of us. A crackling fireplace is tucked into a corner on the other side of the room. In front of it is an elegant coffee table cluttered with unopened mail, empty bottles, and an ashtray packed with cigarette butts. A large portrait of Naomi and Kyle hangs on another wall, both of them smiling as they embrace each other.

"Did my bitch of a sister send you two here?" Naomi demands. She stumbles past us and collapses onto the black sectional couch.

I take a seat beside her, shocked to hear her use such vulgar language, but Liam remains standing.

"No," he says. "We haven't talked to her since you left. We wanted to check on you."

"How sweet," she says sarcastically. Reaching under the couch, she pulls out a half-empty bottle of clear liquid. The stickers that were once on the glass have been scratched off, leaving a discolored residue. She twists off the cap and takes a long swig. The smell intensifies, and I almost gag.

"Want some?" she asks, holding the bottle out to me.

"No, thank you," I say. "What *is* that?"

"Vodka," Liam answers for her.

"Where did you get that?" I ask. "Alcohol is—"

"Illegal?" She laughs. "I know. Prohibition was attempted in the Old World, too, but there's always a way to get it."

"Are you okay, Naomi?" I ask. "I know Mom made you upset, but even before that you weren't yourself."

Slowly shifting her gaze to the portrait, she says, "It's nothing you would understand."

"So help me understand." I inch closer to her. "I know losing your husband must hurt, but I can tell it's something deeper, too. Is it the rumors?"

"Those sure as hell don't help." Another drink.

"When you were at our place," Liam says, "you said 'they' took him from you. Do you know something about his murder?"

"Of course I know." Leaning forward, she studies both of us. "He was innocent, but they still took his life. And it was all because of your father."

My stomach drops. "He left before all of this," I say. "How is it his fault?"

She laughs and stands up. Clutching the alcohol in her hand, she paces the room, hardly able to walk in a straight line. "You really are a naive little girl, aren't you?"

I look to Liam, who has his eyes locked on our aunt.

"For once, open your eyes!" she yells. Her slurring is getting worse. "You think this is any way to live? Never being able to have your own opinion or disagree with the Society. Never being able to succeed if you're not born into fucking wealth. It's bullshit! We're trapped in their disgusting game, and there's no way out."

"Are you saying the Society killed Kyle?" Liam asks. "Why would they do that?"

"To keep us in line," she hisses, jabbing a finger at the air. "They want to scare us into submission. And it's working!"

I stand up and gently try to pry the bottle from her, but she jerks it away. "Naomi, calm down."

"No! They're all in on it! The police, the Elites in the Red Zone—and they're watching. They're *always* watching!"

In one swift motion, Naomi hurls the bottle across the room. Liam ducks out of the way, and it shatters against the front door. Shards of glass spray the room, and vodka soaks the door's surroundings. My heart is racing and my hands are shaking uncontrollably. We shouldn't have come here. Nothing we say can calm her down. Her mind has been tainted by the alcohol and whatever else she may have gotten her hands on. Maybe she's been listening to the false propaganda of the few, quickly dying resistance groups. Or maybe Kyle's death has sent her over the edge, sucking her into a bottomless pit of paranoia. We've learned in school what an immense amount of pain and stress can do to humans. We are a weak species. As strong as Naomi has displayed herself to be in the past, she is not exempt from that failing.

"We can get you help," I say slowly. "I promise we won't tell them about the alcohol."

But she doesn't listen. Liam has disappeared, and I'm left alone with Naomi while she drunkenly rambles and stumbles around the room. My heart breaks for her. I know she feels alone and defeated; a piece of her died with Kyle. Opening up a new bottle that she's pulled from her stash under the couch, she chugs it and continues with her babbling. Her slurring has gotten so bad I can hardly make out what she's trying to say, and her voice crescendos with every word.

A high-pitched whine pierces the air. It starts off as a distant, annoying noise but rapidly gets closer. I turn to one of the windows by the front door as blue and red lights stream into the house through the spaces in the boards. I try to get Naomi's attention but she yells over me, and I don't have enough time or patience to silence her. While her back is to me, I escape the room to find my brother.

Navigating the maze of rooms is a challenge. I have no idea where to look or why he would be roaming her house. Passing through the kitchen for the second time, I begin to worry that he left. The sirens are closer now. Naomi's yelling grows louder, briefly interrupted by what I imagine is another sip of her liquor. Without any luck downstairs, I decide to try the second floor. The sirens are screeching now. They'll storm this place any minute. A door slams outside. Or is that my imagination?

I'm running to the staircase as Liam descends it.

"We need to get out of here," he says. "Now."

"What's going on?"

"Ivy? Liam?" Naomi calls. The rage in her voice is replaced with fear.

A crash echoes through the house, and Liam runs past me, grabbing my arm and pulling me through the house. Dogs bark viciously. Men shout orders. Naomi screams and begs, continuing to cry out our names. We make it to the kitchen, where an exit awaits us. As we pass the doorway looking into the living room, I catch a glimpse of what's going on. Three officers surround Naomi and shove her to the floor. Two more are flipping furniture and tearing into anything they can. Another leads a German Shepherd into a different room. My stomach twists into a knot, and I have to force myself to keep running.

"Hey!" one of the officers shouts. "Stop!"

Boots pound against the hardwood floor. Liam swings the back door open, and we barrel out of the house. He lets go of me as we race behind the neighboring abandoned houses. Another vehicle comes to a screeching stop in the driveway, kicking up gravel. Against my better judgment, I look back. We've made it a few houses down, but the officer who saw us is desperately trying to catch up. He fumbles with his belt and produces a gun, aiming right at us.

"Liam, look out!" I scream.

He whips his head around. *"Shit!"*

Reaching back, he grabs hold of my neck and forces me to crouch. We dive between two houses, and my knees slide on the grass. I catch myself with my hands before my face hits the ground, and Liam shields my body with his. A pop splits the air. A plume of dust erupts from a brick where the bullet collides. Scrambling to our feet, we continue to run, Liam maintaining a strong hold on my arm. Cold air bites into my lungs, and everything in my peripheral vision becomes a blur of colors and silhouettes. My legs burn and my head is pounding. The wind whips at my face as we cut through a field, attempting to avoid twisted metal and other debris that sprouts from the frozen ground.

After what feels like an eternity, we finally stop. I press my back against a crumbling house identical to the others cluttering the area. Gasping for breath, I hunch over, resting my hands on my knees. "What the hell was that about?"

Liam ignores me. He's pacing the small strip separating the two properties with his phone pressed to his ear. He walks around to the front of the house where I can't hear him and returns a couple of minutes later, shoving the phone in his pocket.

"We need to keep moving," he says. "We're not far enough, and I have a feeling they're going to search the area."

"Why? We didn't do anything."

"They don't know that. We were in that house with illegal substances and our aunt who was spouting some unnerving things about the Society."

"Only one of them saw us, and he didn't even get a good look."

"We need to assume the worst. Come on."

We walk in silence, keeping our eyes peeled for police. Liam glances at his phone every so often and responds to a text as soon as he receives one. Guilt settles into my chest for leaving Naomi behind. I know she broke the law and I know she needs help, but I wish we could have been the ones to help her. Her calling our names like a frightened child replays in my mind, making my heart wrench even more.

I've never seen anyone in that state before, and it was utterly terrifying. Naomi accused the Enlightened Society of killing Kyle. That's an insane enough statement on its own, but something else she said bothers me more: It was my father's fault.

The only correlation I can see is that he was a police officer, and maybe her blaming him stems from her irrational hatred of the government. But he's been gone for a few years now. There's no way he had anything to do with it. With the Society still keeping an eye out for him, it would be impossible for him to have been in contact with Kyle without being found. The idea of him communicating with our uncle after abandoning us infuriates me. I remind myself that Naomi was clearly drunk almost to the point of oblivion. Nothing she said holds any truth.

"Ivy," Liam says.

"Yeah?"

He's about ten feet ahead of me, frantically surveying our surroundings. "Are you okay?"

"Fine. You?"

"Yeah. Just a little farther. Nixon is waiting for us."

"I thought he was busy."

He doesn't say anything, and we keep walking. We come to the end of the road, where Nixon leans against his car behind a strip of buildings.

"Are you guys okay?" he asks when we approach, mainly focusing on Liam.

"Yeah, we're good," Liam replies.

The three of us get into the car, and it's quiet for a while. Liam stares straight ahead, bouncing one of his legs. He seems more shaken up than I am. Usually he's good at handling stressful situations. Nixon periodically looks over at him but doesn't say anything. Twenty minutes of agonizing silence later we're in our city again, and there's still another twenty-five or so to go until Liam and I are home.

I want to say something, anything, to break the silence, but all that's running through my mind is Naomi. Not knowing what's happening to her scares me. To my knowledge, this is her first offense. She should only face a few months of re-education. I'm debating whether I should tell Mom. Part of me blames her for all of this. If she hadn't fought with Naomi, none of this would have happened. She'd still be safe and sober at our apartment.

How did the police even know? What made them invade her house? The three of us were the only ones there. There's no way anyone else could have known. Unless…

My heart drops. Liam did disappear for a while, and he's been glued to his phone today. He was the only other person there besides me. And what reason did he have to snoop around Naomi's house?

I desperately try to think of other possibilities. Maybe they really have been watching her since Kyle died. Maybe she's been acting out in other ways and they caught on. After all, I haven't seen her in a while. Grief changes people. But still, why would they show up today while we were there? Every theory leads me back to Liam.

The worst part is, I don't know how to confront him. Angering him by throwing out accusations won't do anything except make him close himself off. He seems anxious, and being in the presence of his friend doesn't help either. I need to get him alone when his guard is down, whenever that will be.

Testing the waters, I nonchalantly ask, "Who do you think reported her?"

"I don't know," he says.

"It's just kinda weird, you know? No one else was there except us."

Nothing. He runs a hand through his hair and starts bouncing his leg again. Is he feeling guilty?

"You need to calm down," Nixon tells him. "Everything's going to be fine."

"It's just… You know."

Nixon purses his lips. "Do you want to come back to my place? I'll fill you in on what happened earlier."

"Yeah. Let's drop Ivy off first."

Nixon takes a left toward our apartment complex.

"Wait!" I protest.

"This doesn't concern you," Liam says. "Tell Mom I'll be back later."

I roll my eyes but don't push it. Nixon pulls up to our building. Without saying anything to either of them, I get out and climb the stairs to the second floor.

4. Secrets and Lies

As soon as I enter the apartment, I hear the all-too-familiar line, "Olivia, where were you?"

Mom comes out of the kitchen, wiping her hands on her dress. "You've been gone for hours. I was getting worried. And how many times do I have to tell you to take your phone with you when you leave?"

"I'm sorry. I'll remember it next time."

"Where's your brother?"

"With a friend. He said he'll be back later."

She sighs and goes back into the kitchen. "A little heads-up every once in a while would be great. By the way, the police called for you two."

Halfway through unlacing my boots, I freeze. Liam was right: Expect the worst.

She comes back out to the living room and sits on the couch. Sifting through a pile of papers on the coffee table, she continues,

"They wanted me to tell you they were sorry if they scared you. One of the officers was trying to catch up with you and make sure you were okay. His gun came loose and accidentally fired when it fell."

"That's not true! He purposely shot at us!"

"Maybe it seemed like that because you were scared. They can get in a lot of trouble for unlawfully firing at unarmed citizens."

"I know what I saw." I kick off my boots and take a seat beside her. "Mom, he was *trying* to shoot us. You can ask Liam."

"Why did you go to Naomi's?"

"Liam told me what happened after I left. We wanted to check on her."

She tears her eyes from the document in her hands and looks at me, cupping one of my hands with her own. "Your aunt is in a very dark place right now, sweetie. She's not well. I've been worried about her. That's why I made the call."

I jerk my hand from hers. "You what?"

"She's sick. She's a danger to herself and possibly others. I had to do something. Re-education can help, and after the first month, she's allowed visitors."

"*We* could've tried to help before sending her off!"

Naomi obviously wasn't in the right mindset today, but I feel like Mom could have tried a little more to be there for her sister. I do trust the Society, and I know she'll be taken care of. Most people who are sent to re-education return to their normal lives. However, thinking of Naomi, scared and alone, angers me. When Kyle died, I asked Mom if we could go see Naomi on multiple occasions, but she always insisted that she needed her space and time to cope. Wanting to avoid conflict and trusting that Mom knew her sister better than I did, I let it go. After seeing her today, I wish I hadn't.

"God, how could you do that?" I demand. "Do you know what re-education is like? You shipped her off without even trying! And for what? So she won't be your problem anymore?"

"That's enough!" She slams a folder down. "I did what I had to. Re-education has helped a lot of people. It's completely safe. There's nothing I could have done to help her." Standing, she gathers the stack from the table. "I made you and your brother dinner. It's in the fridge."

A yellow envelope slips from her arms, fluttering to the floor behind her.

"Mom, wait." Scooping it up, I follow her. "You dropped something."

Spinning around, she snatches the envelope from my hands, but before she tucks it back with the other documents, I see my name scrawled across the front.

"What is that?" I ask.

"It's nothing." She keeps walking.

"It has my name on it. Tell me what it is."

She sighs in frustration, her hand clenching the knob of the front door. "It's just stuff for the shop. I have a lot of work to do." She hesitates for a moment then turns around, planting a kiss on my forehead. "I'll be home soon." Grabbing her keys from the bowl by the door, she leaves.

Last night's lack of sleep starts to creep up on me. I fill the first couple hours of being alone by lounging on the couch, watching the only news station we have. The anchor is droning on about the seven spots available in the Red Zone again. Twice a year, the Elites of the Red Zone allow a few citizens from different zones to apply for residency. Anyone can apply, but only those who pass the interview process and have a substantial amount of money are accepted. Sometimes they'll transfer exceptional members of law enforcement there. Mom had always urged Dad to apply, assuring him that we would be accepted with his position. He didn't want to leave our home, though, which triggered a couple of arguments between them.

My brain refuses to focus on the news anchor. Now that I'm alone, it keeps slipping back to last night. The spotless crime scene is enough to make me think I've gone crazy. If the victim's helpless screams weren't still sending shivers up my spine, I'd be sure it was all a bad dream. But by the way Liam was acting this morning, I assume he somehow knows something about it, too. The reminder that there's a killer out there makes me nervous to be home alone, and even more afraid for Mom and Liam right now.

Remembering my phone is still in my bedroom, I get up to retrieve it. The anchor switches to the topic of resistance groups, claiming police have two members in custody from the Yellow Zone and are closely monitoring the Green Zone. My body relaxes at hearing those reassuring words, and I'm optimistic they'll find the man from last night.

My phone is plugged into the charger on my nightstand, where it has remained for nearly forty-eight hours. I have a few unread texts. A few are from my friend Addison, and some are from Mom when I was out earlier. The most recent is from Liam, saying he won't be home tonight. I text back, asking why, and within a couple of minutes, he responds, *"I just won't. I'm busy."*

He's used that excuse a lot lately. Even when he's not at work, he tries to stay away from home. I can't say that I blame him, but after last night and today, I can't imagine being anywhere but home, and there's no one I want to talk to other than my brother.

I respond with, *"I have to talk to you. It's important."*

Phone in hand, I head back out to the living room and resume my spot on the couch. The TV is still broadcasting the same middle-aged man behind his desk, saying something about increased resistance activity and the slander of the President—both things I already know. Mom still isn't back. It's getting close to curfew, but I'm hoping she stays out a little bit longer so I have time to talk to Liam without her hearing. If he's as busy as he says, though, I don't know if I'll have a chance.

On top of him acting more distant than usual, he seems pretty caught up in whatever it is he and Nixon are doing together. I've met nearly all of Liam's friends over the years, and he pretty much cut ties with them not long after Dad left. I'd never even heard him speak of Nixon, though, and I know for sure they weren't in the same graduating class. The way they talked to each other wasn't how he normally talked with his friends, and I'm curious as to what 'information' Nixon wanted him to gather, as well as what he had to update Liam on.

My phone vibrates in my hand. Liam's name pops up on the screen, and I swipe to answer it. "Hey."

"What do you need to talk to me about?" he asks with an underlying tone of irritation.

There's a man's voice in the background, followed by static and another, more distant voice. I'm about to speak when Liam tells me to hold on. Everything momentarily goes silent on the other end, and I pull the phone from my ear, making sure the call hasn't dropped. Then he cuts back in, telling me to go on.

"At Naomi's," I say, "that officer shot at us, right? When we were running, I mean."

"What? Of course he did."

"Okay, well… Mom got a call from the police today. About us. They said it was an accident—that his gun fell and it somehow went off. And they wanted to apologize."

"That's bullshit."

"I know, but—"

"Wait. She knows we were there?"

"Because they called her, yeah. But there's something else." I pause, twisting a loose thread on the cushion around my finger. I don't want to say it—somehow, keeping it bottled up makes it feel less true—but he needs to know. The news anchor switches topics again, cutting to a woman in our city with a microphone clenched in one hand. Some girl has gone missing—plucked up off the streets, leaving her parents distraught. "Mom is the one who reported Naomi. She told me herself."

Liam doesn't say anything. He's been angry enough with her the past few years, and this definitely doesn't help. I'm angry with her, too, but in a way, I can understand where she's coming from. Re-education—twenty-four-hour surveillance—is the only way Naomi will get the help she needs. She isn't well, and it was only a matter of time until she did something drastic. I just wish Mom had been there for her more.

"Liam?" I ask.

The TV cuts back to the man behind the desk. A picture of the missing woman appears in the top-right corner. At first glance, she looks like any other passerby I'd see on the streets—a faceless person floating through life. Leaning closer, I recognize her. In the picture, she's smiling, but when I saw her, her eyes were wild and desperate pleas were escaping those very same lips.

"I'm here," Liam says.

"Liam, turn on the news!"

"Why?"

"Just do it! Hurry!"

"Okay, I'm doing it." There's a pause, and then the anchor's voice comes through the phone. "Shit. Nixon, come here."

"That's her!" I tell him. "That's the girl I saw last night!"

"This is bad," I hear Nixon say.

"Are you sure it was her?" Liam asks me.

"Yes. One hundred percent. The place where you found me to-day… That's where it happened."

"But there was no—"

"No blood or even crime-scene tape, I know. But I was there! I know it was the same place."

"They covered it up."

"We need to tell someone."

"No!" It's Nixon. "You can't tell anyone."

"Why not? I know what happened to her, and the police are looking for her! She has a family!"

"You know what will happen," Liam says. "You were out past curfew. And they might pin you as a suspect."

"I'm willing to take that risk."

There's a noise on the other end that sounds like his phone was dropped or the mic is being covered. Liam's voice is muffled as he talks. Another faint voice—I'm assuming Nixon's—responds to what-ever he said.

Not wanting to hear any more of the story, I shut off the TV. The front door closes, and I jump up from the couch, spinning around to see Mom. Without so much as a glance in my direction, she disap-pears to her room. Wanting to put distance between the two of us so she doesn't hear my conversation, I walk down the hall, stopping be-tween our bedrooms.

"I think he saw me," I say, lowering my voice.

"What?" Liam asks more clearly.

"Before I hid, the man came running into the alley. He was more concerned with her, but… I don't know. I *felt* him looking at me.

And after she was… you know… he stopped on the other side of the dumpster. He just stood there. But he left me alone."

I lean back against the wall. Why didn't he kill me, too? I'm not even certain he actually saw me, but I almost feel guilty for still being alive while that innocent girl had her life taken. From the picture shown, she didn't look like one to cause any trouble. Now her parents are left wondering where their daughter is, unaware that she's never coming home. The news mentioned increased surveillance of our zone due to an influx of resistance activity. They claimed it was because of the posters, but I have a feeling it's something more.

It had to be the resistance—or terrorists, as we call them. Someone involved with a terrorist group must have killed that girl. It isn't a surprise that the media isn't reporting it. That would cause widespread panic across the country. The police may not know she's dead yet, but it's only a matter of time, and remaining groups will be the top suspects. They thrive on chaos and have an insatiable hunger for power. Unless there's another mass extermination like the last days of the Old World, we'll never be completely safe.

"Liam?" I say again.

"Yeah, I'm here. Let me take care of it. You don't need to get involved in all of this."

"How are you going to take care of it?"

"I just am. Look, I really am busy. We can talk more about this tomorrow."

"What are you so busy with?"

"I'll talk to you tomorrow." And he hangs up.

The apartment is quiet. Mom must have gone to sleep for the night. Knowing Liam won't be home tonight makes me uneasy. I know he's snuck out after curfew a few times, but that was before I knew a murderer stalked the streets. And there's something about Nixon I don't like. Sure, it was nice of him to give us a ride, but my gut tells me not to trust him and I don't know why. Liam acts like he's attached to him, and I don't like the way Nixon orders him around as if he's his pet.

There's something going on that he doesn't want me to know. Liam and I have never kept secrets from each other. We've always been open and honest, and I thought the past few years had made us closer. The first year after Dad's absence, we both isolated ourselves, but we still talked to each other. When Mom wasn't around, we were each other's support.

He's become secretive lately, and I never found out what was bothering him this morning. It's possible that it was about his missing friend, but how could he have already known before I told him what I saw? Tonight was the first time the news broadcasted it, and he was asleep when I got home last night. All throughout the day he was tense, and he was more eager to talk to Nixon than me about what happened at Naomi's.

Straightening up, I take a couple steps forward and open his door. Automatically, guilt sets in. I've never gone through his room before. Under any other circumstances, I wouldn't invade his privacy, but something's not right. Pushing the guilt down, I go in.

Nothing looks out of the ordinary. Clothes are scattered across the floor, and his bookshelf is overflowing. On the dresser is a white frame, holding an old picture of Mom, Dad, Liam, and five-year-old me. Dad has me up on his shoulders with a beaming grin, and Mom is crouched with her arms wrapped around a distracted Liam. Smiling to myself, I recall the night the picture was taken. Dad had just been promoted, and the Green Zone came together to throw him a party. He was ecstatic, and Mom was beyond proud of him. He always loved his job and our country, but the new position took a toll on him as time pushed on. We were able to tell how stressed he was, although he tried not to let it show.

Stepping over articles of clothing, I scavenge the rest of his room. Everything I move I'm cautious to put back exactly the way I found it. While trying to wiggle under his bed, my stomach growls, and I remember the food Mom said she left in the fridge. I haven't eaten all day, but the thought of food somehow isn't appetizing. Adrenaline courses through my veins and the paranoia of being caught at any moment looms over me, despite the fact that Liam isn't coming home.

The underside of his bed is a dud. Nothing but lint and a pair of tennis shoes. Having checked every inch of the room, and starting to feel frustrated, I try one final untouched place: the closet.

I throw the doors open, causing one to come off the track, but I don't care anymore. I'm irritated. Irritated with myself for doing this and with him for leaving me no other choice. I have no idea what I'm expecting to find or what I should be looking for. All I know is there has to be something that will give me an idea as to why he's been acting the way he has. Maybe he still hasn't healed completely from Dad leaving. I haven't either, but for the most part, I've returned to my normal self. Nixon could be a new friend Liam's found to fill that void, which is great, but it's unnerving how attached he is to him—almost like he owes him something.

The closet is packed with winter clothes and empty boxes. At first, I take my time looking through everything, checking the pockets of every coat and pair of jeans. But as waves of fatigue crash over me, I carelessly rip clothes from hangers and shelves and toss the boxes aside. It's almost completely bare, and I've had no luck. A small stack of clothes remains tucked in the corner of the shelf. Standing on my toes, I stretch my hands up to grab it. It's heavier than I expected a jacket and a few shirts to be. Placing one hand on top and the other underneath, I pull them down. There's a thud as something falls out of the pile.

Squeezing my eyes shut, I expect Mom to come rushing in, but the apartment remains as dead as the rest of the city. Exhaling, I open my eyes and search for what made the noise. I involuntarily drop the clothes to my feet when I see it lying on the floor inches from me.

A gun.

5. Go to War

A flurry of snow swirls on the other side of the enormous window. Addison sits across from me, sipping her coffee and scribbling in her notebook. Bustling workers and their chatter buzz around us, and the warm air is filled with the smell of freshly roasted coffee beans and pastries. We're nestled in the front corner of the dimly lit room, away from potential prying eyes and ears. Mom suggested I get out of the house after what happened with Naomi. Luckily, my best friend was free and is always willing to let me vent.

I haven't told Addison about what happened in the alley or what I found in Liam's room. Even though she's not a hardcore supporter of our government, her dad took my father's position as Chief of Police here in the Green Zone, which has deterred me from telling her everything. She's always been someone I can trust with absolutely anything, but I'm nearly certain she would tell her dad. I could probably deal with questioning from the police, but I don't want Liam to get in trouble. There's no reason he should have a gun, and they won't go easy on him if they ever find out.

Addison's not exactly against the Society, but she's one of many who believe the investigation of Kyle's death was a sham. On top of that, she loves a good conspiracy theory. I've told her everything that happened yesterday afternoon, and she decided to write it down to try to make sense of it all.

Liam didn't come back this morning. He hasn't answered any of my calls or texts, and I know he doesn't work today. I decided I wouldn't tell anyone about the gun—at least not until I've talked to him first. Firearms are strictly for police officers and military personnel. There's no telling what he's gotten himself into, and I have no idea how I'm going to bring it up with him. Interrogating him won't get me anywhere, and finding a time when he isn't busy seems to be impossible.

"Ivy, are you listening to me?" Addison's green eyes peek up at me.

"Yeah, I heard you."

"So what did I say?"

I rack my brain for a shred of what she was talking about. Usually it's like a sponge, absorbing things even when I don't want it to, but in this moment when I need it most, it's blank. With a sigh, I say, "I'm sorry; I'm distracted. A lot has happened."

Leaning back, she gathers her straight brown hair in her hands and pulls, tightening her ponytail. "I would be, too. But that's why you have me: to help you work through this and distract you from the chaos that is your life." She offers one of her signature brilliant smiles. "What else happened? How did Liam react when your mom admitted to calling the police?"

"Liam left with his friend after dropping me off. I had to tell him over the phone." I shrug. "He didn't say anything. I don't know— maybe he expected it. You know how he's been toward her these past few years."

"True." Chewing on the cap of her pen, she drums her fingers against the dark wooden table. "Okay, so Naomi mentioned your dad, saying he had something to do with your uncle's death. Did Liam say anything to that?"

"Nothing. And she never brought it up again. It threw me off, but I think she just wants someone to blame, and he's an easy target since he was a cop."

"Could be. The stuff she said about the Society is pretty interesting though."

"You actually believe that?"

She drops the pen to the table and rests one side of her face in her palm. "I mean, not completely, but there's a little truth in everything."

"She was drunk and had a mental breakdown. There was no truth in any of it. Does your dad know anything about Kyle's death?"

She shakes her head. "He couldn't work the case since he and Kyle were friends. If any of his cop friends talked to him about it, he hasn't shared it with me."

"How does he like being Chief?"

"He loves it, but I think he feels guilty." Furrowing her brow, she adds to her notes.

More people have filed into the cafe, the line growing longer. Two more baristas have assumed their positions behind the counter. On the other side of the window the city square is alive again, although not as much as yesterday. The flurries have stopped for now, and the clouds have lightened.

Addison's eyes are glued to her phone, and a smile tugs at the corners of her mouth.

"What are you smiling about?" I ask playfully, leaning across the table to get a look.

She giggles, pulling the phone closer to her body. "Nothing."

"It doesn't seem like nothing. Who is it?"

Locking the screen, she sets it aside. "No one. This guy, but it's nothing. We're just friends."

"*Suuuure.*"

The screen lights up with a text notification. Addison swipes her phone from the table and drops it in her lap, but not before I see the name.

"What was that about?" I ask.

"What was what about?"

Laughing, I take a sip of my green tea, which is lukewarm at this point. Addison picks up her pen and jots down the names of my dad and uncle.

"You're texting my brother," I say.

"Where do you think your dad could have gone?" she asks, avoiding the accusation. "Do you think he left the country?"

"We've been over this, Addison. The borders are constantly patrolled."

"But if he was Chief of Police, he'd know the ins and outs of everything."

I shrug. "Anything is possible, I guess."

Her phone vibrates again and clatters to the floor. "Damn it." Scooting her chair back, she ducks under the table and resurfaces with her device.

"So are you two…?"

"*No!* God, no. We're just talking." She blushes and drops her eyes to her notebook. "You know I've had his number for a while. The three of us used to hang out all the time."

"Yeah, but I've never seen you smile like that when you text him."

I'm slightly annoyed that Liam finds time to talk with my friend but is too busy to return any calls or texts from me. Maybe he needs time to gather his thoughts from yesterday. Talking things out always helps me, and I guess by now I should know that Liam is the opposite.

She smiles and rolls her eyes. "So I may have a *tiny* crush on him, but don't say anything!" Sinking back in her chair, she covers her face with her hands. "My life would be ruined."

"I won't. But *Liam*? Seriously?"

The two of them always got along, and like she said, we all used to hang out together constantly. But I never expected a relation-ship—or even a crush—to blossom from it. Addison has always been like another sibling.

"I can't help it!" She laughs again.

"Well, since you two are *so* close, did he mention anything about yesterday?"

She sits up. "All he said is that it was rough, and I'm guessing that's why."

"Has he said anything else?"

Arching a pierced eyebrow, she gives me her full attention. "No. Why? Is there something you haven't told me?"

It's possible I'm reading too much into Liam's behavior. There are probably things he doesn't want me to know, just as I have secrets I prefer to keep to myself. I'm relieved that he's at least keeping in touch with Addison; his standoffish nature could be due to something going on between them that she's not telling me about. For now, I'll leave that part alone.

I shake my head. "He's been acting weird, is all."

"He's your brother. He's always been weird."

"Yeah, but he was, like, really distant yesterday."

"So maybe he needs some time to himself or with his new friend. If it would make you feel better, I can try and talk to him."

"Yes, please. I just want to know if he's okay… and if this friend, Nixon, has dragged him into something."

She focuses on her phone, which hasn't lit up since the last unopened text from Liam. "Like what?"

"I don't know. I just don't trust him."

"You don't know him, though. If Liam trusts him, I'm sure he's not as bad as you think."

"There was something weird about him."

"Again, Liam's weird. Of course he'll have weird friends."

"Good point."

Her phone lights up again, displaying an unsaved number. She finishes her coffee and excuses herself to the bathroom, taking the phone with her.

Minutes pass, and more bodies shuffle in and out of the shop. A toddler a few tables down spills her drink and begins to cry. The father comforts the devastated child while the mother cleans the mess. My phone chimes from my pocket, and I pull it out to see a text from Liam.

"I'm not mad," it reads in response to the last text I sent three hours prior, *"I have a lot going on."*

As much as I want him to tell me what's bothering him, aside from the obvious, I leave it alone. Pushing the subject when he's tense will be counterproductive.

A police car races by outside, its lights flashing and siren screaming. Passersby stop to look. Other cars squeeze into one lane to let the officer through. Moments later, a second patrol car zooms toward the same direction. I glance around the cafe to see if anyone else has noticed. Some are staring out the window, but the majority are carrying on with their business. Addison returns as the third wailing car comes into view.

"What's going on?" I ask her.

Shrugging, she plops back down in her chair. "Dad says crime is increasing, and the Society is trying to figure out how to stop it before we backtrack."

"How do they plan to do that?"

"Hell if I know. Maybe they'll re-educate us all." She checks the time on her phone. With a groan, she shuts her notebook and stuffs it in her purse. "I gotta go. I promised my mom I'd be home to help her plan my sister's baby shower."

I completely forgot that Addison's older sister is due within the next couple months.

"I'll talk to you later," she says, standing with her purse on one arm. "And *don't* say anything to him."

Smiling, I roll my eyes. Addison leaves, and one of the baristas thanks her for coming on her way out.

I hang out at the coffee shop for another half-hour or so, scrolling aimlessly through news articles on my phone. No updates on the missing girl and no mention of my aunt, which I am thankful for. One article restates the threat of resistance groups around the country as well as an increase in petty crimes and stresses the importance of our after-dark curfew. It goes on to say that the government is looking into new ways to protect our citizens and catch criminals before they strike.

When the shop gets too crowded and too loud for me to think, I leave. A barista calls out the same parting words as when Addison left. Zipping up my jacket, I navigate the busy streets. My brain is working overtime to keep up with the insanity that has rapidly unfolded. One secret turns into another. They grow and grow, and I know there's more to each story. Naomi might be a little crazy right now, but why did Mom feel the need to report her without actually trying to talk to her about it? It infuriates me the more I dwell on it.

And that innocent girl. For now, she's considered a missing person, but I know the truth. I witnessed someone take her life. I heard her final scream, her final desperate cry for help. No one else knows except Liam, and it's weighing on my conscience. He doesn't understand, and insists I keep it to myself. Two days later and it's eating me alive. If only I could go back and change it.

I find myself nearing the edge of our city, heading toward the unincorporated area where my aunt lives. Cars and trucks slowly make their way through the evening traffic, and I stand with a group of people waiting to cross to the other side. My phone goes off and I glance at the screen, seeing that Liam has texted me, asking where I am. Unlocking my phone, I start to type back, but my fingers are so numb from the cold, I give up within seconds. I don't owe him any kind of explanation, anyway. The crosswalk light signals for us to walk, and I follow the throng of people into the street.

Halfway across, someone ahead of me says, "Hey, what's that?"

I look up to where he's pointing. A thick, black trail of smoke lines the mostly clear sky near the horizon. Within seconds of us spotting it, a massive combination of orange, red, and yellow engulfs the world above us.

Time stops, and everything around me freezes. All of my senses seem to shut down except my vision as we stare in awe at the cloud of fire. Seconds later, the sky sounds as if it's being ripped in half like a piece of paper. It's so loud, my heart stops for a moment and my body instinctively jumps.

I can't move. My mind is begging me to run, but my legs won't listen. The sound of the explosion fizzles away and the shrieks and cries from those around me pierce my ears. Panic takes over. Vehicles on the street race away from the chaos, ignoring the traffic lights. Pedestrians disperse in all different directions, desperate to get away.

Smoke billows above the site of the explosion. Fiery debris plummets to the ground in the distance. All I can do is watch. Military trucks screech to a halt down the road, and dozens of soldiers in full uniform spill out into the panicked crowd. They're shouting, ordering everyone to remain calm, but the stampede continues in every direction. Bodies bump against mine. People climb over one another to escape. A larger man hurtles toward me but doesn't see me. We collide and I lose my footing, falling to the ground. On my hands and knees, I try to get up but am pushed back down. I crawl in the same direction the crowd is moving, hoping to find a place where I can stand. A hand grabs my arm and jerks me to my feet, putting me face-to-face with a soldier.

"Th-thank you," I force out. I know my voice is drowned out by everything that's going on, but he must understand because he nods.

"You need to go home!" he shouts.

"What?"

"The Green Zone has entered a lockdown. We have one hour to clear the streets before making arrests."

I manage a nod and shove my way through the waves of people. Breaking away from the crowd a few blocks up the road, I round a clump of buildings, finding my way to a quieter road, and run as far as my legs will let me. The city is crawling with soldiers and police officers. I get about half a mile before having to stop. My chest and legs burn. The cold makes it hard to catch my breath, and my fingers feel like they're about to fall off. There's no way I can make it home in time.

I pull out my phone, which has at least twenty missed calls and text messages. Ignoring them for now, I open my contacts and click on Liam's name. It rings and rings and rings, then goes to his voicemail. I hang up and immediately redial. No luck the second time either. Cursing under my breath, I try one more time.

Finally, he answers on the fourth ring. "Ivy! Where the hell are you?"

"I need your help." My voice is shaking uncontrollably. "I was with Addison and I went for a walk. I was close to Naomi's and there was this explosion. Everyone went crazy. And they have the Army out here! The fucking *Army!* We're on lockdown and they're about to start making arrests!" I press my hand over my mouth as my voice cracks.

"Try to calm down."

"Please come get me. I can't make it home."

"Okay, tell me where you are."

For the first time since stopping, I take in my surroundings. It's a residential area with a small cluster of brick houses. Up ahead, the downtown area opens back up, and two police cars are parked in front of a tan building. The Northern Unity's flag—a black background with an owl, its wings extended, encircled in thirteen white stars—whips violently in the wind in front of it.

"I'm near the police station."

"I'm not far from there. I have another call coming in that I have to take, but I'll see you in a few, alright?"

"Okay."

He hangs up, and I start toward my destination. As I get closer, sirens blare and a patrol car pulls out of the station garage. It swerves around another car whose driver isn't paying attention to the flashing lights and drives toward the edge of the city.

The world feels broken. We're supposed to be safe.

A curtain of smoke blackens the sky, and the smell of gas hangs heavy in the air. Cries from my fellow citizens grow faint as I press on. Curtains are drawn in every home I pass. When I reach the end of the road, every business in my vicinity is dark, with 'closed' signs hanging on the doors. Parking lots are vacant, and I haven't seen anyone else. In less than an hour, our city has turned into a ghost town.

I reach the police station, stopping at the flagpole. Liam's white crossover appears minutes later, and I climb in.

"You alright?" he asks, taking off before I have a chance to put on my seatbelt.

I can't respond. My hands tremble and my brain doesn't want to work properly. Everything was normal, and out of nowhere came an explosion. Everyone turned into manic animals. I want to be home. I want to be safe. And more than anything, I wish my dad were here.

"Addison called me, freaking out since you weren't answering your phone," Liam says. "She wasn't sure if you made it home. I've been driving around looking for you."

"Thank you," I whisper. I tuck hands underneath my thighs and focus on the world outside, silently repeating a variant of the mantra that calmed me the other night. *I'm with my brother. I'm safe.*

"They're calling it domestic terrorism," he says. "That was a plane you saw being shot down. The media is already covering it."

"So, what, someone stole a plane?"

He shrugs. "That's what the news is saying. Military launched a missile. It was allegedly headed to the Red Zone. They suspected terrorists were going to fly it into the Capitol building."

"Were there people on board?"

He hesitates, pursing his lips. "I don't know." But by the look in his eyes, I can tell he does know, and my heart drops.

6. Waking Up

A loud boom jolts me from my sleep. My mind immediately conjures up the idea that there's been another explosion. Sitting up, I squint at the glowing red numbers of my digital clock, the only light in my pitch-black room. 2:13 a.m. I listen for the sound again, but it doesn't come. In fact, it's unusually quiet. Liam's snoring isn't filling the silence. Did that sound wake him, too?

Muffled voices stir outside. Doors open and close, and then glass shatters. The sound comes again. Three times.

Bang, bang, bang.

Not an explosion. Knocking. I hear Mom's voice, followed by the voice of a man. Heavy footsteps thud against our floor. Jumping out of bed, I run to my door and swing it open, seeing Liam's light on across the hall. He's not in his room.

"Olivia, this way," Mom calls. She comes down the hall and grabs my hand, dragging me alongside her while clasping her robe closed with her other hand. Two soldiers are in the living room and one in the kitchen. Couch cushions are thrown to the floor and dishes are being pulled from every cabinet. One soldier flips one of the couches and cuts the fabric underneath.

Mom pulls me outside, where another soldier waits with a gun at his side. Our neighbors across from us are also out of their apartment—a young couple and their three-year-old son. The father holds his wife and their sobbing child close, murmuring comforting words to the toddler.

"It's okay, buddy," he says. "We'll get to go back in soon."

Liam leans against the metal railing of the balcony, his back to us, watching everything unfold in the other buildings. The complex is a rave of red and blue lights, and the heavy snow is confetti falling from the sky. Shouts, cries, and arguments fill the night. The soldier grabs me by the shoulders and spins me around.

"Hands on the wall!" he commands.

Heart racing, I do as I'm told. I know better than to question him. His hands pat down almost every inch of my body and make one final trail down my sides before he says, "You're clear."

I move from the wall, and Mom takes my place as the soldier pats her down. He finishes his search, and Mom walks across to stand with our neighbors. I lean against the railing beside Liam. He glances at me but doesn't say anything. We watch soldiers pour in and out of people's homes. Families stand out in the freezing cold as their apartments are torn apart like ours. After the attempted terrorist attack, they can't be too careful.

The evening news confirmed what Liam told me. Underground resistance members have reached an entirely new threat level. They hijacked an airplane and were attempting to fly it into the Capitol building in the Red Zone—a method once used in the Old World. When air traffic control noticed the plane had changed course, they contacted the pilot and insisted on an emergency landing. The hijacker refused to cooperate and military action was taken. They had no choice but to shoot down the plane.

Fourteen people were on board. Fifteen lives were lost, including the terrorist. Innocent people lost their lives because of a group of selfish individuals with a vendetta against the Enlightened Society.

Now we all have to suffer through surprise raids and whatever other consequences there may be. Anything remotely suspicious will result in arrest, interrogation, and re-education—if the perpetrator is lucky. The Yellow Zone has already turned to public execution in order to rid their cities of terrorists. We've always been more lenient than them, but after yesterday, I wouldn't be surprised if the Green Zone embraced it too.

A new wave of fear washes over me as I realize that one, if not all, of us will be taken into custody tonight. Our military is thorough in everything they do, and a raid is no exception. Something is tucked away in our home that will raise red flags: Liam's gun.

Panic consumes me. With our father being an AWOL cop and our aunt having harbored illegal substances, they won't go easy on us. It's as though this family is cursed. I glance at Liam, who looks as calm as ever. He rubs his eyes and lets out a frustrated sigh. I look over my shoulder at the soldier, who's pacing the small walkway between the two units, looking mildly irritated.

Figuring that now isn't the best time to directly ask Liam about what's hiding in his room, I try a different approach. "You look annoyed."

"I am," he says. He props his elbow up on the rail and presses his cheek to his palm, letting out a long yawn. "I want to go back to bed. This is stupid."

"It's to keep us safe. Anyone could have illegal possessions that could be used to hurt themselves or others. I mean, look at Naomi."

He rolls his eyes. "Not my problem."

Three soldiers exit our neighbors' apartment, giving them the okay to go back in. The family returns to their home, and the soldiers descend the flight of stairs. My blood boils at how careless my brother is being. He's willing to bring us all down, and for what? What purpose does he have for that weapon?

Time crawls by at an agonizing pace. At any minute I expect a soldier to come out, tackle us to the ground and put us in cuffs. Mom stands off to the side with her arms wrapped around herself. The cold is brutal, but my anxiety keeps my mind off it. Bringing my thumb to my mouth, I nibble on my nail, a bad habit I picked up in middle school.

"Nervous about something?" Liam asks.

"As if you don't already know," I scoff.

He raises his eyebrows. "I don't. Care to explain?"

The soldiers assigned to our unit appear, giving us permission to go inside, and leave with the man who has been standing guard without another word to us.

They didn't find it. How did they not find it? Entering the apartment proves their search was as thorough as I knew it would be. Furniture is flipped. Cabinets are bare. Papers, books, and clothes are strewn throughout the hall between mine and Liam's rooms. I'm relieved that I won't be spending the rest of the night in a cell, but it doesn't make any sense.

We spend the next hour straightening up the apartment, mainly focusing on standing furniture back up and fixing the kitchen. Mom tells us to gather our things from the hallway and worry about putting them back after we get some sleep. She bids us goodnight and goes to her own trashed room.

Another hour goes by silently sorting through the mess in the hall and piling it in our own rooms. I finish gathering my belongings before Liam and offer to help him. In return, he helps me move my mattress back on top of my box spring.

When he leaves, I remake my bed, longing for at least a few hours of uninterrupted sleep. But I know that, like the last couple of nights, sleep won't come easily. My nerves are shot. The security I've felt all my life is gone. Is this all coming out of nowhere, or has danger always been lurking in the shadows and I never noticed? All other things aside, one question still burns in my mind: What happened to the gun? I have to ask him. With him home and no one else around, this is the best time.

Before I can change my mind, I march across the hall and barge into his room, not bothering to knock.

Unstartled, he tosses a pillow onto his bed and groans. "Whatever it is, can it wait until later? I'm exhausted."

"Where is it?" I demand.

He collapses onto his bed and runs his hands down his face. "Where's what?"

"The gun!"

"What are you talking about?"

"Cut the bullshit, Liam!"

"God, you're so annoying."

Ignoring his comment, I open his closet. It looks to have only partially been searched during the raid. Half of the clothes that I saw before remain inside and the pile of boxes has toppled over. The stack of folded laundry in the far corner remains untouched. When I pull it down, it's lighter than when I was here last night. Still, I shake out every article of clothing, tossing each one to the floor.

"What are you doing?" he asks, pulling me away from the closet.

"I saw it last night! You had it hidden in your clothes. What did you do with it?"

"You went through my room while I was gone?"

"I'm worried about you!" It comes out louder than I meant it to.

He studies me for a moment. His eyes go from furious to gentle. "God damn it." Moving aside the toppled-over boxes, he tugs at the carpet that meets the base of the back wall. Pulling back the padding underneath, he wedges his fingers under a plank of wood, ripping it up. He reaches into the gap he's revealed, retrieving something.

"Here it is." He stands and turns to me, holding the gun in his hand. It's pointed down at the floor and his index finger rests across the frame. "Happy?"

"Why do you have it?"

"It was Dad's."

"That's impossible. Mom returned everything that belonged to the police department."

He returns the weapon to its hiding place and pushes the boxes back over the spot. "Yeah, well, I was able to snatch it up before she did that."

"But why?"

"Why do you ask so many questions?" Brushing past me, he sits on his bed. "They weren't going to find it, if that's what you've been worried about."

"You don't know that."

"We're not in jail, are we?"

As much as I hate to admit it, he's right. No one would think to look in that specific place under the carpet. I don't blame him for keeping a memento of our father—I have his old nametag stuffed in the top drawer of my dresser. I just wish it were something less lethal and more legal.

"So what's this about you being worried about me?" Liam asks.

"Nothing. Forget it." I start a retreat to my room, but he stops me.

"You already invaded my privacy. I think I at least deserve an explanation."

"Later? After you get off work?"

He considers it for a moment, then says, "Fine. Now get out of my room."

Steam rolls out behind me as I exit the bathroom. I didn't hear my alarm this morning, and I'm scrambling to get ready before starting the day. Mom has already left, and she's going to kill me if I don't turn up soon. The apartment is still atrocious, adding more chaos to my morning, and I frantically search the kitchen for my keys.

We've never had a raid in the Green Zone. After the attack, I understand taking more precautions to keep everyone safe, but barging in and tearing apart our home feels excessive. Did everyone have to endure last night's events, or did they target our area?

Liam comes around the corner dressed in his full black uniform and slides past me. "What are you doing here?"

"Overslept." I pull the microwave away from the wall, checking behind it and running my hand underneath. Nothing. Getting on my hands and knees, I scan the floor. Muddy footprints plaster the white linoleum. Mom probably had a panic attack when she saw them.

Finally, I spot them. Swiping the keys from under the dishwasher, I spring to my feet and run to the living room to grab my shoes.

"Need a ride?" Liam asks as he comes out of the laundry room. He pulls his car keys from his pocket and ties his maroon apron around his waist.

"Nah, I walk there all the time."

He rolls his eyes. "Stop being stubborn. Come on."

Shrugging on my jacket, I stumble out the door behind him. I lock up and take the stairs two at a time on my way down. Liam starts the car as I slide in and pulls out of his parking spot in front of our building. We don't say much during the drive. Yesterday and last night are weighing heavily on my mind, and from how dead the city is, it's obvious everyone else is shaken up, too.

Soldiers aren't flooding the streets anymore, but there is the occasional police officer strolling up the sidewalk, throwing an accusatory glance at each person who passes. The sun is out but brings no warmth. Pedestrians carefully check their surroundings when crossing the street and approaching others. Some look up to the sky, like they're expecting another plane to be shot down any minute.

Liam is more relaxed today. He tries a few times to bring up the subject we left off with last night, but I shoot down each attempt. It's not that I don't want to talk about it—I do—but I'm so out of it I can barely keep my eyes open. Fragments of the past few days replay in my head. Has it only been a few days? It feels more like weeks. Nothing makes sense anymore.

"What's bothering you?" Liam asks, no longer trying to beat around the bush. "Are you still worried about the gun?"

"No." Rubbing my eyes, I lean my head back. "Yes. I don't know. I'm just tired, okay?"

"I know a lot has happened lately, but that's not something you need to worry about. They're not going to find it."

"You don't know that!" I snap. "You're not stupid, Liam, so stop acting like it!" A wave of irritability washes over me and passes a moment later. Even with waking up late, I feel sleep-deprived. "I'm sorry. I'm stressed."

"I understand." He sighs. "I could've been there for you more, especially after what you witnessed."

"Yeah, you could have."

He pulls up to the flower shop and puts the car in park. The small lot is empty, although the neon sign boasts that the shop is open for business. Aside from a couple of special orders that were placed weeks ago, I suspect we won't be very busy today. I love working here—it's always been a bonding experience for Mom and me—but slow days are torturous.

"But we're going to talk when I get off, right?" he asks.

"As long as you're not busy."

"I won't be." He gives me a smile and nudges my shoulder before I get out.

The bell on the door rings when I enter the shop. Poinsettias and wreaths are the prominent arrangements this time of the year, making the interior feel festive with their bright reds and greens. Bouquets of fresh pansies and sweet alyssums toward the front give the store a softer tone. The white string lights tacked to the top of the walls and the spotlights are dimmed, and the marble floors are as immaculate as ever.

Behind the white counter, the small TV in the corner is on, broadcasting the news at a low volume. I pull my white apron from a shelf under the counter and clock in at the computer. Mom comes out from the back, dropping two sealed cardboard boxes beside me.

"You're late," she says, barely sparing me a glance. "By two hours." Her hair is coming loose from the low bun at the back of her head. As usual, she's painted her face, but it doesn't take away from her bloodshot eyes.

I grab a pair of scissors from the drawer and slice the tape on the boxes. "I'm sorry. I had trouble waking up."

One box is the usual supplies we receive on Mondays—floral wire, sleeves, ribbon, tape, notepads, etc. The second box contains the white tablecloths we ordered over a month ago.

"The raid took a toll on everyone, but that's no excuse."

"I know, I know. I'm sorry."

She unpacks the box of supplies, carefully putting each item in its respective place. I turn up the volume on the TV and take it upon myself to dress the tables throughout the shop. The media recaps the raid that shook the entire Green Zone. Nothing illegal was found. No one was taken into custody. All it did was terrorize innocent people—which is good, in a way. It will keep people from doing something stupid like hijacking another plane. The Society has confirmed that random searches will be a regular occurrence in our zone until further notice. They're desperately trying to prevent us from turning into an execution zone like the Yellow Zone. The Yellow Zone wasn't always that way, but terrorist activity continued to rise, and they had no other choice. It's calmed down since then, but public execution is still used when needed. Aside from the Red Zone, where the politicians and Elites reside, ours is the most peaceful. At least it used to be.

Authorities suspect the hijacker wasn't working alone, and they're searching for the person who orchestrated the attack. They will be charged with domestic terrorism, treason, and fourteen counts of first-degree murder. The Society will punish them accordingly, along with anyone else who is discovered to have ties to them.

A customer enters the store, and Mom cheerfully greets her. I move on to the second table out of the four that are spaced down the center of the showroom. Clearing the vases from the top, I smooth the tablecloth over the scuffed wood, then carefully replace the arrangements. The woman selects a bouquet of snowdrops from one of the display racks and meets Mom at the register.

"I can't believe what's happening," the lady says, shaking her head.

Photos of last night's raid flash across the TV screen, followed by the ruins of the aircraft.

"Ungrateful kids, these days," she goes on. "They have no idea how lucky they are to live in the world they do."

"I agree," Mom says.

I move on to the third table. The anchor on the screen switches topics, reporting the most recent breaking news. I ignore it at first, focusing on my task at hand. The woman pays for her snowdrops, still chatting with my mother about last night. Mom doesn't like talking politics with customers, so she politely smiles and gives an occasional "Mm-hmm" as the woman rambles. Finally, she thanks both of us for the flowers and waddles out of the store. While returning the displays to the table, I catch a glimpse of the missing girl—the murdered girl—on the screen. I close my eyes for a moment and reopen them, but the photo remains.

"Police were called to the scene just after sunrise this morning when a body—"

The screen goes black, and my gaze shifts to Mom, who tosses the remote aside.

"Wait, I want to see what that was about!" It had to be a mistake. I must have imagined it. Sleep deprivation and immense amounts of stress can cause paranoia and hallucinations. But as much as I don't want it to be true, I know it is. At least the girl has been found, and her family will get some sort of closure.

"You're supposed to be working," Mom responds. "Besides, I don't need any of those depressing stories in the background when customers come in."

I finish up with the tablecloths and return to my normal spot behind the counter. Opening the drawer beneath the register, I fish out our organizer and read over what's on the list for me to do today. Our two large orders are already crossed out. No other arrangements are due, so we're left to wait on someone to come in. Mom asks me to man the front while she disappears to the back to start this week's audit.

Working alone doesn't usually bother me—I've done it plenty of times—but I'd give anything to take my mind off what's been going on. We have three part-time employees who rotate shifts throughout the week, and I usually work part of the day with at least one of them. For the next few hours, though, it's just the two of us. Someone will come in to relieve me this evening.

In an attempt to distract myself and pass the time, I start on the cleaning list that's scrawled on the whiteboard behind me. I start with wiping down the display racks, taking my time spraying and scrubbing every crevice. Moving on to the coolers, I clean both sides of the glass doors. Some have already managed to accumulate oily fingerprints despite the signs asking customers not to touch the glass. My phone rings on the counter, but I ignore it. Although it's slow, Mom isn't fond of her employees using their devices while on the clock, and I'm held to those same standards. It goes silent after the fifth ring, and the text tone sounds seconds later. I finish the final cooler and gather the cleaning supplies, storing them in the cabinet in the hall.

Checking to make sure Mom isn't looking, I grab my phone. The missed call and text message are both from my brother.

"They found her."

So he's seen it, too. I can't imagine how he's feeling right now if she truly was one of his friends. Hearing it from me is one thing, especially since she was originally reported as kidnapped. That could still be true. She could've tried to escape her kidnapper the night I saw her. But having the news and police confirm she's dead makes it much more real, even for me.

I start a reply, trying to think of something to say that can comfort him. "I'm sorry" sounds too generic. "I know" is too insincere. No words can change it. Nothing will bring her back—so I go with the same response our dad would always give us when something bad happened in the world. *"They'll find whoever did it."*

Bright rays of radiant sunlight pour in through the double glass doors and full-length windows, making everything glow. The activity outside has picked up, but it's nowhere close to what it normally is at this time of the day. Fatigue and irritability fight to consume me. My mind is cloudy and my body is drained of energy. Resisting the urge to lay my head on the counter for a quick rest, I tackle the chore of reorganizing our area behind the counter. The shelves beneath the register are full of clutter and layered with dust. Employees' empty plastic cups have been pushed to the back. Something that has spilled coats a folder in a sticky red substance.

Removing each item from the first shelf, I dust and wipe it down, spraying and scrubbing vigorously to remove the sticky residue. I toss all of the trash and disinfect everything I've pulled out. While I'm scraping the folder clean with my fingernail, the bell on the door chimes. Pushing everything aside on the floor, I pull myself to my feet.

"Hi! What can I do for you?" I ask in the liveliest voice I can manage.

The customer's back is to me as he browses our showroom. The beanie on his head bulges from the hair stuffed inside. Delicately brushing his fingertips against the petals of a centerpiece, he turns his head, and the sunlight illuminates the jagged scar along his jaw. Nixon. "I was hoping you could help me with an arrangement for a memorial service."

"Did my brother send you here?"

He turns around, studying me as if trying to remember who I am. "I'm sorry?"

I plaster a smile on my face. "Nothing. I'm sorry to hear that. What kind of arrangement are you looking for?"

"Something simple. It's a small gathering."

"Of course. I have some options you can look at if you want." Pulling out a catalog, I open it and turn it toward him. Nixon approaches the counter and silently flips through the laminated pages. As he searches, I make myself busy by returning everything to the shelf I cleaned. I purposely move at a slower pace, organizing and reorganizing, then move on to cleaning the middle shelf.

Arrangements for a memorial service aren't orders we receive often. Rarely, in fact. Since nearly everyone who passes is cremated and formal funerals can only be afforded by the Elite, hardly anyone outside of the Red Zone cares to hold a ceremony. If they do, flowers are the least of their worries. At the most, we'll sell a couple dozen roses.

For someone planning a memorial, he doesn't appear to be especially bothered. Everyone mourns in their own way, but he's as nonchalant as he was when I met him the other day.

Unable to tolerate another second of the uncomfortable silence, I say, "If you don't mind me asking, who is the funeral for?"

"A friend," he says, studying one of the pages. "I'm sure you've heard about the girl who was found today."

I freeze mid-cleaning, remaining crouched behind the counter. "That was your friend?"

"Mm-hmm." Resting his temple on his fist, he turns the page. "She was Liam's friend, too."

He pauses, fixating his eyes on me. For a moment, they look defensive.

"I'm his sister," I say.

"That's right." Realization floods his face. "I thought you looked familiar. Ivy, right?"

"Yeah."

He turns his attention back to the book and points to one of the items. "Something like this."

Standing up, I look at the easel and heart-shaped wreath he's chosen, consisting of carnations, phlox, and pink camellias. I grab an order form and jot down his name and the item he's chosen. "Perfect. Anything else?"

"I think that's it."

"Alright. That does include delivery and setup by one of our employees." I slide the form and pen to him. "If you can just put the date and time as well as the location, and a phone number we can reach someone on if needed."

While he fills out the form, I enter the order into the computer. Once he's finished, he hands it back to me. I sign my name at the bottom and rip the top page off, handing him his copy. I recite the total to him, and he pops his card into the chip reader. The system takes longer than usual to accept the payment, but it finally goes through.

Handing him his receipt, I say, "I know this might be a bad time, but I have to know. The other night when I talked to Liam about your friend—"

"I heard you."

"So what happens? Are they going to find who did it?"

He shrugs. "If whoever did it was able to scrub the crime scene like that, I doubt it."

"You told me not to tell anyone."

Letting out a deep breath, he glances around the shop as though making sure no one else is around, then returns his eyes to me. Leaning closer, he lowers his voice.

"I know what it's like to want to tell someone about the bad shit you have bottled up—it eats at you. But I promise it will be a lot worse for you if you tell anyone. It's best to keep it between you and your brother."

"What about you?"

"You won't be seeing much of me, but I can keep a secret, especially when Liam is involved." Shoving the receipt in his pocket, he saunters to the door. "Thanks for your help."

7. Do You Realize

Getting home early feels unnatural.

Mom was in a foul mood when I went back to give her the order form. I volunteered to deliver the wreath in three days, but she insisted she could find someone else to take care of it.

"I won't be in on Thursday," she said. "I have some things I need to take care of, and I need you here to train the new girl."

She hadn't mentioned hiring someone else before, but I'm thankful that we're getting extra help.

Three more customers came in after Nixon, but I can hardly remember taking care of them. Mom came out when the last one was in the store because she heard me stumbling over my words. After we finished with him, she sent me home, promising she would be okay until the other scheduled worker came in. To make up for leaving two hours before my shift was over, I promised I would clean the mess at home.

I start some coffee and tackle the rest of the kitchen while waiting for it to brew. I sweep, mop the floor, and rearrange the dishes that we haphazardly stacked in the cabinets last night. When the coffee is done, I prepare myself a cup and sip from it as I go. Gradually, I move from room to room, avoiding Mom's and Liam's bedrooms. The last thing I need right now is to find something else that isn't meant for my eyes. I'm harboring enough secrets, and I don't think I could handle any more.

The front of the apartment is finally straightened up, but knowing Mom, she'll go back over it a million times before she's satisfied. In the safety and comfort of my room, I set my coffee mug on my nightstand and work on tidying my own space. Clothes are returned to their rightful place, trash is tossed, and other miscellaneous items receive a new home throughout the room.

I still feel guilty for not performing my best at work today. I'd like to think my mom understands, but she wasn't very happy about it. She and Liam experienced the same thing last night, and they're functioning normally. She can't understand because she doesn't know all that I know. Everything I've buried deep is gnawing at me, scraping at my insides to escape. It's killing me.

So what if I do tell her, or Addison, or someone else? The police may think I was involved in the murder, but surely I can get myself out of it somehow. Pinning it on a terrorist would be an easy solution, and I can live with a couple weeks of re-education for breaking curfew. As for the gun, I'm not sure what to do. It's understandable that Liam would keep something of our dad's, but out of all the things he could have chosen, why that? I don't want him to get into trouble. I don't want him taken into custody and questioned. Sooner or later, someone else will find out, and the confrontation he'll face will be much worse than being yelled at by his sister.

I don't care what Liam and Nixon tell me. They don't understand either. They didn't see what I saw. I need to let it out.

Finishing up my room, I shove my phone in my pocket and head into the now orderly living room. The doorknob wiggles when I make it to the end of the hall, and I freeze. My brother enters, tossing his keys into the bowl on the table beside the door.

"What are you doing home early?" I ask, clutching my key in my hand. He still has another hour until his scheduled leaving time, and even then he usually gets held over.

"Got cut," he says. "We weren't busy enough for me to stay on the floor." Removing his jacket and shoes, he looks me over. "Where are you headed?"

Shifting my weight from one foot to the other, I pretend not to have heard him. He rolls his eyes when I don't answer and pushes past me, disappearing into his room. I stand at the opening to the living room for a few moments, conflicted over whether or not I should go. We have two police stations in our city—one on the outskirts near Naomi's house and one in the heart of the city where our dad worked—and the one closest to us isn't too long a walk. I can make it in about fifteen minutes if I hurry. If I don't go now, I'm not sure I'll have the courage again.

I tiptoe to the door. I have to do this. With my fingers wrapped around the doorknob, I twist, hesitating before pulling the door open.

"Where are you going, V?"

Jerking my hand away, I spin around to see Liam with his arms crossed over his chest. He's traded his uniform for sweatpants and a T-shirt.

"Did you forget your promise?" he asks.

"No, I didn't," I say.

"So where are you going?" He moves to the kitchen and searches the fridge. Pulling out a plastic storage container full of leftovers, he tosses it in the microwave.

I remain frozen, feeling like a little kid who got caught doing something they shouldn't have.

"Nowhere," I lie.

"Doesn't look that way." He grabs a fork from one of the drawers, and when the microwave beeps, he removes his food and takes a seat at the table.

The intensity of the past few days is crushing me. Knowing I have no choice but to go to the police is terrifying, but I know deep in my soul it will bring some sort of relief. I'd give anything to have someone to trust, someone who could give me answers. Confiding in Mom or Addison won't do any good. Nothing will change by telling them.

Fear, confusion, and desperation take over. The feelings grow stronger with every second I meditate on it. I want to scream. I want to cry. I just want everything to be okay again.

"I have to tell someone," I finally say. "I can't deal with this anymore."

"Sit down. Talk to me."

No matter what he says, I'm going, but I could use a few minutes to collect myself and figure out exactly what I'm going to tell the authorities. Taking the seat beside him at the circular table, I wait for him to speak. I have nothing to say to him.

"You were going to tell the police?" he asks in between bites of lasagna. The smell of marinara and cheese makes my stomach grumble, but I can't imagine eating right now.

I nod. "Save the speech. I know you don't want me to."

"You can do what you think is best, but you need to think about how it will affect you."

"I know she was your friend."

He takes a couple more bites. "She was."

"So you should be upset. You should *want* me to report what I saw."

"Believe me, I am. It's not that simple, though."

"Then tell me what to do!" Tears build up in my eyes, and I blink them back before they can spill. "I just want everything to go back to normal. Between this and Naomi and the gun and whatever is going on with you, I feel like I don't have control over anything."

"None of this is your fault though. You need to understand that. I already told you about the gun, you weren't the one who killed Elizabeth, and you can't control what Mom did."

"I just want to help."

He sighs and pushes the now empty container to the side. "I know, but like you told me earlier, they'll find whoever did it." He keeps a poker face, but I know he doesn't believe that. Nixon pointed out that it will be nearly impossible to track the killer with the way the crime scene was cleaned, and Liam knows that, too.

Even if I do report what I saw, I didn't get a good look at the murderer. My testimony would be useless. Taking all of that into consideration, I can only hope they find some trace of his DNA.

"Why the gun?" I ask.

"I don't know. I thought maybe it could be useful if something were to happen. If it will make you feel better, I can get rid of it."

It would make me feel better—knowing there's a weapon in our home with no other purpose but to kill scares me—but if it's something for him to remember our father by, who am I to take it away?

"No," I say, "just keep it hidden. I'm sorry about Elizabeth."

He shrugs, but by the way he averts his eyes, I can tell it's weighing on him. "Why have you been worried about me?"

"You've been acting weird. The other day when you came into my room, you were so... off. You seem so distant, and you always say you're busy. After watching what happened to Elizabeth and what happened at Naomi's, I really could've used you. And then there was that plane that was shot down and the raid..." Propping my elbow on the table, I cover my eyes with my hand.

"I was upset the other day because of Elizabeth. We were supposed to meet up with some other friends early that morning. She never showed, and no one could get a hold of her. I was already assuming the worst, and I didn't want to believe she was who you saw."

The dam breaks and the tears erupt, spilling from my eyes and seeping between my fingers. I'm trying to understand, trying to make sense of it all.

"What have you been so busy with?" I croak.

"Some stuff you wouldn't understand, but that's no excuse for brushing you off, and I'm sorry."

I pull my hand from my face, smearing the tears, and wipe the moisture on my pant leg.

"I'm fine, though," he continues. "There's nothing for you to worry about."

"You didn't answer my question."

He picks at the top left corner of the woven placemat in front of him. "I've been… trying to find Dad—or at least an idea of where he went."

So Liam's tried looking for him, too. I tried searching the entire first week after his disappearance. That's when I started going out after curfew. I walked the city as well as the outskirts for hours. I went through Mom's phone multiple times, hoping maybe she was secretly staying in touch with him. After seven nights without any luck, and one traumatic experience, I gave up.

My fingers slide along my collarbone, stopping at the smooth scar.

I'd quickly learned how to avoid the police patrols and become an expert at blending in with the darkness. I was out for close to six hours that night, with my heartbreak still fresh. I waited in the shadows, watching the police station, hoping Dad would show up. Of course, he never did, but I was too stubborn to let it go. An hour before sunrise, I took a shortcut home, one I'd learned didn't have much police activity. Two neighborhoods over from our apartment complex, I heard footsteps. Instinctively, I turned around to see a man in street clothes following ten feet behind me. As soon as I started running, he picked up his pace, tackling me to the ground.

I tried to fight him off, but he was twice my size and had me firmly pinned to the sidewalk. My heart pounded furiously against my ribcage; with every kick or attempted punch, he applied more pressure to my torso with his knee. Digging my nails into his arm resulted in a strike to my cheek. He produced a knife, seemingly out of thin air, and held it to my throat with a shaky hand.

"Stop resisting," he grunted, "or I'll kill you."

I let my body fall limp underneath him, and he pulled the knife away, keeping it clenched in one hand. He relaxed a bit and let up on my torso, but before he could do anything else, I sucked in as much air as I could and screamed as loud and as long as my lungs would allow me. Startled and angry, he made one swift swipe with the blade across my collarbone. Searing pain burned through me, and blood trickled down my chest. I screamed again and again and kicked and clawed until he leapt off me and ran. Pressing my hand to my wound, I ran home.

I went to Addison's dad the next day and reported it. I lied, saying I'd been on my way to work when I was attacked. Because I'd seen my attacker's face, I was able to identify him, and he was arrested. Apparently he had a record of assaulting multiple young women and already had a case built against him.

I never told anyone else about what happened—not even the fabricated version—and that was the last time I tried to look for my dad. I took it as a sign to give up all hope. For an entire year, I didn't sneak out. At the one-year mark of my attack, I ventured out again. Not because I thought I could find my dad—it was obvious by then that he wasn't coming back—but because I found the idea of roaming the city during those forbidden hours both calming and exhilarating. It became a new way for me to clear my head and find peace at a time when it was truly quiet.

Apparently, Liam *hasn't* given up hope. It's inspiring… and also incredibly stupid. If Dad cared at all, he would have come back already, or wouldn't have left in the first place.

"So why is Nixon involved with that?" I ask. "With the way he talked about you 'gathering information', I assume he's involved."

He finishes typing something on his phone, then sets it aside. "Nixon has been there for me through all of this. He's a good friend— one of the only ones I can always rely on."

"Well, it's none of his business. You're not going to find Dad anyway. He obviously doesn't want to be found."

He doesn't say anything, just continues picking at the placemat. I'd never realized how angry I've been with our father until now.

"I think the terrorists killed Elizabeth," I blurt out.

He looks up at me. "What?"

"Think about it—who else would be fucked up enough to murder an innocent person? I mean, look at the attack they planned for the Capitol. Fourteen civilians lost their lives because of them."

"What reason would they have to kill her?"

"They don't need a reason. Their goal is to ruin this country and drag us back to the Old World. We're among the safest and most progressive nations in the world, and now—"

"Spare me the history lesson. I learned all of that just like everyone else." He shifts in his chair, glancing at his phone when it lights up then back to me. "I don't think they were behind her murder, though."

"Who else could it be?"

"If I knew, I wouldn't be talking to you about it right now." Closing his eyes, he lets out a long breath. "Let the police do their job, okay? At least wait until tomorrow to go up there."

"I'm sorry I keep bringing her up."

He opens his eyes. "It's fine. I understand."

"I just… I hate them, this resistance that's sprung up out of nowhere. Everything was great—it has been for decades. And now all of this is happening so close together. It's not fair to the rest of us."

"I get it." He stands up, pushing the chair back under the table, and takes his dish to the sink. "Hey, do you remember Dad's homemade hot chocolate he always made?"

The mention of it brings back tons of memories, from childhood all the way up until I started high school. Cold nights were spent with the four of us cuddled on the couch, watching movies and sipping the rich, silky-smooth cocoa. When we were old enough to work the stove, Dad taught us his secret recipe. It was like a magical potion that could melt away any form of stress. He made an extra-large batch for me and him when my first boyfriend broke up with me in the eighth grade. We sat in my room and drank the remedy while I cried to him for hours.

Despite my newfound anger toward him, it brings a smile to my face. "Of course I do."

Liam finishes putting the dirty dishes in the dishwasher and pulls a stainless-steel stockpot from one of the cabinets. "Let's make it. I have a feeling it'll make you feel better."

I join him in the kitchen. He pulls the ingredients needed from the fridge, and I grab the dry ingredients. We talk, laugh, and reminisce as we pour and stir the ingredients over the heat. Before the concoction is even complete, it's already doing its job. My stress melts away.

Mom comes home from work, and a smile flickers over her lips when she sees us. Coming up behind us, she wraps the two of us in her arms. Her eyes look tired with a hint of sadness. Although it's something so simple, this recipe is something that's special to all of us, and I can only imagine what memories it brings back for her. She plants a kiss on each of our cheeks and tells us she loves us.

"I'm exhausted," she says. "Save me a cup. And get some sleep, Olivia."

When the hot chocolate is ready and Liam is ladling it into separate mugs, there's a knock at the door. I look to Liam, who shrugs. With twenty minutes to curfew, there shouldn't be anyone here.

My first thought is a dumb, childish one: Maybe the cocoa *is* some sort of magic potion that has lured our father home. The next idea is much darker but still irrational: The Society knows I was at the murder scene and has come to arrest me.

Liam doesn't move from his station, and Mom hasn't emerged from her bedroom. Another light knock.

"Don't worry, I'll get it," I say sarcastically, nudging my brother with my elbow as I pass by.

Two petite arms throw themselves around my neck once the door is open. Addison pulls back with a toothy grin. "Surprise!" She lets herself in, and I lock the door behind her. "Ooh, it smells amazing in here!"

I follow her to the kitchen, where Liam tops our cocoa with marshmallows and pulls a third mug down.

"What's going on?" I ask, giving Liam a questioning look.

He avoids my gaze while he fills the final cup. When he passes Addison and me our drinks, he finally looks at me with a smile. "I thought you could use a friend."

8. True Colors

Two weeks have passed, and everything has gone back to normal for the most part. Work has been especially busy. After all of the bodies from the plane wreckage were identified, people poured into our store, purchasing bouquets, single flowers, wreaths, and more. A rally was held in our zone two cities over, and a massive order was placed for thirteen arrangements. President Hoffman came to speak, and Mom was ecstatic to have the honor of crafting different masterpieces for her visit. The President spoke of the atrocities that have plagued our zone and gave her condolences to those who lost their loved ones. During her speech, she assured everyone that the Enlightened Society is working diligently to locate and arrest the remaining terrorists. She insisted there are few remaining and urged everyone to follow the 'see something, say something' rule. Toward the end of her speech, she answered the unspoken question everyone had been wondering: Will we embrace executions like the Yellow Zone?

No. But the raids will continue at random to ensure everyone's safety.

We did have two more raids across the Green Zone. One was late at night again, and the other was during the day, targeting businesses during their open hours. They weren't as nerve-racking as the first one—they were more annoying than anything. Knowing the gun was hidden in Liam's room kept me on edge, but I reassured myself they wouldn't find it. And they didn't. The three of us repeated the same cycle of cleaning the apartment and catching a few final hours of sleep before starting our day.

I've made it a priority to spend more time with Addison. After our shifts and on our days off, we've made time for each other. I've let her in a bit more on what's been going on, but she still doesn't know every detail and, for now, it's better that way. Spending as much time as possible with her has helped keep my mind off everything. I've been sleeping better and have been a lot more productive at work. The night Liam surprised me by inviting her over was exactly what I needed.

Liam has disappeared a couple more times, claiming to be busy. I haven't pressed the subject of his search for Dad again. It's better he has something to motivate him—even if it is a false hope—than for me to crush his dream of our family being reunited. When he has been home, he's been more present and has silently listened when I need to rant about my growing hatred for the resistance groups. And as he's listened on those late nights, I've realized that it's something he's gotten better at. He always used to be the type of person who would interject with an unsolicited opinion or advice. Now, he sits back and absorbs every word, only speaking when asked directly.

We were supposed to visit Naomi at her one-week mark since being admitted to re-education. The day of our scheduled visit, Mom received a phone call from the ward. Naomi had been refusing to cooperate or complete any treatment. She exhibited violent behavior and underwent multiple psychiatric evaluations before they decided to put her in solitary. Contact with the world outside her cell is forbidden, as it may hinder her progress or trigger another mental breakdown. She'll be allowed monitored phone calls in a few days, and if she finally decides to cooperate, they'll reschedule our visit.

The alcohol obviously wasn't her only issue. Whenever Liam or I ask why Naomi is acting the way she is, why she's refusing treatment, Mom says the same thing: "She's suffering from losing Kyle." To a certain degree, I understand. I know how awful it is to lose someone close to you, regardless of the relationship. At the same time, I see it as incredibly selfish. Naomi doesn't have children, but she has us, her family, and her husband's family, who are all struggling with the loss of the same person. We all want answers. We all want justice. Everyone has their own secret battles, but we don't break the law and refuse help when it's offered. And the Society *is* trying to help. They could have refused her re-education and sent her directly to prison for the possession and consumption of illegal substances. Given the circumstances, they went easy on her, but she's made it worse for herself.

I finish braiding my hair and emerge from my room. Liam and I are both off today, and it's no surprise that he's still asleep. What I don't expect is for Mom to be seated at the kitchen table when I enter. Her laptop is open and she scrolls through whatever's on the screen while sipping from her black mug.

The apartment smells of its usual scent: Fresh coffee mixed with seasonal candles and an underlying trace of all-purpose cleaner. It's familiar and comforting. Although one of us four is missing, it's still home. We're still a family. This has become our new normal. I fought it for a while, refusing to believe that this was how my life was supposed to turn out. But after all that our family has endured recently, I'm content with it. In a way, it's brought the three of us closer, and I wouldn't have it any other way.

My father is out there somewhere. He can run as much as he wants, but we'll always be connected, forever tethered by fate and the will of the Universe.

Mom looks up at me with a smile. "Good morning, sweetie."

"Good morning," I respond, plucking a banana from the fruit basket on the counter. "Aren't you supposed to be at the store today?"

"After working nine days in a row, I need a day off. The store's fully staffed, anyway."

"Any plans today?" Biting into the fruit, I sit beside her.

"Not really; just want to relax." Her eyes widen and she angles her laptop so I can see the screen. "Isn't this beautiful?"

The open tab displays a realtor website specifically showing houses in the Red Zone. She clicks through the pictures of the house she's selected, pointing out everything she loves. It's a three-story Victorian home with a white wrap-around porch, consisting of seven bedrooms and three-and-a-half bathrooms. Restored hardwood floors glow under the immense amount of natural light on the first and second floors. The kitchen is modest in size but boasts dazzling quartz countertops, snow-white cabinets, and brand-new stainless-steel appliances. The white walls make everything brighter and are complemented by the black banister on the staircase and matching doors.

For a moment, I imagine what it would be like to live there or any other place in the Red Zone. I've never left the Green Zone, and it's not a bad place, but I've always been curious about the rest of our country. I think the Red Zone is intriguing to everyone. Aside from knowing that's where the Elites reside, it's shrouded in mystery. For those of us who weren't born into extreme wealth, the only way in is through the residency program. It's a generous offer but incredibly difficult to be accepted, and spots are limited. The seven openings this round are the most I've ever seen. Usually there are only two or three spots available, and it's not uncommon for one of the semi-annual programs to be cancelled.

"It is," I agree. "What, are you hoping to move there or something?"

Rubbing her thumb along the handle of her mug, she turns the computer back toward her and stares longingly at the house. "Maybe one day."

I toss the banana peel in the garbage and check my phone. Addison has messaged me, confirming that she'll be leaving her house soon to meet up for our run. It's one of the new hobbies we've picked up together. Liam suggested it as a way to blow off steam and clear my mind in place of sneaking out at night.

"Your father could've been transferred there, you know," Mom says. "We could be living there right now."

"He didn't want to though. He wanted to stay in our home." I keep my eyes on my phone while I respond to Addison.

"Obviously not," she mutters.

I return to the seat next to her. "Do you have any idea why he left?"

Her index finger brushes the touchpad beneath the keyboard and she taps it once, selecting another mansion we could never afford. Liam emerges, heading straight for the coffee pot and giving Mom the same puzzled look I probably did.

"Mom," I say.

She glances at the dainty silver watch on her wrist. "No, and it doesn't matter."

"What do you mean, it doesn't matter? Don't you wonder where he is? It's been nearly three years, and you're telling me you don't have any idea why?"

She shuts the laptop and takes a deep breath. "He clearly didn't want to be here anymore."

"But *why?* You have to know something."

Her eyes harden when they meet mine. I look to Liam for backup, but he's not paying attention—or at least he's pretending not to. He's leaning against the counter, coffee in hand and eyes glued to his phone.

"If you're insinuating it's my fault—"

"I'm not," I cut her off. "I just… I want to know why he left us."

Her eyes flick to Liam, then back to me. Downing the rest of her coffee, she rises from the chair and crosses the kitchen to the sink. "If I ever find out, I'll let you know."

"But Mom—"

"Ivy, drop it," Liam says. "She doesn't know anything." He shoots me a warning look, and when Mom's back is turned to me, I give him the finger. He does it right back with a smile.

Mom tosses her mug in the dishwasher. Filling it with detergent, she presses 'start' and the hum of the machine fills the kitchen. She checks her watch again as if she's waiting for something. Remembering my plans with Addison, I jump out of my chair and grab my boots from beside the front door. Sitting on one of the couches, I lace them up and send Addison a quick text, letting her know I'm on my way. She's notorious for being late, so she won't notice I'm running a few minutes behind. I promise myself I'll try talking to Mom again later when Liam isn't around.

My anger toward Dad has fizzled somewhat, and at this point, I simply want closure. Anything will do. After that, I can move on.

"Where are you going?" Mom asks, coming into the living room.

"Going for a run with Addison," I say, heading down the hall and into my room.

Pulling open the top drawer of my dresser, I search for another top. I settle for the first long-sleeved one I can find and change out of the T-shirt I already have on, throwing it to the side.

Digging deeper into the drawer, I retrieve the familiar silver rectangle. *B. Clearson.* I turn it over in my hand, tracing a finger over the letters engraved in the worn metal. His job was the one thing he loved as much as his family. To leave it all behind without any explanation is beyond strange. As crazy as it sounds, I'm beginning to believe Naomi was on to something. Maybe Dad's disappearance and Kyle's murder are linked somehow. The way she spoke, she made it sound like my dad killed her husband, but I don't think that's the case. She knows something, and when I'm able to talk to her again, I plan to find out.

A banging on the front door makes me jump. I toss the name tag back in the drawer, covering it with clothes before shutting it away. In the living room, Mom makes her way to the door as the banging continues.

"Another raid?" I ask Liam, stopping beside him.

He shrugs. "Wouldn't surprise me."

Mom unlocks the door, and I mentally prepare myself to be searched and deal with the clean-up afterward. Three men barge in and she steps aside. They look nothing like the usual soldiers who carry out the raids. They're dressed in black suits and pork-pie hats with dark sunglasses. One holds a black briefcase and another carries an overstuffed manila envelope with the words "TOP SECRET" stamped in bright red on the front.

Neither soldiers nor police—but they are without a doubt linked to the Enlightened Society. The third man looks directly at me and Liam. Although they're shielded, I can feel his eyes boring into us. His hand rests on his hip, where a gun peeks out from beneath his coat. I look to my brother who, for once, looks at least half as fearful as I feel. I try to rationalize the situation, but everything comes back to one possibility: They're here for Liam.

"Mrs. Clearson," the briefcase man says.

Mom doesn't appear to be afraid at all. In fact, she smiles at the man, and not once does she look back at us.

"That's me," she says in the same customer-service voice I've heard her use at the shop.

The man with the envelope produces a thick packet of papers stamped with the same red letters. Removing the pen from his breast pocket, he nods to the empty-handed stranger, then focuses on Mom. "We just need you to sign these."

The third man passes me and Liam and wanders down the hall. My heart is beating furiously now, pounding in my ears and drowning out the hushed conversation between my mom and the other two men. I'm frozen in place. The air grows heavier by the second. Every thud from each step he takes reverberates in my skull. He reaches the end of the hall, standing in between the two doors. I hold my breath, awaiting his next move. I try to convince myself that this isn't happening. That this is all a bad dream. But the knots in my stomach and hammering against my chest confirm that this is reality.

As I expected, he turns to his right and twists the doorknob to Liam's room. The hinges groan as he pushes it open. I brace myself for what's to come.

But Mom's voice cuts through the roaring in my ears and stops the man in his tracks. "Wrong room."

No. I must've heard her wrong. This has to be a mistake.

The man quickly turns around and opens my door, letting himself in. Moments later, he returns, carrying an old backpack I've had since my senior year. One of my shirts dangles out of the slightly unzipped main pocket. I snap my head in Mom's direction. She finishes signing the last of the papers and hands them back to the man. He stuffs the packet back in the envelope, and his partner passes her the briefcase.

"We appreciate your contribution," he says without emotion. "This is the agreed-upon payment."

"Mom," Liam says slowly, "what's going on?"

She doesn't answer him, doesn't even look at him. Clutching the briefcase to her chest, she thanks the two men in front of her.

"Olivia Clearson," the man holding my backpack says, "we're going to need you to come with us."

My heart stops.

"What did I do?"

I frantically look around the room. All eyes are on me—except hers. Liam repeats the question, which is again left unanswered. I want to run, but can't bring my legs to move. The room spins, slowly at first, then picking up speed. Faces blur into one another. Hands reach for me, grabbing at any part of my body they can touch. There's yelling and orders being barked. Liam is shouting, cursing at Mom, the men, me.

I'm being shoved toward the door. Screaming penetrates my ears. Liam reaches for me but is swatted away. One of the men draws his weapon, warning my brother not to come any closer. I'm suddenly lifted from the floor and carried outside. Liam yells my name, followed by other words I can't make out. My mind struggles to make sense of anything.

Only when we're outside do I realize the screaming is coming from me. I look back before being toted down the stairs. Closing the door, Mom finally looks at me. Her caramel eyes are dead, absent of any light.

9. Missing

Nothing could have prepared me for this.

One of the men stays behind with Mom and Liam while the other two carry me to the blacked-out prisoner transport van that awaits us. Seeing the vehicle is enough confirmation of where I'm going. It's the same type of vehicle used for all criminals and troublesome civilians when they're taken to re-education. Being escorted by men in suits, however, is out of the ordinary. Local police in normal uniform are always assigned to detain and transport the lawbreakers, except during the raids.

They know that I was out past curfew—that I witnessed Elizabeth's murder. They have to. There's no other reason I would be taken to re-education. No updates have been aired about the investigation since the day the body was found. Police have neither confirmed nor denied whether they have any suspects, and as far as I can tell, the alley has remained absent of police activity. Despite all of that, they must have somehow found out. But that doesn't explain the briefcase or the papers Mom signed.

Whenever the vehicle makes sharp turns, I'm jerked in one direction or another. Thankfully, I'm the only prisoner back here and don't have to worry about bumping against someone else. Handcuffed and buckled in, I attempt to reposition myself. The plastic bench is uncomfortable and the compartment itself is cramped. Before I can fully extend my legs, my feet make contact with the metal wall across from me. There's enough room on the bench beside me for two—maybe three—more people if we were all scrunched together.

Leaning my head against the cold metal wall behind me, I focus on my breathing and rapid heartbeat. Anxiety surges through me, flooding my veins with its venom. No mantras or comforting words can help me this time.

The way Mom looked at me during those last seconds was nearly as frightening as being taken. All of the love and comfort I've always known vanished. It's as if she knew something I didn't. If I'm being pinned for the murder, rather than just a witness who snuck out at night, she may believe I did it. She's always clung to every word spoken by the Society and law enforcement. I have, too. That's what we're taught to do. But she *has* to know I would never do that. I've never been a troublesome child. The worst I've ever done is sneak out, and it was never to do anything malicious. If that's the reason I've been arrested, the briefcase could have been reward money for reporting information about Elizabeth's murder. Maybe Mom heard Liam and me talking one night and called in a tip.

I'll serve my time for being out past curfew—that *is* something I'm guilty of. But there's no way I'm going to take the fall for killing someone.

In a way, I can't blame Mom for reporting me, assuming she overheard one of our conversations. Out of fear for my own life, I'd probably do the same if the tables were turned. It must have been a difficult decision for her to make, but I'm determined to prove to her and the Society that I'm innocent.

The muffled voices of the men up front travel through the wall that separates the cab. One of them laughs, and the sound of it brings my blood to a boil. I'm furious with them, and the fury toward my mother continues to grow too. I can't believe she turned me in. She didn't even look like she cared. No goodbyes or hugs or apologies. She was a zombie.

And then there's Liam. It feels misplaced, but the anger is aimed toward him as well. It was out of his control, I know that, but part of me wishes he could've done something like putting that gun to use. I immediately scrub the thought from my mind. That's something the terrorists would dream up. I'm the polar opposite of those twisted people, and expecting that of my brother is horrible.

The cuffs dig into my wrist every time the van hits a pothole. I'm pushed back in the seat, my arms trapped between my own weight and the wall. One especially large bump in the road forces me back farther, and I let out a yelp. Sitting up, I readjust myself for the tenth time. I don't know how long I've been back here. An hour maybe; no more than two. The day has hardly begun, and already I'm growing tired.

I wonder what Addison thought when I didn't show. She has to know something is wrong, especially if she tried calling my phone. Liam could've let her know what happened, or as much as he knows anyway. Or he may keep it to himself, not wanting her—and her dad—to get involved. He's had this mentality lately that he can fix everything by himself. While I'd love for him to come to the rescue, I'm afraid there's nothing he can do.

The vehicle comes to a stop. Doors slam and voices get closer. I close my eyes, saying a silent prayer that this isn't as bad as I'm expecting it to be. My chest tightens and my throat squeezes shut. The entire time I've been back here, I haven't shed a single tear. Now the pressure builds up in my head as I try to hold it back. Dim light seeps through my eyelids, followed by the screech of metal. Drawing in a deep breath, I open my eyes. One of the men hoists himself up into my compartment and removes the seatbelt. He helps me to the ground and takes me by the arm, walking beside me while the other man walks a few feet ahead of us with my backpack slung over his shoulder.

I frantically scan the area. Eight vans identical to the one I just exited are parked in the open gravel space. The large concrete building stretches out before us with nine garage doors lining the wall. Vibrant coniferous trees surround the building, filling the air with an earthy scent. The man guiding me gives me a nudge, and I pick up my pace. We reach the single metal door at the far end of the garages, and the lead officer holds it open for us to enter. I'm pushed inside, and the heavy door slams.

A bright room opens up that reminds me of a waiting room for a doctor's office minus the chairs. Pushed against one wall is an aquarium full of multicolored fish obliviously swimming about. Potted plants decorate the otherwise colorless room, and a receptionist area is centered on the back wall with a set of beige double doors beside it. The guard who has my arm drags me to the desk while the other remains at the entrance.

The heavy-set woman on the other side of the glass barrier looks up from the book on her desk. Her eyes skate over me, locking on my chaperone and giving him a courteous smile.

"Good afternoon!" she says. "Who do we have today?"

"Olivia Clearson, number 974," he responds flatly.

"Perfect. Let me see here." She swivels her chair to the computer adjacent to her and adjusts her glasses. Her fingers fly across the keyboard, the screen casting a glare on her lenses. Her forest-green polo captures my attention. Looking closer, I see the gold letters embroidered above the left breast pocket. *TCG.*

Transport Center Green. Every zone has several of its own transport centers five miles from the border of its neighboring zone: TCG, TCR, TCB, and TCY. They're used as a form of customs when traveling from one zone to another. Belongings are searched, bodies are probed, and people are held for hours, answering questions about their reason for crossing the border. It's a brilliant way to prevent illegal items from being smuggled to another zone and protect the civilians on the other side. It can be a stressful experience for anyone, but it keeps us safe.

Since the Green Zone is in the heart of the Northern Unity, I don't know which center we're at or why I'm being taken to another zone. From my understanding, crimes committed are dealt with in the zone in which they took place.

"Why am I here?" I ask. My voice is pathetic, like that of a scared child. Shaky and mousy.

They ignore me.

"Why am I here?" I ask again, forcing myself to be louder. The pressure in my head grows. Heat radiates throughout my body.

Clearing her throat, the receptionist hands a laminated band to the man beside me, which he slaps on my wrist underneath the cuff.

"You're good to go!" she says, keeping the same excitement in her voice. "If you'll escort her to the double doors, I'll buzz you in."

He pulls me away from the desk, and we veer left. There's a click and then a groan as the beige doors open. He and I step forward but he stops me in the doorway, removing his hand from my arm. There's jingling, the sound of metal clanking against metal, and a tug at my wrists before they're freed. I'm pushed through the portal, where two guards await; I stumble toward them as the doors shut.

One of the guards scans my body with a beeping wand and the other pats me down when his partner is finished. Then I'm guided down the dim hall, each guard keeping a firm grip on my shoulders. Everything happens in clips, fragments of a movie sloppily pasted together. The hallway stretches on, eventually opening up like a mouth ready to swallow me. Nearing the opening, I see barred cells lining the walls of the circular room, and I gasp at the sight of them. It's loud enough for the guards to hear, and the one to my right chuckles.

"That reaction never gets old," he says.

The one to my left releases me and moves ahead. He selects a cell and fishes a heap of keys from his pocket. As the other guard and I approach, he shoves the key in the keyhole and tugs the door open.

I can't hold it back anymore. My vision blurs. Everything is underwater. The unbearable pressure in my head lets up, turning into a dull throb. The tears come like a monsoon, but I don't bother wiping them away. The same guard laughs again, shoving me into the cell, and the door screeches shut.

Blinking away the tears, I spin around, gripping the bars, and they stare back at me from the other side. One smiles, amused by my reaction, by my capture. The other's face is emotionless, his eyes a void.

"Why are you doing this?" I sob. My cries bounce off the brick walls and vaulted ceiling on the other side, ringing louder than I intended. Quickly scanning the cells behind them, I realize I'm the only prisoner here.

"We're following orders," the emotionless one says.

"Is someone going to tell me why I'm here?" A deep, shuddering breath. "I'm innocent!"

"This isn't a matter of innocence or guilt," he says, holding eye contact.

The obnoxious one rolls his eyes. "Just leave her alone. It's not your job to give an explanation." He clamps a hand on his partner's shoulder. "On that note, I'm heading out. I thought we were going to get more in today. Thanks for picking up, New Guy." And with a parting glance my way, he strolls out of the room of cages.

The remaining guard stares after him until the pounding of boots fades to nothing.

"Tell me what's happening," I beg. "This has to be a mistake."

"There's no mistake," he says, keeping his eyes trained on the exit. "You're exactly where you're supposed to be."

"So why am I being taken to re-education in another zone?"

He turns his attention back to me. "I'll check on you later. Try to calm yourself down, and don't do anything stupid. I'm authorized to use any force necessary."

"Wait! Please!"

But he's gone, and like the fish in the waiting area, I'm trapped. Tears pour out faster, stronger. Pressing my hands to my face, I crumble to the floor and let out a scream. I scream until my throat is raw and my lungs feel like they're about to cave. No one comes. No one checks if I'm okay. I'm left with my echoing sobs and jumbled thoughts.

Long after the tears stop flowing, I remain on the floor. With my cheek pressed to the cold Silikal, I stare through the bars, willing someone to come to the rescue. Liam. Mom. Addison. Anyone. To hear one of their voices right now would be enough to keep me from spiraling into insanity. I knew re-education awaited me but it didn't truly set in until we reached this place. I don't know much about the process, but this can't be part of the protocol.

The silence eats away at me. My sense of time is obscured. No windows or clocks to give me an idea of whether it's day or night. How long has it been since that guard left?

I don't remember moving, but at some point I got up and lay on the cot at the back of the small cell, focusing on the ceiling panels. My eyes are swollen and heavy. Sleep, a temporary escape, beckons me. As enticing as it is, I force myself to remain conscious, too afraid of what might happen if I give in.

I replay happier memories to ease my mind, starting with childhood moments all the way up to the most recent: Addison, Liam, and me sitting in the living room drinking the magical chocolate potion. We watched movies and talked and laughed. We reminisced and embraced the nostalgia that crashed over us. We poured out the secrets we were brave enough to share. Closing my eyes, I imagine myself in that moment again, surrounded by love and people I trust, and I hold on to it for as long as possible.

Rattling bars pull me out of the trance I've slipped into. I sit up, feeling groggy, my head cloudy. The emotionless guard has returned, holding a plastic tray and small cup.

"Dinner time," he says, shoving the tray through the small rectangle in the center of the cell door. The bag of chips leaps from the tray as it clatters to the floor, but the plastic-wrapped sandwich stays in place. He slides the cup on the floor through the bars and steps back.

"I'm not hungry," I croak.

"You have to eat."

I lie back down, not having the energy to argue. Turning to my side, I hug my knees to my chest with my back to him. He doesn't say anything. I can feel him watching me, and I wish I had a blanket I could hide under.

"I want to go home," I murmur, closing my eyes again.

"I'm afraid that's not possible."

I'm in and out of sleep for a while—back and forth like a tide. The first time I wake, the lights are dimmed, projecting ghostly shadows throughout the room. Occasionally, I get up to use the metal toilet in the cell or pace the tiny area before returning to the cot.

At one point, I wake up to the sound of the guard's boots passing by my cell. An itchy wool blanket is draped over me; the tray of untouched food has been taken away, but the cup remains on the floor. I can hear the guard's voice somewhere outside of my cell but don't get up.

"She's not doing well," he says in a low voice. Is there a hint of sympathy there, or am I imagining that? I don't hear a response to what he said. I hear his footsteps again and a few seconds later he says, "Tomorrow morning. Ten o'clock. She'll be taken to…"

Before I can hear the rest of his sentence, he's gone. His footsteps fade and his words follow; I'm still left without an answer as to where I'm going. If someone would just tell me, maybe that would ease the anxiety a little. Maybe that would alleviate this pit of fear. The not knowing is killing me.

Crossing over to the dream realm is a short-lived tranquility, but knowing it waits for me each time I close my eyes is enough to soften the blow of reality. If I can escape into my imaginary world forever, everything will be okay.

I'm offered breakfast in the morning but refuse it. I've been awake for a while, lying under the blanket and staring at the ceiling. Sleep won't take me anymore. The fruit and bowl of oatmeal are still on the floor when the guard returns, and he shakes his head at the sight of the wasted food.

"You're going to wish you ate something later," he says, pulling his keys from his pocket. He unlocks my cage and steps over the tray. Sitting up, I realize he's carrying my backpack. He tosses it at me and says, "Five minutes. My shift is about to end, and they're ready for you."

He exits and locks the door but doesn't leave my sight. Instead, he turns his back to me and just stands there. Of course he wouldn't leave me alone with anything that might aid an escape—not that I know the first thing about breaking out of a jail cell.

Jumping up from the cot, I unzip the bag. I'm anxious to leave this place and scared of the next unknown destination at the same time. A travel-sized toothbrush and tube of toothpaste rest on top of my clothes. I grab them first and brush my teeth at the sink, thankful that they at least thought of my dental hygiene. I retrieve the first outfit I can find and toss yesterday's clothes into the bag. My hair is knotted and has fallen from its braid, and I can't find a brush anywhere.

"Time's up." He turns around just as I finish twisting the elastic band around my ponytail. He re-enters and instructs me to turn around and place my hands behind my back. I do as I'm told, and the cuffs are fastened on my wrists again.

"Where am I going?" I ask, not actually expecting an answer.

He grabs my backpack and rotates me toward the door. "Somewhere better than here."

For now, I'll accept that. It's the most information I've received. I just hope he's right.

Once again, I'm guided across the room of cells and down the empty hall. I keep up with him this time, still nervous but more alert. Screams erupt from the other side of the double doors I came through yesterday as we near them.

They have someone else.

The guard tenses up for a fraction of a second. This job must take some getting used to, and I almost pity him. Almost. He signed up for this.

When we're a few feet from the doors, he steers me toward a single metal door on the right. He swipes a small, blue key fob across a black panel on the wall. *Click.* We enter through the mysterious portal and take a left. Another swipe, and we enter a garage on the other side of the door. An unmarked vehicle awaits, engine humming. A man in a suit stands by the driver door of the van and climbs inside when he sees us. The back doors are already open, taunting me.

We descend a small set of stairs, where another guard stands. She passes a clipboard to my escort; he scribbles something in a box on the chart and hands it back to her. Silent and seamless, like everything else about the Society.

He helps me up into the compartment on the left and pushes me into the seat closest to the exit.

"I've never been to re-education before," I say as he fastens my seatbelt.

He pauses. "Just lie low." Finishing up, he steps back, seeing that I'm strapped in and not going anywhere. "Be sure to do exactly as you're told and you'll be fine."

Jumping out of the van, he shuts the cage doors, and the black ones slam right after. Darkness envelops me again. There are two slaps on the back of the van, followed by metal screeching. Then the vehicle is in motion, transporting me to pay for a crime I didn't commit.

The road is bumpy, but smooths out the longer we drive. Anxiety swirls in the pit of my stomach, churning until I feel I might be sick. I want to cry, but I don't have any tears left. I wasted them all over being locked in a cell when the real trouble lies ahead.

Re-education has always been a mysterious thing to the general public, and to an extent, we've been okay with that. It's like we've had this mentality that whoever goes is a stain on society and we try to distance ourselves from them in any way possible. Deep down, though, people have to be curious. Liam and I were fascinated with the idea of it from a very young age. Our father never told us anything about it when we asked, except for repeating the same thing everyone else says. *"It's an effective way to help people turn a new leaf and become productive members of society."*

I still believe that. There's hope for Naomi if she cooperates. There's hope for the thugs tied up in these terrorist organizations. Anyone can start a new life. But I'm not like them. I will never be like them.

The van slows down. As it drives over a hump in the road, I'm briefly lifted out of my seat and sway to the right. Another hump, and it picks up speed again. The vehicle suddenly swerves, jerking my body forward. Caught by the seatbelt, I'm slammed back against the metal wall. Pain immediately radiates from my head down to my neck; a scream scrapes through my throat. Tires and brakes squeal. The men in the cab yell, continuing to swerve and toss me around in the back.

There's a deafening bang as something collides with the vehicle, followed by the crumpling of metal. The van spirals out of control, yanking me in every direction before it comes to an abrupt stop. A brief moment of silence follows, and a door closes. Then the gunshots come, one after another, the pattern hideously rhythmic.

Bang! Bang! Bang! Bang!

Heart pounding furiously, I squirm on the bench, bending my arms in unnatural ways to try and reach the buckle. I give up on that attempt after realizing it's impossible and settle for working my way out of the handcuffs. Twisting and yanking with all of my strength only leads to the cuffs digging into my wrists, and I let out a yelp as one slices the skin. Panic paralyzes me.

Bang!

"Shit!" I mutter through the pooling tears. My breathing quickens. Unable to see what's happening fuels the panic. Re-education doesn't seem too bad at this point.

The doors swing open, and I'm blinded by the sunlight that pours in. For a moment, I'm relieved. But that relief is shattered when a masked man hops into the van with a gun strapped to his back and my backpack slung over one shoulder.

10. The Stolen Child

"Who the hell are you?"

He reaches for me, and I instinctively swing my foot up. Catching it before it makes contact with his groin, he forces it down and uses the other hand to unbuckle me.

"Leave me alone!" I yell, elbowing him as he hauls me to my feet. It collides with his ribs and he grunts.

"I'm helping you," he says calmly. He fidgets with the handcuffs, and seconds later they fall to the floor and my hands are free.

At this moment, I'm grateful for being freed, so I take his gloved hand when he offers to help me out of the van. As soon as my shoes hit the asphalt, I turn my head to the front of the van, where another car has smashed into the cab on the driver's side. The wall separating this zone from the next is visible on the horizon, and I can make out the first checkpoint a few yards ahead. The gate is absent of its border patrol, and considering what's taken place, I have a feeling the other three up ahead are also empty.

Circling the van, I get a better view of the destruction. The vehicle that hit us took pretty severe damage, its front end unrecognizable. The driver's side of the van I was in is a heap of twisted metal and plastic and the door is caved in. Blood is sprayed on the interior of the windshield, and the other side of the glass is a web of fractures and bullet holes. The passenger door is open, a puddle of crimson already forming beneath it. I know what's on the other side of the door, but my mind refuses to accept it. My legs carry me closer.

Debris crunches under my boots. All feeling and emotions leave my body, and I'm watching myself from another realm. One step at a time, slow and hesitant. One of them has to be alive. I can't stomach the sight of another lifeless body. Not this way.

Before I reach the other side, a hand grabs me from behind and yanks me back. I'm teleported back to my vessel, and emotions I never knew existed flood my racing mind.

"Ivy, we have to go."

My feet leave the ground and I'm carried away.

"Let me go!" I scream, kicking and scratching. "*Let me fucking go!*"

He tightens his arms around me, pinning my arms between my back and his torso. We circle back around the wreckage, and he ducks into the treeline off the side of the road. Bringing my hand to his arm, I snake my fingers up the sleeve of his jacket and sink my nails into his flesh until I feel bits of skin collect underneath them.

"I said, *let me go!*"

He curses and drops me, but grabs my arm before I have a chance to move. The more I try to pull away from him the tighter his grip becomes, and I wince as his fingers press into the bloody wound on my wrist.

"Relax! It's me!" He throws his hood back and tears off the mask.

Nixon? What the hell is *he* doing here?

"Your brother told me what happened," he says.

"I don't understand."

"I promise I'll explain everything, but we have to go."

Releasing me, he wanders deeper into the forest, and I reluctantly trail behind him. The road disappears behind us, and every so often, Nixon looks over his shoulder at me. The weapon on his back glimmers in the morning sunlight, its deadly nature impossible to ignore. Knowing what he did with it makes me want to follow him even less.

I slow down, letting the space between us grow. Surrounded by bark and leafless branches, I can't see any sign of civilization. Without any idea of where I am, it would be a risk to venture off on my own. It's also a risk to follow a man I don't really know without any sort of explanation. If Liam did contact him—which I doubt—the chance of him finding me was slim. Immediate family doesn't even know where someone is taken for re-education until a visitation date is approved by the Society.

Nixon picks up the pace, and I do the same. There's a break in the trees ahead. Buildings jut out of the ground, and parked on the back side of one of them is the same black car he picked Liam and me up in. I don't recognize the area, and being so close to the wall confirms how far I am from home.

Home or not, the Green Zone's authorities are all the same. Someone will be at the first checkpoint soon if they're not there already. Seeing that I'm missing, they'll hunt me down, and they won't stop until I'm found.

Nixon glances at me one more time as he reaches the clearing, and when he nears his car, I turn to my right and break into a sprint.

"Ivy!" he yells.

But I ignore him. Maybe Liam can trust him, but I can't, and I can't dig myself into a deeper hole than I'm already in. I'll find a police officer or a passerby. Anyone. I'll turn myself in, as well as Nixon. Maybe my punishment will be less severe if I report him, too. Whatever happens to him isn't my problem. I'll serve my sentence and go home. It'll be as if this never happened.

I push farther into the temporary safety. Looking back, I don't see any sign of him or hear him following me. While it's slightly warmer than it has been, the wind still slices through me, and I wish I'd grabbed a jacket before I was forced from my home. My stomach gnaws at itself and black spots pop up in my vision. In the past twenty-four hours, all I've had is a banana and no water. The guard was right; I'm definitely regretting my hunger strike.

I finally stop and lean against a tree trunk, hunching forward with my palms on my knees. Several deep breaths later, I look up, scanning my surroundings. Birds fly overhead, black specks against the brilliant blue sky. Trees stretch for as far as I can see. If I weren't wanted by the government and didn't have a stranger trying to kidnap me, I'd probably take the time to explore this new place. Our zone is huge, and I've only seen a small portion of it.

After a couple more moments of rest, I start moving again, slower this time. In the endless maze, I pick another direction to walk while keeping an eye out for Nixon. I'll wind up finding civilization eventually. Not for the first time, I fiercely wish Addison were here. Her dad has always been obsessed with the idea of being a survivalist, and has bragged on many occasions of knowing the entire layout of the Green Zone. Addison was forced to absorb it all from a very young age, and I know her parents took her to visit and memorize the grounds surrounding each border. She could easily guide me to where I need to go.

There's movement fifteen feet or so ahead. I inch forward, expecting it to be Nixon, and prepare to run. As I get closer, though, I see the twinkle of metal under the sun, and relief washes over me. The lone officer cautiously prowls the area, weapon drawn, and a hopeful thought latches itself to my mind: *Maybe the others caught Nixon.* As cruel as it may be, I don't feel guilty about it.

Nearing the officer, I try to gather my thoughts on what I'm going to say. I'll be questioned for sure, and I need to make it known I'm innocent in this circumstance. A twig snaps under my weight, and the officer whirls around, his full focus on me.

"Freeze!" he barks. "Hands where I can see them!"

Coming to a halt, I throw my hands up in the air, and he walks toward me, keeping his gun pointed at me.

"I was—"

"Quiet!" he yells. "Where's the person you escaped with?"

I swallow hard. My legs are shaking so badly I fear they might not hold me up. "I don't know. I got away."

Lowering his weapon, he reaches for the handcuffs clipped to his belt. "You're in a lot of trouble, Ms. Clearson."

"I didn't have anything to do with it!"

"You'll have time to explain yourself later."

There's movement behind him. Something dashes behind a tree, and I take my eyes off the officer to see what it was. He follows my gaze, but the figure doesn't reappear.

"I promise!" I blurt out. "I didn't want to go with him!"

"Hands behind your back."

As I drop my hands behind me, he pulls out the cuffs and closes the gap between us. But at the last minute, the apparition darts out into the open.

Nixon wrenches the gun from the officer's hand and wraps his arm around his neck, pressing the crook of his elbow into the center of his throat. The officer grabs at Nixon's arm, gasping for air.

"*Stop!*" I scream. Before I can stop myself, I'm at his side, yelling and hitting and pushing. "Leave him alone! You're going to kill him!"

But he doesn't let go. He applies more pressure, and the officer's eyes roll back into his head before his eyelids flutter shut. Nixon releases him, and he falls face down to the ground.

"*What the hell is wrong with you?*"

Whirling around, he grabs me by both of my wrists. His eyes are icy, and a vein bulges from his temple. "Do you realize how stupid that was?"

I drop my eyes to the motionless body. I can't tell if he's actually dead or just unconscious.

"I'm trying to *help* you!" he yells. "You're lucky I was here!"

Snapping my eyes to him, I yell back, "You murdered them!"

"I saved you!" The air around us is heavy, charged with tension. He closes his eyes for a moment and draws in a deep breath. "I know there's a lot you haven't been told, and I promise I'll explain what's going on, but we need to get going. We've already wasted enough time." He drops my wrists. "And I have permission from Liam to do whatever's necessary to make sure you come with me."

"Is that a threat?"

"Try something like that again and you'll find out." He turns me around and keeps a hand on my shoulder. "Start walking."

Once again, we're navigating the forest, and I haven't been told a damn thing about what's going on. No answers for the multitudes of questions cycling through my brain. I don't even know where to start asking, and I don't know if he'll give me a real answer.

I didn't care for him the day I met him, and at the time, I didn't know why. Now I despise him for his cockiness and this superiority complex he seems to have. He ordered Liam around like he was his pet, and he's trying to do the same with me. I can't imagine my brother giving permission for someone to take me forcefully, and I still doubt he actually sent Nixon. Liam isn't the type to have other people handle his problems for him. He always faced them on his own.

"Liam was supposed to tell you," Nixon says. "I told him to come clean after you called that night he was at my house."

"What are you talking about?"

He steers me a little to the left to avoid a dangling tree limb. "Your brother is part of the resistance, Ivy."

"You're lying."

Liam is stupid in his obligatory brotherly way, but not like that. Aside from holding onto our father's gun, he's an ideal, law-abiding citizen. He's always helped others. He puts everyone else's needs above his own. Even with the feud between him and Mom, he's still stayed at home to help her out.

"And I'm the Green Zone's resistance leader."

My fear intensifies, accompanied by boiling anger, and I'm not sure if the anger is directed toward Liam, Nixon, or whoever else dragged my brother into this. If Liam gets caught, he'll be locked up for life or worse. I don't know what that entails, and I hope to never find out. Mom and I wouldn't be exempt from punishment either. We'd endure interrogation after interrogation, and at the very least, we'd be kept under a microscope for the rest of our lives. But Dad's disappearance has already raised the Society's suspicions of our family; I have a strong feeling that we'd face far more severe consequences.

I stop walking, forcing my weight against him as he tries to push me forward. "Tell me you're lying," I say.

"I'm not lying. Come on." He gives another light push, but I keep my feet planted.

"Then why isn't he the one 'saving' me?"

"He's not exactly in the position to be leaving home right now." Another push, and I stumble forward. "I can tell you whatever you want to know, but we need to keep moving. We already saw one cop, and the rest won't be far behind."

Part of me wants the police to come, but I know Nixon being caught will inevitably lead them to Liam.

While my family and I were carefully watched like lab rats after Dad left, the Enlightened Society helped us. Because of the sudden drop in our household's income, we qualified for government assistance for the first six months. It wasn't a lot, but it helped keep a roof over our heads and food on the table until we were able to get back on our feet. And now Liam is betraying them as if they've never done anything to help him. Not only is it idiotic, it's ungrateful. It's a slap in the face to those who were there for us.

The same clearing as before comes into view, and Nixon guides me to his car. Unlocking it, he opens the back door. One of my jackets is balled up on the seat, and my backpack is sideways on the floor.

"Get in and lie down," he says. When I don't, he pushes my head down and shoves me inside.

Shooting him a glare, I say something that feels incredibly childish yet accurate: "I hate you."

"Good. I'm not here for you to like me."

11. *Inside Voices*

It's been quiet aside from the occasional clicking of the turn signal and the whir of the heater that's on full blast. Lying on my back, I watch the tree branches and scarce buildings pass the window across from me. Clouds cluster in the sky, blocking out part of the sun.

Neither of us have spoken since getting into the car. I don't know how long we've been on the road, but I do know we're still in the Green Zone. A tiny sliver of hope embedded inside me tells me that Nixon's taking me home. Knowing that's not possible, I snuff out the thought. Home is the first place the police will look.

I wonder how Mom will react when she finds out that I managed to escape my fate. Surely it will be passed along that I didn't go willingly. The Society may consider me a danger due to my silence on Elizabeth's murder, but I've never tried to outrun the law. They know my record is clean.

Addison and her dad probably know everything by now. If I'm ever able to go home, I know she'll never speak to me again, and if she finds out who Liam truly is, her heart will be broken. Even though she played it off as nothing at the coffee shop, I know she's head over heels for him. She's always been like that with her crushes, but Liam is different. She grew up with us, so that bond is stronger than with the guys she swooned over in the past.

"Where are you taking me?" I finally ask.

"Somewhere safe."

"Why do you care whether or not I'm safe?"

"I don't." He takes a sharp left and I slide forward, having to push my arm into his seat to keep from falling onto the floor. "But your brother does, and he asked me to do this."

"I still don't believe he sent you."

"I don't expect you to."

I'm tempted to open the door and jump out. I still have a chance of turning myself in as well as Nixon. If he's truly Liam's friend and leader, he won't rat him out.

"Is this what you guys do—murder people?"

He sighs, tightening his fingers around the steering wheel. "Only if we have to."

"So Liam—"

"No. He's never been put in that position… and I hope he never is."

But that's not something he can promise, not really. Anything can happen, and if Liam really wants to associate himself with these criminals, it's bound to happen sooner or later. I know he's not like them, though; he's never harmed a living being in his life. This has to be a phase—some short-lived act of rebellion. He probably felt alone after Dad left and needed some kind of support to get him through his dark times. I was dealing with the same pain in my own way, and I hate myself for not being there for him more. Maybe this could have been prevented.

I'm angry at him for not telling me what he'd gotten himself into. Nixon said he'd told Liam to come clean to me after we had escaped from Naomi's. Maybe he'd wanted to but didn't know how. Maybe he was scared of how I would've reacted. Or maybe he did try and I pushed him away. I've been so absorbed in the things that have been happening to *me*, he didn't have a chance to open up about his own personal life. He pushed so hard for that talk we had a couple of weeks ago and, once again, I made it about myself and demonized the resistance to his face. It's no wonder he didn't tell me. Now all I want to do is go back in time and change the way that conversation played out. Or, at the very least, apologize to him.

The trees become denser on the other side of the glass and any buildings have vanished from my view. I prop myself up with my arms as Nixon passes another car and merges back into the right lane. In the rearview mirror, I catch a glimpse of the upper half of his face. His eyes are dull, nowhere near as vibrant as the day I met him. With an elbow propped up on his door, he rests his temple against his fingertips, making small circular motions against his skin.

While his eyes are locked on the road, I lunge for the door and tug on the handle. It pulls toward me, but the door doesn't budge.

"Child lock," Nixon says, not even looking back at me.

Releasing the handle, I jam my finger against the button for the window.

"Windows are locked, too." He's sitting in the same position. The only other way out is through the front. Before I can move, he readjusts himself, shooting his right arm out to block the gap between the two front seats as if reading my mind. "Don't even think about it."

Slumping back in the seat, I cross my arms over my chest. "I hate you."

"I know, you've said that already." He keeps his arm draped over the seat, but doesn't order me to lie back down. I doubt anyone could see through the dark tint on the windows anyway. "And you're annoying me."

"I'm scared," I admit.

He doesn't say anything.

What could he say? He's one of the things I'm scared of. I'm in the back of a terrorist's car, being taken to another unknown place. He and Liam are the people we've all been warned about, the ones who kill and destroy. If we were to get caught right now, the Society would either view me as a hostage or an accomplice. While I hope for the former, they'd more than likely assume I'm an accomplice, since I haven't put up much of a fight. All of my attempts have failed, and Nixon is somehow a step ahead of me.

I was so close to being out of his clutches in the woods. There was an officer in reach; everything was perfectly laid out in front of me. Maybe if I hadn't been as hesitant those few seconds before he saw me, it would've been enough time for things to play out differently.

I can't change any of that now, but I need to figure out how to get away. Nixon is clearly capable of doing something horrible, and I don't want to be around long enough to find out what he has in store for me. Terrorists don't have morals or empathy; they're animals, ready to kill at a moment's notice. He's made that obvious.

"How did you find out where they'd be taking me?" I ask. "Surely Liam didn't know."

"Your guard from TCG, Sebastien, is one of my guys. When he wasn't checking on you, he was relaying information back to me, and I kept Liam in the loop as much as I could."

"But Liam's not here."

"Believe me, he wanted to be. He came by my place as soon as he could and told me about his plan to rescue you. This is all part of *his* plan, but it would've been too risky to have him out searching for you. The Enlightened Society is keeping a close eye on him and your mom." He moves his arm from the seats. "I was under the impression you already knew about him being in the resistance, which would've made all of this a whole lot easier."

"Yeah, well, I didn't, and I'm not happy about it either."

"Obviously." For the first time since he started driving, he glances over his shoulder at me. "I don't expect you to trust me, but at least have an open mind."

Taking a right, he drives down a narrow road wedged between two endless barren fields. Neglected houses are spaced out along the road, dotting the land with the illusion of civilization. From the overgrowth of weeds and the busted doors and shattered windows, it's obvious that no one has occupied this area in a while. Most of the houses are missing chunks of shingles and others are graffitied. Some of the graffiti is random—illegible words overlapping one another, skulls and crossbones, and streaks of colors bleeding into one another—but there's one piece of vandalism that's painted on almost every house we pass: three black horizontal lines stacked on top of one another. The recurring mark is faded and painted over in a lot of areas, but others are fresh.

This entire area feels like a post-apocalyptic wasteland when, in reality, everyone just moved closer to the cities as affordable housing became more available. The Enlightened Society funneled massive amounts of money into revamping the cities that were neglected by the previous government. They lowered the costs of the new and re-modeled homes and created enough jobs for everyone. Our economy is flourishing, breaking records those in the Old World could never imagine, yet there are people such as Nixon and Liam who want to burn it all to the ground.

Nixon pulls into one of the worn driveways and follows its winding pattern down the other side of the hill. A small single-story house emerges. Like the rest of the dwellings in this area, it's tattered and covered in words and symbols.

"What are we doing here?" I ask.

"We'll be staying here for the night." He nears the end of the driveway and stops at the detached garage behind the house. "I've been up for over twenty-four hours, and we still have a long way to go." Getting out of the car, he walks up to the rusted garage door; it screeches as he heaves it open with a grunt. He left his door open, and I'm tempted to crawl over the seat and make a run for it. The temptation is fleeting, though, as I remember his threat.

Sliding back in, he pulls the car into the garage and shuts it off.

"Grab your stuff." He presses a button to his left and the trunk pops open.

While he's gathering his things from the back, I pull on my jacket and slide my arms through the straps of my backpack. He opens my door, his own bag over one shoulder and his gun on the other. Keeping my eyes fixed on the weapon, I hesitantly step out of the car. We exit the garage and he pulls the door back down, the gears scraping against each other and cutting through the silence.

The blast of cold after being in the warmth for so long sends a shock through my body, and I pull my jacket tighter. This part of the

Green Zone is much more daunting once I'm outside. Nixon starts toward the house and I follow, scanning the surroundings for any sign of another person, someone I can go to for help. But we're alone out here.

Nixon climbs the three steps of the small concrete back porch, unlocks the door, and waits for me to catch up. The blanket of dead leaves crunches under my shoes as I follow up the stairs, and he does a quick survey of the yard stretching out behind the house before following me inside. We enter a small living room, and Nixon locks and latches the door behind us.

It's almost as cold inside as it is outside. The only difference is that the walls and the windows—which are surprisingly intact—block out the wind. The smell of mildew and rot assaults my nose, and I bring the cuff of my jacket to my face. A shadeless lamp lies on its side in the corner of the room, its bulb busted, and a sheet of dust coats everything in sight. There's a kitchen directly across from us. Cabinets hang from their hinges, exposing their bare shelves, and beams of plywood are nailed across the front door.

Nixon props his gun in the corner closest to the door and disappears into one of the two rooms adjacent to us. Staying put, I peek inside. It's empty save for a ripped box-spring on the floor. Two rolled-up sleeping bags are tossed into the living room, sending a plume of dust into the air. Nixon emerges, carrying a small propane tank with an attachment on top.

"No electricity," he explains, placing the tank on the floor and turning the valve. The mesh center of the top piece glows a dim orange. He disappears again and returns with a jug of water and a couple of plastic cups.

"Where are we going after this?"

He twists the cap and the seal breaks with a pop. "A safehouse farther away from here." He pours some water into one of the cups and hands it to me before pouring some for himself. "This one is only really used in the case of an emergency." He shrugs off his backpack; it drops to the floor with a thud and he unzips it, producing a flashlight. Although enough natural light comes through the two windows for me to make out the general layout of the house, he turns it on and sets it upright, brightening the space.

I take another look around the place and steal a glance through the window closest to me. "For a safehouse, it doesn't seem too safe."

"Stop being so damn ungrateful."

I snap my head back to him. "I didn't ask for this."

"Neither did I. You think I *want* to be here?" His eyebrows furrow, and he takes a small step toward me. "I had to drop everything on short notice for *you*. Because your brother asked me for a favor. My group and I are risking everything to keep you safe!"

"Being saved by terrorists? That's ironic."

"We are not terrorists!" he yells. "You're so ignorant, and you're not even *trying* to work with me. Look, if you don't want my help, you can leave. Survive on your own out there, turn yourself in, do whatever you want. I'll go back home and tell Liam I tried but you refused to cooperate."

Folding my arms over my chest, I turn my back to him. I know I'm acting like a brat, but I don't know how else I should act. My world has been turned upside-down. Everything has been ripped from me in less than forty-eight hours, and I'm still clinging to the idea that it will all go back to normal. It has to. I don't want to go to re-education, but it's better than being viewed as a fugitive.

"You're not my hostage," Nixon says, his tone a tad softer. "Seriously, I won't stop you this time if you want to leave, but you won't last very long and I'm trying my best here."

I keep my back to him and my eyes glued to the window. The parted, tattered curtains and chunks missing from the blinds allow me a glimpse of the wasteland outside. Miles and miles of unknown territory surround us. This morning, I had some idea of where I was—near a border. I could've found help if I'd wandered around long enough. Here, it's different. There's no telling what kind of people lurk amongst these ruins.

"I want to go home," I say. It's the same pathetic line I said to my guard at TCG.

"That's exactly where the Society expects you to go, and the faster you realize I'm on your side, the better this will be for both of us."

A bird swoops down from the sky, landing on a lower branch of a tree beside the house. Its beady black eyes zero in on me before it takes off again.

"I don't mind going to re-education." I turn toward him again. The room is a bit warmer now.

He purses his lips and mimics me by crossing his own arms, resting a shoulder against the doorframe of the bedroom. "This is the safest place you could be right now. Following today's events, I expect there to be raids across the zone, if not the country. It's unlikely they'll search here, but if they do, I'm prepared."

"As long as I'm with you, I'm not safe."

He lets out a quick, sardonic laugh, dropping his arms and taking a seat on the floor beside the propane heater. "Are you staying or leaving?"

I look to the gun beside the locked door. "At least let me talk to Liam."

"I would, but I don't have my phone. Can't risk them tracking me." He rummages through his bag again. "Sit down," he says with the same assertive voice he used on the phone the first day I met him. "Ask me whatever you want."

"Are you going to kill me?"

"Okay, ask me anything as long as it's not stupid." He tosses something to me, and I catch it before it hits the floor. "Your guard at TCG told me you refused to eat." He tears open his own package and takes a bite out of the protein bar.

Slipping the bag off my shoulders, I take a seat on the opposite side of the room and pull my knees up to my chest. I set the cup of water beside me and turn my protein bar over in my hands. I have millions of questions as well as doubts that, for some reason, I can't put into words. So I tear open the wrapper of my bar and eat in silence, keeping my eyes down. Nixon stays quiet, crumpling his trash and shoving it in his bag when he's finished.

The natural light slowly shrinks away, allowing the flashlight to take over. Finishing my food, I ball up the wrapper in my hand, running my thumb along the wrinkled, metalized plastic. I try to dig up more pleasant memories that I've kept safely locked away over the years—a family vacation, a festival in the city, sleepovers with friends, anything. But my brain decides to plague me with the most recent past instead. Fragmented thoughts force themselves together like mismatched parts of different puzzles.

Naomi was taken away. Kyle was murdered. Liam and I ran from the police. Addison and I talked with each other at the coffee shop. And there was the terrorist attack which led to the start of the raids.

"The hijacked plane that the military shot down," I say, looking up at him, "did you have anything to do with that?"

Back against the wall and eyes closed, he tilts his head up, his scar illuminated by the light. "Yes."

My heart stops, and a new fear ignites. "Fourteen people died because of you."

One corner of his mouth twitches upward into a disgusting smirk that makes me want to smack him. "I'm flattered that they assume we could pull that off, but no one died. There wasn't even a pilot."

"The news said—"

"I know what they said, but that doesn't mean it's true. It was a cargo plane carrying weapons and ammunition for the military—self-flying. No passengers. No fatalities."

"But you were still going to fly it into the Capitol building."

"Nope. We hacked the system and changed its course to fly outside of the Northern Unity where other resistance members reside. And if you don't believe me, you can ask Liam whenever you see him again. He was the one in charge of the hacking."

"Why?"

He opens his eyes and brings his cup to his lips, his words echoing when he says, "Why what?"

"Trying to steal those weapons… What was the point?"

"They killed one of my members."

It takes me a minute to catch on. "Elizabeth."

His silence is enough of a confirmation.

It doesn't make sense. I didn't get a good look at the killer, but he wasn't dressed in any kind of uniform, and the Enlightened Society doesn't patrol the streets themselves. If they knew Elizabeth was part of the resistance, it's unlikely they'd just kill her out in the open, regardless of it being after curfew. She should've been arrested and reeducated or questioned about other members. That's how it works. The Society is all about maintaining order.

Nixon didn't act upset about Elizabeth's murder the day he came into the flower shop, but now it seems to be a difficult topic. Terrorist or not, I'm not going to push the subject and potentially hurt him more, so I make a mental note to get more details at a later time.

"How did you and Liam meet?" I ask.

"His job. He waited on me one of my first days in the Green Zone."

"So you're not from here."

He shakes his head, sipping on the water again. "Blue Zone. Liam only joined the resistance... I don't know, six months ago—maybe seven—but we've been friends for a few years." He focuses on the window beside me. Clouds blanket the sky, giving the house more of an eerie feel. The flashlight's beam showcases the water stains on the ceiling directly above it.

"Liam told me you were helping him locate our dad."

Shrugging one shoulder, he stands up. "In a way, yeah. I tried to look into his disappearance." He crosses the room and pulls the curtains over the window, then does the same to the ones in the kitchen. "It was a dead end, though. I know as much as you do."

The flashlight is the only source of light now. Nixon materializes out of the darkness, resuming his spot across from me. Curfew must be nearing, and the idea of being here overnight makes my stomach knot.

"One more question," Nixon says, "then it's lights out. I don't want anyone knowing we're here."

While thinking of what to ask next, I take my first sip of water and end up downing the whole cup. Nixon shuts his eyes again. Patches of purple and blue have formed on the right side of his face, starting at the edge of his forehead and circling underneath his eye. They must be from the wreck earlier.

"What's going to happen to me?" I ask.

"We'll head to a safehouse tomorrow, lie low for a bit. The Commander, my boss, will give the orders from there."

"In other words, you don't know."

"I didn't exactly have much notice to plan the entire future of someone I don't know."

My heart sinks. No certainty or even an idea of what's going to happen. At least in the custody of the Society, I'd know what the next step would be… although I wasn't really given much of an explanation when I was taken by them either.

If I was destined for re-education, I don't understand why Liam cared so much as to launch an entire mission to save me. To my knowledge, he didn't do that for Naomi. He didn't even say anything when I told him Mom was the one who turned her in. Like me, Liam has never been fond of Naomi, but he wouldn't be heartless enough to rescue me while leaving her to endure her punishment.

"What was Liam so worried about? Why did he send you to 'save' me?"

"I said *one* question." Leaning forward, Nixon reaches for the flashlight in the middle of the room. I dive toward it at the last second, and my hand wraps around it at the same time as his.

"You also said you'd explain everything." I tug on the flashlight, but he doesn't let go.

"Maybe you should ask the important questions first."

Another tug, which he counteracts with his own force. Something inside me snaps. Maybe it's fatigue or the stress of it all, but my next words come tumbling out before I have a chance to think them through. "Tell me, or I swear I will turn your ass in the second I see someone."

Inches away from each other, the space between us is electrified with tension. He narrows his icy eyes and tightens his grip, but I don't back down. My body stiffens and my pulse quickens, realizing how dumb it is for me to confront him like this—to be this close to him. As far as I'm concerned, he's the enemy.

I attempt to rip the flashlight from his grasp again, but he pulls back. Removing one hand, I try to pry his fingers from it, using my nails to aid in my attempt. With his free hand, he grabs my wrist, pressing his thumb into my wound. Crying out, I instinctively recoil, and he pulls the flashlight out of my reach but doesn't turn it off.

Blood beads up on my arm where the scab has broken. I'd completely forgotten about it, but now the pain comes rushing back. I don't know how deep it is. It's hard to tell in the dim lighting, but the skin around it looks pink and raised. A dried red ribbon streaks the inside of my arm from earlier today.

"Give me your arm," Nixon says, dousing a cloth with water. Not waiting for me to comply, he grabs my hand and dabs at the injury with the cloth. When he's finished, he tosses it aside and pulls a box of rolled gauze from his bag.

"Even if I did tell you," he says, wrapping the fabric around my wrist, "you wouldn't believe me." Cutting the gauze, he secures it with tape and releases my hand. "And I don't appreciate being threatened, especially after what I've done for you."

12. Torn in Two

The silence is unbearable, even worse than when I was in the jail cell. I got up a couple times to use the bathroom (having to fill the toilet with water to flush) and Nixon was still awake. The first time I came out, he was pacing the dark living room, an indistinct shadow figure barely visible in the dull light of his heater. The second time, he was sitting against the wall beside the door, writing in a small notebook. Neither of us spoke, and my eyes only briefly passed over him. His sleeping bag was still rolled up in the same spot he'd tossed it earlier. I've heard his footsteps again since coming back to my room. They've stopped by my door a couple times, then faded into the kitchen before returning to the living room.

He refused to answer my final question earlier, but promised he'd explain more tomorrow. "This is a lot to process," he said, "and you're obviously not ready to know everything yet."

There was no more talking after that, no matter how much I pushed for an answer. He remained silent aside from explaining how important it is that we stay as quiet as possible. No more speaking or lights until dawn. So I continue to lie here, listening to the underwhelming white noise of the heater, inhaling the musty scent that clings to the air, changing positions for the hundredth time. His footsteps start up again, followed by the sound of the sleeping bag unzipping.

Curled up in my own sleeping bag, I toss and turn. Night fell long ago, and despite how exhausted I am, I can't shut my mind off. The second propane heater emits a dull glow, invisible to anyone who may pass by the house. I'm on the floor of the bedroom while Nixon stays in the living room. The window of this room is boarded up, which is why Nixon insisted it would be best for me to sleep here—to keep me safe.

All is still. Closing my eyes again, I will sleep to come. Thoughts become puddles of problems to be solved another day. I imagine them as murky water, swirling around a drain, being flushed away. I suppress my fears and worries, remind myself that nothing can be done about them right now. Answers will come tomorrow. Everything will make sense tomorrow.

I'm ripped out of my sleeping bag some time later. My eyes snap open, all senses on high alert, and a burst of adrenaline explodes from my chest, flooding my body. The heater is off, and the house is shrouded in black. A hand clamps over my mouth once I'm upright, and I freeze.

"It's me, Ivy," Nixon whispers, as if that's supposed to be comforting. "I heard something outside. Stay quiet, okay?"

I nod. He steps away from me, and I hear him stumble through the dark room. Something scrapes against the floor—the box-spring, maybe?—followed by squeaking hinges. I squint through the darkness but my eyes can't adjust, adding to my panic. Nixon's fingers brush my forearm before wrapping around it.

"This way." He gives a small tug and I stumble forward, instinctively reaching out with my other arm to feel for my surroundings. "Step down."

My bare feet meet cold, splintery wood. Another tug. The floor disappears from beneath me before reappearing farther down, and I fumble in the dark for something to grab. One hand swings out, colliding with a rough, slimy surface while my other hand wraps around Nixon's arm. He tightens his grip on my forearm, steadying me. I take another step, keeping my hand against the surface to my left. There's noise somewhere outside. Voices. A prickling sensation creeps up my neck.

Nixon lets go of me, and I impulsively press my fingers deeper into his skin. "What are you doing?" I try to whisper, but it comes out as more of a soft cry.

"Hold on." He shakes himself from my grasp, and I hear him slide past me, bumping against my elbow. Hinges squeak again, and there's a muffled thud. Nixon moves toward me, his hand finding my shoulder, sliding down my arm, and he's in front of me again. "Okay, follow me. Watch your step."

He guides me deeper into the abyss without a single misstep. It's obvious he has the house memorized. Soft, silver light illuminates the final step and large underground room. Two small rectangles at the top of the far wall allow the moonlight in. The basement is nearly empty save for a ripped sofa, pallets of wood stacked along one of the walls, and my backpack at the foot of the stairs. The smell of mildew is more pungent down here, and I stifle a cough.

Nixon lets go of me, and I take the final step into the basement, shivering as my feet hit the cold, rough concrete. My jacket was left upstairs along with my sleeping bag, so all I have to protect me from the bitter cold is the thin sweater I threw on before leaving TCG. I listen for the voices and any other abnormal noises, but everything is quiet.

Nixon crosses the room, motioning for me to follow. Grabbing my backpack, we round the sofa and he takes a seat against the wall underneath one of the windows. I do the same, keeping a good distance between us and setting my bag beside me like a barrier. He readjusts his gun, laying it across his lap with the butt toward me. In the moonlight, I can make out goosebumps on his arms.

The sudden burst of energy I had has dissipated, leaving me to deal with the fatigue I briefly forgot. It feels as though I only slept a few minutes before being woken. My eyes are heavy, my brain foggy.

"What exactly did you hear?" I whisper, staring at the back of the sofa in front of us. Yellow stuffing bulges from the rip across the fabric that's spattered with brown stains.

"I'm not sure—I fell asleep."

"Do you think it's them?" I can see my breath when I speak. Hugging my legs, I rest my chin against my knees. A gust of wind makes the house groan, a haunting sound that reverberates in my bones.

Before he can answer, a beam of light pours into the basement from the window, exposing everything from the cracks in the cement floor to the exposed rusted pipes along the ceiling. Nixon tightens his hands around the gun, his head tilted back and eyes fixed on the window above us. I can't bring myself to look up. An irrational idea pops into my head, telling me that if I don't look, it's not real, they won't find me.

A piece of me does want it to be the raid soldiers here to take me away, but I fear I'm too deep into this now. Nixon gave me a free pass to leave and I didn't take it. If they find us, Nixon would almost definitely inform them of that to cover his ass. That's what terrorists do.

Then the light disappears. Muffled voices circulate outside, their words swallowed by the wind and carried away from my ears. I look to Nixon, who simply touches a finger to his lips and focuses his attention on the opposite side of the room where the staircase is. We remain frozen. The cold gnaws at me no matter how much I try to ignore it. Slowly unzipping my backpack, I grab the socks I threw on top earlier and shove my frozen feet into them. I bury my hands under my armpits and clench my teeth together to keep them from chattering.

I listen again for sounds of intruders—a door being kicked in, windows shattering, guns firing into the night—but there's nothing. Nixon stands up, instructing me with a hand motion to stay put, and slowly makes his way to the stairs. By the fourth step he's sucked into the shadows, and I stay seated with my back pressed against the wall and my knees to my chest. I keep glancing up at the window, expecting someone to peek in here, then back to the stairs. There's no sound from the room above me, and I didn't hear the door to the basement close. Although I don't think the visitors saw us in here, they could be staking the place out, waiting for any sign of life inside the house.

A sleeping bag comes rolling down the stairs and slides across the floor, its waterproof shell catching on the rugged surface. Nixon follows behind it, carrying the second sleeping bag and one of the heaters.

"It's clear," he whispers when he reaches me, plopping the sleeping bag on the floor. "We'll stay down here in case someone comes back."

"And what if they do come back?"

Positioning the heater on the floor, he turns the valve, and the gentle orange glow returns. "I'll take care of it. Stay here and get some sleep—we have a long day tomorrow." And he shuffles to the other side of the room, sitting beside the stairs.

I get as comfortable as possible in my sleeping bag, using one of my balled-up shirts as a pillow. Concealed by the sofa, I lie awake and anxious—anxious to be sleeping in the same room as Nixon, anxious that someone might barge in while we're unconscious. My body thaws as the room gradually warms up, and my fingers and toes prickle as blood finds its way back to them. The wind whips angrily outside, its howling almost like a warning—though what its warning is, I'm not sure.

Nixon's quiet. I haven't heard him get into his own sleeping bag or move at all since crossing the room, and I don't know if I'm more uncomfortable with the two of us sleeping in the same room or him staying awake while I sleep.

Exhaustion wraps around me like a cold and lonely blanket, making me shiver. The sounds outside and white noise from the heater melt away as my brain slowly clicks off each of my senses. At one point I'm dozing off, slightly aware of my surroundings, when I hear the creaking of one of the steps. It momentarily pulls me back to reality, but when no other sounds follow, I tell myself it was probably Nixon and allow myself to surrender to sleep again.

When I wake, dull morning light streams into the warm basement. The musty smell fills my nose once more on my first conscious inhale. I hear the growl of a zipper, plastic crinkling, and movement across the room. Sitting up, I'm groggy from the interrupted sleep but thankful nonetheless. We survived the night. I immediately think back to the first raid the Green Zone endured and Liam's gun tucked away in his room. After all of this, I wonder if it's still there or if he got rid of it, knowing this would happen.

With one final stretch, I force myself out of the sleeping bag and pop up from behind the sofa. Nixon has all of his stuff stacked beside the stairs, but he's nowhere in sight. Unsure of what else to do, I roll up the sleeping bag and carry it along with my backpack across the room, dropping them beside his belongings. I circle the room, trying to shake the grogginess as I wait to be told what to do next. My mind begins to conjure up all the possible worst-case scenarios awaiting us, from capture to killing or being killed—or both.

"Ready to go?"

Standing at the end of the room near the pallets, I spin around. Nixon crosses the room and shuts off the heater, then grabs the sleeping bags and starts back up the stairs.

"Grab your backpack," he calls down. "And try to use the bathroom. We won't be stopping for a while."

I hesitate, waiting for him to reach the top of the stairs. After a few more seconds, I head to the staircase, plucking my bag from the floor on my way up. The door at the top is open, and there's just enough light to see where I'm going. The staircase isn't nearly as daunting as last night when Nixon guided me in the dark.

As I make it farther upstairs, the air becomes colder. At the top, the door opens up into the false closet of the bedroom I slept in for the first part of last night. Nixon finishes storing the sleeping bags in another closet when I emerge. Without saying anything, I grab my boots and jacket that were left in the middle of the room and slip out as he goes back downstairs.

Light filters into the living room through the now-parted curtains. The door is still locked and the windows are intact. Whoever was lurking around last night didn't bother coming in. Pulling on my shoes and jacket, I go to the bathroom and shut the door, flicking on the flashlight that's on the counter and dropping my bag to the floor. In the grimy mirror, I untangle the elastic band from my knotted nest of hair and run my fingers through it a few times before throwing it back up again. Wiping the oils that have coated my fingers on my pant leg, I wish more than anything that I had access to a functioning shower.

I hear Nixon's footsteps in the living room, and the anxiety swallows me. We're destined for a new safe haven. I'm a fugitive and he's aiding and abetting. It may not be a big deal to him, but this is a whole new world for me, one I never wanted any part of. With a deep breath, I shoulder my backpack, grab the flashlight, and twist the doorknob.

Beside the front door, Nixon stands with his bag and rifle, ready to go. I approach him, passing him the flashlight, and in return he hands me another protein bar. Dark circles rest under his bloodshot eyes, and I wonder if he ever went back to sleep after we went to the basement. The bruises on his face have darkened and there's a small knot above his eyebrow. He opens the door and we're greeted by the furious wind and relentless cold. Locking the door behind us, he takes the lead toward the garage, and I keep up with him this time.

The sky is a swirl of pink and blue as the sun creeps up over the horizon. The giant door is already open and his car is running, puffing clouds from the exhaust pipe. Without being asked, I crawl into the back seat, and Nixon stores his belongings in the trunk before getting in and backing out into the driveway. He jumps out, pulls the garage door down, then gets back in, and we're on our way to the next safe-house.

Like yesterday, it's quiet, but this time, I'm content with it—at least for now. I'm too tired to argue or absorb any new information, and I know he must be, too. So I tuck the protein bar in the side pocket of my backpack for later and lie in the back seat, focusing on the window across from me.

13. *Sympathy*

Two long, agonizing hours of driving have passed in silence, and it's taken everything in me to stay awake. Sleep would mean losing what little control I have of this situation.

We've stopped at a gas station, and Nixon has gone inside to pay. The place is vacant save for a white SUV parked two pumps over. I keep watch for any prying eyes that may spot me, although I'm not sure what I'd do if someone did recognize me.

The woman fueling her SUV doesn't seem interested in anything other than getting back into the warmth of her car. Through the space between the pump and a pole, I can see her hopping from one foot to the other over and over as she watches the screen. There's a man bundled up in a thick jacket with the gas station's logo leaning against the front of the building, puffing on a cigarette with a cellphone pressed to his ear. When the embers burn down, he tosses the cigarette butt to the ground, stomping it into the sidewalk, and returns to the store.

The double doors swing open seconds later and Nixon comes out. I quickly sink down into the seat behind his, but I'm certain he's already seen me. He circles the car and without sparing me a glance, starts fueling the vehicle. Crossing his arms, he leans back against the door closest to me. A blacked-out pickup truck pulls up to the pump next to us, and I force myself farther down until my back is touching the lower part of the seat and my head is level with the door handle. The truck's door swings open, and the glaring badge on the driver's chest is the first thing my eyes are drawn to. His eyes gravitate in our direction, his face pinched into a permanent scowl. I glance to Nixon, whose back is still to me. He has to have noticed the officer, too.

The officer goes straight to the pump, pays with a card, and waits. On the other side of the bed of his truck, I can see him scanning the area. The woman with the SUV has left, leaving the two of us and him. I slump farther down while staying focused on him. I'd be on the floor if it weren't for my backpack being in the way. He flashes another look toward Nixon, who seems completely unaware.

The click of the nozzle makes me jump. Nixon returns the hose to the pump and calmly slides into the car. The officer does the same, his truck purring to life. Nixon wordlessly starts the car and loops around to turn out onto the road, and the truck is right behind us, turning in the same direction.

"Don't move," Nixon says. His eyes dart back and forth between the rearview mirror and windshield.

The road splits into two lanes, and I expect the officer to go around us. But when I carefully reposition myself, I can still see him following dangerously close in the mirror on Nixon's door, and my heart hammers against my chest. Any second, I anticipate the hidden lights to flash and siren to sound. The car will be searched, and he'll find not only me but the gun and whatever else may be stored in here. And my brother's friend will be taken into custody. What they're doing is illegal, but at this point, I'm not much better.

Nixon veers to the right, taking a ramp onto the interstate, and I breathe an audible sigh of relief when the truck continues straight. I pull myself up into the seat, stretching my legs as far as they can go before my feet hit the door. It feels more cramped back here than it did yesterday, and I'm beginning to get restless. To make things worse, I still don't know where we're going, not exactly, and the uncertainty of it all eats at me.

"Are you going to answer my question from last night?" I ask, staring at the fabric on the ceiling.

"Which question was that?"

I roll my eyes. "Why did Liam send you? Why is he so worried about me going to re-education?"

He drums his thumb against the steering wheel, not giving an answer right away. "You wouldn't believe me if I did tell you."

I turn my focus to my wrist, brushing a finger over the bandage that's spotted with dried blood. The gauze catches on the wound underneath, and I wince. "Tell me anyway."

He sighs. "You weren't going to re-education. You were sold by your mother as a participant for the Elite Auction of the Red Zone."

"Wait, *what*?" I prop myself up with my arms so I can see him, ignoring the pain that shoots through my wrist. "What the hell is that?"

"It's complicated, but basically, it's this underground auction held twice a year where select Elites bid on people. Think of it as a human trafficking ring. Usually, their 'assets', as they call them, are kidnapped and brought to the Red Zone, but there are the occasional circumstances like yours where a parent, spouse, or whatever will sell someone for quick cash."

"Shouldn't that be illegal?"

"Technically, yes, but the Enlightened Society is well aware of what's going on. They're the ones who started it, and many of them take part in it."

"My mom would never do that to me!" The words are more to convince myself than him. Mom always valued Liam and me over everything else. She always prided herself in being an outstanding mother, and she was. Up until recently, she was someone we could talk to and seek support from. Both of our parents were phenomenal people all around, until Mom crossed a line by turning in Naomi; regardless of her breaking the law, Naomi is family. Family is always supposed to be there for each other.

"Well, she did. She wanted the money."

"But *why?*"

"Think about it—what else is going on in the Red Zone right now?"

My mind is reeling. It's hard to think straight. Everything about the Red Zone is so secretive; the rich don't want to be disturbed by the rest of us. While we're a unified country, they take their status seriously, and with members of the Enlightened Society residing there, extra precautions are taken to ensure their safety. But twice a year...

"The residency program," I say. She always wanted to go, and I remember the house she showed me the morning I was taken. And the way she looked at me as I was being carried out of the apartment, like I was nothing to her anymore. If what Nixon's saying is true, then she's been planning this for a while. I was her ticket to becoming one of the Elites.

"Exactly."

"You really think that's why she did it?" I don't want to believe it. I don't want to think my own mother would sell me like cattle, but in a way, it makes sense. It explains the briefcase and the 'TOP SE-CRET' envelope presented by those men.

"I don't know for sure, but that's how a lot of people come up with the money to get in." When I don't say anything, he continues, "I know that's not something you wanted to hear, but you did ask for the truth."

"People who are taken to the auction... what happens to them?"

"The Elites who attend bid, highest bidder wins. Once they're paid for, anything goes, and I mean absolutely *anything*. It's some pretty dark shit."

I collapse onto my back, trying to absorb it all. My stomach tightens, threatening to squeeze out what little I ate last night, and every breath is shallow and rapid. This can't be real—not in the Northern Unity. Our government is a thousand times better than that of the Old World, and they exterminated every remaining corrupt politician when they took over. We all learned this throughout our school years.

Everyone knows the horror stories of the United States; we're reminded of them every day so history doesn't repeat itself.

"Do you believe me?" he asks.

"I don't know," I choke out, and I truly don't.

What would Dad do if he were still around? Would he have stopped her? As Chief of Police for the Green Zone, I doubt he knew anything about the auction. He went to the Red Zone a handful of times that I know of, but never spoke of anything like this. I know a lot of things in his line of work were confidential, but he still let us in on little secrets such as cases he and Addison's dad worked on together or information he received about the executions happening in the Yellow Zone. He was always an open person, and if anything was bothering him at work, we knew about it.

There was one night he came home late. Liam, Mom, and I were seated at the table, waiting for him to get home before we ate dinner. When he finally arrived, he was quiet and looked like all of the life had been sucked out of him. We ate in silence; none of us wanted to pry. After dinner, while he and Mom were performing their nightly ritual of cleaning the kitchen together and Liam and I watched TV in the living room, she asked him what was bothering him, and he broke down. Earlier that day, someone had reported their neighbors for reasons I still don't know. He and two other officers went to the couple's house, and they were taken to re-education. What destroyed him was that the couple had a daughter who was only a few years old, and while his men took her parents away, he had to calm the toddler who was screaming for her mom and dad. I never knew what happened after that, but it haunted him for months.

I can't imagine him being able to stomach something as wicked as the auction.

"I need you to know that I'm here to help," Nixon says, "and I have no reason to lie to you. Whether you believe it or not, that's on you, but it's true. I do what I do because of shit like this."

Not wanting to talk about it anymore, I change the subject. "You said you're from the Blue Zone. Why did you come here?"

"The Commander thought the Green Zone was too quiet—not enough resistance activity—so he had me move here and appointed me the leader."

"So you're the reason crime has spiked."

"Part of it."

"And this Commander of yours, how did you meet him?"

"I've never met him in person. I got involved with the resistance back home through one of my friends, if that's what you're wondering."

"How long have you been doing this?"

He reaches over to the passenger seat, grabbing a second jacket I didn't notice. "Since I was sixteen, so a little over six years." He tosses the jacket to me. "I need you to get on the floor and put this on top of you."

"What? Why?"

"We're about to cross a border."

"What border?" The fear is obvious in my voice. I sit up, spotting the wall up ahead, and my body turns to ice as the identical wall from yesterday pops into my head. "Where are you taking me?"

"Calm down. We're going to the Blue Zone, but we have to get past Border Patrol first. I promise everything's going to be fine."

"How do you plan on getting through without stopping at TCG?"

Leaning forward, he pops the glovebox open with one hand and extracts a stack of documents paperclipped to a manila folder. "Already got that figured out. Just stay still and stay quiet, and we'll easily make it to the other side."

Without much of a choice, I shove my backpack out of the way enough for me to curl up behind his seat. I drape his jacket over my body, careful not to leave any part of myself exposed, and hear my bag being unzipped. Another light item is tossed on top of me, followed by the bag itself. The vehicle slows down, rolling over a speed bump just like when I was in the back of the van.

Wrapping my arms around myself, I close my eyes and wait. My heart is beating so violently it roars in my ears and I'd swear Nixon can probably hear it, too. We roll over another hump and the car comes to a halt. I hear the motor of the front window and a man asking Nixon for his license and documentation from TCG. After a few moments of silence, Nixon's cleared to continue on through the next two gates. The guards at both checkpoints let him through without an issue. Then we stop at the fourth gate—the final checkpoint before crossing over to the Blue Zone. I open my eyes, though I'm unable to see anything. My nerves calm down a bit as I take comfort in knowing we're almost there.

Like the other guard, this one asks Nixon for his license and documentation.

"Everything checks out," I hear him say. "Would you mind if I did a quick search of your vehicle?" From his tone, it's obvious he's not really asking for permission, and the split second of calm is broken.

"Actually, I do," Nixon responds firmly, while maintaining the same politeness he had with the other guards. "I have orders from President Hoffman herself to investigate resistance activity in the Blue Zone, and I'm already running late."

My chest tightens. I want to jump up and scream, to beg the guard for help. Everything I was just told was a lie, an elaborate story he put together to lower my guard.

"Your tardiness isn't my problem."

"Oh, but it is. I'm on an important mission, given to me directly from the Commander-in-Chief."

"I understand that, sir, but—"

"But nothing!" Impatience creeps into Nixon's voice. Papers rustle and I hear him shift in his seat. "I'm limited on time, and if I can't get to where I need to be *now*, I'll be sure to tell her whose fault it was. None of the other guards had an issue when I crossed into this zone from the Red Zone. I have the papers right here if you happen to have a top-secret clearance."

Defeated, the guard mumbles, "I don't."

"Then I suggest you let me through, or you can put me in contact with your commanding officer. I'm sure Mr. Tackett would love to hear about this."

"No, no, that won't be necessary." He hesitates but finally says, "Go on ahead. I'll have them open the gate for you."

"I appreciate it."

The car lurches forward, passing over one last speed bump, and Nixon rolls up his window. Metal scrapes against metal somewhere outside, and although my face is covered, I can sense the shift in the light coming through the windows. It's as though night has fallen, but it only lasts for a minute or two before we're back in the daylight. We're not stopped again, but I remain where I am for at least ten minutes before Nixon tells me I can sit up.

"What the hell was that?" I demand once I'm no longer buried. I'm on the opposite side now, behind the front passenger seat, sitting upright.

"What do you mean?" he asks coolly, which only angers me more.

"Top-secret information? Orders from the President?"

Glancing over at me, he smirks, and for a moment, I'm teleported to the first time I met him. "You bought it, too? Damn, I'm good."

"What are you talking about?"

He reaches over to the seat beside him, grabbing the manila folder he pulled out of the glovebox, and passes it to me. The front is stamped with the same bold, red letters as the envelope presented by the men who took me from my home. Shaking the fresh memory, I open the folder stuffed with papers, pulling all of them out in one big stack. "TOP SECRET" is the only thing printed on the front page. When I move it to the back of the pile, the second page is blank. And the third. And the fourth. I thumb through what must be fifty pages— all of them empty.

"You were bluffing," I say.

"Of course I was."

"What about the documents from TCG?"

"Forged along with my ID. I told you I had this figured out."

"So, what, you pose as a private investigator of the Society to avoid being searched?"

"Something like that."

If what he said about the auction is true, it's comforting to know that he can pull something like this off—he can lie and deceive our way to safety. But that means he's just as capable of lying to me, too. Ultimately, it boils down to choosing between the lesser of two evils, which is exactly what started the downfall of the Old World. It's smart, I'll give him that.

"Why didn't you mention yesterday that we'd be going to another zone?" I ask. Stuffing the papers back in the envelope, I toss it into the front seat and sit back. Being in another zone feels wrong. It's not only the fact that it's new and unfamiliar—I don't know anyone here. I'm alone. If anything were to happen, there's nowhere for me to go, no one for me to turn to.

"You didn't really give me a chance to explain much. Do you need a reminder of the altercation near the Red Zone's border?"

"You don't know that I won't try to escape again."

"I gave you the opportunity yesterday, but feel free. I'm not going to keep playing these games."

"Isn't that what I'm doing—going along with this game of yours?"

"How about you ask some real questions instead of throwing out threats and accusations? Honestly, I couldn't care less what you do. I wasn't planning on babysitting."

Rolling my eyes, I cross my arms and stare at the blur of trees and billboards. "Yeah, well, I wasn't planning on being kidnapped back-to-back."

"Look at you, you're catching on!"

"What?"

"You acknowledged that you were kidnapped."

"By you."

"That's not what you said—you said, 'back-to-back'."

"I didn't mean it like that. They were just…" Just doing their job? What kind of sick people would want a job like that? How could the Enlightened Society condone it? "They probably weren't doing what you thought. I don't care how powerful you think your group is, there's no way you know everything."

We pass three more exits before getting off the interstate, and after a few turns, we're on a congested city road. There are a lot more vehicles here than back home and fewer people walking. Buildings are spaced out rather than scrunched together, and even inside the car it feels more open—more breathable—here. I love my home, but everything being so close together can be overwhelming. Under different circumstances, I probably wouldn't mind being here.

The longer we drive, the farther we get from the city. Shops and homes become more spread out, and the sky has turned gray. Snow blankets the ground and weighs down tree limbs, some looking like they may snap under the weight. I fidget in the seat, trying to get comfortable. Long drives have never been something I like, and I'm desperate to get out and stretch my legs. I've been confined the past couple of days. From the cell at TCG to staying out of sight since being with Nixon, I feel like a caged animal—no control over myself or my surroundings. All I want is to be free like I was before.

We stop at a small convenience store in the heart of a lazy town. Multiple tire marks have packed the snow tighter into the asphalt parking lot, creating a thin layer of ice. Three vehicles are parked in front of the building. An unattended delivery truck is at the edge of the parking lot, its open door revealing cases of different beverages stacked on top of one another. Posters and advertisements for everything from cigarettes to food plaster the windows of the store, making it nearly impossible to see inside.

"Still have that jacket?" Nixon asks, pulling into a parking space directly in front of the door. Fishing it from the floor, I offer his jacket to him but he shakes his head. "Put it on and keep the hood up."

"Why?"

"We're going in, and while I don't think anyone is here looking for you yet, I want to be safe."

"Okay, but why exactly am I going in with you?"

"Stretch your legs, use the bathroom, whatever." Shutting the car off, he unbuckles his seatbelt, and with his fingers around the door handle, he pauses, looking back at me. "If you're wanting to 'escape,' now's your chance." Then he gets out, opens the door behind his, and waits for me.

The cold rushes in, slamming into me. With his jacket still balled up in my lap, I hesitate, unsure whether this is some kind of trick. He doesn't say anything, doesn't rush me to get out. He waits, patient and silent. The glass door of the store swings open, and a woman carries a paper bag to her car. Nixon has one of his arms propped on top of the door, and while he appears to be relaxed, I can see the seriousness in his eyes as he surveys the area.

I pull on his jacket, his scent—an earthy smell—filling my nose as I zip it. Throwing the hood up, I make sure all of my hair is tucked away underneath, brushing back the loose strands that have escaped my ponytail. I slide across the back seat and exit the vehicle, following Nixon to the entrance of the store. A bell chimes when he pulls on the door, and he holds it open, gesturing for me to go in first. Keeping my head down, I flee to the women's bathroom at the back of the shop.

The stalls are empty. The smell of bleach stings my nostrils, masking the scent of Nixon's jacket. All of the stall floors are littered with shreds of toilet paper and walls covered in writing and drawings—names, dates, curse words, and the three-lined symbol etched into the paint. I pick the cleanest of the four and lock myself inside. Nixon's words replay in my head. *If you're wanting to escape, now's your chance.*

Of course he knows I'm not familiar with the Blue Zone, and there's no way I could get through the wall. Unlike the resistance, I don't have forged paperwork from any of the transport centers and it would be impossible to leave this zone without that. So even with his offer of letting me go, he and I both know it won't happen. I'll either be caught or end up finding my way back to him. The idea of turning both of us in looks grim at this point. I don't care too much about what happens to him, but if the Elite Auction is real, I'd be walking right into it.

At this point, I don't know what to believe, where to go, or how I should feel. I'm shut in the grimy little bathroom of a convenience store far from home with one of my kidnappers walking the aisles, waiting for me to make my decision. This is all wrong. What my mom did, being tied up with a resistance leader, the Society and their secrets. And there's Elizabeth—Liam's friend and one of Nixon's members. The Society killed her, either because they saw her as a threat or for other unknown reasons. I listened to her pleas and cries. I heard her attacker split her skull. And he knew I was there—he must have—but

I wasn't a threat, not at the time. They let her family believe that she went missing one night, then planted her body and launched an investigation as if it were some sloppy homicide. Because they're so powerful, they can get away with it and no one can stop them.

Now I'm left with a choice that I'm not prepared to make. Three days hasn't been enough time to absorb all of what has happened or get all of the details surrounding my kidnapping. The door is open for me to walk up to the next person I see and beg them for help—or I can follow the person my brother apparently trusts the most to the next safehouse and wait for whatever comes next. Either way, I'm putting my own wellbeing in someone else's hands, and whichever I choose, what happens next is out of my control.

High heels click against the tile floor, pulling me out of my head. The stall door beside mine squeaks as it's closed, and I quickly stand, stumbling as I jerk my pants up. The toilet automatically flushes behind me, making me jump. Unlocking the stall, I push my way out toward the two sinks. As soon as I start the water, there's a second flush, and another door squeaks open. I dispense a glob of soap into my palm and shove my hands under the water that hasn't warmed up yet. The clicking returns and I keep my eyes on the sink. The woman turns on the sink beside me, and I try to act natural, rubbing my hands together under the water. In my peripheral, I think I see her staring at me. No, she *is* staring. Her gaze is fixed on my arm, and I look down at the stained gauze peeking out from beneath the jacket's sleeve.

I shut off my sink, and when I do finally look at her, her eyes meet mine. They hold a look of concern as well as fear, and I can only imagine how she's thinking that wound got there. She parts her lips, but before she's able to utter a single word, I turn and make a beeline for the door, drying my hands on my pants and adjusting my hood.

I scan the store, passing a few aisles and avoiding other people while searching for Nixon. I find him by the coolers just as he pulls out two bottles of water and turns around. He raises an eyebrow.

"I'm going with you," I say, keeping my voice as low and level as possible in case anyone overhears.

"Good choice."

14. Get Out Alive

After Nixon pays, we get back in his car. He turns it on but doesn't make any attempt to leave. Instead, he passes me a bottle of water and one of the wrapped chicken sandwiches that were under the heating lamp near the register. I thank him and we eat in silence. I don't have much of an appetite, but I force myself to eat as much as I can with my back against the door and legs stretched out in the seat.

"The safehouse isn't far," Nixon says after a swig of water. "We'll be staying there with a few members of the Blue Zone's resistance."

The thought of being surrounded by others like him makes me uneasy, but I don't voice it. Reality is setting in and a curtain of dread falls over me. I can't turn back. I've made my decision and I have to go through with it.

"I'll update the Commander," he continues, "let him know you're safe, and we'll wait for his orders on what to do next."

"I thought this was your mission."

"It is, but I still have to report everything to him and get his approval." He shifts in his seat, pressing his back against his door to face me and folding one leg underneath him.

"And where is this Commander of yours? Shouldn't he be more involved in all of this?"

He shrugs. "Like I said, I've never met him in person. He operates from somewhere outside of the Northern Unity."

"And you just... take orders from someone you don't know? How do you know he really stands for what he says? Or isn't, like, a double agent or something?"

He smirks. "You're smart. Try using that kind of thinking when it comes to the Society, though." Balling up the wrapper from the sandwich, he tosses it into the center console. "I know plenty of people who have met him—one being Eli, the leader of the Red Zone—and in a way, we're all double agents, doing whatever we have to to get information and stay off the Society's radar."

"Why are you the one doing all of this? I mean, you have an entire group of people back home you could have sent."

"Liam assumed you'd be a little more comfortable with me since you'd seen me before, but we saw how well that went, didn't we?"

Dropping my eyes, I twirl the broken plastic seal around the top of my bottle. "I'm sorry."

Half of me says it because it feels like an obligation, but the other half is actually remorseful. Liam put all of this into action. He was looking after me, like he always has. Despite all that has shaken our family, despite how he closed himself off, he made sure I was safe. In spite of that, I still don't want to accept this new reality, and I'm clinging to the idea that one day I can return home. Maybe that will change with time, but right now, I'm content with resisting the resistance.

"Me too."

Surprised, I look up at him. "Why are you sorry?"

"I snapped on you last night, not taking into consideration that you needed time to adjust. I didn't expect this to be easy by any means, but..." He lets out a long breath. "Honestly, I would've assigned a woman to make you more comfortable, regardless of what Liam insisted on, but Elizabeth was my only female member." Something flashes in his eyes—something that makes him appear more human—but it's gone in an instant.

Of course, he's still mourning the loss of his friend—which makes me feel more guilty.

"I'm sorry," I say. "Really, I am."

"It happens."

"Well, it shouldn't have happened. What they did was fucked up." And it was, regardless of my stance on the resistance or the Society. That night has haunted my dreams, and it's obvious now why Liam was acting so weird the following morning. He knew something was wrong before ever speaking to me, and I only confirmed what he was already thinking.

A sad smile pulls at the corner of his mouth. "That's nothing compared to the rest of the shit they do." He holds out his hand, eyeing the wrapper and mostly-eaten sandwich in my lap. Pushing the small remaining pieces of bread into the little bag, I hand it to him, and he stores it in the console with his. Turning around, he fastens his seatbelt. "We should get going. You can sit up, just don't move around too much."

Sliding my legs off of the seat, I start to buckle myself in but realize I'm still wearing his jacket. I remove it, and as soon as my seatbelt clicks, the car is in motion. When I lean forward to drop his jacket in the seat in front of me, he stops me, saying, "Keep it. You might need it." I doubt it, but keep it beside me anyway.

He's hard to read, and that's another thing I don't like about him. Stealing quick glimpses of him while he drives, I look for some sign of emotion. Liam displayed his concern for Elizabeth the day after she was killed, and although he said they weren't close, I was able to tell how deeply he was wounded when we talked about her. But with Nixon, there's hardly anything there. He's his cool, indifferent self. I guess you become desensitized to these kinds of things when you dedicate your life to a rebellion. He's been doing this for six years, so I'm willing to bet that wasn't the first time one of his comrades has died.

It's such a dangerous lifestyle, filled with uncertainty, and I don't understand how anyone can devote themselves to it. The Enlightened Society may be darker than we've been led to believe, but if they're as powerful as Nixon makes them out to be, the resistance won't be able to stop them. Not now, not ever. One day, they'll see that.

I find myself biting at the skin surrounding my nails, wondering again about the safety of my brother and the sanity of our mother. He's stuck there with her, forced to face her every day that he actually decides to be home. And if what Nixon said is true, Mom's probably shopping for houses in the Red Zone, if she hasn't already bought the one we looked at together. Every day she has to live with knowing that she sold her daughter for that filthy money, and I hope it haunts her. I want it to eat her alive.

"You can keep talking," Nixon says. "Or ask questions."

But I don't know what to ask or what to say. There are too many questions, and I'm not sure if I want to know the answers to them. My world has been plucked off its axis and plunged into eternal darkness. I'm following a stranger through another zone where I'll meet more strangers who, for whatever reason, also play a part in this mission to protect me.

It's funny how the world works that way. One minute everything is fine, near-perfect even, and the next, you're doing something incredibly stupid, forced into a new world you don't understand, a world you never knew existed. And for what?

I'm a strong believer that everything happens for a reason. Sometimes that reason isn't revealed until much farther down the path of life, but it's there, waiting. So what's the reason behind this?

"I want to know about you," I say, pulling my finger from my mouth.

"Me?" He peeks at me in the mirror. "What do you want to know?"

I shrug. "Anything. If I'm going along with all of this, I should know a little about the person I'm stuck with."

"I've already told you some stuff."

"Hardly, and that doesn't count anyway. The resistance isn't who you are."

"I'm afraid I'm not that interesting a person."

Rolling my eyes, I straighten up. "No wonder you and Liam are friends—you're both so secretive. You said you moved to the Green Zone from the Blue Zone. Do you have family here?"

He purses his lips. "I did."

"Did they move with you?"

"No. Look, this isn't something I really want to discuss." Another glance in the mirror. "It's not you, I just—"

"You don't have to explain. I get it." I rack my brain for something more lighthearted to ask. I've forgotten how hard it can be to get to know new people, let alone a resistance leader. With Addison, I can talk about anything and everything. She and I are always open with each other. No conversation is off-limits and no topic too taboo—not until recently. "Okay, so you said you've been doing this for six years, since you were sixteen, which makes you twenty-two now."

"Mm-hmm." That makes him one year older than Liam, three years older than me.

"How long have you actually been in the Green Zone?"

"About three and a half years."

"That's almost a year before our dad disappeared. Are you sure you don't know anything about him?"

"I never said I didn't know anything about him. I don't know why he left or where he went."

I narrow my eyes at him. "So what *do* you know? Aside from the obvious, because he was still Chief of Police when you came to our zone."

"Do you really want to know?"

His words drip with a cautionary tone, making my stomach cave in. He knows something that I don't—something I shouldn't—but no matter how awful it is, it might help me put the pieces together. If only a sliver of light can be shed on the mystery of Dad's disappearance, it might bring me closure. I've accepted he's never coming back, but the reason behind it all—the unknown—is what kills me.

Chewing on the inside of my lip, I nod.

"We're not a hundred percent certain, so this is technically all still in theory, alright?" He pauses, allowing that line to sink in. "We have reason to believe that your father played some role in the Elite Auction. It's not uncommon for Police Chiefs of any zone to be involved, but the thing is, the Enlightened Society has to *select* you for the job. As I said earlier, this whole thing is an underground organization, so most of the police and even the military have no idea it exists—much like the Black Hats."

"The what?"

"That's another story, but basically, those are the men who showed up at your apartment, as well as the person you saw in the alley. Mercenaries who do the Society's dirty work. Anyway, your dad made multiple trips to the Red Zone which happened to be around the times of the auctions, and his stays lasted three to four days at a time."

My brain is working overtime to take this all in while simultaneously rejecting everything he says. There's absolutely no way my father would do anything like that. It's true that he went to the Red Zone, but he informed us it was for work—they were just meetings for all high-ranking officers. "So what part are you unsure of?"

"Why they chose him and exactly what his purpose was. Based on what we dug up prior to his disappearance, he worked closely with the prisoners. My guess is that he was some sort of escort, if you will, taking them either to the auction or wherever they were supposed to go after being purchased. Again, this is all in theory. For all we know, he could've unknowingly taken people who the Society considered criminals to the Red Zone without ever actually witnessing the auction."

"But you're assuming the worst."

"I'm just speaking on what my team and I know. He *could* be innocent, but it's unlikely, considering how the Society works. If he wasn't in on it, I can't imagine that they'd let him get that close. As for why he left, I don't know. There hasn't been any trace of him since then."

Sitting back, I run my hands down my face and draw in a deep breath. "I'm guessing Liam knows?"

"He does."

"How did he take it when he found out?"

"Honestly? Not well. He was in denial for a bit even after seeing the proof for himself."

Liam harboring this secret knowledge about our father would explain his reaction when I tried prying information about him out of Mom. What I thought was a look of irritation was actually much more. He knew what Dad did, and Mom probably did, too. Once again, I've been kept in the dark—and for a moment I wonder… If I had known all of this then, would things have played out differently?

"You'll see your brother soon," Nixon says. "Once things cool down, he'll head up here and meet us at the safehouse."

"Liam's coming *here?*" I perk up at the thought. What a relief it will be to have at least one person I can fully trust with me. "When?"

"About a week. He'll be able to confirm everything I've told you."

Nixon turns onto a narrow road that barely looks wide enough to fit a passing car. Similar to the neighborhood we stayed in last night, this one is in a rural area, but in much better shape. The houses are larger and well kept, each at least a half a mile from one another, and most of the driveways are absent of snow, signifying that people actually live out here.

"It's not that I don't believe you." Or is it? He's offered reasonable explanations for everything that has happened, so why is it so hard to trust what he says? He and Liam are putting everything on the line to help me. "It's confusing, and it's hard to make myself go along with what you tell me when I don't even know you. As someone who's in the resistance, you don't just trust anyone who tells you they're on your side, do you?"

"No, I don't, and I don't expect that of you. This is all new to you, I understand that, but you have to *let* me help you." The car slows down. "If it will make you feel better, I'll tell you a bit about myself once I get some sleep."

I'd forgotten he mentioned that he hadn't slept in twenty-four hours when we got to the first safehouse. He admitted to falling asleep last night before we relocated to the basement, and, as Liam would say, he looked like shit this morning between the clear signs of exhaustion and the bruising on his face. He probably stayed up to keep watch last night while I slept.

"Should you even be driving?" I ask.

"Probably not." He turns left, driving up one of the cleared driveways and parking behind the car at the end. "Leave your stuff. We'll grab it after you meet everyone."

The house is noticeably bigger than the last, and like everything else, the property is covered in blinding white. Daggers of ice jut down from the roof, and a dangling shutter sways with the wind. Nervousness creeps up on me as I realize I'll be surrounded by more people I don't know who are part of the same thing as Nixon, but I push it away. Liam will be here soon. Nixon will explain more. Everything is going to be okay.

Nixon's outside, opening the door for me, and I brace myself against the cold. We walk along the side of the house toward the back. Multiple footprints are imprinted in the snow, overlapping each other. Nixon notices them, too, slowing his pace as he eyes them. I silently beg him to hurry up. My face is already stinging, and small clouds float into the air with every exhale. He looks over his shoulder past me as if expecting someone to be behind us.

Approaching the corner of brick that shields the back side of the building from my view, he stops, throwing his arm out to stop me. He peeks around the corner and does another scan of the area.

"What's wrong?" I ask, trying to peer around him.

He snaps his fingers, and I take it as a cue to be quiet. A few moments pass before he trudges on, motioning for me to follow. The footprints wrap around the house, leading to the back door, and as we near it, he slows down even more, barely inching forward. We step onto the concrete platform that hardly passes as a patio, where the footprints are so clustered that the snow is tinted brown. The back door is ajar, and from where I'm standing behind Nixon, I can see fractures on the inner part of the door frame. With one foot, he pushes the door farther open and takes a hesitant step inside.

Once we're both inside, he nudges the door partially closed. The warmth envelops me and heat rushes back to my hands and feet. Flames crackle in a brick fireplace across the den. White residue coats the dark wooden floor, and a coat rack lies on its side beside the entrance. Holes riddle the far wall and white sofa in the center of the room, its armrest smeared with red. Nixon mutters something under his breath and moves about the house, weaving in and out of the surrounding rooms. The house is quiet, save for the crackling fire and Nixon's footsteps.

I try to rationalize what's going on. Maybe they had a mission of their own. Maybe they didn't expect us to be here yet and went out before we arrived. But with the way Nixon darts from the kitchen, back to the den, and disappears into the room ahead of me, I know it's worse than that. I'm frozen, useless. My eyes are drawn to the stain on the sofa, and I tell myself it isn't what I think it is.

"*Damn it!*" Nixon yells. He sounds farther away, and when I look around, I can't see him.

Forcing myself to move is a task in and of itself. My legs are gelatin, as though the bones and muscles have dissolved. It feels like the heat has been sucked out of the house. Every room I pass through in search of him is a warzone. Holes in this wall, more white residue in that room. Doors hang from their hinges and splinters of wood litter the floor. My heart's hammering and my palms are sweating. I'm so cold—why am I sweating?

I hear movement and head toward it, wandering down an empty hallway. Red streaks the wall to my left, a deformed handprint at the end of its trail. More footsteps, closer now. I approach the room they seem to be coming from, stopping in the doorway. It's some sort of office, complete with an executive desk and bookshelves covering the walls. The leather chair is on its side. Pages with all different kinds of writing have been carelessly thrown to the floor, and books are toppled over. The desk drawers are open, one pulled off its track, and blinds have been torn from one of the broken windows.

And there he is, crouched on the floor with his back to me, blocking what I already know is there. A metallic scent fills my nose. My throat tightens. The room is spinning. A pool of crimson stretches out to Nixon's left, seeping into the spaces between the wood and dotting the front of the desk. Two legs extend to his right. He rises, a cellphone clutched in one hand.

"Nixon?" I barely squeeze out his name.

He whirls around, jaw clenched and eyes icy. I enter the room, but he steps forward at the same time. Peering around him, I see the rest of what was being hidden: a motionless man with a hole torn through his chest, his white shirt soaked with blood. Tears pour down my cheeks, and I try to push my way toward the body.

"*What the hell happened?*" I can't help but yell.

Nixon's hands are on my shoulders, pushing me into the hallway. He's saying something but I can't hear him over the roar of my pulse, and I'm pushing back, trying to get to the victim. Although I know it's futile, a stubborn part of my brain insists we can save him. I ask the same question again. The sobs are coming all at once now, convulsing my entire body.

Nixon guides me away from the room, stopping only when I'm no longer fighting back.

"Ivy, I need you to calm down," he says. His voice is stern yet gentle. Gripping my shoulders, he keeps a distance between us. His eyes soften, but the underlying anger is still there. "Calm down and listen to me!"

Wiping my eyes with the back of my hand, I try to steady my breathing while focusing on him. Soon the sobs come in small bursts rather than endless waves.

"We're okay," he assures me.

"But he was… They—"

"Stop!" He closes his eyes, sucking in a deep breath. "I have to check one more room. Stay here. Do not move. Do not touch anything. Got it?"

Without giving me a chance to answer, he disappears, almost jogging down the hall. Wrapping my arms around myself, I frantically look around, expecting an enemy to appear. I'm standing beside the bloody handprint, and it makes me wonder how many more victims there are. How many people lost their lives today? And will we be next?

Nixon returns, nostrils flaring. "Let's go," he orders, brushing past me.

"What? We can't!"

He stops, spinning around to face me. "God, for *once* can you just listen to me?!" He grabs my wrist and drags me down the hall. "A cleanup crew will be here soon, and we don't want to be here when they arrive."

"But Liam is supposed to meet us here!"

"Yeah, well, he won't be able to meet us at all if we're dead, too."

In the den, he pushes the door open with his elbow, and we're outside. I wriggle from his grip and we sprint to the car, both of us scanning our surroundings. Everything is calm, peaceful, a stark contrast to the horrors inside.

Nixon starts the car as soon as we're inside but doesn't leave immediately. He stares ahead, focusing on the snowy landscape that extends behind the house like he's lost in a trance. Then, in one swift motion, he slams a fist against the top of the steering wheel with a force I can feel through the floor. Huddled in the back seat, I'm unsure of what to do. Nothing I could say would help the situation. Nothing will bring them back.

Nixon backs out of the driveway and leaves the same way we came, grating his teeth against his lip. His shoulders are rigid, and he's gripping the steering wheel so hard his knuckles are white. He must've known them, the members who were supposed to be waiting for us. If he worked with them when he still lived in the Blue Zone, I'm willing to bet they were close. To him, this is a lot deeper than the safehouse being compromised. This is about seeing more of his friends die. If this is what being in the resistance is like, I can't see why anyone would want to do it.

He stops at a small park, consisting of a couple of picnic tables and a brightly painted playground. As expected in this extreme weather, it's vacant. He fishes the cellphone—a basic flip-phone—from his pocket and punches in a number on the keypad.

"Give me five minutes," he tells me. "I know where we can go, but I need to contact this zone's leader first." Pushing the green call button, he puts the phone to his ear and opens his door. "By the way, you don't have to sit in the back if you don't want to," he says as he slides out, taking me by surprise. Just before the door is closed again, he says, "Hey, it's me," into the phone. He puts about five feet between him and the car, pacing and gesturing with his arms while he talks. I can't hear anything he's saying, but by his exaggerated movements and the way his brow furrows, I know it's not good.

Trying not to focus on the panic, I look to the front passenger seat, considering what he said. I couldn't tell if that was an offer or a command because of his tone, his words still thick with assertiveness, and I'm not sure how comfortable I would be sitting so close to him. Back here, it sets more of a barrier between us, and in a way, I'm content with that. But at the same time, being stuck back here *has* made me feel more like his hostage than his equal. Regardless of how he said it, perhaps it was his way of opening up a bit. If I don't accept the attempt now, he may not try again.

He's still on the phone, pacing, with one hand balled into a fist. When he turns his back to me, I crawl to the front, shoving the folder that's on the seat back into the glovebox, and wait, anxious for whatever is going to happen next.

Now that Nixon's gone, my sobs start to come in stronger waves again, swelling in my chest before pouring out, and I bury my face into my hands to muffle my cries. The same phrase repeats over and over in my head: *This can't be happening. This can't be happening. This can't be happening.* But the hot tears drenching my face and hands and the image of that man reminds me that this is real. The tightening of my chest with every sob that forces its way out of me confirms that this isn't a dream like I so desperately wish it was.

Nixon and I are safe, at least. The safehouse was compromised and he lost people he knew, but we're alive. There's another place for us to seek refuge where we'll wait for Liam, and the rest of the mission can be carried out. Focusing on that one glimmer of hope helps calm me down enough to where my tears come in silent streams and my breathing is more manageable.

Nixon wraps up his phone call and pries the back panel off the device, removing the battery. On his way back to the car, he drops the separated phone and battery in a nearby trash can. He doesn't say anything when he gets in, nor does he acknowledge that I've moved up front, but he does seem to have calmed down a little. His shoulders are more relaxed and he doesn't have a death grip on the wheel, but I spot him gnawing on his lip a few times as he drives.

I've subconsciously pressed myself against the door with my arms wrapped around my torso. I want to ask what the Blue Zone's leader said but know it's not my place. Whatever it was, I'm thankful it took the edge off his anger. While the blood and the body are seared into my brain and my heart still feels like it's going to leap from my chest, I'm no longer violently shaking or blinded by tears. I'm in this weird limbo between hysteria and numbness.

"Are you okay?" I ask Nixon.

"Yeah, I'm good." His voice is soft, tired. "What about you?"

"I'm fine," I lie, discreetly wiping away my tears.

"I'm sorry. This wasn't supposed to happen."

"It's not your fault." At least I don't think it was. Without any way to communicate with other members the past couple of days, there's no way he could've known or prevented it. I find myself wondering what he saw in the final room he checked, what piqued his anger. Before I can stop myself, I ask, "How many?"

He sighs. "Three. Two more escaped, and one is missing."

"Do you… Do you think they knew we were coming?"

"No. There hasn't been any talk of you around here yet. Piper thinks the Black Hats tailed one of them when they were returning from a mission, which inevitably led to an attack."

Piper must be the Blue Zone's leader. With increased resistance activity in the Green Zone, it makes sense that the Society would have their people step up their game across the country.

"It was a coincidence," Nixon continues, "nothing more. If they suspected you were coming, they would've held off until you arrived. But that's behind us now. I have a friend in the area who can help us." He offers something that resembles a smile. "We're okay."

Physically, we are okay. Exhausted, sure, and Nixon has some gnarly bruising, but overall, we're unharmed. Mentally, though, we've been through hell. At least, I know I have. I wasn't built for a life like this, and rather than easing into it, I've been thrown to the wolves. From losing my home to finding a corpse in the safehouse and every-thing in between thus far, my mind is reeling.

Sitting up here does make me feel a little better, more grounded. It instills the thought that we're on the same side in a way. I'm not part of the resistance, nor will I ever be, and I don't necessarily agree with what he does. But at this moment, we have a common goal.

Survive.

15. Breathe

"Nixon!" the woman exclaims when she opens the door. She throws her arms around him, pulling him tight into her tiny frame. "It's so good to see you!"

"You too, Lacey," he says, returning the hug before breaking away from her grasp.

"Oh, honey, your face! What happened to you?" She places her worn hands on either side of his head, tilting it to inspect his injury.

"I'm fine, I'm fine. Can we come in?"

"Of course!" She drops her hands and moves aside for us to enter.

As soon as I step inside, the smell of something cooking—a multitude of spices blended together—makes my mouth water. She leads us through the elegant house, all the way back to the massive kitchen.

"Adam isn't home yet," she calls as she rummages through the freezer. She retrieves an ice pack and swipes a towel hanging from the stainless-steel double oven. Wrapping the towel around the ice, she hands it to Nixon and motions toward the two black bar stools tucked underneath the raised portion of the granite counter.

Nixon and I take a seat, and he holds the compress to his face. A stock pot on the flat-top stove pipes a steady cloud of steam into the air. Lacey rests her elbows on the countertop opposite us.

"And who is this?" she asks, surveying me with a sweet smile, the corners of her eyes scrunching up. "Your girlfriend?"

"No!" Nixon and I say in unison.

She does a little playful pout, panning her eyes back to Nixon. "Too bad. I think you two would make a cute couple."

Heat rises to my cheeks and I drop my eyes to the counter. Nixon clears his throat and says, "This is Ivy, my second-in-command's sister. It's a long story, but I'm on a mission, helping her."

"A mission all the way out here?" she asks.

"She was being taken to the auction, and the Green Zone isn't safe. Piper didn't tell you any of this?"

Standing up straight, she shakes her head. "I had no idea. And you know Piper, always busy. But the auction… that's awful." She looks at me with sympathy in her dark eyes. Her face is kind, with gentle creases in her brown skin. "I'm so sorry you're going through this, Ivy, but you're lucky to have Nixon with you. He was one of the best when he was here." She crosses the kitchen, lifting the lid from the pot, and a plume of vapor engulfs the space above the stove, strengthening the aroma that swirls through the kitchen. "Always willing to help others and putting their needs above his own. You're in good hands." Pulling a wooden spoon from a nearby drawer, she stirs the contents of the pot. "So what brought you here, sweetie?"

I know the question is directed at Nixon, but he doesn't answer immediately. He switches hands to hold his compress and leans forward onto the counter.

"We need a place to stay," he finally says. "The safehouse I had planned for us to stay at is hot. There was an ambush before we got there."

Lacey freezes with the spoon halfway out of the pot. "How bad is it?"

"Two are with Piper right now. Three were inside, KIA. Kase is—missing." He chokes out the last sentence.

She purses her lips, setting the spoon aside and smoothing out imaginary wrinkles on her skirt. "Does the Commander know?"

"Not yet. We're supposed to have a radio meeting with him tonight." Sliding off the stool, he walks to her. He lowers his voice, but I can still hear him when he says, "This is the only other place I know is safe. I don't want to risk going to another safehouse that may be compromised. I know you guys don't do much with the resistance anymore and I've been gone for a while, but I *really* need your help right now." There's a fleeting hint of desperation, but it's hidden well under his confident demeanor and steady voice.

She smiles, cupping his face with her hand. "You know you're always welcome here." She turns to me. "Both of you."

I return the smile, and Nixon breathes an obvious sigh of relief. "Thank you," he says. He hands the ice pack to her and pulls his keys from his pocket. "I have to grab some stuff from my car." As he leaves, he says, "Stay here, Ivy."

As soon as I hear the front door open and close again, Lacey returns to her spot in front of me, but doesn't lean in as close as when Nixon was sitting here. With my hands in my lap, I pick at my already-short fingernails, unsure of what to say. She seems nice. In fact, she reminds me a lot of how my mom used to be, and I think that bothers me more than being in a stranger's house.

"How are you holding up, dear?" she asks.

It's a loaded question that I don't know how to approach. After being betrayed by my own mother, I'm hesitant to trust anyone. Lacey seems like the type of person you could tell anything to and she'd gladly listen without passing any judgement, but I don't know where I would even start. She and Nixon seem close, too, and I don't want to say anything about him that might upset her or make her think I'm ungrateful for what he's done. I *am* grateful, but the adjustment is difficult, and today has added to the weight of it all.

"I'm okay," I say. "Thank you for letting us stay here."

"Oh, don't thank me. I'm happy to help, and if you need anything at all, I'm here."

"Thank you," I repeat. "I really appreciate it."

"How long have you and Nixon known each other?" She arranges and rearranges four identical white canisters that are pushed against the backsplash of the counter.

"Uh, not long. I met him briefly a few weeks ago through my brother." And again when I was at work, but I don't tell her about that. It was such a meaningless encounter, and he didn't even recognize me. "We've been kinda forced together these past couple of days. He saved me before I made it to the Red Zone." Has it really only been a couple of days? It feels like I've been on the run forever.

"So you aren't part of his group?"

"No. Actually, I didn't know he and my brother were part of the resistance until he showed up to save me."

She nods, taking in everything I say. "So this is all very new to you." A look of concern flashes across her face and for a moment, I assume she's thinking I might turn them in—I'm not one of them. But the gentle smile returns, and she locks her eyes with mine. "Well, like I said, you're safe with Nixon. He worked closely with Piper—that's my daughter—and my husband when he still lived up here. He's basically family. He can be reclusive, though. Poor kid has been through so much."

The front door opens, and Lacey excuses herself. I hear her tell Nixon where to put our things, and when she offers to help him, he refuses. She returns moments later as his footsteps fade into an unknown part of the house.

"That boy is so stubborn," she says, almost to herself but loud enough for me to hear.

"So the Blue Zone's leader is your daughter?" I ask.

"She sure is!" She beams with pride. "She took over after her father retired a couple years ago."

"And you and your husband… you're not part of the resistance anymore?"

"I never officially joined," she says, sweeping her jet-black hair behind her ear. "I couldn't do it, but I supported it from the sidelines. My husband is still involved in a way. He's a doctor, so he provides medical supplies whenever he can get his hands on them."

And probably works on injured members, I think.

"Piper was fascinated with the resistance since she was a little girl," she continues. She leans against the counter again, smiling at the memory. I wait for her to go on, partially because I don't want to interrupt her train of thought, but also because her talking makes this all less awkward. "She always wanted to be like her father. And I remember the first time she brought Nixon over when he was hardly fourteen."

"Gross, don't talk about me," Nixon says playfully as he re-enters the kitchen.

Lacey pulls him into a one-armed hug, planting a kiss on the side of his forehead. "You're the son I never had. I always talk about you." Releasing him, she goes back to the pot and stirs the simmering concoction. "Dinner will be ready soon. You two must be starving."

"And exhausted," Nixon says, opening one of the doors of the black stainless-steel refrigerator. Grabbing two bottles of water, he brings one to me and says, "Follow me. I'll show you where we'll be staying."

"Make yourselves at home!" Lacey calls as he leads me out of the kitchen.

We pass through the dining room, living room, and foyer again, rounding the staircase near the entrance. Every room of the colonial-style house is spacious and bright, with a homey energy pulsing throughout. We turn down a hallway and step through the third open door on the right. The room is mostly empty save for a white club chair and matching ottoman in a corner beside the window, a floor lamp, and a small bookshelf. Two and a half walls are painted a calming gray, a project that was obviously abandoned. The rug in the center of the room has been flipped over on itself, revealing an open hatch in the wood floor.

Nixon descends into the secret space, and I hesitate at the edge of the hole, staring down the glossy staircase. He notices and, looking back, says, "It's better than the last place."

It's not how luxurious it may or may not be that bothers me, but the fact that we're expected to stay underneath the house for who knows how long. I don't start my descent until he reaches the bottom, and even then I take my time as he waits patiently. As soon as I get to the bottom, I find myself searching for alternate exits aside from the trap door. There are none.

The finished basement looks like an underground apartment, complete with a full-sized kitchen and bathroom. The living room and bedroom share a space, but it's large enough to feel like they're two separate rooms, minus a wall, and the entire ceiling is covered with foam. A made-up king-sized bed is on one end with a nightstand on either side. On the wall adjacent to it is an empty mahogany wardrobe, one of its doors ajar. In the center of the living space sits a leather sofa with a glass coffee table in front of it and a massive TV mounted to the wall. The warm lighting and neutral walls add to the feeling of being in an actual apartment, almost making me forget we're in a hidden basement. Our backpacks are on the bed, and Nixon's gun is perched in a corner behind one of the floor lamps.

"We'll be safe here," Nixon says as I make my way around the basement. "Especially since Adam and Lacey aren't as involved with the resistance anymore." He props one shoulder against the wall by the stairs and takes a drink of water.

For a moment, I think I might believe him, but the moment is fleeting as reminders of the last safehouse crawl to the front of my mind. Remembering the man's bloody chest and vacant eyes, I bite back the urge to cry—the heat of my tears burning behind my eyes. I turn my back to him, surveying the area again and focusing on the single bed.

"You're staying down here, too?"

"I have to. My babysitting job isn't over yet." There's a trace of a smile in his voice. Then, as if reading my mind, he adds, "Don't worry, I'll take the couch."

"That's not what I meant." My face gets hot, and I'm thankful he can't see it right now. "I just… I wasn't sure if you *had* to stay down here, since you're not the fugitive."

"My mission is to keep you safe, so it looks like I'll be stuck down here, too."

A door closes somewhere upstairs. Footsteps thump against the floor and a man's muffled voice makes me jump.

"That's Adam," Nixon says. "Ready to go back up?"

I turn to him again. He's nearly finished his water, while my unopened bottle is still clutched in my hand. "Yeah." I look to the bathroom door across the room, remembering my longing for soap and warm water. My skin suddenly feels disgusting, itchy and crawling. "Actually, I'm going to take a quick shower and then I'll head up."

"Do you need me to wait for you?"

"I think I can find my way out of here."

"Alright, come up whenever you're done." He climbs the steps, leaving me alone.

I fish the last of my fresh clothes from my backpack and nearly run to the bathroom, locking myself inside in case he comes back. Fear and anxiety bubble up inside me, and everything I've experienced crashes over me like a wave, pulling me under. So many questions fire off in my overtaxed brain. What if they find us, too? What if they find Liam before he gets here? What if I'm not strong enough to handle all of this? It could've been us. Had we arrived any sooner, I could've been one of the casualties, or hauled off toward the Red Zone again.

The idea that everything is a lie adds to the mental torment. Do we really live in a world where our government murders innocent people, traffics their own citizens, and tears families apart? The Society has torn mine apart in more ways than one. My dad worked for them, my mom sold me to them, my brother made the choice to fight them, and my aunt is being re-educated—whatever that entails—by them. And I'm stuck in the middle of it all, not knowing which side I should be on or how much of what I've been told from either side I should actually believe.

I want to trust Nixon, I do. There's no real reason for him to lie to me, but the Society is something I have known and trusted my entire life—we all have. Why would they lie and hide these dark parts of themselves? What do they gain from it all? Secrecy was the invisible monster that brought the Old World to its knees. All this time, I believed we'd come so far from what our country used to be. We've combatted nearly everything, from the epidemic of mental illness to homelessness, all while exterminating the corrupt politicians who let it go on so long. People celebrated when they finally had a voice, when they gained knowledge that had been stowed away only for the higher-ups. But now it seems like there are layers upon layers of lies, even in the Society.

Turning the handle of the small walk-in shower, I let the water get as hot as I can stand. I peel off my clothes, tossing them in the empty wicker laundry basket, and try to avoid seeing myself in the mirror. Just from a quick, unintentional glance, I can see that my cheeks have sunken in and my eyes are puffy. Stepping into the shower, I allow the scalding water to beat on my sore back and shoulders and let out a soft sigh. The solitude in this moment is blissful. No guards or soldiers. No resistance members leading me to one place or another. If I could stay like this forever, I'd be okay with that.

I run my fingers through my knotted hair underneath the water, feeling the oils coat my hands and run down my back. I pump a generous glob of floral-scented shampoo in my palm and work it through my hair, digging what's left of my nails deep into my scalp before rinsing it out. With one of the sponges, I lather my body with soap—gently at first but then scrubbing vigorously. I scrub away the dirt and grime and memories and hurt. The mesh material catches the scab on my arm, peeling it back, but I don't care. I grate the sponge against my flesh until it's red and raw and a mixture of blood and water streaks the floor. But it's not enough. Nothing can wash this away, not completely. There will always be reminders, a stain on my subconscious no matter how many pleasant things I try to bury it with.

I find myself sobbing. The water masks the tears but the shallow, shuddering breaths that ripple through me can't be hidden, and I'm thankful Nixon went back upstairs. All I want is to collapse onto the slippery tiled floor and allow the water to melt me into a puddle, to wash me down the drain with all of the disgust I feel.

Kyle, Elizabeth, and the members at the safehouse. Five murders. One missing. Six innocent lives. Kyle's case went cold, but something tells me the Society was behind that, too. Naomi could have been on to something, and Mom probably knew it. The bitch was able to betray her daughter, so why not her sister, too? But there's no way of knowing that now, not with Naomi in re-education and me in another zone. Unless Liam is able to contact her before he heads out here.

I rinse the suds from my body, and after a few more minutes of standing under the heavenly stream, I shut off the water and step out, reaching for one of the towels hanging up. Not wanting to be alone with my thoughts, I quickly dry off, get dressed, and rid my hair of any remaining knots with the hairbrush on the counter before leaving the basement.

Lacey and Nixon are in the kitchen with a man who I'm assuming is Adam. Nixon is seated at the counter, and the other two stand on the opposite side. Adam has his arm wrapped around Lacey's waist, and she leans her head against his chest. He's not much taller than she is, but his frame is at least twice her size. I enter quietly, not wanting to interrupt them. Adam says something about Kase, the missing member, but doesn't finish his thought. I guess Nixon filled him in on what happened at the safehouse.

"If they don't hear from him by tomorrow, I'm going to look for him," Nixon says.

Adam runs his hand through his short, salt-and-pepper hair. "I know he's your friend, but this isn't your zone anymore. You need to trust that our group is doing everything they can. There's nothing you could do differently."

I'm halfway in when Lacey's eyes click to me and a smile lights up her face. "Ivy!"

All eyes are on me, and I hope no one can tell I just had a breakdown in the shower.

"This is my husband, Adam," she says, giving him a squeeze.

"Nice to meet you," I say, with a smile I'm scared might look as forced as it feels.

"You too," he says. "Lacey and I are happy to have you here."

"Thank you. I'm happy to be here." I am. At least for now. If I can get more answers, I'll be even happier. When your world is falling apart, knowledge can be your best friend. I've always been one to plan, search for answers, and try to fix things. Uncertainty has always been my enemy, even in the smallest of things.

"Let's eat," Lacey says, removing the pot from the stove. She carries it into the dining room and we all file in after her.

The black marble dining table is already set with a bowl and spoon in front of each of the four upholstered chairs. Lacey sets the pot in the center beside a plate of garlic bread and begins ladling chili into each bowl. I take the last empty chair—between Nixon and Lacey and across from Adam—after everyone else is seated. We eat in silence at first, spoons clanking against crockery. Nixon updates Adam and Lacey on the entirety of his mission, going into more detail than he did earlier. When he mentions the auction and my mom again, Adam flashes me a look of sympathy, making me want to fold up inside myself. Nixon goes on about how Liam put all of this into motion and how he was supposed to meet us at the safehouse, and Lacey assures us that he'll find his way here.

Adam and Nixon do most of the talking. After discussing the events that have unfolded over the past few days, they move onto lighter subjects such as Adam's work and Nixon's adjustment to the Green Zone after stepping up as a leader, and I take it all in. Nixon hasn't had any contact with Adam or Lacey since moving, out of fear of getting them in trouble if he were ever caught. The only reason he still communicates with Piper is because she's one of the leaders, and all four leaders are required to meet with each other monthly. Adam cues me in a few times, asking the same questions I already received from Lacey, and I give the same answers.

Kase is momentarily brought up again, but Adam shoots down Nixon's request to go search for him, stressing that it's too dangerous for either of us to be roaming the Blue Zone, with everything that's going on. From there, he presents us with some ground rules while we stay here.

Rule number one: No going outside, ever. While raids haven't crept into the Blue Zone yet, curfew is upheld here just like it is in the other zones, and Adam and Lacey's neighborhood isn't far from a military base that regularly surveys the area with helicopters. The outdoors has always been my sanctuary and cabin fever has already set in, but I remind myself that we won't be here too long. I'll survive.

Two: We are to stay in the basement whenever Adam and Lacey are asleep or aren't home. Nixon and I are welcome to come upstairs at any point other than then or if someone comes over who isn't part of the resistance.

Three: No use of cellphones or any other device to contact the outside world. The only exception is a radio they'll provide so Nixon can communicate with the Commander and other resistance leaders.

And rule number four: We can't leave for any reason until given direct orders from the Commander. If either of us needs anything, Adam or Lacey will go get it for us. No exceptions.

After everyone is finished eating, we all work on cleaning up and putting leftovers away together. Watching Adam and Lacey, I'm reminded of how my parents used to be, and just for a moment, it feels like I'm back home with both of them and my brother when everything was normal. But all too quickly, that reminder fades, replaced with the things I've learned about my family. When the dishes are done and the food is stored, I thank Adam and Lacey for dinner and excuse myself to the basement while they migrate to the living room.

"You don't have to go down there yet," Nixon whispers to me before he joins them.

"I know," I say. "I just need to lie down." And before he can say anything else, I disappear to my new temporary home.

Moving our bags to the couch and turning the lights off, I crawl underneath the heavy blankets and sink into the fluffy mattress. It's completely dark save for the small beam of light from the open hatch that barely reaches the bottom of the stairs. The only sound comes from the vents blowing a steady stream of heat into the spacious room. I don't really want to be alone right now, but I didn't want to intrude on Nixon's unexpected reunion. Adam and Lacey are more than welcoming, but I know quality time with them, with people he's close to, is something he needs right now.

It's amazing how much more relaxed he is here. From the way his body softened to the way he speaks around them, I can tell he feels safer. Until now, I never stopped to think about how this may affect him, too. I assumed that, because he's been doing this for a while and made the conscious decision to join the resistance, he's basically heartless, void of all emotions. He has to have seen plenty of people die before. His reaction to the ambushed safehouse was anger, but it must run deeper than that. With the way he insisted on searching for his friend, I know he isn't the monster that the Society wants us to believe the resistance members are. The Society has made it seem like the resistance has been dwindling rapidly and what's left of them is poorly organized. From what I've seen, I already know that's a lie, and I've barely scratched the surface of their organization.

Lacey is probably the nicest woman I've ever met, and I know Addison would adore her if she ever had the chance to meet her. I find myself missing Addison more now. Whatever obstacles I faced, she was there, making them exponentially easier to beat. I'd like to think she'd be on my side now, when I need her more than I ever have. Again, I wonder if Liam has told her anything, or if he's allowing her to believe I've vanished from the face of the Earth, and I don't know which I prefer. If Liam tells her the truth, he'll have to tell her everything, ultimately exposing himself and the rest of his group—which I'm sure would one way or another lead to Nixon and me being caught. She's the current Police Chief's daughter; if the tables were turned and I didn't know what I know now, I would've told my dad.

When Addison and I were at the coffee shop a few weeks ago, I didn't even tell her everything that was going on. I purposely omitted certain topics such as Liam's gun, assuming she would go and tell her dad. Another blade of pain slices through me, knowing I don't have anyone I can fully trust. If this all blows over and I'm one day able to return home, there are certain things I'll have to hide from certain people. Parts of myself will have to be buried so deep that even I will forget about them, and I don't know how I'll be able to do that alone.

I know sleep won't come—not now at least. Still, I lie in bed, changing positions every so often while begging my brain to shut up. I'm too restless. Nights like this back home would usually drive me to roam the city, avoiding areas I knew to be hubs for police. Then I'd go home to our cozy apartment, the familiar sound of Liam snoring, and the calming smell of whatever candle Mom had burned throughout the day. I don't want to sleep because I'm scared that I'll relive the horrors in my dreams. The nightmares from Elizabeth's murder only recently became more infrequent, and now my mind has the fuel to force me to relive even worse.

What feels like hours pass, and I'm still wired. I'm so deep in my thoughts, I don't hear Nixon enter. The lights flick on, and I sit up, startled. Dots float into my vision as my eyes adjust to the sudden brightness. He pauses at the bottom of the stairs, holding a basket full of clothes, and looks as surprised as I probably do.

"Sorry," he says, unfreezing himself and setting the basket on the coffee table. "I didn't think the light would wake you. Lacey found some of Piper's old clothes for you."

"It's fine. I was already awake."

"Not tired?"

I shrug. "Just can't sleep. Anxiety, I guess."

"We'll be fine here." He looks like he wants to say something else but doesn't.

The silence stretches longer than I'd like. Neither of us moves, though I'm tempted to lie down and bury myself under the blankets. Finally, he unzips his backpack and pulls out the same jacket I was covered with when we went through the border.

He tosses it to me and shrugs on another jacket. "Put that on and follow me."

"Where are we going?" I put it on, zipping it up and folding the too-long sleeves over my wrists. Pushing off the covers, I swing my legs over the side of the bed and pull my boots on just as he finishes lacing up his. "They told us we can't go outside."

"Just for a few minutes. I won't tell if you don't."

Without any other protest, I follow him up the stairs and through the house. All of the lights are off except for the single bulb over the stove. Adam and Lacey must be asleep, which means we're breaking another rule. As desperate as I am for some fresh air, I feel guilty disobeying the people who have opened their home to us, and I'm scared of being caught, either by them or a lurking officer. I'm about to tug on Nixon's arm and tell him we should go back, but stop myself. Just a few minutes; what could it hurt?

Nixon opens a door that leads us into a sunroom, and then another that takes us out to the wooden porch on the back corner of the house. Kicking away the snow that found its way to the top step, he sits down, and I take a seat beside him, scrunching my body against the railing to my right. Neither of us speaks, but I'm content with it. I inhale the crisp winter air. It's like shards of glass cutting into my throat and lungs but, at the same time, refreshing. It's a feeling other than fear or depression, something external rather than internal, so I embrace it and soon become numb to it.

The clouds have cleared out, exposing thousands of twinkling stars and a magnificent full moon. Living in the city, the sky was usually distorted by our artificial lights and clouded with whatever pollutants factories pumped into the air, but here, I can see everything. The moon bounces off the snow, illuminating everything in sight with a gentle, silver light. Almost instantly, I'm at peace. The beauty of it is so serene, so surreal. For a moment, it feels as though I'm not really here, like I'm in some sort of dreamland. All is still, all is calm. From the motionless tree limbs to the sparkling snow, it's like a picture you can't take your eyes off, something you'd want to tuck away safely and look back on to put your mind at ease in the midst of chaos.

From the corner of my eye, I see Nixon gazing up at the sparkling sky, the moonlight highlighting his jagged scar. For a second, I wonder if he got it during one of his missions, and I feel an irrational pang of anger that turns into worry. If he can be injured in this line of work, what's stopping that—or worse—from happening to Liam? No matter how hard he tries, he can't keep everyone safe. He can guide and take precautions, but he can't protect everyone all of the time.

I push the thought away, not wanting to taint this taste of freedom. I remind myself of the positives, chanting them over and over in my head. *I'm safe. I'm not in a cell. I'm not being auctioned. I'm not being chased. I'm safe.*

"Sitting outside at night always helped calm me down when I lived up here," Nixon says, and I wonder if he used to sneak out like I did before he joined the resistance or if that was only behavior he exhibited afterward. I have so many questions for him surrounding the resistance and his own personal experience with it, but don't want to seem like I'm prying into his personal life. On top of that, I know he must be exhausted. "I thought it might help you, too."

"Do you miss it here?" I ask.

"Sometimes… But there's nothing here for me anymore."

I find that hard to believe. Adam and Lacey treat him as if he's their own, and from how he spoke of some of the other members at dinner, it seems like he has a lot of friends here. Moving to the Green Zone and becoming their leader wasn't his choice; it was an order. Uprooting and starting anew must have been hard for him. I know it has been for me, and only now is it clear that it's not his fault. He's only tried to help. He's doing his job. If it weren't for him, Liam would have made the attempt himself, and I'm not sure he and I could have made it this far.

"Thank you," I say. "For everything you've done. I know I've been difficult."

Snapping one of the icicles from the railing beside him, he turns it over in his hands. "You're human. It's natural to doubt and fear things you're not familiar with." He presses the icicle into the snow on the step below us and crushes it with his boot. "I was kinda the same way when I was younger—resistant to the resistance. Never had to be rescued from the auction, though."

"Yeah, that's still a concept I haven't quite grasped."

"I'll know more about it after my meeting tonight. And hopefully some insight on where we go from here."

"Shouldn't you rest? You've hardly slept."

He directs his gaze to me, arching an eyebrow. "Are you worried about me?"

"You're *human*," I mimic him. "It's normal to get tired and sleep."

He smirks. "Alright, smartass. Yes, I'll rest after the meeting."

"Good. It would suck if my *babysitter* died on me."

"You're not going to get that lucky." He rises to his feet and scrapes the snow from his shoes on the edge of the deck. "Let's go back in."

16. The Hunted

The last five days have been painstakingly slow, but a blur all at the same time. I wasn't able to hear any of Nixon's meeting with the Commander, and he didn't share any of it with me except for a brief layout of the plan to get Liam here. Whenever he feels it's safe, Liam will travel at night with another member to the wall between the Green Zone and the Blue Zone. Once they reach the wall, Liam will continue alone through service tunnels that run beneath the zones. A member from the Blue Zone will be waiting for him to emerge somewhere on the other side, and from there, he'll be escorted to us.

Originally, Nixon said Liam would be here in a week, but every day that I've asked if Liam has left home yet, the answer has been no. A couple of days into our stay here, Nixon found out that Liam is being tailed. The Enlightened Society has hired someone to follow his every move, which has resulted in Liam not being able to communicate with the resistance without risking bringing everyone else down.

Nixon isn't sure if they suspect he's part of the resistance, but he's lying low just in case.

"It's probably nothing," Nixon said when I brought up my concern for my brother. "They were watching him after they took you anyway. They probably just extended their surveillance, since you've been missing without any leads. He'll contact me as soon as he can."

The Green Zone's other members are watching Liam, too, making sure he's safe and isn't given any trouble from the Society or any of their puppets. For the time being, the Green Zone is reporting to Piper, who then reports back to Nixon, and he updates the Commander on the mission.

Nixon and I have been getting along. No longer do I search for reasons to discredit what he says or to hate him. As Lacey said the day we got here, he can be reclusive. Getting him to open up is a chore, and when he does let his guard down for a split second, he only offers crumbs of information about himself. He still hasn't spoken of his family. I've found out he's an only child, but that was the extent of it.

He told me he originally didn't want to let Liam into the resistance. Liam had no idea Nixon was the leader—or involved in any way—the first couple years of their friendship, but he somehow found out and begged Nixon to join. Nixon denied it for a while but eventually came clean, still refusing to let Liam in. It started out with Liam asking about our dad. He assumed Nixon knew something about his disappearance.

"He was persistent," Nixon told me. "He refused to take 'no' for an answer."

When I asked him why he was so against Liam joining if they were such good friends, he responded, "That's exactly why I was against it—because he's my friend. And with him in my group, I became his boss and responsible for his life."

Although Nixon doesn't talk much about himself, he's a great listener. He's patiently listened to me rant and express my fears, only speaking after I've finished and offering whatever reassurance he could. There was one night I had trouble sleeping and had already endured multiple nightmares, and he stayed up with me and let me talk and ask questions until I felt better. I've offered countless times to take the couch so he can sleep in the bed, but he's refused every time, insisting he doesn't mind.

We've spent a lot of time with Adam and Lacey when they haven't been at work. Adam works the most, sometimes staying overnight at the hospital if they need him to. Lacey is a genetic engineer, and when she's not at work, she's usually in the greenhouse out back. Although Adam doesn't technically do anything with the resistance anymore—save for swiping medicine every now and then and working on injured members—he still stays up to date on everything that happens and keeps in contact with the Commander.

Every afternoon around three o'clock, Nixon radios members of his group to check in on everything from Liam to whatever other missions are being carried out. I try not to bother him when he's in the middle of business, and I know it's not my place to be listening in. But there was one day I came downstairs, unaware that he was still in the middle of a call, and heard bits of his conversation. He addressed the other man as Isaiah and was instructing him to have his squad prepare for another hijacking, stressing the importance of getting weapons to the groups outside of the walls. The mention of that brought back memories of their first attempt, how I'd been trapped in the chaos on the streets as it happened and the raids that followed, something I still haven't fully recovered from. I backed out of the room quickly after that, not wanting any more reminders.

Nixon and I went outside again on the fourth night. It was after one of my nightmares that happened during one of his meetings. The Commander gave him permission to cut out early to check on me. We didn't stay out long, just a few minutes again, but it helped tremendously. That was the night Nixon opened up a bit about the friends he has in the Blue Zone. He was closest to Kase, who still hasn't been found. They'd been scouts together, and Kase showed him the ropes when Nixon shadowed him on his first mission. In his entire time in the Blue Zone's group, Nixon lost two of his friends, witnessing one of their deaths personally. He didn't go into much detail, but said it was a mission gone wrong, and that he held his comrade as he took his last breath.

Since he's been in the Green Zone, there's been only one casualty—Elizabeth. She wasn't on a mission. She wasn't even outside when the Black Hats came for her. They broke into her home, expecting her to be asleep, when she was actually getting ready to go to a resistance meeting. She fought back and fled her home, injured, which was how we crossed paths. Nixon assumes she was trying to make it to a safehouse in the area where the resistance has weapons stored, but before she could get there, they found her. She was already panicked and hurt, and didn't have any other members with her for backup. Somehow, they knew what kind of work she did, but weren't able to tie her back to the organization. Thinking she was acting alone, they took her out to prevent widespread fear of an uprising. It wasn't until the plane hijacking that they realized the resistance ran deeper.

The bathroom door opens, and I look up from my place on the couch. Nixon steps out, and the heat from his shower radiates into the room. He pulls his shirt over his head, covering his bare torso. His damp locks fall over his shoulders, leaving wet spots on the fresh shirt.

I turn my eyes back to the book in my lap and ask, "Anything about Liam?" as he grabs some food from the kitchen. I've started asking the same question multiple times a day, partially to annoy him but also because I'm hoping he got an update when I wasn't around.

"Nope," he responds. He comes back into the room with a bag of chips in hand and plops down on the opposite end of the couch. "Chill. He'll get here."

"It's been almost eight days since the Society lost track of me, and—"

"And this stuff takes time. Here, eat." He shoves the bag toward me, and I grab a handful of chips.

"I have another question for you." Finishing the snack, I shut the book that I was hardly paying any attention to, one Lacey insisted I read, and set it on the coffee table.

"What's up?" he asks around a mouthful of chips. The bruising on his face is almost completely gone. A few yellowish spots linger, but you can hardly tell it's there.

"You remember the first day we met? You drove Liam and me to our aunt's house." It feels like forever ago. He nods, and I continue,

"Liam was offering to go with you after you answered that phone call, but you told him to stay with me and 'collect more information.' What information were you looking for that concerned Naomi?"

He studies me for a moment. "Think about it."

So much happened within those couple of days. It all bleeds together. What was said in his car that day is especially hard to remember. I wasn't fond of Nixon then, either. I was so angry with Liam, thinking he'd been the one to report Naomi and that he only wanted to come with me to spy on her. The way the two of them talked about her infuriated me. Maybe the latter is still true, but what reason would he have to spy?

"Kyle. You were looking into Kyle's death." Pulling snippets of that day from the depths of my mind, I add, "You told me I can't trust everything I'm told."

"Knowing what you do now, why do you think the police closed the case?"

I know exactly what he's implying, and I know he can see the sudden realization all over my face, but I don't say it. "But why? Was he part of your group or something?"

"He was definitely part of something to make their hit-list, but it wasn't anything to do with my group—or any group. I wanted Liam to try and find something around that house that could give us some insight as to why."

"Naomi said our dad was involved."

"I know, but we couldn't find any correlation. Your dad had been gone for a while."

"But she knew the Society was behind Kyle's death."

He rolls up the bag, setting it aside. "She was probably there when it happened or right after, and they tried to keep her quiet."

"But the report said—"

"Fuck what the report said. She was spot-on with a lot of the stuff she told you guys, regardless of the state she was in. Your uncle did something to piss the Society off enough to shut him up for good, and the only reason they didn't do the same to Naomi is because it would've raised suspicion. My best guess is that your dad told him about the auction, because from what Liam's told me, they were close.

After your dad was out of the picture, they targeted Kyle." He shrugs. "We were still looking into it when I was told they'd taken you."

Reaching for the remote, he turns on the TV, which has stayed on the news channel since we arrived. Adam insists we stay up to date on what's happening locally in case there are any announcements of raids or any action being taken against the resistance. So far, everything has been normal save for the ambushed safehouse, but of course, they haven't reported that. Nixon has made sure to tune in for the morning, evening, and late-night news every day since we got here, even if it just plays in the background while we talk.

The news anchor for the evening appears, spouting off the same scripted bullshit about the slots available in the Red Zone. With only two left and the deadline to sign up for residency quickly approaching, the anchorman urges everyone to get their applications in, insisting, *"This is the opportunity of a lifetime! Imagine starting your New Year among the Elites..."*

Rolling my eyes, I stand up and head toward the stairs. I'm sick of hearing about this program. It's the same thing every six months, and knowing there's a possibility my mom sold me in hopes of being accepted makes all of it more nauseating.

"Where are you going?" Nixon asks, keeping his eyes on the screen. He absorbs everything that's reported, dissecting every word and looking for any clues that can be used to the resistance's advantage.

"Going to see Lacey," I respond, climbing the stairs.

Lacey's on the couch in the living room, a laptop and open binder sprawled on the table in front of her. The news is on up here, too. I'm unable to escape it.

Lacey looks up from her work as I enter and smiles.

"Hey there, sweetie."

"Am I bothering you?" I ask. The TV cuts to a commercial.

"Not at all!" She motions to the two armchairs beside the couch, and I take the one closest to her. Removing her thick-rimmed glasses, she shuts her computer. "How are you feeling? I hope Adam and I have helped make this transition easier for you."

"You guys have been amazing. I can't thank you enough. Where is Adam, anyway?"

"Working overnight again, but thankfully, he gets the next three days off." She leans against the arm of the couch, pulling her legs onto the cushion. "And Nixon has been treating you well?"

I smile, remembering what she said about us when we came here. Ever since then, she's looked at us as if expecting more to come from this mission. "Of course. He's been great."

She smiles again like a mother would when complimented on her child. "Good. He can be impatient at times, especially when he has a lot on his plate like he does now."

"I think I may have triggered some of that impatience. I wasn't exactly cooperative at first."

"Oh, he should know what that's like. He *hated* the resistance when he first started staying with us. Ironic, isn't it? Adam was the leader of this zone back then, Piper was getting ready to join, and I was giving my support any way I could."

The news anchor's voice returns in the background, but I ignore it, intrigued by the story Lacey has started telling and hoping to find out a little more about Nixon. She repeats some of the things I've already been told, such as what age he was when he moved in with them and how close he and Piper were, but I don't stop her. One quality I love about Lacey is that she can go on and on about any topic, filling any awkward silence. It's a gift I wish I had.

"It took him maybe three or four months to come around," she continues, finding her train of thought again. "And nearly two years later he made the decision to join himself. I'll never forget—"

At the sound of my name—my *full* name—she stops, and we both direct our attention to the TV. My senior picture from high school is displayed on the screen. It's a year old, but I don't look much different. My blood turns to ice and my stomach churns.

The man drones on with a feigned look of concern on his face as he reads from his script. "*…Has been missing for seven days. She was last seen near the Red Zone's border, accompanied by government officials to re-education. Police have extended their search from the Green Zone to all other zones, believing that she has escaped and is responsible for the tragic* *death of multiple officers, including Border Patrol. At this time it is unclear if she acted alone, but authorities urge everyone to be on the lookout and consider her a threat…"*

Lacey places her hand on my leg, but I don't look at her. "This was to be expected, hon," she says. "You're safe here."

I know she's right, but actually seeing my face on TV and being painted in such a negative light is something I didn't expect. The man mentions a reward that's being offered for any information leading to my arrest. It's unbelievable how much money the Society is willing to shuffle out in order for me to be a 'participant' in the Elite Auction.

Then the picture on the screen changes, and I feel I might be sick. Liam, with his styled, dark hair and our father's eyes, stares back at me.

"Liam Clearson, age twenty-one, is also missing, as reported by his mother. He was last seen at home yesterday evening and disappeared some time before curfew was lifted…"

Lacey starts to say something, but before she can get anything out past my name, I'm on my feet, storming out of the room. How could Nixon lie to me? I finally start to trust him, and he keeps *this* from me? He promised to keep me updated every step of the way of Liam's journey, especially since he'll be travelling part of it alone.

I take the steps two at a time, nearly losing my footing. My anger has melted the ice in my blood, making it boil and pump furiously throughout my body. In the basement, the TV is still on, but Nixon is no longer on the couch. The bathroom door is open, so I check the kitchen, where I find him standing against one of the counters with his back to me.

"What the hell, Nixon?" I yell as I approach him. "You lied to—"

He spins around, slapping a hand over my mouth. "Shut *up*," he mouths, holding up the mic.

Static cuts through the radio that's nestled in the corner of the counter. Then a man's voice says, *"I'm afraid we don't know, sir. We lost him. Over."*

Nixon slowly pulls his hand away from me and lifts the mic to his mouth, pressing the push-to-talk button on the side. "I gave you orders to keep tabs on him until you escorted him to the border. Have you called him? Or checked his house? Over."

A crackling fills the air before a response comes through. *"Affirmative. No luck. Over."*

Nixon's jaw clenches, and he closes his eyes, sucking in a deep breath before responding, "I want you to search *everywhere* and stay in contact with the other group. If I don't receive an update by morning, I'll have your asses when I get back. Over and out."

"Copy that. Over and out."

Shutting off the radio, Nixon leans back against the counter and drags his hands down his face.

"What's going on?" I demand.

"Liam's gone, and my group had no idea until the news segment aired." He shakes his head. "He didn't tell anyone, and the guy who was supposed to take him to the border isn't with him. As far as we know, Piper doesn't know where he is either."

"What do you mean he's 'gone'? How could they *lose him?*" I can't keep myself from yelling.

I'm not mad at him—I know it's technically not his fault. Before all of this, I didn't care to know where Liam was every second of the day. With both of us working and maintaining our separate social lives, we'd go days at a time without seeing each other aside from at dinner with Mom or on the nights he slept at home, which gradually became more sporadic. Now, I *need* to know where he is. I need to know he's safe.

"Apparently they can't function properly without me there," Nixon says. He sighs and mutters, "The Commander is going to be pissed."

I stalk out of the kitchen, a tsunami of emotions crashing over me. My body seems to move on its own without my brain telling it what to do. With shaky hands, I throw the doors of the wardrobe open, pulling out one of the thicker sweaters and a jacket that belonged to Piper. I have to get out of here. I don't know what I expect myself to do that the resistance can't, but I *have* to find my brother.

Nixon comes into the room just as I slip into the new sweater.

"What are you doing?" he asks.

Ignoring him, I shove my feet into my boots and zip up the jacket. Liam can't have gotten far in less than a day, especially if he happens to be on foot. Then it strikes me that he may not have left willingly at all. I start toward the stairs, but Nixon cuts into my path.

"Move," I say sternly, trying to push past him, but he blocks me again.

"What are you expecting to do, Ivy?" he asks.

"I'm going to look for him."

"You know that's stupid, right?"

Another attempt to go around him fails. "He's my brother, and we have no idea where he is!"

"And there's nothing you can do to change that." His voice remains level and his eyes gentle. It's hard to stay angry when he's so calm. "You'll get yourself caught in the process."

"I have to try! You expect me to just sit here and wait?"

"That's exactly what I expect of you. Liam's smart. With or without help, he'll be here."

Biting down on the inside of my lip, I look away, focusing on his gun in the corner behind him. Liam's not dumb. He wouldn't leave without notifying his team, let alone his leader. This mission was his idea. There's no reason he would unexpectedly change plans.

I swallow past the lump in my throat. "You don't know that." I attempt to blink back the tears, but they spill over at the last second. "What if they took him, too?" My voice cracks and I close my eyes, willing the steady stream flowing down my cheeks to stop.

As terrible as it is, I wouldn't put it past Mom to sell her son, too. I'm sure she'd love to add to her newfound fortune, and I imagine they haven't been getting along since I was taken. Or the Black Hats who were tailing him could've snatched him up when the resistance members assigned to him had their guard down. He could be on his way to the Red Zone right now, fulfilling the fate that was sealed for me.

Nixon's arms suddenly wrap around me, and my body becomes rigid. I open my eyes, tempted to pull away from him at first. Neither of us have touched the other aside from when he carried me away from the Red Zone's border, before I knew it was him, and when we fought over the flashlight at the first safehouse. This is the first real form of physical contact I've had with anyone since being taken from my home, and because he's the only one close to understanding even a fraction of what I feel, I accept his effort to comfort me. Hesitantly circling my arms around him, I rest my forehead against his shoulder, allowing the tears to flow freely.

"Everything's going to be okay," he says. "I have someone inside TCG, remember? If they had him, I would know." He pulls back, keeping his hands on my arms, and waits for me to find his eyes before saying, "If I don't hear anything tomorrow, we can come up with a plan to find him, okay?"

Using the heel of my hand to wipe away my tears, I nod.

"I'm worried about him, too, but I know he can take care of himself." Releasing me, he takes a step back. "Go upstairs. Lacey is probably worried about you. I'm going to touch base with the Commander."

"What can he do about it?"

"At the least, he'll notify the Red and Yellow Zones' leaders of what's going on… and probably chew out my group." Then he playfully adds, "I promise I'm a decent leader. I mean, I've kept you alive so far, haven't I?"

A small smile tugs at my lips. "Taking the small victories?"

"Hey, don't act like you were easy to deal with."

"Don't act like you weren't a douche."

He smiles, holding up his hands in surrender. "You win. Am I a douche now?"

I shrug, walking past him. "You're decent."

I fill Lacey in on Liam's disappearance, and despite Nixon having cheered me up, it takes everything in me to hold myself together. When I mention what Nixon said about looking for him if we don't hear anything, she objects.

"Absolutely not!" she says, making me pause as I set the table. She doesn't exactly yell, but an assertiveness has crept into her voice that surprises me. "You should know by now how dangerous that is. Your face is everywhere."

"I couldn't live with myself if something happened to him," I whisper, setting the third plate on the table.

"Well, let's hope it doesn't come to that." She finishes shoveling spaghetti onto the last plate and returns the pot to the kitchen. When she comes back, she rubs my back and gives one of my shoulders a light squeeze. "Try to stay positive, sweetie. I'm sure he'll be here before you know it."

We take our seats at the table, but wait for Nixon before we start eating. Lacey lightens the mood a bit by talking about a million different things, but I'm most intrigued when she brings up that she's traveled all around the Northern Unity. Apparently Adam has attended dozens of conferences for the top doctors in the country, and she was able to tag along. They visited the Yellow Zone before executions were introduced, and the Green Zone nearly a decade ago. When she talks about the Red Zone, she scowls, saying that while it's an extraordinary place, she can't stand the people who reside there. Like my father, Adam was offered a job there but declined for obvious reasons, whereas my dad simply didn't want to leave our home. Adam used Piper as an excuse, claiming he didn't want to uproot her while she was still in school, but that didn't stop them from asking.

"He still gets an offer every so often," Lacey says, "but he tells them we're comfortable here."

Nixon finally comes up, taking the seat between Lacey and me. His expression is hard to read, and despite the 'stay positive' advice Lacey gave me, I fear for the worst. None of us speak at first, and I force myself to choke down my first few bites. Nixon took the edge off my anxiety downstairs, but my stomach is still in knots.

"Anything new?" Lacey asks, breaking the silence.

He nods and finishes chewing. "Eli and Nadia will be informed."

"How mad is he?" she asks.

"He's… definitely not happy. But I did find out what's going to happen once Liam gets here." He looks at me, and my heart skips. "Congratulations, Ivy, you'll be escaping the Northern Unity."

17. Neon Brother

"What?" I nearly spit out my food.

"Orders directly from the Commander," he says around another bite.

"That's his plan for keeping me safe? That's a death wish!"

"Hold on," Lacey says. "How does he plan on doing that? An aircraft wouldn't work—one was shot down over your zone. Not to mention that she's considered a high-profile fugitive."

She's heard about the plane Nixon's group hacked and hijacked, too. The Society fabricated a story, making sure to stitch in over a dozen faux casualties when it was really just a cargo plane. But if that's the route I take, there actually will be a death. Even if I make it outside of the Unity, I won't be able to survive there alone. There's nothing out there. It's been uninhabited for decades.

Nixon shrugs, taking a drink of water. "I assume he's working on that."

"I can't go out there!" I protest. "I *won't* go."

"If you stay within these walls," Nixon says, "sooner or later they'll find you. The auction is a week away, and if they can't find you before then, they'll throw you into the next one. We have groups outside of the walls. You'll be fine."

You'll be fine.

Fine isn't exactly what I've been hoping for. I want some sense of normalcy to return. If I have to start over, that's okay, I can live with that. Take on a new identity, move to a new zone, whatever it takes. But leaving the country and living somewhere we all know is absent of any civilization isn't something I can handle. No longer being under the Society's microscope would be a plus, but having any semblance of a real life would be impossible.

"And Liam will be with me?" I ask.

Keeping his eyes down, Nixon twirls the pasta around his fork over and over, but never brings it to his mouth. I look to Lacey, who eats in silence. Aside from questioning how I'll make it out, she hasn't looked the least bit surprised.

"Nixon."

"That hasn't been determined yet," he says.

"You said—"

"Liam will escort you to the outside, and from there, the Commander will determine whether or not he'll stay permanently. You have to understand that he's still part of my group, and getting you out of here doesn't mean the Society will stop what they're doing."

This has been the plan all along, and Nixon had to know or at least suspect it. I didn't give him the opportunity to explain at first, but over the past five days, he's had plenty of chances to tell me.

"You'll be safe, Ivy," Lacey says, reaching across the table for my hand, "and that's what matters."

I help Lacey clean up once we're finished eating. She offers as many comforting words as possible, such as, "This is what's best," and, "I'm sure the Commander will let Liam stay with you." Even if Liam does stay with me, that doesn't change the fact that we'll be outside of the Northern Unity, and who's to say the Society won't look there, too? Liam isn't the fugitive, but if they find him with me, he'll face the consequences. So will Nixon, Lacey, Adam, and whoever else I cross paths with. Perhaps it's best if Liam does go back to the Northern Unity, assuming he'd be relatively safe here.

This is all because of Mom's disgusting greed. I could've lived my entire life without knowing this perverse layer of our country exists, and I would've been perfectly fine with it. Once again, I tell myself that this never would've happened if Dad were still around—although he isn't a saint either. All this time, I thought he was perfect—he could do no wrong—but like everything else, that was a lie, too.

A new hatred for the two of them comes to life, festering inside me. I wish I could find them. I wish I could hurt them the way they've hurt me. Their selfishness ripped our family apart. They destroyed our lives.

When the kitchen is clean, I tell Lacey I'm going to head to bed, despite not actually being tired. She doesn't object, but pulls me into a tight hug, murmuring another optimistic line she must've read somewhere before retiring to her own room. I start toward the spare room that leads to the basement, stopping only when I hear her bedroom door close and see that Nixon isn't around. Then I turn around, backtracking through the house and out to the back porch, thankful I kept my jacket and shoes on after Nixon stopped me from leaving earlier.

The waning moon reflecting off the snow offers enough light to see the landscape nearby, but nowhere near as much as my first night out here. Fewer stars are visible in the inky-black sky as clouds have begun to move in, blocking out their beauty. I sit on the top step, resting my head against the snow-covered railing, ignoring the sharp cold stabbing into my skin like thousands of tiny needles. It feels wrong yet exhilarating being out here without Nixon. He's been my safety net throughout all of this, even if I didn't see it at first. Adam and Lacey have been great, too, but he's the one who has seen me cry, listened to my late-night ramblings, and ultimately saved me from my fate. While Liam was the one who arranged most of this, Nixon put it into action.

As grateful as I am for the resistance's many sacrifices for me, I want to run—not to turn myself in like I wanted before, but just to get away. To be free. I don't know where to go or how I'd survive, but I have this impulse to get out. The treeline fifteen feet ahead of me looks so tempting, dense enough to be concealed but clear enough to find my way through it. It's calling for me. I can hear it in the whistling wind and branches bumping against one another.

I pull myself to my feet, taking a tentative step down. The untouched snow crunches under my weight, and I freeze. The two opposing parts of my consciousness conflict: One tells me to go, if only for a few minutes, and the other orders me to retreat into the house. Another step down, and the world pulls at me like a magnet. The rational side of me is screaming, begging me to turn around, insisting that nothing good can come from this. My foot hovers over the ground.

"Going somewhere?"

The illusion of freedom shatters.

With a groan, I turn to face him. "What do you want?"

Nixon stands beside the door with his arms crossed. "Thought I'd check on you, but I didn't expect you to be out here."

"I just needed some fresh air."

"You really shouldn't be out here without me."

Turning my back to him, I gaze at the trees, wondering if I could still make it. "You're out here now, aren't you?"

His shoes thump against the deck, then become muffled by the snow on the stairs. "I understand if you're scared. I've never been outside of the walls either."

"You knew."

"I didn't, I promise."

"Then what did you expect to happen?"

He reaches for my arm, and it takes all of me not to shake him off. "Come on, let's go inside. We can talk."

"Talking isn't going to change anything."

"No, but it can't hurt either. We shouldn't be out here anyway. Surveillance is going to be heavy after that news segment." Standing behind me, he gently tugs on the sleeve of my jacket, and I take one final, longing look at the open space in front of me before following him to the basement.

"Talk to me," he says, facing me as we sit on the couch. There's noticeably less space between us than there has been the past few nights we've sat here together, but he's still a comfortable distance away. I've removed my boots, but keep the jacket on and fidget with the zipper at the bottom.

I don't know what to say. All of my thoughts have dried up like a desert, and I'm left with a single infantile thought: *I don't want to go.* I feel like a kid whose parents are trying to drag her to a doctor's appointment, terrified of what's going to happen although I know deep down it will only benefit me, even if it's in a way I don't fully comprehend.

"I don't want to be alone out there," I finally say. "I've just learned about the resistance, and I'm expected to go out there and pretend I'm okay with all of it when there are things I still don't understand." I run my thumb up and down the teeth of the bottom half of the zipper's track. I probably sound so dumb to him right now. He's put his trust in his boss and this entire operation. "If Liam doesn't get to stay, I'll have no one, and if he does stay, I'll not only feel guilty for him having to leave our home, but I'll be scared for him… I guess I'd be scared of him staying here, too." I shake my head. "I'm probably not making any sense."

"You are," he says, watching me intently with his hands folded in his lap.

I reposition myself, pressing my back against the arm of the couch and crossing my legs in front of me. "I'm grateful for everything you've done, I mean it, but I never wanted this to happen—I never *expected* this to happen. My dad left, my mom pulled this bullshit, and I've already had to leave everyone else I care about behind, including my brother, who happens to be the only family I really have left who's not in re-education." The words pour out now without any barriers, and with every sentence I speak, I do feel a little better. Nothing can change what's going to happen, but letting it out and having someone who listens lightens the load a little. "I don't expect you to understand."

He purses his lips and breaks his eyes away from me, focusing instead on the book I left on the coffee table. He looks to be debating what he should say, and the longer he lets the silence stretch on, the more I fear I've somehow offended him. I know he's lost people he cared about, but it's not the same. We're part of two different worlds with two different goals. I want to survive. He wants to fight.

Finally, he speaks in a low, detached voice, refraining from looking at me. "My dad was part of the resistance, but I never knew until he was gone. He worked under Adam back when he was the Blue Zone's leader."

I'm thrown off by him suddenly bringing this up, not understanding how it's relevant, but I don't interrupt.

"He died when I was fourteen—I know he was on a mission, but I never cared to find out the details. My mom was a wreck; she hardly left her room. Even though she was still there, at home, it was like he took her with him. A month later, she killed herself. I kinda expected it would come to that eventually. She just didn't have the will to live without him." He untangles his hands from each other, dropping them between his legs.

I have an overwhelming urge to reach out and hug him, or at least take one of his hands in my own—anything to let him know I'm here and I'm listening. But that might make him close himself off again.

His jaw tightens, and he closes his eyes, taking a deep breath before continuing. "Piper and I had been friends for a while, and she was my only form of support at that time. She brought me here after my mom was gone, too, and I stayed here for a few weeks before Adam and Lacey petitioned for custody of me. I didn't have any other family that I knew of, so they became my legal guardians. Only after that did I learn the truth about my dad and that Adam and Piper were involved with the resistance as well. I hated them. For a long time, I blamed them for what happened to my parents." He opens his eyes, finally looking at me again. "I didn't want anything to do with the resistance, I didn't want to stay here, but after a while, it grew on me. Adam and Lacey, and even Piper, who was new to the resistance, taught me a lot.

"Two years from the time I came here, I joined, and I was fucking terrified. I was a scout, and every time I went on a mission, I thought it was going to be my last. I had to learn to trust the Commander, my zone leader, and my comrades, and it wasn't easy. I watched my teammates, my *friends*, get hurt, and a couple died. I've been hurt and have come close to death a couple of times, but that comes with the job. So I do understand, and even though you didn't make the choice to join the resistance like I did, you made the choice to trust me to some extent. Otherwise, you wouldn't be here right now. The Commander and those members outside of the walls… I trust them, and I trust that they'll take care of you. If I didn't think it was safe, I wouldn't send you out there."

I search for something to say or do to make him feel better, but I know nothing can. He carries the weight of his past so well; I assumed the resistance was always something he'd lived and breathed.

"I'm so sorry," I say, but the words feel empty. There's nothing I could say that would hold any weight.

He shakes his head. "Don't be sorry. I didn't tell you that to get your sympathy. I want you to know that I've been in a similar situation, but you'll get through it, and you know you can talk to me."

There's a muffled thud upstairs, so quiet I probably wouldn't have noticed had Nixon been talking a little louder. He must've heard it, too, because he jerks his head toward the staircase and springs to his feet. We hear it again and I'm on my feet, too, following close behind as he moves toward the stairs. I try to tell myself it's just Lacey, but know there's no reason for her to be in the nearly empty room directly above us. Nixon freezes on the second step, leaning forward to listen for any other noises while I stand at the bottom of the staircase.

Ever so faintly, I hear Lacey's strained voice say, "We started painting in here but never got around to finishing," followed by three small taps at the top of the stairs, and I can tell she's standing on the hidden door in the floor. Another voice responds to her, but I can't make out what it's saying or who it might belong to.

Nixon lingers on the stairs a moment longer before he swiftly descends, sliding past me and grabbing his gun. With one hand on my shoulder, he gently guides me from the stairs and against the wall beside them, shielding my body with his. He presses a finger to his lips, and I nod obediently as a shiver shoots up my spine.

Anonymous voices and footsteps continue to circulate above us, and I strain to hear what's being said. Nixon turns his back to me with his gun in front of him. He reaches behind him, extending his hand out to me, and I hesitate before taking it. As soon as he feels my skin touch his, he uses his elbow to push down on the light switch beside us, and we're cloaked in darkness.

I should've expected a raid after the news this evening. But this raid is different from the few I experienced in the Green Zone. There, we were ushered out of our homes while the soldiers tore everything apart, leaving us to clean up their mess. If this is a raid, Lacey shouldn't be allowed to remain in the house. Whatever it is, Nixon think it's dangerous enough to grab his weapon.

With every passing second, my heart beats faster. I'm being hunted, and my predators—however many there are—are right over our heads, searching tirelessly. They'll scour every home in hopes of finding me, and the safehouses throughout the country won't be an exception. For a moment, I think that if they prioritize finding me, they'll brush off Liam's disappearance long enough for him to get here safely. But I know the Society is always thinking ahead, and they're likely confident that if they find one of us, they'll find the other, too.

Something scrapes against the floor upstairs, and I hold my breath, expecting the hatch to swing open at any minute and the basement to be swarming with soldiers or Black Hats or whoever is here. But it doesn't happen, and everything becomes unnervingly quiet. No footsteps. No voices. Just my hammering heart and Nixon's quickened breathing. After a couple of minutes of silence, I think they're gone, but the air is still thick with tension and my gut is telling me something much worse is coming.

A dog barks, confirming my intuition. I impulsively squeeze Nixon's hand, and he squeezes back. It briefly eases my mind, reminding me I'm not completely alone in all of this. I hear the creature's nails clicking and scratching against the wood, and it barks again, reverberating in my skull. They're tracking my scent. If there was any hope I'd make it through the night, it's gone now.

The voices return. They'll be here any second. There will be bloodshed, and I have a feeling Nixon will lose the gunfight. I can't tell how many there are, but back home, raids were performed by groups of three. If that's the case here, we're outnumbered. Even if Lacey can wield a weapon, I'm dead weight.

The air grows heavier with suffocating tension. Seconds feel like hours.

At last the dog's barking fades along with the voices, including Lacey's, but Nixon doesn't turn the light on. We remain against the wall in chilling silence, my hand still gripping his without any intention of letting go. I'm afraid to move or whisper a single syllable, paranoid they can sense me through the walls and floor.

When the hatch opens and light floods in, my entire body becomes stone. Nixon gives my hand a final squeeze before letting go and readying his gun.

"They're gone," Lacey's tired voice says.

Nixon steps into her view, lowering his weapon. "How did you manage to do that?"

"I told them they were picking up the scent of a dog we had that passed away yesterday. And Adam is well-known around here. They know not to question either of us."

Nixon relaxes his shoulders and smiles. "Thank you."

"You two need to be careful. They'll be back."

"We will."

The hinges of the secret door whine, and right before she closes it she says, "And no more going outside." Then it slams shut, and the darkness returns for a few seconds before Nixon finds the light switch.

"We won't get that lucky again," he says, returning his gun to its designated area and taking a seat on the edge of the bed. "You okay?"

Still pressed against the wall, I nod, although my heart is threatening to leap out of my chest and I can't bring my body to relax. They were so close. Their dog picked up my scent, but Lacey lied for me. They have to know that. They'll be back, and next time they won't be so quick to believe her. Liam is out there somewhere while all of this is happening, too, and while I do want him here with me, I'm beginning to question how selfish it is. He's living a dangerous lifestyle regardless, but he'd be undoubtedly safer if he stayed in the Green Zone without me.

"We're still safe, right?" I ask.

"For now."

Nixon is already awake, and seems to have been for a while. I find him in the kitchen, pouring himself a cup of coffee. He's pulled his hair up into a ponytail that sticks out at all different angles.

"Nothing on Liam," he says as I enter.

My heart sinks, but I pretend I don't care. Nixon has enough to worry about and doesn't need my millions of questions he can't answer piled on top of it. After last night, I can almost guarantee we won't be coming up with any plans to find him. Even if Nixon wanted to, Adam and Lacey would forbid it.

I grab a mug from one of the cupboards and prepare my own drink. Nixon takes a seat at the small kitchen table, eyeing the radio as if expecting new information to come through any second. As the Green Zone's leader, I know he has to be worried about his missing member—his second-in-command, as he called him. After all that's happened, I find that I have an immense amount of respect for Nixon. He's handled all of this with ease, making sure that I'm comfortable and aware of all that's going on throughout the process.

"How are you holding up?" I ask, sipping on my coffee. I've only asked if he was okay once—after the attack on the second safehouse— the entire time we've been together, and that was only because it felt obligatory.

He looks to me, arching a once-bruised brow. "I'm fine. Why?"

I shrug, leaning back against the counter. "I don't know how you deal with all of this and keep it bottled up."

"I'm used to it. What, are you warming up to me now?"

"What if I am?"

Leaning back, he smiles and takes another drink before responding. "It's about damn time. But I seem to recall you saying you hated me… twice."

Thinking back to how I acted our first day together, I laugh. "Oh, I did."

"What changed?"

"Guess I realized you're not a *total* dick. Your face looks better, by the way."

"Wow, so generous with compliments this morning. I'm sorry my face deterred you from liking me after I saved your life."

I roll my eyes but laugh, and his smile widens, reaching his eyes. "No, the bruises—they're gone."

"Oh, yeah." He brings a hand to the side of his face that was injured. "That shit hurt. How's your arm?"

I flash him the wrist that was injured by the handcuffs. The wound has healed, leaving a permanent reminder in the form of a raised, purple scar. "Better. Although, I would've preferred it if you hadn't dug your thumb into it at the first safehouse."

He shrugs, tracing the handle of his mug with his thumb. "I would've preferred if you hadn't threatened to turn me in."

Tugging on my bottom lip with my teeth, I drop my eyes to my coffee. I'd forgotten about that. It was a stupid thing to say, no matter how upset I was. I can't recall what made those words spill out. We'd been fighting over the flashlight after I asked something about Liam. It feels like a lifetime ago, and I honestly can't believe how much I despised him at first. "I'm sorry."

He crosses the kitchen and cleans his cup in the sink beside me. "We're good now, right?"

"Right."

Reaching behind me, he returns the cup to its designated cupboard. "And about Liam—"

"It's fine. I can wait a little longer."

"I was going to say I can go look for him if you want. After last night, it wouldn't be smart for you to leave the house."

When all of this started, I would've jumped at the offer. I would've *expected* Nixon to go out and look for my missing brother. Now, I'm hesitant. The Society has their people scouring every zone for me, and if something happened while Nixon was away, I know he'd blame himself. Although he's the one in charge of the Green Zone, he'd have to explain himself to Liam, and knowing my brother, he wouldn't take it well. During my time with Nixon, I've gathered that he's patient and understanding. Liam, for the most part, is the opposite, especially when it comes to his family.

Nixon's right, it wouldn't be smart for me to leave—at least not until it's time to flee the Northern Unity—but I don't want anything to happen to him either. He's done enough for Liam and me, putting his life on the line and temporarily leaving his team behind, and regardless of my views of him at first, I know the guilt would eat me alive if he left and got himself killed. We've made it this far, and the smallest mistake could burn this mission to the ground.

"I trust you," I say. "If you believe Liam is safe, then so do I."

Footsteps pound against the staircase, and before either of us have a chance to react, Adam appears, still dressed in his work attire—dark blue scrubs and a white lab coat. By the bags under his eyes, I can tell he's had a long night at the hospital and hasn't slept much, if at all. He studies the two of us for a moment, his brown eyes flicking back and forth between us, and I unconsciously sidestep from Nixon.

"Kase is here," Adam says.

"What do you mean, 'here'?" Nixon asks.

"He's in the living room. He came into my ER early this morning." Adam hesitates, running his fingers through his hair—something I've noticed he does when he has bad news. "He specifically asked to talk to you."

Nixon draws in a deep breath. "Does Piper know?"

Adam nods. "She's here, too. I contacted her as soon as he came in. Another member brought him here after he was discharged."

Nixon shoves his hands in the pockets of his jeans. "Why me?"

His response surprises me. After learning Kase was missing, Nixon was insistent on finding him. Kase was Nixon's closest friend and mentor during his time in the Blue Zone, though, so I understood. Now that Kase is here, Nixon doesn't seem to be very excited about it. Sure, Kase is hurt, but he's safe nonetheless.

"He trusts you," Adam says. He glances behind him at the stairs, and although there's no way Kase would be able to hear him from the living room, he lowers his voice and says, "Something doesn't feel right. I don't know what happened, he wouldn't tell me anything.

Piper feels like she's only getting part of the story, but considering how close you two were, you can probably get him to talk."

Without either of them outright saying it, I quickly put the pieces together. Kase has been missing for a week and was the only person from the safehouse who was unaccounted for. The other two members who escaped the attack met up with their leader, but he remained absent. Without contacting Piper or anyone else that we know of, he went into Adam's hospital, knowing he'd fix him up and possibly cover up that he was ever there.

He has to have been abducted by the Black Hats during that isolated raid, and for whatever reason, they've let him go—something even I know is unusual. They had no issue killing Elizabeth, and if they're not murdering members of the resistance, they're hauling them off to the auction. There's only one reason they would keep Kase alive: He gave them information.

"How bad is he?" Nixon asks.

"His physical injuries aren't too severe," Adam says. "He was dehydrated and has a couple broken ribs and bruising on various parts of his body—nothing life-threatening. Mentally, though… He's obviously been deprived of sleep, although he won't tell us everything he's been put through."

"Let him sleep. I'll talk to him later."

"He wants to see you now."

"And I want him to rest at least a couple hours before we talk." Although Adam is essentially Nixon's father-figure, Nixon speaks to him as though they're equals—two resistance leaders, regardless of Adam's retirement, swapping information and giving orders.

Adam hesitates, obviously wanting to say more or argue with Nixon's decision. Instead, he starts toward the stairs, calling over his shoulder, "I want him out of here before Lacey gets home."

18. Fallout

"We're fucked," Nixon mumbles again, pacing back and forth with his hands clasped behind his head.

I haven't said a word since Adam went upstairs. This isn't my business, and I know nothing I say will change what we're both thinking.

Kase has flipped.

"If they took him, he shouldn't be alive," Nixon says, confirming my suspicion.

Kase has to have given the Society something in exchange for his life—what that is, we don't know. He knew we were going to that safehouse. He and the rest of the Blue Zone's group were aware of what was going on before it made the news. Information on my whereabouts could have been the key to his freedom, likely with strings attached. The Society could have begun a manhunt across the country before notifying the public. Secrecy is the foundation of this wicked empire they've built, after all.

If Kase knew Nixon would come here after the safehouse fell through, then he knows I'm here, and if my theory of him selling us out is true, the Society knows, too. They're just waiting for the right time to strike.

I shift in the chair, crossing one of my legs over the other. Nixon continues pacing, clenching and unclenching his jaw as he works through everything in his head. Again, I'm scared more for Liam than myself. I at least have Nixon with me. As far as we know, Liam is alone.

"We can't stay here," I say, as much as I don't want to. I don't want to imagine leaving this house without my brother. I don't want to be out there again in search of a safe place, but I know that's exactly what we'll have to do. "He knew I'd be with you. If the Society got him to admit to it—"

"I'll tell him I lost you once we got into the Blue Zone," Nixon says.

"It doesn't matter if he's already told them otherwise, and you know that. Even if that *did* change anything, they know you're here, and you played a role in all of this."

"And we don't know if he's given them the locations of the other safehouses either." He stops beside me, pressing his hands against the top of the table and taking a deep breath as if attempting to ground himself. "We don't know anything yet. If I feel that it's no longer safe here, I'll take you somewhere else, and someone will have to let Liam know, if they ever find him." Dropping his shoulders forward, he sighs. "I'm sorry."

"It's not your fault."

"I don't know everything Piper and her group work on. The Black Hats could've been looking into that specific squad for some reason. If they suspected Kase knew anything about you going to that house, they wouldn't have attacked when they did. That's one thing I'm sure of."

"Liam always says to assume the worst." He told me that the day we ran from the police after I insisted they didn't see us, and he ended up being right. They called Mom before I got home, lying their way out of attempting to shoot us but confirming they knew who we were. I'm hoping his motto doesn't prove to be true this time.

"In most cases, yes, but the Society wouldn't go through all of this trouble if they knew where you were headed less than forty-eight hours after losing you."

"I hope you're right."

We kill time over the next couple of hours by flipping through channels on the TV but always end up circling back to the news. No new information has been reported on Liam or me. The same story about me is spewed by a different anchor, but there's no mention of Liam at all. He's not their priority, but I'm almost certain they're still watching for him, hoping he'll lead them to their prize.

Waiting around down here is mind-numbing. I'm itching to go outside again—day or night, I don't care. The small doses of fresh air and openness have kept me somewhat sane. I'm desperate to be free, and this new obstacle has added to my anxiety and fear of what's to come. But I don't cry again. I don't show any emotions, because I know Nixon is in the same position as I am. There's nothing either of us can do right now. Not about Liam or Kase or leaving the Northern Unity. So we wait, and we talk about things that distract us from the haze of doubt and uncertainty looming over us.

Nixon opens up about his life before his parents died, before he joined the resistance himself. His mom was a journalist and his dad was a high-school teacher. He talks about how different the Green Zone is from his home, but in a good way. It was an escape for him that he never knew he needed. I let him do most of the talking, not only because he knows plenty about my life from Liam, but because I like watching his eyes light up when he recalls a happy memory from his past. I like hearing his laugh when he tells me something embarrassing he did as a kid.

Slowly, the walls he's built around himself crumble. They're still present, but weakened enough for his true self to slip through the cracks. At some point, I block out the background noise of the TV and focus solely on him. I'm hanging on to every word he says, and soon it's as though nothing else matters. Nothing else is real.

Since the resistance consumes most of his life, it's hard to avoid the topic completely, but he talks about the optimistic side of it, such as how close-knit everyone is. It's like a family, and they all look after each other. When he moved to the Green Zone, it was difficult for him to adjust, and the handful of remaining members who had worked under the leader prior weren't too happy about Nixon taking over. But within the first six months of taking power, he recruited more than thirty new members, and from there, they continued to grow both in numbers and strength—no drop-outs, and only one fatality as far as we know. He's proud of the work he's done in the resistance, both as a scout and leader, but he's also humble.

When he asks me to go upstairs with him, I'm reluctant. This isn't my mission or my group, and I don't want to interfere, but he insists I need to hear him question Kase. So we make the short journey upstairs and find Adam and Piper in the kitchen. They cease their conversation when we enter, and Adam excuses himself to inform Kase that Nixon is on his way up. We wait with Piper for him to return. She has the same dark hair and eyes as Lacey but a blend of both her parents' skin tone—not as light as Adam but not as dark as Lacey either—and her facial features aren't as gentle as her mother's.

"You know she can't be in there with you, right?" Piper asks Nixon, eyeing both of us. She's perched on a stool, bouncing one of her legs.

"Nice to see you, too," Nixon responds.

"Seriously, if Kase sees her and he's—"

"I know what I'm doing. Why did you have your team bring him here in the first place?"

"He knew you'd come here, and he's refusing to talk to any of us."

"You're jeopardizing my mission." Nixon remains calm, but there's an obvious warning in his voice. "What would you have done if I weren't here? This is *your* zone. I have my own to worry about."

Piper rolls her eyes. "This isn't exactly the family reunion I expected either. He would've wanted to talk with you anyway. He was closer to you when we were teammates. You know that."

"That doesn't matter. You're his leader and he reports to you." Crossing his arms, he glances around the room as if he's expecting someone else to be here. "Did you check him for a tracker?"

"Of course I did."

"Were you followed?"

"Not that we could see."

"Have you informed the Commander?"

"Not yet. God, *stop*. I know how to do my job."

"Really? Because it doesn't seem that way."

Piper narrows her eyes at him, and her face becomes stony. Nixon matches her glare, awaiting her response.

Her eyes pan to me, and seeing how uncomfortable I must look, she says, "I'm sorry, Ivy, my *brother* can be a dick sometimes."

She says 'brother' as if it's a slur, and I don't understand why until Nixon says, "She already knows."

Piper raises her eyebrows and leans against the back of the stool, smiling. "Wow, you actually opened up to someone outside of us." She directs her gaze to me once again. "You must be *special.*"

Heat floods my face like when Lacey made a similar comment. Nixon doesn't entertain her speculation. Instead, he gets back to business by asking, "Do you want him dead or do you want him to walk?"

Piper's face drops, and all signs of playfulness evaporate. Fear flashes in her eyes but she composes herself quickly, save for the leg-bouncing. "That depends on what he's leaked."

"I'm not making that decision for you."

"I never asked you to."

Adam returns, telling Nixon that Kase is ready for him. Either he doesn't notice the tension pulsing between his kids or he doesn't want to get in the middle of it, because he doesn't say anything else. I follow Nixon out of the kitchen, and when we're on our way up to the second floor, I reach out, brushing my fingers against his elbow. Stopping halfway up the stairs, he turns to me.

"I think Piper's right," I whisper. I don't know how close we are to Kase's room and don't want to risk him hearing me. "Seeing me can put us in more danger if he's caught up with the Society."

"You'll stand outside the room. I want you to hear what he says for yourself."

"You don't think I'd believe what you tell me?"

He smirks. "You don't exactly have the best record of trusting me. Besides, it's better if you hear everything firsthand."

Before I can protest any more or admit that I'm actually scared, he continues up the stairs. I follow as quietly as possible, making sure not to put all of my weight into each footfall. Upstairs, we stop at the second door in the hallway. Nixon points to the wall beside the door frame, and I take my place there. He lifts his hand, curling his fingers and hesitating before rapping his knuckles on the door. A man's raspy voice tells him to come in, and Nixon looks to me, mouthing, "It's okay," before entering.

"Hey. How are you feeling?" Nixon asks, stepping into the room, sounding as friendly as ever. He pushes the door with the back of his foot, leaving it open just enough that I can see his back through the small crack.

"Awful," Kase croaks. "This has been a nightmare."

"I was worried about you. When I went into that safehouse and saw you weren't there… What the hell happened?"

"Black Hats stormed the place soon after Jace and Isaiah got back. They had stun grenades. After three were gunned down, the other two and I tried to escape."

"But you didn't make it."

Kase is quiet for a moment, and I hear him suck in a breath like he's trying to keep himself from sobbing. When he speaks again, it's as if he's struggling to force the words out. "I tried. I was so close. I… I tried to fight back."

"Take a breath. You're safe now." Nixon leans against the other side of the door frame. "I need to know what happened after you were captured. Where did they take you? What did they do?"

"I was blindfolded the entire time. Whenever we reached our destination, I was left alone for I don't know how long, maybe a day— no food or water. Any time I dozed off, they'd wake me up with loud noises or questions or beatings… or all three."

My heart aches for this faceless man. Weeks ago, when I was swimming contentedly in the Society's sea of lies, I probably would've thought he deserved his torture. Now that I'm frantically trying to stay afloat and seek shelter in truth—the *real* truth—I hate them for what they've done to him.

"What kinds of questions?" Nixon asks.

"A lot, some stuff I don't even know about. I was so tired and scared… I can't remember everything. What's going to happen to me?"

"What do you want to happen?"

Kase doesn't answer immediately, and even from out here I can feel how much weight Nixon's question holds. If he's been in the resistance as long as Nixon told me, surely he knows his options. Nixon asked Piper if she wanted him dead or if she wanted him to walk, but I can't imagine the resistance killing one of their own teammates. They're supposed to have each other's backs.

"I want out," Kase says. "I want a normal life. After what I went through, I can't do it anymore. It's too much."

"You and I both know you shouldn't be alive right now. Not without giving them something in return."

"I lied to them. I gave false information to save my ass."

"What kind of information?"

"They asked who's in charge, but I told them I only report to the head of my squad, Jace, who they'd already killed."

"What else?"

"Safehouses. I gave them the locations that aren't in rotation anymore. That's it. I held out as long as I could."

"You knew I was coming to your safehouse. Did you happen to let that slip?"

"What? No! You know I'd never rat you out. I wouldn't do that to any of you. I care about every person I've worked with."

"Would you care about a refugee?"

"She's safe?"

"It's not your mission, so that's not something I can discuss with you, especially not if you're wanting out."

"Why is it such a big deal that I want out? Plenty of people leave."

"You're right, they do, but none of them escaped the Black Hats. After witnessing what they did to your teammates, I find it hard to believe you don't want to fight back."

"You weren't there, Nixon. You weren't their prisoner. You haven't gone through what I have, and I hope you never do. It was hell."

"I'm sorry you had to go through that. It's not your fault that you were abducted."

"But you don't believe me, do you?"

Nixon pulls away from the door frame, spreading his arms as he says, "I want to, but I don't have much to go off. You know we need proof that you're not compromised."

Kase chuckles bitterly. "I took you under my wing after your parents died, Nixon. I showed you everything there is to know! *I* was the one you looked up to and came to for everything because, deep down, you still blamed Adam for your dad getting killed. And now that you've been promoted to a leader and moved to another zone, you can't trust me?"

"I do trust you, but this isn't my zone anymore. Whatever happens is out of my hands. You said you wanted to talk."

"And I'm being fucking interrogated."

"You're my friend, but I need to know what happened. I care about you, but I also need to know my group isn't in any danger."

"I don't know shit about your group."

"I'm a leader of the resistance, and we ultimately all work together. We're just trying to figure this out."

"There's nothing to figure out. I was captured and tortured, but I didn't tell them anything. I'm innocent."

"I'll let her know. Don't worry, you'll be out of here soon. Get some rest." Nixon turns toward the door but stops with his hand on the handle. "Oh, one more thing. You said you gave the locations of the dead safehouses. If I remember correctly, two of them are on unmarked roads. How did you explain to them how to get there?"

Kase lets out a frustrated sigh. "They gave me a map of the zone and had me circle them."

"Okay."

Nixon exits the room, lingering outside the door after closing it behind him. His impenetrable mask has returned, concealing all emotions, a look I know all too well from the beginning of our time together and meeting him prior to being sold. It's unnerving how easily he can switch from the transparent man I've recently seen to the cold, detached leader I originally hated. An electric current shoots through me when he grabs my hand and pulls me away from the wall, leading me down the stairs.

Piper is sitting on the same bar stool in the kitchen with Adam beside her. Nixon releases my hand when we enter, but Piper has already spotted it. Her eyes linger on us a second too long, and I brace myself for whatever comment she's about to make. But, to my surprise, she doesn't bring attention to what she saw.

"How did it go?" Adam asks. He's changed out of his scrubs and into jeans and a T-shirt.

Nixon leans forward, folding his arms over the top of one of the chairs tucked under the table. "What did he tell you, Piper?"

She shrugs. "Not much. They tortured him and he made it out."

"Is that all?"

"Yes."

Nixon nods slowly and looks at me. "Ivy, after what you heard, how do you think it went?"

I resist the urge to squirm under the other two pairs of eyes that pan to me. My gaze goes from Adam to Piper then settles on Nixon, all of them awaiting my response. I don't know what to say or why I'm the one being asked. Nixon was the one in the room and asking all of the questions.

"I don't know," I finally say. "I wasn't in there. It sounded like he was telling the truth."

It did. Aside from the few details of the past that Kase brought up, he sounded like a true victim, a terrified man who has been broken down. Nixon didn't seem to like that Kase wants out of the resistance, but after what he's been through, I can't blame him.

"It did, didn't it?" Nixon says, tapping a finger against the chair. "He said he was blindfolded the entire time. Did he tell you that, too, Piper?"

Piper nods.

"He mentioned giving them the locations of the dead safe-houses in exchange for his freedom," Nixon continues. "How did he say he directed them to those houses, Ivy?"

Crossing my arms, I shift my weight from one foot to the other. "I don't understand why you're asking—"

"Answer the question," he says.

"He circled them on the map they gave him." As I say it, it clicks.

"Exactly."

"Shit," Piper mumbles, closing her eyes and rubbing her forehead.

"He's traumatized," I say. "He probably can't think straight." I don't know why I'm jumping to this stranger's defense—he doesn't mean anything to me—but I can't help myself. My brain works to come up with any plausible reasons as to why Kase couldn't keep his story consistent.

"Maybe," Nixon says. "But I've known Kase for a long time. He didn't look like a man who was traumatized. He looked guilty, and instead of wanting to avenge his fallen comrades, he wants to quit."

"You think he sold us out?" Piper asks.

Taking a deep breath, Nixon straightens up, keeping his hands on the chair. "He definitely told them more than he's letting on, but I'm not sure what."

"He could've promised to lead them to you," Adam says, running his fingers across his chin. "He could easily go back and confirm that you're here, leading to the capture of a resistance leader and their missing product all at once."

I cringe when he uses the word *product*.

"They would've shown up already if they had any suspicion," Piper says. "And Nixon isn't wanted."

"The Black Hats don't go off of suspicion," Adam says. "They need proof. Your mom was able to cover when the dog picked up Ivy's scent last night, but if Kase tells them he saw Nixon here and knew of his mission… At the very least, he should be in re-education right now."

"Fine," Piper says, leaping to her feet. "I'll take care of him myself."

"Kill him now and you won't get any information he may have," Nixon says, stopping her at the kitchen's entrance.

She spins around with a fire in her eyes, ready to make Kase pay for something we're not even sure he did. "If I let him go, we're fucked, and that includes your group."

"I'm not telling you to let him go. Hold him prisoner and get him to talk… then kill him."

"He *won't* talk," she spits.

"Okay. Do what you want, but I can't help you any more with this. I have enough going on."

She rolls her eyes, pulling a phone out of her back pocket. She types something and waits a minute before saying, "One of my teams is on their way to help me get him out of here."

"How long?" Adam asks.

"Five minutes. They're just up the road."

"Ivy, maybe you should go downstairs," Adam says, standing up.

I'm not about to protest, but Piper jumps in, saying, "No, she should see him. Mole or not, she needs to see what the Society does."

"You don't have any authority over her," Adam argues.

Piper fixes her gaze on Nixon, who avoids looking in her direction but must know she's waiting for his input. I've already seen what the Society is capable of from the safehouse and Elizabeth's murder. They'll do whatever it takes to get the information they want or to keep people quiet. I may not have wanted to accept that before, but I understand it now.

"You should see him," Nixon says eventually.

"What happened to not letting him know I'm here?" I ask, but it's more than that. My first thought when we were downstairs and heard about Kase being here was that he'd flipped—he'd given in to the Society, putting at least two of the resistance groups in danger. After hearing him talk to Nixon, I couldn't help but feel sorry for him. The slip-up about being blindfolded the entire time he was in the Black Hats' custody was the only inconsistency Nixon could pinpoint, but that was enough for him to discredit everything Kase said, whereas I immediately jumped to his defense. My empathetic nature took over, clouding my rationality. There's a shred of me that still believes he sold all of us out, but I'm afraid that actually seeing him in his current state will make me totally blind to his transgressions.

Nixon shrugs. "It's not like he's going to live long enough to tell anyone." He says it so nonchalantly, and his face remains blank. This is his friend he's talking about. How can he be so indifferent toward what's about to happen to him?

I'm so torn over how I should feel about this. The resistance kills people on the opposing side when needed. I've come to terms with that. As long as innocent people aren't harmed, I can accept it to an extent. What I can't fathom is taking the life of a civilian, especially someone who has fought for the resistance itself, even if it means saving my own.

Piper checks her phone and motions for us to follow her. We file into the foyer, where she opens the front door, letting in two of her men. They wordlessly climb the stairs with their leader close behind. Nixon and I stand off to the side at the bottom of the staircase and Adam remains beside the door, peeping through the blinds every so often. We wait in strained silence, listening to the muffled voices and movement above. Someone shouts, and I can't tell if it's Kase or one of the other men. Neither Adam nor Nixon react, and I try my best to look as calm as they do, pushing back the urge to bite on my nails or do anything that might make me appear nervous or closed-off.

After a few minutes of shuffling around upstairs, the four make their way down. Piper leads the way, and her two members are on either side of Kase as they assist him down the stairs. With an arm draped over each of their shoulders, they carry most of his weight. Deep purple welts cover his face, neck, and what I can see of his arms, and one eye is so swollen it's obvious that he's struggling to keep it open. As the three men near the bottom of the stairs, Kase spots us. His mouth twitches upward into something that resembles a smile, threatening to split open a wound on his lip.

"So she *is* here," Kase says with amusement. He studies me as though memorizing every detail before focusing on Nixon. "Let's hope you don't get her killed like you did Elizabeth."

Although they're directed at Nixon, his words cut through me, too.

Pulling a handgun from her waistband beneath her jacket, Piper whirls around, jerking Kase's head back by his hair and shoving the muzzle of the gun beneath his chin. With her face inches from his, she sneers, "Keep talking shit and I swear I'll blow your fucking jaw off right here. That wasn't his fault and you know it!"

Kase doesn't falter, though. He holds her glare and his smile widens, causing the scab on his lip to crack and bleed. I steal a quick glance at Nixon beside me, expecting Kase's words to have impacted him, but he remains calm and quiet. Like him, I keep my composure on the outside, but inside I'm burning with hatred toward this man, and whatever pity I had for him is gone.

Releasing him, Piper steps aside, waving the men forward and concealing her weapon once again. "Get him out of here. I'll be right behind you."

Adam opens the door and they half-carry, half-shove Kase outside, the disgusting grin still plastered on his swollen face. As soon as they're out of the house, Piper pulls Nixon into a hug, saying, "Don't listen to him. He's pissed because he knows he got caught." She gives him a squeeze. "I love you."

"Love you too," he says. "Be careful."

"You too." She breaks away from him and flashes me a smile. "It was nice meeting you, Ivy, although I wish it was under different circumstances. Good luck on the outside." She finishes her goodbyes with Adam, planting a kiss on his cheek and promising she'll come by soon for a visit.

As he shuts the door behind her, I turn around to see that Nixon has disappeared. The sound of the back door closing gives away his location, but before I make it out of the foyer, Adam stops me by placing a hand on my shoulder as he passes by me. "Give him some space."

"He needs to know it wasn't his fault," I say, following him into the kitchen.

He digs through the fridge and pulls out a container of left-overs. Reading the piece of paper taped to the rubber lid, he smiles, and by the bubbly handwriting and excessive amount of hearts, I can tell it's a note from his wife. Removing the lid, he sets the glass dish in the microwave. "Nixon's strong. He'll be alright."

Strength comes in many forms, and Nixon seems to embody them all. But everyone has a breaking point, and little by little, his mask is slipping. I got a glimpse of it our first night together when he talked about hijacking the cargo plane and said the Society killed one of his members. He got quiet when I said her name. I saw it again when we left the ambushed safehouse. He expressed his grief with anger. The closest I've ever got to actually seeing the real him was last night when he shared a piece of his past with me. This time, he's isolating himself. He knows his mask is falling and he's trying to hide it, trying to appear as a leader who has it all together.

After all that Nixon has done for me, after listening to me cry and complain while helping me understand what's going on, I want to reciprocate at least a fraction of that. It's the least I can do.

"That was a fucked-up thing for Kase to bring up," I say angrily.

"It was." Adam pulls his food from the microwave and jabs a fork into the pile of pasta. "Because the two of them have been friends for so long, Kase knew just how to hurt him."

"But Nixon knows it was bullshit, right?"

He makes a face that tells me he's unsure. "Nixon was… reluctant, to say the least, when the Commander selected him to take over the Green Zone. There were many reasons why, but the main one was because he isn't exactly confident in his leadership skills. As I'm sure you've witnessed, though, he's pretty damn good at it."

"I don't really know what it takes, but I definitely agree."

"Compare him to Piper—she's impulsive but still good at what she does. Nixon, on the other hand, carefully plans every move he and his group make, and only one fallen member in three years is impressive." He takes another bite of his food and finishes chewing before saying, "People die in the resistance; that's how it always has been, and always will be until we're no longer needed. Eventually, he'll learn not to beat himself up over it."

As Adam finishes eating, Nixon comes inside. Adam asks if he's okay and he responds with a simple, "I'm fine." He avoids looking at me, but I could swear that when he passes by, his eyes are red. I look to Adam in hopes of a gesture telling me to go talk to him, but he shakes his head. As much as I don't want to, I obey, telling myself that he knows Nixon better than I do.

In the living room, Adam and I watch the news, and I'm relieved to not be staring at myself on the screen. There's a brief clip about Liam, confirming no more than what we already know: He's still missing with no leads. The anchor seamlessly switches topics, reading over her script about the Red Zone's residency program. All applications have been reviewed and interviews completed, and a list of the seven lucky winners consumes the screen. I mindlessly read through them—two from the Blue Zone, four from the Yellow Zone, and one from the Green Zone.

The Green Zone. Bracing myself, I focus on the name beside my home zone.

Evalynn Brooks.

I'm not the least bit surprised. I knew this was coming, and I've gradually numbed myself to the fact. But what really infuriates me is that my mother has used her maiden name, severing all ties to Liam, me, and our missing dad.

19. Innocence

With or without Liam, I'll be leaving the Northern Unity in three days. Originally it was two, but Nixon talked the Commander into allowing a little more time for my brother. It's been arranged for me to be smuggled out on a cargo aircraft, but instead of attempting to make it over the walls, it will land in the Red Zone. Upon landing, their team will get me outside. Eli, the Red Zone leader, and a few of his members have crossed over multiple times without being caught, and Nixon promised I'll be safe with them. When I asked if he'll be with me, seeing this mission to the end, he ignored the question. In fact, he didn't stick around to answer any questions after coming upstairs to relay the vague plan for my escape.

Just as Lacey came home from work, Nixon returned to the basement, where he has remained ever since. Lacey immediately took notice of his unusual behavior, and when she asked what was wrong, Adam told her he'd explain later. It's been hours since Piper and her men left with Kase, but Adam has insisted countless times that I let

Nixon have time to himself. The longer I leave him alone, though, the worse I feel. So when dinner is nearly ready, I politely tell Adam and Lacey I'm not hungry and make my way downstairs, figuring out what I'm going to say to him.

I haven't been in the position where I'm the one to comfort Nixon before. He's normally well-versed in concealing whatever he's feeling, and although he's opened up to me more than he apparently usually does with others, I don't know him all that well. At home, I was good at defusing potentially explosive conflicts, but with him I'm at a loss. I haven't had to experience what he has, and I don't think I could even imagine it. No matter how hard I try to put myself in his shoes, I can't comprehend what it must be like to be in charge of other people's lives and the sense of failure that must follow when one is lost. The best I can do is listen, if he lets me.

In the basement, Nixon is seated on the couch with an elbow propped up on the armrest and his forehead pressed into his hand. The TV is on but the volume is low, quiet enough not to hear exactly what's being said but loud enough to provide some background noise. I slowly approach him, picking through various words of comfort in my head, all of which feel hollow. As I near the opposite end of the couch, he becomes aware of my presence and looks up, eyes still red, although not as much as earlier.

Without being prompted, he says in a quiet voice, "I'm okay."

I take a seat beside him, keeping a respectable distance. "It wasn't your fault. You know that, right?"

He rolls his eyes. "I'm fine, and I don't need sympathy from you." He sees the sting of his words and immediately backtracks. "I'm sorry. I didn't mean it like that."

Pretending not to care, I continue, "I was *there*. It was out of your control."

"I'm supposed to keep my team safe, and have to assume responsibility for whatever happens to them."

In a way, I understand that, and it's admirable. He obviously cares for everyone he works with; Adam was right—after years of working closely together, Kase knew exactly how to hurt him. It was cruel and clearly rooted in something other than anger toward his situation. Jealousy, perhaps? Kase made it a point to bring up Nixon being promoted to a leader and switching zones, almost as if he was mad at him for it.

Nixon presses his head against his palm again, slightly angling his body away from me. He doesn't say anything else, just sits quietly, his face unreadable and eyes locked on the floor. I've become used to sitting in silence with him—comfortable even, not feeling obligated to fill it—but in this moment, it's excruciating. All I want is to ease the pain I know he feels but refuses to show, if only a little. I don't know why I care so much—probably my overactive empathy again—but I can't shut it off.

Inching closer to him, I try again, recalling what Adam said to me earlier. "I know next to nothing about being in the resistance, let alone being a leader, but if you've only lost one person, it sounds like you're doing a pretty good job."

Nothing.

"I know Liam looks up to you," I continue, "from the couple of times he talked about you. And all Lacey did was praise you our first day here."

The urge to reach out for him returns, similar to when he opened up about his past, and unlike that time, I give in. Hesitating at first, I gently place a hand on his forearm. He tenses up when my skin meets his, but quickly relaxes.

"Nixon, look at me."

Dropping his hand from his face, he turns his head, avoiding my eyes at first. When they meet mine, he's put that familiar mask back on. As broken as it is, he wears it well.

"I trust you," I say. "Elizabeth's murder was *not* your fault. I don't care what that asshole says. He was mad, I get it, but that doesn't make it right or true. I know I said I hated you at first, and I'm sorry, but even then, I never thought what happened to her was any fault of yours." At this point, I'm not thinking my words through. Like a faucet, they pour out, and I just hope they somehow get through to him. "And because of you, I'm not being auctioned off to some sadistic Elite. You've kept me safe while leaving your entire group behind, and they're using what you've taught them to stay alive. You're good at what you do, and everyone can see that."

There's a faint curve to his lips, but his eyes remain somber. "I appreciate what you're trying to do, but…"

"But that's not the only thing that's bothering you."

He nods, as if just realizing it himself. I slowly pull my hand back, having forgotten it was on his arm, and turn the front of my body completely to him. Bringing my knees up, I rest my head against the back of the couch.

"So tell me." Running my finger along the stitching of the top cushion, I try to keep my eyes off him. I can feel him watching me, though, analyzing me as though determining whether he can trust me.

Leaning forward, he rests his elbows on his legs and lets the quiet linger between us, and I do, too. I don't push for a response or attempt to fill the void. I want him to know I'm here and open to listen to whatever he has to say, even if we sit here all night—talking or not. I push back any thoughts that pop up of what may be bothering him.

"Kase was always one of the strongest," Nixon finally says, "physically and mentally. He could take on anything that was thrown at him." He pauses, closing his eyes like he's visualizing what he should say next, and I wait patiently, focusing on the tiny threads of the cushion and their bumpy texture beneath my finger.

When he starts talking again, he speaks more softly, a tinge of vulnerability in his voice. "If they were able to break *him* down and get him to talk… I don't know how I'd survive. I don't want to think I'd give up my group or any of our secrets, but if I did—if they pushed me beyond my limits—I'd hate myself for it." Opening his eyes, he sinks back, tilting his face up toward the ceiling.

I allow his words to sink in for both of us. The old me, who ignorantly hated the resistance, would've thought they deserved whatever torture the Society used. The current me empathizes with them, specifically Nixon.

"You're a good person," I say. "You wouldn't sell them out."

"How do you know?"

I shrug. "Just a feeling. You can be… intimidating at times, but I can tell it's to protect the people around you. And I think you're stronger than you give yourself credit for."

"Sometimes I wonder if my life would be different had my mom stuck around."

The statement takes me by surprise. I drop my hand and look at him. "Do you regret joining the resistance?"

"No, not really. I just… I feel like there's more to life than this, even in this country."

"You have to find a balance." Although I imagine it's difficult locking away another half of yourself to carry out a somewhat normal life, living a double life until you're sure you've found someone you can let in completely. "You can't let the resistance consume you."

"If it's not the resistance, it's the Society, and I'd rather feel like I'm making a difference than live a self-serving life."

"Do the other leaders feel the same way you do?"

He shrugs. "I don't know Nadia well. Eli works in the Red Zone, so he's forced to keep the resistance separate from his everyday life. And Piper grew up learning about the resistance. She never knew any different, so I guess it's easier for her." He turns his face to me. "I love her, and she gets shit done, but she's a bit more reckless than I am."

"You plan missions out with your members' lives in mind."

"I try to."

Maybe his overprotectiveness is a product of what happened to his parents. He knows it was out of his control, but he tries to make up for it now with his group, desperate to keep everyone alive, to keep everyone close yet distant at the same time. Getting too close to someone makes the hurt worse when you inevitably lose them. I know that all too well from my own past, although I've never looked at it that way until now.

After Dad left, I changed. We all did. Liam closed himself off, Mom immersed herself in her work, and I clung to the people I had left, living with the constant fear that they'd leave, too. Whenever a fight brewed between my mom and brother, I was quick to jump in and establish peace, or at least have them back off until I wasn't around.

It wasn't the arguing itself that bothered me—save for the few times Liam made it a point to throw Dad's disappearance in Mom's face—but the lack of control of the situation. I wanted everything to be okay. I wanted to keep the people I cared about as close as possible, but the more I tried, the worse everything seemed to get. The tension was constant between Mom and Liam. Liam spent less time at home and, I know now, more time with the resistance. Kyle died. Naomi went to re-education. And Mom turned her back on me.

"You can't protect everyone," I say. "You need to trust that your team knows what to do. After all, you're the one who trained them."

He sighs, sitting up. "You're right. Thank you."

"Thank you? I didn't do anything."

"You did more than you know."

I sit up too, suddenly hyper-aware of how little space there is between us, and have to force myself not to back away. "Is what Piper said true? That I'm the only person you've told about…?"

Smiling, he looks away. "Yeah."

"Well, I'm happy you feel like you can open up to me."

An idea pops into my mind, something that seems childish but has always helped me in my darkest moments. If it's something that can potentially lift his spirits, I'm willing to try it. Grabbing his hand, I drag him into the kitchen with me and release him to search the pantry and refrigerator that Lacey always keeps fully stocked. She keeps a stockpile of nearly every ingredient imaginable and went shopping for all of the perishable items after we got here.

I set out all of the necessary ingredients on the counter and pull a saucepan out from one of the lower cabinets.

"What are you doing?" Nixon asks, watching me turn on the front burner and empty the milk into the heated pan.

"Something my dad always did for us when we were upset."

Once the milk gets hot, I adjust the temperature and begin whisking in the other ingredients one at a time. The billowing steam carries the rich scent of chocolate, and something that was once a remedy, if only temporary, to whatever stress I carried is now bittersweet. Not only do the memories of my dad come rushing back, but of Liam and Addison, too. The last time I made this, I had no idea what was awaiting me in the weeks to come.

Nixon offers to help, but I insist that I've got it. Sharing this with someone outside of my family is one thing, but allowing him in on the process feels wrong. No matter how simple it is, it's a sacred ritual that I don't want to be tainted by someone else's hands. So he stands arm-length from me, watching me concentrate on my miniature cauldron as I concoct the perfect potion. My worries are melted with the chocolate and my stress swept away with the clouds of steam. Focusing on the trails left by the whisk as I stir is therapeutic. Nixon watches me carefully, quietly. The desperate need to fill the silence no longer hangs over me. The tension has dissipated, and while there are still so many unspoken struggles between us, I take comfort in his presence. I would've loved for my brother to have been by my side through all of this, but I'm thankful to have had Nixon.

"Liam and I made this together not long before I was… taken," I say, retrieving two mugs from a cabinet. Ladling the hot chocolate into each of the cups, I top them with marshmallows and pass one to Nixon. "It was kind of a family tradition whenever something bad happened. As dumb as it sounds, it helped. We stopped once our dad left, but Liam suggested we make it after the first raid."

"So that's what he was doing when I let him skip our meeting," he says playfully. "That was the night he said he was going to come clean to you."

"I think he tried in his own way. I wasn't very receptive though."

The night of the first raid, Liam wanted to talk after I said I was worried about him and he admitted to having the gun. He agreed to put the conversation off until the following evening when we both got off work. The following morning, he promised he wouldn't be busy, which I now realize must have taken some convincing on Nixon's part. What I thought was going to be a heart-to-heart conversation about the struggles the two of us had been dealing with was actually supposed to be his way of letting me in on his deepest secret. That makes me feel worse. Not only was I closed-minded, but I was expecting Liam to be there for me and understand all of my problems when I wasn't trying to understand his. Keeping that part of himself hidden without being able to tell anyone must have been eating at him so much.

"Shocker," Nixon says sarcastically, taking a sip of his hot chocolate. "What did you say?"

I shrug, poking at one of the marshmallows floating in my mug. "I didn't really give him a chance to say much. I'm pretty sure at the first mention of the resistance, I called them—you—terrorists and accused you of killing—" I stop myself, not wanting to bring her up again. "I'm sorry."

"You've learned. I just hope you never go back to thinking like that. Thanks for this, by the way." He raises his cup. "It does help."

Smiling, I take a drink of my own and push back the memories that cloud my mind. My father is gone. I have to accept that. My mother betrayed me. I've come to terms with that. The wound is still fresh, but with time, I know it will heal. So here's to making new memories, and whether I'm inside the Northern Unity or not, whether I'm surrounded by people I love or new ones I'll learn to love, everything will be okay. That's one thing I'm confident of.

Although I'm ready to put everything that's happened in the past, there's one thing I have to bring up. Partially because I want to get it off my chest—release it into the open and be free of it—and partially because I want him to know I do trust him. Completely.

"You were right about my mom," I say. "She used that money to buy herself a house in the Red Zone. It was announced today."

He sighs. "For once, I wish I hadn't been. I'm sorry."

I wave it off. "It's fine. I mean, I should've expected it after everything. She used her maiden name, too, like she's done with all of us."

"Are you okay?" His voice is gentle, melodic, and his eyes are pools of empathy. The ice has melted in them, drawing me in. Whatever I previously thought of him has vanished. He's not the bloodthirsty, radical killing machine I was programmed to believe him and his people to be.

I nod, taking another drink, focusing on the warmth of the liquid as it envelops my insides. Having made just enough for the two of us, I grab the pan from the stove and bring it to the sink. Turning on the faucet, he stops me by placing a hand over mine.

"I've got it," he says with a smile, the most authentic one I've seen since meeting him. Seeing it makes my soul flicker with joy, and knowing my childhood remedy has helped him makes that joy radiate throughout my body. No matter what tribulations we face, the small things still have an enormous impact.

He sets his hot chocolate on the counter, and while he washes the pan and whisk, I return what's left of the ingredients to their designated spots, being sure to leave everything exactly the way Lacey had it. When he's finished, he grabs his mug and takes a seat at the table.

"I'm going to miss this," he says as I shut the pantry.

"The Blue Zone?" I ask, picking up my drink and sitting across from him. I sip on my now lukewarm cocoa, watching as he eyes his half-empty cup.

He leans back, resting one leg on top of the other, and takes a drink before saying, "Yeah," though he sounds unsure of his answer. There's something else on his mind; I can tell by the way his brows come together as though he's trying to figure it out himself. When he continues, he keeps his eyes locked on his mug, tracing the handle with his thumb. "It's been nice having someone to talk to outside of the resistance."

"I thought you told me I annoyed you," I tease.

He smirks. "You still do, but in a good way."

"A good way?"

"Yeah, like when I want to be alone, you're always right there, talking to me and trying to make me feel better."

"You can tell me if you want me to leave you alone. I tried to give you some space today."

He breaks into a smile again and shakes his head. "No, don't. When I'm upset, I don't…" He slowly lifts his eyes to mine and drops his hand from the mug to the table, tapping a finger against the black wood. "…I don't realize I actually need someone to talk to until you get me to open up. You've helped me a lot."

"Like I said, I'm happy you feel like you can open up to me. You can talk to me whenever you want. You know that by now, right?"

Pursing his lips, he nods. He averts his eyes, gazing in my general direction but looking past me. "I tried to convince the Commander to let me escort you and Liam outside of the walls."

"He wouldn't go for it?"

He shakes his head, takes another drink, and props an elbow on the table, resting his head against his fist. "The most I can do is get you to the Red Zone. Eli will take it from there."

"And you'll go back to the Green Zone?"

He nods again, and my heart sinks a little. He's the only person I've had by my side this entire time. I remind myself that I'm starting a new life, that everything will be just fine, but the anxiety still crawls over me. Nixon was a stranger and an enemy to me, but he's so much more now.

"You have a group that needs you," I say, attempting to snuff the anxiety. "And you'll be safer there than with a fugitive."

But of course I'd much rather have him with me, especially as it looks like my brother won't be showing. Nixon insisted Liam would be here, but my hope is quickly fading.

"*You* don't need me anymore?" he asks, and his eyes snap to me. It's a lighthearted question but holds some weight to it, almost as if he's wanting me to say that I do.

"I need to get as far away from the Society as possible, and I trust that the other members will help get me safely outside of the walls." I internally cringe at how scripted I sound.

He sits forward, pressing his torso against the edge of the table. "Do you? Because it seemed to take a lifetime for you to even trust me, and we had met before on a couple occasions."

I roll my eyes. "Briefly. That hardly counts."

He sits back, taking another long drink. "Whatever you say." Standing up with his mug in hand, he asks, "You done?"

I nod, and he takes both of our cups to the sink. Turning on the water, he scrubs the chocolatey residue from the inside of the dishes. He cleans in silence, his back to me. Our conversation ended so abruptly, and I'm not sure if I should say something else or bring up another subject. The need to talk to him, to stay up for as many hours as we can handle, is overwhelming. Whatever direction the conversation flows, I don't care. It's a way to fill the void that threatens to swallow me, to ease the anxiety that continues to pull at me.

"You've helped me a lot, too," I say. "I'm safe because of you."

He shuts off the water and dries the cups with a paper towel. "Your brother planned it out."

"But you approved it and put it into action."

"And the Commander approved of me going out to rescue you." The cups go back in the cabinet and he turns to face me. "You shouldn't consider yourself safe yet. This isn't over."

"I know that. Is something else bothering you?"

He's not necessarily being hostile, but the open, vulnerable man I saw minutes ago has disappeared.

"Nope, just a little tired," he says, obviously faking a yawn. "Interrogating one of your traitorous friends takes a lot out of you."

He exits the kitchen, and I'm quick to follow.

"I thought you were feeling better," I say. "I mean, I know it's not something you just get over but—"

"I was—*am*. I am better." Grabbing a pair of pants and a shirt from the wardrobe, he disappears into the bathroom, sparing me a small smile in passing.

With a sigh, I pull out some clothes for myself, refolding some things that have been moved around. Whatever else is bothering Nixon—and I know there is something else—I need to know for no reason other than I care about him.

I don't know why. I don't want to. When I leave the Red Zone and he's no longer with me, I want to be able to forget him. Caring about him in any way will make him impossible to forget, and I'll inevitably worry about him. He and Liam will be together, and I'll constantly wonder whether they're keeping each other safe and whether or not they're being tailed by Black Hats.

It all ties back to how overly empathetic I am, and for once, I wish I could shut it off. Nixon doesn't seem to have that issue. He can seamlessly transition from empathetic to apathetic in seconds, as though he has a switch in his brain that turns off all emotions. It's infuriating at times, but one thing I envy about him.

Nixon emerges from the bathroom and I take his place, changing into the shorts and shirt that once belonged to Piper and tossing my outfit from today in the nearly full basket. I quickly brush my teeth and make my way out into the main room, wanting to catch him before he lies down. Tired or not, I want to know what else has got to him, especially if it pertains to this mission. I at least have a right to know that, and he didn't say much about his conversation with the Commander earlier.

The TV that I'd forgotten has been on this entire time is now off. Nixon's opening the small closet beside the bathroom as I reappear. He glances at me while reaching to the top shelf for the blanket and pillow he's been using every night.

"You don't have to sleep there," I say as he tosses the items on the couch. Every night since arriving here, I've offered him the bed, and with every offer, he's insisted he doesn't mind. One night he even claimed he prefers sleeping on the couch, but I know that's a lie. It's fairly comfortable, but hardly big enough for an average-sized adult to sleep on. He's too tall to stretch out his legs, and before falling asleep, I've heard him toss and turn.

"I've told you multiple times I don't mind." Unfolding the blanket, he drapes it over the couch.

"You're just trying to be nice. Seriously, let me take the couch."

He chuckles. "It's fine. It's only for a couple more nights."

Moving from the bathroom doorway, I plop down on the couch, pulling part of the blanket down with me. "Looks like I'm sleeping here."

Rolling his eyes, he smiles. "Then I'll feel like an asshole." He grasps one of my hands, giving it a light tug, and when I don't budge he playfully says, "You're being annoying again."

"Good—so go over there." Smiling back, I cock my head toward the bed.

With another stronger tug, he pulls me to my feet, but I remain planted in front of him, blocking the couch. We stare each other down, like two friendly predators battling over prey neither of us really wants.

"A couple more nights," he repeats. "It's not a big deal." His smile reaches his eyes, which are soft again, enticing even. From this small distance, I can see where a tiny scar cuts through his right eyebrow. It must be what's left of the injury from crashing into the prisoner transport vehicle.

Glancing down, he abruptly releases my hand as though just remembering he was holding on to it. I resist the idiotic urge to reach for his hand again and cross my arms over my chest. But my brain persists, insisting I need to feel his touch, however small, and when I don't comply, it digs up the memory of him hugging me. Something I never gave a second thought now fills my mind, making me crave it.

He gives me a nudge, and his touch sends a current through me like it did before. I take a few steps toward the bed but stop to look back at him. Before I have a chance to process what I'm about to say, I blurt out, "You can sleep in the bed."

"I've told you I—"

"No, I mean…"

My cheeks burn, and he must be able to see it. Wrapping my arms around me, I curse myself. Stupid, stupid, stupid. I desperately search for something to say to get me out of this, but the part of my brain that puts together coherent sentences has shut down.

He arches an eyebrow, and his eyes flicker with amusement. "With you?"

My heart lodges itself in my throat, and I struggle to squeeze my response past it. "It's… It's big enough for two people."

"You want me to, though."

"No!" *Yes? Maybe?* Wiping the moisture that has collected on my hands on my shirt, I follow up with the first excuse I can come up with. "I just thought I'd offer, since you won't let me take the couch. I feel bad."

"You're cute when you lie. Too bad you're terrible at it." Shoving his hands in his pockets, he looks to the stairs as if expecting someone to come down. Now desperate to escape the humiliating position I've put myself in, I subconsciously take a couple of steps back. I want to shut off the lights, bury myself under the blankets, and forget this ever happened.

"Liam would freak out if he knew," he says.

"He doesn't have to know. We're just sleeping." I can't make myself shut up. I want to retreat, but don't want there to be any awkwardness between us. With a couple of days left, I couldn't bear things going back to how they were when we were first forced together. The words blurt out of me. "I won't tell if you don't."

"It wouldn't be weird to you?"

I shrug, backing away from him and climbing onto the bed. With more distance between us, my nerves let up a bit. "All of this has been weird." I pull the sheet and comforter over my lap and remove my hair from its restraint, slipping the elastic band on my wrist. "You can say no if you *really* want to sleep on the couch. Or I can sleep there, like I originally offered."

Without so much as glancing at me, he crosses the room, stopping at the light switch beside the stairs. He hesitates with his finger hovering over the switch, and my mind broadcasts another memory: the second time we actually touched in a real way. In that exact spot, we stood hand-in-hand in the dark, listening to the men search the house above us. When we heard the dog bark, I squeezed Nixon's hand, once again finding comfort in his presence.

"I won't tell," he says, and the lights go out.

Moments later, I hear the delicate sound of sheets brushing against one another and feel his weight on the mattress. Lying down, I stare into the darkness, nowhere near ready to go to sleep. Only the sound of our unsynchronized breathing fills the room, and the occasional rustling of the sheets when Nixon moves. The awkwardness intensifies, and although he's lying a few feet away from me, it feels as though we're miles apart.

"I'm happy I met you," I say, and count the empty seconds until his response. Twenty-three.

"Why's that?"

"You've taught me a lot, and despite what I thought of you at first, you're a good person."

Another long pause, and I can hear him reposition himself. "I've done a lot of bad things."

I don't know everything he's had to do, and I probably don't want to. Some things are better left unsaid. I know he's killed people—how many is another mystery—but not in cold blood like the Society does. From what I understand, he only does it when he has to protect himself and others.

I turn on my side, facing his general direction. "Sometimes you have to do bad stuff for the greater good, but that doesn't make you a bad person."

"That's easy to say when you haven't had to live through it or witness it. You've only seen what I've done in order to protect you."

"But you don't hurt innocent people. You're not like them."

He sighs and when he speaks again, his voice is closer, slightly muffled. I imagine him facing me with half of his face buried in the pillow. "At the end of the day, those people on the opposing side are still human. Some of them—the soldiers, police, or whatever—probably don't fully understand what they're doing or why. They're following orders, trusting that the Enlightened Society has the people's best interest in mind. To me, that makes them innocent, and innocent people do get hurt if they're blindly following the wrong side."

I inch forward. Part of my mind tells me to keep my distance. But that yearning for his touch—to comfort him and be comforted—overpowers it, pulsing through me. With some distance still between us, I feel the heat radiating from his body, coaxing me closer.

"You can't help that," I say, lowering my voice to a volume hardly above a whisper. I tentatively reach my arm out, and my fingers brush against his shirt. He doesn't tense beneath my touch as he did earlier.

"I know," he says, covering my hand with his and pressing it to his chest. The steady beat of his heart drums against my palm, and the beat of my own picks up. "I'm happy I met you, too." He gives my hand a squeeze and my heart races.

"Why did you ask the Commander to go outside the walls with Liam and me?"

"To make sure you get there safe."

"You don't trust Eli to keep us safe? Or that Liam knows what to do?"

"No, I do, and I'm not worried about Liam."

"You're worried about me?" Wriggling my hand, I lace my fingers through his, and that overwhelming need is satiated. "Weird, I remember you telling me you didn't care if I was safe or not."

He laughs, and the melodic sound of it makes this moment more beautiful. "You've grown on me."

"I've *grown* on you? Is that your way of saying you have a crush on me?"

He laughs again. It's softer this time, almost nervous. I didn't think that was possible for someone so sure of himself. If the lights were on, I'm sure I'd catch him blushing or avoiding my gaze at the very least. But in the dark, where we can't read each other, it's more relaxed. I don't think I would've asked such a direct question if he were able to see me right now.

Under the protection of the blankets and masked by the darkness, it comes easier. Hushed words flow freely, absorbed by the pillows and sheets.

"If I said yes," he whispers, drawing me in closer, "would that make you uncomfortable?"

I bite down on my lip, holding back the blossoming smile. Closing the gap between us, I press my body against his. My head rests against his shoulder, and I breathe in his familiar scent. "No," I whisper, tightening my fingers around his. His chin brushes the top of my forehead, the few prickly hairs that have appeared over the past few days tickling my skin.

"Then yes," he says. He frees his hand from mine and circles his arms around my shoulders. His heart beats against my chest now and mine against his, and this moment becomes euphoric. It's something I never want to end... but I know it will all too soon.

"Even though it's unlikely we'll see each other again after this," I say.

I hate to say it or even think about it right now, but we both know it's true. After this mission is complete and I've left the Northern Unity forever, there's no reason for us to be in each other's lives anymore. I'll start over again and he'll go back home. I'll be under the Commander's supervision, but I doubt he'd let me speak to Nixon. If he knew my reason for wanting to, I imagine he'd be even more against it. I don't know what kind of person he is, but it's clear he takes the resistance seriously. Allowing me to continue having contact with Nixon would only be a distraction.

"I wish I could go with you," Nixon says.

"Me too. Just promise me you'll take care of my brother if he comes back here."

"I promise. Try to get some sleep. I'm actually tired."

I bury my face into his chest, inhaling his intoxicating scent, savoring his warmth. His heart thumps heavily against my face, reverberating in my skull. "Can we stay like this?"

My brain warns me not to let this go any further in my remaining time here. Getting any closer will make leaving harder. I already care about him—there's nothing I can do to change that. I'll worry about him the same way I'll worry about Liam and Addison and Naomi. But if I can distance myself from him now, maybe leaving him behind will be less traumatic.

"As long as you want," he says with a smile in his voice.

When he tightens his arm around me, molding me into him, I promise myself I'll start tomorrow.

20. Be Careful What You Wish For

Last night feels like a dream—the first pleasant one I've been graced with in a long time. If I could turn back time and relive it, I would over and over again. When I awoke, Nixon was gone, but the warmth of the sheets beside me confirmed that last night was real, leaving me confused, elated, and even more uncertain of the future.

I'm scared to face him. The promise I made to myself last night pushes itself to the front of my mind as well as the reminders of his warmth, his scent, and the security of being close to him. I know I need to distance myself from him—it will be better for both of us in the long run—but I don't want to hurt him, and I don't want these newfound feelings to disappear yet. If what he said last night was true, he'll get hurt either way, but after how much he has opened up to me, I don't want to be the one who lets him down. At least if we're forced apart, it won't be my fault.

This was never supposed to happen. He was simply meant to be my guide, my protection from those who are after me. Nothing more, nothing less. Once the mission is complete, he's supposed to go back to the Green Zone and continue leading the invisible fight against the Society. We both knew that all along, so why did we allow ourselves to surrender to our emotions? And if we hadn't been forced together the way we were, would there have ever been anything between us?

The news is a faint murmur in the background as I make the bed. I stopped listening after the same story was spewed about my escape and the list of participants accepted into the Red Zone was repeated. Liam hasn't been mentioned again, which worries me. Either they've given up searching for him or they've caught him, and both equally terrify me.

As terrible as it may be to think, I'm a little happy it's taking Liam so long to get here. Had he shown up already, last night never would've happened. As Nixon said, Liam would freak out if he knew—not because Nixon is his friend, but his leader. Liam trusted him to find me and keep me safe, which he has, but it shouldn't have gone any further than that. If I can put a stop to whatever this is between Nixon and me now, Liam won't have to know. It'll be as if it never happened.

When I'm done with the bed, I grab my coffee and turn up the volume on the TV. The anchor is saying something about increased military presence in the Green Zone, but before I can hear any details, Nixon says, "How'd you sleep?" as he descends into the basement.

I don't look at him. I can't. "Fine. What about you?"

"Fine," he says slowly. He approaches me, but stops behind the couch. I can feel him there. "Everything okay?"

"Yeah." I feign interest in what the anchor is talking about, when in reality I couldn't care less. The Green Zone isn't my home anymore. I'll never be going back.

"You're lying."

"No, I'm not."

Letting out a dramatic sigh, he circles the couch and sits down, and when I instinctively look toward him, he nods at the opposite end.

"Tell me what's bothering you." Keeping one foot planted on the floor, he extends his other leg out on the couch.

Halfway sitting on the arm of the couch, I glue my eyes back to the screen. I had no issue talking to him last night after the lights went out. Everything felt natural when he couldn't see me. Now that I'm exposed again, I've curled up inside myself. He's easy to talk to in general, but not when it comes to my feelings toward him, partially because I'm not completely sure of them myself.

In the open, he can see through me, read me the way he does everyone else. It's something I love and hate. I like that I don't really have to say anything for him to know something's wrong. Most of the time, he can guess what's bothering me before I tell him but still allows me to explain it in my own words before offering any kind of feedback. I hate it because I can't keep anything from him, and this is no different.

"Is it about last night?" he asks, and I can't help but notice the tinge of hurt in his voice. He overthinks things like I do, though he's quicker to rationalize, whereas I fall down a rabbit hole of unrealistic ideas.

"Not really," I say, knowing that's hardly an answer. He deserves more than that to ease his mind so he doesn't obsess over the idea that he may have done something wrong, but I just don't know what to tell him.

"Not really? So it's bothering you a little. Look, if I made you uncomfortable, I—"

"You didn't. It's not that."

"So tell me… Please?"

I look away from the TV, still reluctant to lock eyes with him. He's level-headed and understanding, and I don't want to see him hurt. I've seen that from him before and it was devastating enough, but this time I'd be the one hurting him.

I focus on my nearly empty cup, watching the few stray coffee grounds swim around in the light brown liquid. Anxiety washes over me again. I can feel him watching me, waiting for me to give him some kind of answer. "Do you want this, Nixon?"

"This?"

"Whatever this is between us… or what it might become. I'm not even sure what it *is*."

He sucks in a breath, and from the corner of my eye, I spot the surprise on his face. I wasn't expecting the question to come out of my mouth either, but in order to explain myself, I need to know what it is he wants.

"I mean, if you do," he says. "I don't want to force you into anything, but I thought it was pretty mutual last night."

"It was… or is. It's just… You're smarter than this."

"What?"

"You know we won't be together in two days and the odds of us seeing each other again are non-existent."

He sighs, and the cushions grate against his pants as he slides closer to me. "Come here." Wrapping his hand around my wrist, he pulls me onto the couch beside him, and I set my cup aside before it slips from my grip. With my back against the armrest, there's maybe a foot of space between us. Sliding his hand down, he threads his fingers between mine. "I'll talk to the Commander again, tell him I need to see my mission through to the very end."

"You've tried that," I say, training my eyes on our hands, resting on his knee. "Even if he approved it, what then? Your group needs you."

"I'll figure something out." Placing two fingers under my chin, he tilts my face up to look at him, and the second I do, all of my uncertainty dissipates. I know I have questions that are still unanswered—and may never be answered—but right now, with him, everything feels okay again. "You worry too much."

"I don't want either of us to get hurt," I admit. "Especially not you."

"Do you trust me?"

"Of course I do." Without any thought to it, I find myself gravitating toward him. Our legs bump one another as I scoot closer, and that foot of empty space becomes a mere few inches.

"So understand that I'll make this work. It's not something for you to stress over."

He brushes his thumb over mine, making my skin tingle. Being this close to each other in this moment is both exhilarating and frightening. Any second, Adam or Lacey could come down here and see us touching, see me practically sitting in his lap. While we're not doing anything wrong, I'm sure there are rules in place for resistance members pertaining to things like this.

"If I wasn't sure of that," he continues, lowering his voice and leaning forward, "I wouldn't allow this to happen."

My heart beats erratically in my chest, so hard it feels as though it might rip its way out. His scent envelops me the closer he gets, drawing me in. My legs are weak, and if we were standing right now, I know I'd collapse. He glides his hand up the side of my face, sweeping back my hair and pulling me closer.

With shaky legs and adrenaline pumping through me, I clumsily climb into his lap, pressing my torso to his. His heat seeps through my clothes, wrapping my body in a warmth I never want to leave. His intoxicating presence makes my head cloudy and melts my thoughts into a puddle. This is the safety I've been craving, and I never would have thought that he'd be the one to make me feel this way.

Closing his eyes, he presses his forehead to mine. His other hand finds the small of my back and we sit like this for a few moments. Nothing else matters. No one else exists. It's only us.

"Just kiss me already," I finally whisper, snaking my arms over his shoulders.

He smirks. "I wanted your permission first." He hesitates with his lips hardly an inch from mine, teasing me now.

The squeaking of the hatch being opened pulls me out of the trance he's put me in. I pull away from him, both afraid of being caught and irritated that we've been interrupted. We were so close.

"They're right down there," Lacey's bubbly voice says.

I resume my spot against the armrest, feeling heat creep into my face, and Nixon sinks back into the couch, tapping his foot. Footsteps beat against the stairs, and I watch, waiting for our unexpected visitor to appear. From Lacey's tone, I know it's not anyone with the Society. I'm expecting Piper to come down with an update on Kase, something I know has been on Nixon's mind but would completely ruin this moment. But it's not Piper or the Black Hats who infiltrates our sacred space.

Addison grins at me as she reaches the bottom of the stairs, and I spring to my feet.

"There's my favorite fugitive!"

Nixon turns around at the sound of her voice, and stands when another figure emerges from the shadows.

"Hey, V," Liam says, walking toward me.

Before he makes it across the room, I tackle him with a hug, nearly knocking him over. At home, he would normally get annoyed and shake me off, but here, he laughs and hugs me back.

"Oh my God, you're here!" I cry. This doesn't seem real. Even as we embrace each other, I think this must be some kind of illusion concocted by my overly stressed mind. "You're both here!"

Every emotion pumps through me in heavy doses: relief that he's safe, ecstasy that he's here, anger that he didn't update anyone. All I can do is cry and squeeze him tighter, too afraid to ever let him go again. Eventually he does let go and has to pry himself from my grasp. Addison stands beside the stairs and Nixon remains by the couch, allowing us to have our moment.

"I've missed you, too," Liam says.

"What the fuck, Liam?" Nixon demands.

The whole room goes quiet.

Liam takes a step forward. "Look, I'm sorry, but—"

"You're *sorry*? You left my entire group behind without telling anyone!" The leader in Nixon comes out with full force. His words are coated in anger and authority, but his face remains composed, for the most part. His voice crescendos with every word, reaching a volume I've never heard from him. "Your sister and I have been worrying about you *every fucking day* after I promised her you'd be safe! I had a team ready to escort you to the wall, and you abandoned them! And then you show up here, unannounced, with someone who isn't part of the resistance?!"

I peek at Addison, expecting her to be uncomfortable, but she doesn't look the least bit fazed. She and Liam must have expected this. While I'm happy to see my best friend and instinctively want to jump to my brother's defense, I understand where Nixon is coming from. This is dangerous for all of us, especially since the Black Hats were tailing Liam before he went missing. So I hold my tongue, allowing the peacemaker in me to sit back and watch everything unfold.

"She can help," Liam says coolly. "Calm down."

With two long strides, Nixon is in his face, narrowing his eyes. "You don't have the authority to decide that! And don't tell me to 'calm down'. We may be friends, but I'm your leader first—you follow *my* orders and ask *me* for permission when changing plans. You may have jeopardized this entire mission by dragging your girlfriend along."

"Girlfriend?" I ask. Only when I say it does Addison look uneasy. Her eyes widen, and she focuses solely on Liam, who stands a few feet in front of me. "Liam, what is he talking about?"

Nixon's gaze clicks to me for half a second. "So you didn't tell her that either?"

"There was a lot going on," Liam says. "I should've contacted you. I'm sorry, but I know you would've shot it down, Nixon."

"Of course I would have! She's the Police Chief's daughter!" Nixon steps back, and closes his eyes, taking several deep breaths.

"Nixon, listen to me—"

"Stop," he says through gritted teeth. "You can't act on impulse. You know that. That's how you get yourself killed."

Liam's shoulders drop. "I'm sorry."

"You need to leave, Addison," Nixon says, massaging his forehead with his thumb and middle finger, "before your dad sends a search party out for you… if he hasn't already."

"I'm not a child," she says. "He doesn't have to know where I am every second." Crossing the room, she stands behind the couch. "How do you plan on getting them out of the Northern Unity, Nixon?"

Opening his eyes, Nixon chuckles. "That's none of your business."

"Nixon—" Liam starts.

"She's not part of my group. She's not entitled to any of that information."

Nixon's right; she shouldn't know any details of the resistance's missions. But it seems Liam has told her more than he ever told me—a conversation I intend to have with him later—and knowing Addison, with her father's survivalist training and her obsessive need to organize, she's already come up with her own plan leading to our escape. Yes, she's the Police Chief's daughter, which puts us in a dangerous situation if he goes by her apartment and realizes she's missing, but being so close to a government official, she potentially has information that could be valuable to the resistance. That's something Nixon doesn't seem to be grasping.

"Aircraft," I say.

Liam and Addison look at me, and Nixon rolls his eyes before shifting his glare to my direction.

"We'll be smuggled into the Red Zone by a cargo plane, and their group will help us from there."

"Terrible idea," Addison says. She pulls a folded sheet of paper from her back pocket and rounds the couch, smoothing the map of the Northern Unity out across the coffee table. I immediately recognize it as one of her dad's. Liam and I migrate toward the table, standing across from her and Nixon.

"Going back through the heart of the country"—she points at the Green Zone—"will undoubtedly get you caught. I think we all remember how your last mission involving an aircraft went down—no pun intended. The Green Zone is crawling with military personnel right now. Let's say you land safely in the Red Zone." She slides her finger to her left. "The closest place you could land is still twenty miles from the border. With the Enlightened Society searching tirelessly for our fugitive here"—she motions to me as if the other two may have forgotten—"and the Red Zone being her original destination, you risk her being captured, even under the protection of the other group."

"The arrangement for their escape was put in place by the Commander," Nixon says, not attempting to mask the irritation in his voice.

"But it risks us being shot down or found upon landing," Liam says.

Nixon chews on the inside of his lip and sits on the couch. Leaning forward, he studies the map with its mysterious markings, some faded and some fresh. "So what do you suggest?"

"Similar to how we got here," Liam says. "We jump on a distribution truck while they're fueling. As long as it's not carrying weapons or medical supplies, they're not locked from the outside."

"Right," Addison says. She folds one side of the map, concealing the Red Zone and revealing times and locations on the backside. "These are the schedules of every truck carrying food from the Blue Zone to the Yellow Zone"—she glides her finger from one zone to the next, then points to the Yellow Zone's northern border—"and into Canada. These drivers have automatic clearance to get through each gate, bypassing TCB and TCY."

"No," Nixon says.

"Why not?" Liam asks.

"In theory, it would work," Nixon says, looking over the schedule and path Addison traced, "but you wouldn't be under the protection of any resistance groups. Piper might dispatch a team to keep watch while you sneak into a truck in this zone, but Nadia won't go for it. She has enough to deal with in the Yellow Zone, which is why she wasn't originally in the loop with this mission."

"We can make it through without a group," Liam says.

"If everything went according to plan, yes. But if things went south, you'd be on your own." Nixon looks up at us, but mainly focuses on Liam. "Ivy's not part of the resistance and has no training. You've been doing this less than a year, and I've never actually put you out in the field. I know your strengths, but a group of police or military personnel would take you out almost immediately without any backup."

"What if you come with us?" Liam asks. "And have a team from the Blue Zone tail us if the Yellow Zone won't do it. I know they have documents to get through the walls."

Nixon taps a finger against his lips and drops his eyes to the map, furrowing his brow. "The Commander would have to approve it *after* being told about the stunt you pulled." He slides his hand down, letting it fall to his lap. "Piper and her group have a lot going on, but I'm sure she could spare a couple of her members. That would leave one problem: If we made it out through the Yellow Zone, we'd be stuck in Canada without any idea of where to go. The Commander wants you two at his camp, and none of us know exactly where that is. Somewhere in this area." He unfolds the left side of the map, drawing a circle outside the Red Zone with his finger. "But that doesn't really help us."

"The Canadians hate the Enlightened Society," Liam says. "There are groups out there that can help us."

"And have you talked with any of them?" Nixon asks, obviously already knowing the answer. "Because I sure as hell haven't, and I doubt the Commander has either. That would leave us stranded in another country, as refugees in their eyes, yes, but that's not the end goal. As far as I know, Canada still extradites, and all four of us have committed crimes in the eyes of the Society—whether they know it yet or not."

"I'm sure the Commander can pull some strings and get us to his camp," Liam says. "This will work."

"So *you* talk to him about it."

"I thought leaders were the only ones allowed to speak with the Commander."

"We are." Nixon stands, crossing his arms. "But I'm not going to take the heat for something you did behind my back. Let's get this over with."

"Wait, right now?"

"Yes, now." He walks toward the kitchen, and Liam reluctantly follows. "Ivy, Addison, wait upstairs please."

Without protest, Addison and I do as we're told.

"So," I say grimly once we're in the living room, "you and Liam?"

Adam and Lacey aren't anywhere in sight, but I can hear Adam's muffled voice, followed by Lacey's laugh. It sounds like they're in the sunroom, giving the four of us space. They must have been just as surprised as Nixon and I were to see Liam and Addison.

Addison wrings her hands together and nods.

"How long?" I demand.

I'm not upset in the least bit that they're together. She admitted to me back home that she liked him, and she's always been equally as close to him as she has to me. I expected it to happen eventually, but not in my absence—not while my world crumbled around me and I was left alone, wanting nothing more than to be with them again.

When I sat in my cell at TCG, crying and begging the guards to let me go home, the only thing that kept me relatively sane was replaying all of my precious memories of them. Meanwhile, they were going on with their lives, building a relationship, and doing normal everyday things—mundane tasks that I've never realized I miss. Instead of following through with the original plan, Liam decided to bring her along without informing anyone. He couldn't bear to leave his girlfriend behind. I envy him for having the opportunity to have the person he cares about most by his side while I have to leave Nixon.

To make things worse, it seems Liam has told Addison nearly everything about the resistance. She's already making plans and talking as if she's known how they work for a while. When she and I talked about Liam at the coffee shop the day of the plane crash, she hardly seemed surprised when I brought up how distant he'd been. I wonder if she already knew everything when I talked to her that day—Liam's involvement in the resistance, his gun, Elizabeth—while I was kept in the dark. Not wanting to get Liam into trouble or share too much of his business, I censored myself, leaving out what could've been critical information, and Addison just sat across from me, allowing me to stress over the well-being of my brother.

"A while," she says reluctantly. "It started before you were taken. I wanted to tell you, and he did too, but he thought it was best to hold off. He had a lot going on with the resistance, and you were going through so much."

"How long have you known he was in the resistance?"

She purses her lips and averts her eyes, focusing on the exit behind me. "I don't know... A few months maybe."

She knew. When I was worried that Liam was tangled up in something sinister, she knew. When I found his gun and was terrified that he'd be arrested any second, she knew.

"And you'd met Nixon?" I ask. He was another topic of conversation, not only at the coffee shop but in the days leading up to my kidnapping. When I expressed how much I disliked him after we met—albeit only a couple of times, but under strange circumstances—Addison either steered the conversation in a totally different direction or urged me to give him a chance.

She nods. "A few times."

I can't look at her anymore. I don't want her here anymore. All of this time I was desperate to see her and my brother, to have someone to share this loneliness with, but now I want them gone. Blood rushes to my head, and I'm blinded by rage. The bitter taste of it builds up in my mouth, shrouding my tongue in words that I know I shouldn't say but need to let out. But not to her. No, the venomous thoughts aren't directed at her. She's played a part in all of this, but Liam is the one behind it all, and I've already made up my mind that he'll be on the receiving end of my wrath. I don't care if I interrupt his talk with the Commander. I don't care about anything.

I storm out of the room, bumping Addison's shoulder as I push past her. She trails behind me, reciting apologies and excuses I know she must have rehearsed, but I couldn't care less and my head is too cloudy to process most of what she's saying. Every room I pass through is a blur, a mixture of colors and objects morphing into one another. Addison reaches out for me at one point, but I shake her off and growl, "Don't touch me."

The hatch is still open in the spare room, and I hesitate momentarily in the doorway as a rational thought tries to emerge from the fog in my brain. But it's almost instantly sucked into the storm brewing in my mind, consumed by anger, and I'm moving again with Addison close behind me. My feet pound against the steps, and I nearly collide with Nixon halfway down. He reaches out, grabbing my shoulders to stop me. His touch temporarily grounds me, but looking past him, I see Liam and everything comes rushing back.

"What the fuck, Liam?" I yell.

"That seems to be everyone's favorite line today," Liam says. Sarcastic and irritating as usual.

I push back against Nixon, but he tightens his grip and blocks my view of Liam. His eyes bore into mine, stern with a touch of tenderness. "Ivy, calm down."

"Get out of my way," I growl. I don't want to hurt Liam, not physically, but I need to see him when I unleash my anger. I need to look him in the eye when he tries to defend hiding everything from me.

"Remember how I said you were annoying me our first day together?" Nixon asks. "You're doing that again. Chill the fuck out." He lets go of me. "I'm going to move, and we're going to sit down and talk… *calmly.* Got it?"

"Don't talk to me like I'm a child," I snap.

"Then don't act like one." He and Liam turn around, retreating into the basement.

Liam and Addison sit together on the couch and Nixon disappears into the kitchen, returning with a permanent marker in hand. There's enough room for me to sit too, but right now I want to put as much distance between myself and them as possible, so I stand off to the side, being sure not to get too close to Nixon.

"Ivy," Nixon says, swiping the map from the coffee table, "say whatever it is you need to say to your brother so we can tell you what's going on."

Being put on the spot makes the anger that was burning through my body evaporate, leaving me cold and hollow. Nixon props his foot up on the coffee table, and with the map draped over his thigh, he adds new markings to it. Addison watches him intently, and Liam's eyes are on me, challenging me. He knows I've never really been one to lose my cool. I've always been the one in our family who avoided conflict while he tackled it head-on, almost embracing it. It was a way for his voice to be heard.

Now *I* want to be heard, and for him to see that I've changed in the time we've been apart—that I'm strong enough to handle the truth. So I collect the remaining droplets of my fury and focus it all on him. It's not as potent as it was moments ago, but it will do.

"How could you keep everything from me?" I begin. It sounds too nice, so I push myself to be more assertive, to sound more like

Nixon when he scolds his members. "I don't care that you two are dating, but I'm pissed that you told her everything while shutting me out! That night we talked after the raid, you continued to lie! I know I said some terrible things about the resistance, but I could've handled it. It would've been a *lot* better hearing it from you than your leader—who assumed I already knew. What else have you been hiding from me? Did you know Mom was going to *sell* me?"

"Of course not!" he says, not bothering to hide the hurt in his voice. "I wanted to tell you everything, and believe me, I'd planned on it that night. But you were so adamant on going to the police, I thought that would've been your tipping point. And there was never really a good time to talk to you after that."

"But you still found time to tell Addison—who stood by and let me think there was something wrong. Had I known, all of this would've played out so differently."

Addison turns to me at the mention of her name, but doesn't say anything.

"I'm sorry, okay?" Liam says. "If I could go back and change everything, I would. I promised both of them I was going to tell you and didn't want you to hear it from anyone else. I would've told you eventually, but what Mom did kind of ruined that."

"Yeah," Nixon says without looking up, "thanks for leaving me with that task."

"I had no idea Mom was going to do that," Liam continues, with an eye-roll for Nixon, "and I went to get help as soon as I could."

As messed up as it was to keep these secrets from me while letting Addison in, I know what he's saying is sincere. That doesn't dismiss what he's done, nor does it completely take away the pain of feeling betrayed, but it does calm me down. He's here, he's safe, and I know what I need to now. That's what matters. I'll squeeze more answers out of him and Addison another time.

"Okay," I say. "Just don't keep shit like this from me again."

"I won't. I promise."

"Now hug," Nixon says, sliding his foot off the table.

"Seriously?" I ask him, to which he responds with a smirk.

Liam stands and pulls me into him, swaying obnoxiously with his arms wrapped tightly around me. "Love you, V."

"Love you too, asshole," I say, before pushing him off me.

Addison stands too, wrapping me in a much lighter hug and whispering, "I'm sorry."

"So," Nixon says, dropping the map back to the table and capping the marker, "this is what's going on. The Commander, as angry as he was with Liam's lack of communication, approved the new plan. Piper will have two of her members follow us to the fueling station here"—he points to one of the circles he drew—"where they'll follow the truck up to TCB. Following beyond that point would be too obvious, but the Commander will work something out with the Yellow Zone so we'll have some sort of protection from them."

"We?" I ask.

Nixon looks up at me. "Yes, 'we.' I'll be going with you." His face remains neutral, but there's a smile in the eyes that I've come to know so well, and I wonder if the others notice it, too. Barely able to suppress a smile of my own, it takes everything in me not to pull him close and cry with joy. "Anyway, when we get onto Canadian soil, Border Patrol will do a routine stop, check the vehicle and all that. One of the officers with the resistance will get us out. From there, we'll fly to the Commander's camp." He drags his finger to the giant black 'X' drawn outside of the Red Zone. "Addison, he approved you to come with us, but you won't be staying. Once Liam and Ivy are settled, you'll go back to the Green Zone with me."

Hearing him say he'll go back to the Green Zone threatens to rip away my happiness, but I don't let it. We have a little more time together, and I believe him when he says he'll figure something out.

"Am I going to be, like, your spy or something?" Addison asks.

"If you want," Nixon says. "We could definitely use you. There is one setback with all of this, though. Since we're not sure you two weren't followed, we don't have as much time left here as we were originally given."

"How long do we have?" I ask.

"We leave tonight."

21. Madness

In the Old World, there were infinite numbers of belief systems. Some died out while others prevail, although Church and State are actually separate today, unlike before. Our family was never religious or spiritual or whatever people call it, but religion was one thing that always fascinated me. In times of turmoil, it gives people something to turn to, an entity much stronger than them who can magically whisk away all of their troubles. I know I've said a silent prayer when I've needed some extra help. Maybe it's superstition, or maybe there is something behind it.

Religion was the first thing I thought of when Nixon told us what time we'd be leaving: 03:00, the time some people call the devil's hour. It's just old-fashioned superstition, but that didn't stop the prickly feeling from creeping over my skin.

Nixon and I haven't had time alone together since Liam and Addison showed up. I'm happy to have them here and to know they'll be with me on my exodus outside of the Northern Unity, but I've grown accustomed to it just being Nixon and me. Sure, we've been with Adam and Lacey, but for the most part, it's been the two of us. I don't want Liam to know that something has developed between us—at least not yet. I guess I have secrets of my own… but nowhere near the scale his are on.

Any time Nixon stood close to me in front of Liam, I inched away before he could notice, and I purposely made a habit of not looking at him for too long when he spoke. At dinner, our final meal with Adam and Lacey, Nixon brushed his fingers against mine under the table, and I inconspicuously pulled away. Sitting across from us, I'm sure Liam and Addison couldn't see, but the paranoia of being caught told me otherwise. Lacey, however, did take notice. She didn't say anything, but gave me an approving smile when I looked her way. There have been a few small instances after that where Nixon got too close to me or touched me when passing by or reaching for something. After the first couple of times, I realized he was doing it on purpose, because he always followed it up with a playful smile. At first I was annoyed, but it soon became exciting, like a game to see how often we could touch without being noticed.

Figuring out the sleeping arrangement was another obstacle. Since we're leaving so early and have hours upon hours of dangerous travel ahead of us, we all retired early after tearful goodbyes from Adam and Lacey—mostly Lacey. Addison volunteered to take the floor with Liam, not wanting to disturb the routine Nixon and I have made for ourselves and insisting she wanted to be close to him. At any point before last night, I would've been content with the set-up, but now, more than ever, I want Nixon beside me.

I've been lying in bed for hours. Nixon is on the couch, and I wonder if he's fallen asleep yet. I wonder if he misses my touch as much as I miss his. Liam and Addison are on their makeshift bed behind the couch, snuggling close under some of Lacey's spare blankets and a mattress constructed of their unzipped sleeping bags stacked on top of each other. Liam's snoring confirms that he's asleep and has been for a while. The sound of it, as annoying as it can be sometimes, fills me with another layer of happiness. I have my brother back, and soon, we'll be out of this hellhole of a country.

Nixon shifts again on the couch, and I imagine him reaching out for me, finding me for the kiss we were so close to sharing earlier. Each time I looked at him today, that was all I could think about, and I had to stop myself. His teasing didn't help either, but in a weird way, I enjoyed it. It felt like we were kids in high school, sneaking around so the teachers didn't catch us doing something so innocent but deemed inappropriate.

After dinner, Liam told me he'd been allowed to visit Naomi. He said she was scared but other than that, normal. The Society has labeled her as insane, diagnosing her with one of the mental illnesses from the Old World, which consists of extreme bouts of paranoia and hallucinations. They currently consider her a danger to herself and others, and by now, she's been transferred to a psychiatric ward where she'll remain indefinitely. My aunt is many things, but crazy isn't one of them. The Society can't kill her without the risk of raising suspicion, so instead, they stamped her with a phony diagnosis in case she one day attempts to expose them. By doing that, they've guaranteed that no one will ever take her seriously.

A hand wraps around my bicep and I jump, scrambling to sit up.

"It's okay," Nixon whispers, lowering his lips to my ear, "it's me."

I move over, making room for him beside me, and he stealthily slides under the covers. "What are you doing? They're going to see us."

He wraps his arms around me, making me instantly soften and melt into him. "They're asleep. I'll get up before them, don't worry." His lips awkwardly brush my hairline, and while it's not the kiss we were so close to earlier, it still sends a rush of warmth through my body and awakens butterflies in the pit of my stomach.

The kitchen light is on when I wake up. I don't remember falling asleep; it feels as though I closed my eyes for only a couple of minutes. Sitting up, I'm groggy and want nothing more than to curl up underneath the blankets and sleep for however long I can before our trek outside the walls. Liam and Addison are still asleep, unbothered by the light pouring into the room, but Nixon is awake, no longer in the bed. This time, I know him being with me wasn't a dream.

I find him in the kitchen, stuffing packaged food and bottles of water into one of the four bags stacked on the table. We already packed all of the clothes we'll need before going to bed, and he's moved his gun in here from the bedroom. The clock above the stove boasts the time in glaring green numbers. We have less than an hour until our departure, but I don't think I'm ready. Time has passed by too quickly, and I want it back. I want to spend more time here where I know we're all safe.

"I told you I'd be up before them," Nixon says quietly when I approach him. He's already dressed and ready to go, but the dark rings under his eyes are hard to miss. "I was going to wake all of you soon."

"Have you even slept?"

He shrugs, zipping the backpack. "A little. I'll be fine. How are you feeling?"

"Nervous."

"Everything's going to be okay." Reaching out for me, he gives my hand a quick squeeze. "I'll be with you the entire time." Unzipping Liam's backpack, he retrieves a handgun that's tucked underneath the clothes—the same gun I found in his closet—and sets it aside on the table.

"Are you scared at all?"

"Not really. I've done worse."

"But you've never left the Northern Unity before."

The Northern Unity is all I've ever known. Traveling outside of the Green Zone was already daunting enough. I know this country isn't the paradise I grew up believing it was; it's dark and twisted, its shadowy secrets ready to wrap their fingers around our throats. The Enlightened Society does help people, through their various programs that assist those in need, and guarantee employment and homes for everyone. But their superficial good deeds can't mask the evil. Still, it's ingrained in my mind that this is the safest place in the world, and although my knowledge of the Society has been forcefully expanded, I can't shake the shred of fear-based loyalty that remains with them.

"The danger isn't out there. It's here." He turns, wrapping me in his warm embrace. "You'll be safe."

Knowing he'll be with me as well as Liam and Addison takes the edge off my anxiety. Knowing that in less than an hour, we'll be on our way to safety—*actual* safety—gives me hope. I've survived this long as a fugitive, side-by-side with a leader of the resistance. I've made it through two raids and, by sheer luck, avoided the ambush of a safehouse. Through all of this, I've become harder, molded into a different person, and I'm not sure if I've lost who I once was or just uncovered a part of myself I never knew existed. But this is just the beginning, and there is so much more learning and growing and changing to come.

"Get dressed," Nixon murmurs into my hair. "I'll get the other two up."

I tighten my arms around him and hold him a moment longer, cherishing this last bit of alone time we'll have for a while. All too soon, he breaks away. I refrain from pulling him back in. We'll have plenty of time together once we're out of here.

The next twenty minutes or so are spent getting dressed, attempting to fully wake ourselves up, and collecting our belongings. As usual, Addison is full of energy and it's contagious, circulating throughout the basement, seeping into the rest of us. It starts as a small simmer, tiny bubbles of optimism and liveliness popping inside me, releasing their power. As we continue to move around and go over the plan one final time, it intensifies, turning into a rolling boil. We're awake. We're ready.

We shoulder our backpacks and Nixon tosses his keys to Liam, instructing him to start the car and wait for him. The license plates have already been swapped out, and Piper's team should be in place half a mile away. This is so surreal. I can't believe that it was only a few weeks ago that my life was ripped away from me. Things will never be the same again, I've learned to accept that, but I'll find a new sense of normalcy.

Liam and Addison head upstairs and I wait with Nixon, despite him telling me to go ahead with them, as he searches through the linen closet for something. Within a couple of minutes, he finds a handgun stashed behind stacks of towels. With his rifle already slung over his shoulder, he tucks the second weapon in his waistband, and we head up.

It's dark, and Adam and Lacey are asleep. Not wanting to draw attention to ourselves, we keep the lights off and feel our way through the darkness with Nixon leading the way. A car door slams outside. Liam and Addison must have already made it out.

The house feels exponentially larger at night—it has every time we've snuck up here—but tonight, it seems even more massive. It doesn't help that Lacey turned off the few lights she usually keeps on before we went to bed, leaving nothing to guide us. Thankfully, Nixon has this place memorized and moves through it with ease, similar to when we were in the first safehouse together. I follow close behind, allowing my ears to guide me, each step falling in sync with his.

A horn blares outside, slicing through the dead silence.

Nixon curses under his breath. "Stay close," he whispers urgently.

There's a pause and the horn sounds again, longer this time. Then Nixon's hand is gripping mine and we're running, our boots thumping heavily against the wood. There's the squealing of tires, gravel being kicked up, clanking against metal. My heart leaps to my throat, making it hard to breathe.

We're close, so close to freedom. I can make out the dim streetlight through the window on the front door. A figure eclipses the light. Then two. Nixon notices, too, and jerks me in another direction while retrieving the gun from his pants, and we're sprinting toward another exit. We're in the kitchen; I can tell by the digital clock that casts an eerie glow. More figures, dark and mysterious, like demons lurking in the night. We come to a halt, and Nixon raises his gun, shielding my body with his.

The door explodes inward, and the figures momentarily disappear as something thuds against the floor. Nixon shoves me back, but he's not quick enough. There's a second explosion and all I can see is white. The blast is deafening, throwing me off balance as it rips through me.

Yelling. Gunshots. Bodies flood the room, barking orders, grabbing at me. I fight back, kicking and thrashing and scratching. And screaming. So much screaming. I frantically search for Nixon and spot him warding off his own horde of demons.

Black Hats.

One of them comes up behind me, grabbing me by my backpack. Without thinking, I slip out of it and attempt to run toward Nixon, but my body hasn't recovered from the shock of the explosion. I'm grabbed again, around the waist this time, and jerked backward. I lurch forward, but he's too strong.

Something pricks my neck and I let out a cry. The edges of my vision blur and my head spins. Something inside pulls at me, silencing all of my thoughts, leaving behind nothing but panic. *Run,* my brain shouts, but my legs buckle underneath me, and the last thing I see is the horde closing in on Nixon.

22. *Hymn for the Missing*

Swirling colors swim onto a canvas, forming broken, blurred figures before fading out again. The darkness swallows me, pulling me deeper and deeper into its eternal abyss. My head burns as though I'm wearing a crown of flames. Pain comes in bursts from multiple points of my body. Stabbing, slicing. I open my mouth to scream, but nothing comes out. The fire has snaked its way down my throat. It swells in my chest.

My cheeks are wet and my mind tries to fight through the haze. I reach out, desperate for something to grab, something to stop me from falling. My fingers graze a smooth surface but it quickly disappears and I'm grasping at air, cold and empty. My arms are pinned down, forced to my sides, and I'm too weak to fight back.

Disembodied voices float around me, but they're so faint compared to the roaring of the fire in my ears. I focus what little energy I have on deciphering their cryptic words, to no avail. The presence of the voices confirm at least one thing: I'm alive. But where am I? Not safe. I can't be.

I'm alone. There are people around me, I can hear them, but I can't see or feel the bodies the sounds are attached to. These voices are unfamiliar. Cool and calculated, not belonging to anyone I know. Fragmented bits of what happened slowly roll in like a weak tide but pull away before I can make much sense of it.

White. Blinding, hot light. Everything turned to chaos after that. We were almost free. Nixon and I were almost out.

Nixon.

Where is he? And Liam and Addison, they were out in the car. What happened to them? Adam and Lacey were in the house, too. I didn't see them during the ambush. I have to find them. Hysteria crashes over me and my body—heavy and tired—convulses, pushing back against the invisible force bearing down on my arms.

The fire lashes violently through me, ravenous and ready to consume me. It rips through one of my arms and I attempt to scream again. It makes its way out this time, though it's muffled. But I can feel it. It tears through me like a shard of glass, building in my chest and surging in my lungs. It scrapes my throat like sandpaper. My fists clench and I feel the flesh on my palms split as I dig my nails deeper.

Another prick at my neck, amplified this time. Everything is amplified. Except the voices. I need to know whose voices those are.

The darkness cradles me, tugs at me again, and I'm tempted to succumb to it. The roaring fire fades to a dull burn. Manic thoughts are replaced with tranquil ones, and the darkness doesn't seem so bad.

Wake up, a voice begs deep within me. *Wake up!*

I struggle to obey, to fight the black blanket surrounding me. The words repeat over and over, bouncing around in my skull. For a moment, I'm pulled up out of the hungry darkness, but it fights back, refusing to release its grip on me. And I continue to fall, not strong enough. I surrender to its gravity, let it consume me.

23. Slip Away

Daggers of light slice through my eyes. The ceiling spins above me as I squint against the blinding bulbs beaming down on me. Nausea threatens to take over; I have to close my eyes and wait for it to pass. When my stomach settles, I open my eyes again and try to sit up but am immediately jerked back down. Alarm roots itself in my gut when I notice the black leather straps binding my limbs to the bed. A needle is lodged into the crook of my right arm with a narrow, transparent tube connecting it to the dripping bag on the metal stand beside me. My palms sting as I clench and unclench my fists. Gauze is taped to the bend of my left arm, and on the inside of my forearm is a trail of thread sewn into my flesh.

My panic grows, blooming rapidly. When did I get stitches? I don't recall being injured—not from the attack at least. How long have I been unconscious? No clocks are in sight. No windows or anything else to give me a sense of time. In fact, the room is completely empty save for my bed and IV bag. There's one door to my right and one on the wall across from me. The walls and floors are a sparkling white, absent of any blemishes.

Hospital. That's the first word that pops into my head. Hospitals are safe, which means I must be safe. But my gut tells me otherwise. No matter how hard I try, I can't bring any details of what happened to the surface of my clouded mind.

There are only two things I'm sure of: I'm alone, and I'm trapped here.

I fight against the restraints a second time, yanking upward and attempting to wiggle my arms and legs free. Of course, nothing comes of it. The leather straps burn as they rub against my skin. After a few minutes of struggling, I give up, scowling at the now still ceiling.

Digging deeper into the trenches of my mind, reaching past the haze, I'm able to pull one detail into the light: Black Hats. I didn't get a good look at any of them, but I know they were the ones who invaded the house. Between the flying bullets and mindless minions of the Society shouting, shoving, and grabbing, time seemed to stop and zip by all at once. Out of nowhere, the world closed in on me, faded away along with our freedom. Nixon was there with me, fighting them off as much as he could. He was surrounded by them before I lost consciousness, and I don't know what happened after that. The likelihood of him having made it out alive is slim. I hate myself for thinking that way. He's a leader of the resistance, damn it, he knows what he's doing.

Liam and Addison were nowhere in sight. They were outside before us, and I want to believe they got away and are safe somewhere. But this *is* the Enlightened Society—the all-knowing, never-tiring corruption that has infected the world. They won't let anyone walk free. Even if Liam and Addison weren't originally their targets, they were there during the ambush, and that makes them a threat.

I try sitting up again—slower this time—and am able to prop myself up with my elbows, lodging the needle deeper into my skin. I strain to see through the slender rectangular window on the door to my right, but it's too far away. Never mind the fact that my eyes have yet to completely adjust to the glaring light and comprehending much of anything right now is a major task.

The door creaks open and a man enters, pushing a metal cart. He's dressed in all white—a stark contrast to his dark skin—and looks to be in his early thirties. From his uniform, I guess he's not a Black Hat, but he's not someone I'm willing to trust either. He walks toward me and I glare at him, imagining my eyes are burning a hole through his body. As far as I'm concerned, no one here—wherever I am—can be trusted. Making eye contact with me, he doesn't react to my dirty look. He must be used to putting up with things like that.

Stopping by the bed, he fidgets with my IV bag, and I train my eyes on the door, wondering if it's locked from the inside. It doesn't matter either way if I can't get out of these damn bonds though. Even if I could, I'm weak. Fighting against my restraints was enough to make my muscles ache, and I know standing will prove to be more difficult, especially with the fog in my brain. I don't want to give up so quickly though. There's got to be a way out.

"I'm surprised to see you're awake, Olivia," the man says. His voice is hollow. "The medication shouldn't have worn off for a couple more hours."

"Where am I?" The words cut against my throat, and I think I taste blood. What was meant to be a demand sounds hoarse and help-less. "Where are my friends?"

Finishing up with the IV, he tosses the empty bag on his cart and, turning his back to me, rearranges its contents. Peering around him, I try to get a glimpse of what he's brought, but he obscures my view and all I can make out is the empty bag and a clipboard. "Your friends are fine."

His words offer no comfort, and before I can press for an actual answer, he spins around with a tray in one hand, shoving a forkful of food in my face with the other. Squeezing my lips together, I jerk my head in the opposite direction, reminded of my hunger strike at TCG. I regretted not eating anything after I left there, but I don't have any-where to run to this time. Until I get some real answers, I'm not trust-ing anything I'm offered here.

He sighs. "I heard you were stubborn." When I hear the tray clank against the cart, I turn back to him. "I'm one of the nicer ones here, but I don't have time to play any games. It would be wise of you to cooperate with me." His tone reminds me of Nixon's when I first met him—assertive and blunt. But he's calm and soft-spoken where Nixon was quick to showcase his authority.

"Where am I?" I try again, forcing my voice to stay firm despite the aching of my throat and dryness of mouth.

He hesitates, but only for a moment. "You're at your original destination."

The Red Zone.

"Had you arrived at your scheduled time," he continues, "you would've been able to complete your Transitional Adaptation course before the auction. But it's too late for that now."

No longer able to hold myself up, I fall back onto the bed. The walls cave in on me and the air becomes thick and hot. I can't breathe. It's as though my lungs have collapsed and there's a weight on my chest, slowly crushing me. The tears come without warning, blurring my vision, making me feel more helpless. My breaths finally come in sporadic, sputtering gasps and my thoughts are an out-of-control carousel. Spinning. Everything's spinning.

The nurse is beside me with something in his hand. He pops off the cap, flicks the barrel, and the glinting needle is piercing my skin.

"Please," I choke out between gasps. "Don't."

"Shhh. It's just to calm you down." And he presses down on the plunger.

The medicine invades my bloodstream, burning its way through my body, and I'm met with the darkness again.

When I come to, another nurse enters the room—a woman with graying hair and a permanent scowl. Other than checking my vitals and helping—and watching—me go to the bathroom, she doesn't acknowledge me. In the short-lived minutes of freedom from the restraints, I'm tempted to break away from her and bolt for the exit. My legs are far from capable of carrying me, though, and I have to lean on her to keep from toppling over. When I attempt to ask questions, I'm answered with a glare that could cut through glass.

I'm in and out of sleep, a side-effect of whatever medication I was given, no doubt. But the darkness doesn't swallow me again. There are no voices or fire, just sleep. Like my time at TCG, it has become my escape. But no matter how much I hibernate, I'm facing my fate this time. It's not something I can outrun, and I was foolish to think otherwise. Just as I feared from the beginning, I've brought everyone down with me.

I don't know how long I sleep for. At first I only wake up when the female nurse comes in to routinely check on me. Slowly, I'm able to wake up by myself but only for minutes at a time. Time stretches on—how long for, I still don't know—and I'm able to stay conscious for longer intervals. My brain fog has begun to disperse, and each time I wake up, I'm a little more clear-headed. The lights stay on, blinding me each time I open my eyes.

The final time I awake, I'm alone. My head is mostly clear; a trace of the haze remains, but it's functioning normally now nonetheless.

The door opens and the male nurse from the first time I woke comes in. To my surprise, I'm relieved to see him. At least he offered up a shred of information and didn't look at me like he wanted to kill me. Another tray of food sits on the cart along with his clipboard, and on the lower shelf is a small pile of folded clothes and my shoes. Upon further inspection, I make out three syringes shoved underneath the clipboard, and my stomach drops. I can't be knocked out again. I'm finally feeling closer to myself.

"How are you feeling, Olivia?" he asks.

I resist the urge to correct him. The only people who have used my full first name in the past decade were my parents, and even they only really used it when scolding me. I don't give him an answer, which he probably expected.

Although he's dressed in the same uniform, he looks different today. I could be imagining it, but he seems to be standing taller, keeping his shoulders squared but tense. A crease forms between his eyebrows as he dislodges the needle from my arm and removes the IV bag from its stand. He begins loosening the strap on my right wrist, and I pray he isn't going to watch me in the bathroom as the female nurse did.

"What's with the stitches?" I ask.

His eyes flit to the delicate threads. "Tracker."

"W-what?"

My arm is freed, and he moves down to my feet. "Every participant in the auction receives one."

I want to ask why, but from my time with Nixon, I know to ask the important questions first. And I'm pretty sure I already know the answer anyway. In a way, I've always been the property of the Enlightened Society—everyone has been and always will be—but this permanently binds me to them. What little freedom I had is gone, ripped away from me in the blink of an eye.

My panic is replaced with anger—no, *rage*. Who the hell gave them the right to do this? We're human beings, the same as them. We aren't their property. We have our own lives—our own families and dreams—and no amount of money should ever be able to take that away from us.

The strap comes off my other arm, and I sit up a little too quickly. Black dots float into my vision, and I squeeze my eyes shut until my head stops reeling.

"What happens to my friends?" I ask, opening my eyes again. I want to yell at him. I want to reach over and strangle him. He's one of them and he deserves every ounce of rage within me, along with anyone else who's here, but playing nice is more likely to get me answers. So I bite back the anger for now. "They weren't supposed to go to the auction."

He tosses the clothes from the cart—a white T-shirt and black pants—onto the foot of the bed. "That's out of my control. But with kidnapping, aiding and abetting, and active resistance, I don't foresee the Society going easy on them."

"How the hell can you support something like this?"

"I never said I did. Stand up for me." He offers his hand but I ignore his gesture, using the rails to push myself up instead. I sway when my bare feet meet the cold tile. He reaches out to steady me and

I shake him off, gripping the railing of the bed. My head is full of pressure and my legs are wobbly.

"If you don't support it," I say between breaths, "then why are you here?"

"To help people."

I scoff. "Is that what you call this?"

Ignoring my remark, he strides across the room. "I'll leave you alone to get dressed. Someone will be in soon to do your makeup, then I'll escort you out. I suggest you eat."

"Escort me where?"

He pauses at the door, his back to me and fingers wrapped around the handle. "The Elite Auction."

24. The Dark of You

As I finish washing my hands, I gaze at my reflection in the mirror, disgusted. With the black bordering my eyes, the unnaturally dark lashes, lips painted a powdery pink, and my hair swept back into a tight ponytail, I look nearly identical to my mother. The liquid foundation slathered on my face makes my skin feel sticky and unclean, and I'm tempted to scrub it all off. I didn't want any of it and protested against it, but the woman who did the makeup said it was required, and like in all other things, I didn't have a choice.

After moving around a bit and forcing myself to choke down some of the food that was left for me, I'm more stable. My head is clearer and although my legs are heavy, they're strong enough to carry me. The woman said the last of the effects from the sedatives should wear off soon. They hadn't planned on keeping me sedated as much as they have, but after multiple panic attacks and my inability to attend the Transitional Adaptation course—whatever that is—they didn't have any other option.

I hear the main door to my room close, and my heart skips.

This is it.

The nurse patiently waits for me beside the cart that's still in the center of the room. Although he said he'd be escorting me to the auction, I expected guards of some sort to be with him. Escorting a fugitive doesn't seem like a job for a nurse. But he's alone and I approach with caution, stopping at the foot of the bed.

"I'm glad to see you ate," he says, eyeing the half-eaten food. "Are you ready?"

What a stupid question. And I respond with a stupider answer. "I'm not going anywhere with you."

He smirks, and I know he can see through my feigned confidence. I'm able to keep my voice steady and stand tall, but my heart is hammering in my ears. Can he hear it, too? By no means am I a fighter, especially not in my current state, and he probably knows that from the way the ambush went. He wasn't there, but I'm sure he heard about it. I did absolutely nothing to help, nothing that was beneficial to us or the mission.

Folding his arms over his chest, he sits on the bed. "I'm responsible for getting you to where you're supposed to be. But if you were to somehow get away from me…"

"I don't understand."

Is he going to let me go? Or is that supposed to be followed up with some sort of threat?

"The guards are preoccupied right now," he says. "You have at least thirty minutes before they do a final sweep of this wing and round up the remaining prisoners."

He's trying to help me, but why? It has to be some kind of trap, something to paint me in an even worse light to the Society. I couldn't care less about what they think of me anymore, but I don't want the fate that's already sealed for me to be made worse. I glance at the door, ten feet away, then back to him. If he were to chase me, there's no way I'd be able to outrun him, even if I had a generous head start. Not only does he look to be in good shape, but I haven't fully recovered from being kept constantly drugged up.

"How do I know this isn't a trap?" I ask. He doesn't have any real reason to set me up that I know of, and out of the three people I've seen here, he's been the most cordial one. I've learned, however, that there are layers to everyone and everything connected to the Society. Nothing is as it seems, and nearly everyone has an ulterior motive.

His eyes linger on the door as if expecting someone to burst in at any moment. Then he stands, turning to face me, and pushes the right sleeve of his shirt up. Licking his thumb, he rubs it against the inside of his wrist, revealing a symbol I've seen before but can't remember where: Three bold, black horizontal lines stacked on top of one another, permanently inked into his skin. He gives me a look that suggests I should know exactly what the mark is and the meaning behind it.

Leaning forward to closer examine it, I ask, "What is that?"

The Green Zone. I saw it in the Green Zone when Nixon took me to the first safehouse. Most of the houses in the battered neighborhood we drove through had the same symbol haphazardly painted on them. And again in the bathroom stall when Nixon and I stopped at the convenience store just inside the Blue Zone.

He pulls his sleeve down, concealing the mark. "Nixon never showed you his?"

My heart leaps to my throat at the sound of his name coming from this man's mouth. He's part of the resistance. The tattoo and the graffiti… It's their symbol. "What?"

"We all have one."

"You know him?"

"I do, very well. We've worked together for a long time." I know my confusion is obvious because he adds, "Go find Nixon, Ivy."

A glimmer of hope is restored, and I know there's a chance of making it out of here, but I have to find the others first. The Society might have chosen my fate for me, but it's not set in stone.

I start toward the door but stop halfway there, spinning around to my new savior again. "Wait, where am I supposed to be going?"

"Your father was a police officer. I'm sure he always used whatever tools were at his disposal."

I'm taken aback by his answer, and my curiosity is piqued. How does he know anything about my dad? His career wasn't exactly a secret, but I'm still surprised to hear this stranger mention him. Maybe he knows him from the times my father worked the auctions—another secret part of my family I wish I'd never known. I almost ask about it but stop, telling myself this is a conversation for another time.

I scan the room for whatever tools he's referring to but it's still the same empty prison, and I wish he would just come out and tell me what he's talking about rather than challenging me with riddles. The cart to my left catches my eye as I do a final sweep, drawing my attention to the clipboard. The nurse watches, as if making mental notes of my every move, as I inch toward it.

The first page is a list of names and room numbers. I spot mine almost immediately, neatly penned in bright red ink: *Olivia Clearson, 974. Room 402.* All of the other names are written in black, and not every name has a number beside it like mine. In fact, skimming down the first page, I only count five other names that are matched with a number. The rest are carelessly scribbled down with only a room number in the column beside them. *974* was the number I was assigned at TCG, so everyone else with a number must be participants in the auction as well. That leaves thirteen people who are here for other unknown reasons.

I read through every single name and room number, stopping at the second from the bottom, where I find Nixon's. *Room 612.* Flipping the page up, I expect to find another list of names—one with Liam and Addison—but am presented with a floor plan instead. My room is circled in the same red ink, and two corridors down from the one I'm in is *612.* There's a gold key taped to the small square. I flip through the remaining pages, desperate to find Liam and Addison, but all I find is more detailed information on me, Nixon, and other people I don't care about right now. I want to read over what the Society has on us, but unfortunately I don't have the time.

"If you're looking for the other two," the nurse says, "they're not here."

Just like that, my optimism is shattered. I've found where Nixon is though—that's a start. He can help me track down the others.

I remove the second page from the clipboard, knocking the syringes out from underneath it in the process. They roll across the surface of the cart, stopped by the tray in their path. Without thinking, I swipe all three of them, shoving them in my pocket with the capped needles pointed down and covering what sticks out with my shirt. When I look back at the nurse, he gives me an approving nod and cocks his head toward the door.

"Thank you," I say, and he responds with another nod and a smile.

I get to the door as fast as my legs can carry me, now filled with a new wave of energy. Swinging it open, I glance both ways down the hall to see that it's completely empty. Just like he said. Fear prickles at the back of my neck. This is stupid. This is dangerous. But it's worth it. So I step out of the room, allowing the door to close behind me, echoing into the emptiness.

Like my room, everything is white. The hallway stretches on for what looks like an eternity in either direction, and the walls are lined with doors all identical to mine. The smell of ammonia burns my nostrils and makes my eyes water. I check my map, studying where I am in comparison to Nixon's room.

I head to my right, peeking over my shoulder every few steps. Surely I would hear if someone were behind me, but the creeping feeling of paranoia won't go away. I refrain from looking through the windows of the rooms I pass. Knowing there are people on the other side who are also prisoners to the Society shrouds me with a sense of guilt. How is it fair that I've been given a second chance at freedom while they're trapped in there?

I know I can't save everyone. I told Nixon something along those lines, too, when he opened up about his fears after interrogating Kase. I believed it then. Now I understand what he felt, albeit on a smaller scale. Although I'm not part of the resistance, I feel this overbearing obligation to do something to help these people. But I know bringing even one along would not only slow us down, but put the resistance at risk.

At the end of the hall, I take a left. I will myself to pick up the pace, but my body feels like lead. Again, there are no guards or other nurses, and I wonder where the nurse who helped me went. If he's part of the resistance, shouldn't he be trying to help Nixon and me escape? He gave me the tools I needed to figure out where I'm going, but with working in the midst of all of this, he should want to do more. He could've rescued Nixon himself.

A door shuts somewhere behind me, and my legs stop moving despite my brain telling them to move faster. The prickling of fear turns into pins and needles working its way down my spine. With my heart hammering, I look over my shoulder, surveying the monstrous facility behind me. No one's there, but I know I heard it. It must've been my nurse finally making his way out of my room. I force myself to move again, on high alert now just in case that closing door was from someone else.

The air conditioning cuts on, making me jump, and every few feet, I think I see something move from the corner of my eye. When I look around, all is still, which only adds to my uneasiness. This is too easy. A place like this should be constantly crawling with guards. I understand today might be chaotic, but that's all the more reason to recruit as much security as possible.

I make it to the second hallway on my left—the one where the key is taped on the floor plan—and stand frozen at the mouth of it. According to my map, Nixon's room is the fifth door on my right, and from here, I can make out its frame down the hall. I've made it this far without any altercations, but I can't bring myself to move. Insecurity and doubt flood my mind. What if I'm not the one he wants to see? Whatever we have between us is irrelevant right now. He needs someone who can actually help him out of here—someone who's trained and familiar with how things work around here. Liam would be more fit for this task, or anyone else in his group.

The third fluorescent light ahead flickers wildly, its annoying clicking stabbing at the silence like it's threatening to disrupt the calm completely. The doors in this area are black rather than white and absent of any windows. It could be my imagination, but the air feels thicker, too. Glowing keypads are mounted to the wall beside each door, and I quickly scan my paper again for some sort of code. The nurse didn't mention anything about this. The only marking on the front is the red circle around my room, and the back is blank.

A distant voice drifts in my direction. No one is in sight but the voice—a woman's—gets closer, bouncing off the bare walls and glossy floors, twisting its way into my head. Suddenly I'm moving forward at a quicker pace than I was previously able to manage. Not quite running, but faster than the sluggish pace I've been maintaining. With every footfall, my body throbs and my heart pounds in my head. She's getting closer. High heels strike the floor like knives. I can't tell how far away she is, but I push myself to move faster, ignoring the aches in my legs.

When I reach the door beneath the flickering light, I search the area for some sort of clue as to what the code is. Nothing. Once more, I check the paper as if expecting the number to magically appear, but the only thing there is the key, which is of no use for this kind of door. With my thumbnail, I scrape at the edge of the tape, peeling it away in small strands. The high heels are louder now, and the voice has ceased to penetrate my ears. I scratch harder against the tape, careful not to rip the paper, and the key pulls away, revealing four numbers: *3013*. I punch them into the glowing keypad and wait as the rotating white cursor processes the code, looking back and forth between the small device and both ends of the hallway.

Please work, I think. *Please, please work.*

When the stabbing high heels sound like they're near the end of the hall, the keypad lets out a soft beep, displaying a green check, and the door clicks. With slick, shaky hands, I fumble with the door handle, losing my grip on it a couple of times. Finally, I secure my fingers around it and push my way into the room, catching the door by its handle on the other side before it slams shut. I close it gently and take a few deep breaths to calm myself, focusing on the stopped clock hanging above the door. When I finally have a grip on myself, I turn around.

With his back to me, Nixon is in the center of the small, empty room, seated in a chair that's bolted to the floor. His wrists are chained behind him and his ankles are hugged by shackles. Hunched forward and shirtless, his shoulders are shiny with sweat and his back is striped with multiple lacerations. Most are caked with dried blood, but a few glisten under the light.

A lump is already forming in my throat. I don't know what I was expecting to see when I found him, but it wasn't this. I guess I should have been after seeing what the Society did to Kase. I swallow back the tears that are so close to spilling over. I can't cry. Nixon has been strong for me this entire time. It's my turn now.

"Nixon?" I say, circling the chair.

He doesn't look up, but his shoulders tense. His body trembles with each breath, and with his head bowed, his hair hangs over his face like a curtain, masking his defeat.

Crouching in front of him, I tentatively reach up, brushing my fingers along his jaw, and he flinches. "Hey, hey, it's okay. It's me."

Slowly, he raises his head, searching my face with fearful eyes. A ribbon of dried blood streaks his chin from the corner of his mouth.

"What are you doing here?" His voice is raspy.

"Nice to see you, too," I say, pulling my hand away from his face. Setting the paper aside, I use the key to free his ankles. "You have no idea how worried I've been about you."

"I've been worried about you, too," he says. "But how did you...?"

Standing up, I move behind him and get to work removing the chains binding his wrists. "A nurse helped me. He said he knows you."

"Knows me how?"

"He said you've worked together." The chains fall to the floor as Nixon pulls his arms forward, and I resume my place in front of him. "He had this tattoo on his wrist, too. Three black lines."

Wincing, Nixon leans forward enough to grab the hem of his pants and lifts it up, revealing the same mark just below his ankle. "Like this?" I nod and he sits up. "So... you've met Eli."

The Red Zone's leader.

"So why isn't *he* the one helping you?"

Pursing his lips, he turns his face away from me. "If he gets too close, he'll get caught. Eli does a lot around here. He's like a ghost, slipping in and out without being noticed." He keeps his gaze on the blank wall to his right, gnawing on his bottom lip. Moisture coats his eyes, and a single tear silently rolls down his cheek.

I grab his hand, giving it a long squeeze, and rise to my feet. "It's okay. We're going to get out of here. Can you stand?"

He shakes his head, redirecting his eyes to the ceiling. "It's not going to happen, Ivy. You need to worry about yourself."

"I'm not leaving you!" I try my best to keep from yelling. I don't know how thick these walls are, but I don't want to risk anyone hearing. My anger returns, raging like a fire. I'm angry at the Black Hats and the Enlightened Society. I'm angry at my mom for forcing me into all of this. But at this very moment, my anger is directed toward Nixon. I'm pissed that after all of this, he's not willing to try anymore. "So that's it? You're just giving up on your mission?"

"My mission obviously failed."

"Not yet, but it will if we don't *try*! We still have time before the auction starts."

"This place is too secure to escape without help from more members. Even if that weren't the case, I don't have any weapons, and I'm not exactly in any shape for hand-to-hand combat."

"Let me take care of it. Just tell me what to do." I'm begging at this point, but manage to keep the tears at bay. One emotion after another crashes over me but I hold onto the anger. It's the only thing that keeps me from breaking down. "You saved me. You've protected me… Let me return the favor."

Looking at me, he musters a small smile, but the defeated look in his eyes doesn't fade. I'm furious at him for giving up, but at the same time, I hurt for him. Seeing him so broken and vulnerable makes me want to hold him, to absorb his pain so he doesn't have to bear it. So I do exactly that.

Taking his other hand, I pull as hard as I can to bring him to his feet. He grunts as he stands, gripping my forearms and leaning into me for support. I pull him close, mindful of his wounds, and allow him to put as much of his weight on me as he needs. Wrapping his arms around my waist, he buries his face into my shoulder, soaking my shirt. I imagine all of his hurt seeping into me with each tear that makes contact with the fabric and my skin. In return, I visualize my new-found confidence and strength flowing into him.

"I'm so sorry," he says softly. "I was so sure we were safe."

"It's not your fault," I say, lifting his face to look at me. "You didn't know."

"I didn't tell them anything."

I smile, brushing a lock from his face. "I know. You're strong. And I need you to be strong a little longer, okay?" When he gives me a doubtful look, I reach into my pocket, producing the three syringes. "Eli let me take these. Can they help?"

He plucks one from my palm, turning it over in his fingers as he studies the label. "Tranqs? They could if we can use them on someone with a gun. But even then it's risky."

"So let's take that risk."

He smiles, a real smile—one I've only seen a handful of times but made my soul light up on each rare occasion. "You've come a long way since I first met you." Confidence returns to his eyes. It's diluted, but it's enough for now. "I'm going to need your help. They've been giving me hell the past couple of days."

A couple of days? At least forty-eight hours have been lost from me being sedated, then. They didn't want me awake until the day of the auction in case I tried to make an escape, blind to the fact that they have a resistance leader working right under their noses.

"You look beautiful, by the way," Nixon says. His eyes have dried, and the leader I've come to enjoy being around returns.

Heat rises to my face, and I know he can see it through the makeup I forgot I had on. I move my hand that's not holding the tranqs to the side of his face, wiping away a stray tear with my thumb. Then I pull him in, closing my eyes and pressing my lips to his, and he tightens his arms around me. Electricity pulses through me, tugging at my heart and zapping away the last of the fog in my head. I inhale his scent—that intoxicating smell that's hidden under the sweat and blood and fear. I twist my fingers into his hair, savoring the moment, his taste, and the movement of his mouth against mine.

I want to stay like this forever. I want the rest of the world to melt away like it did the nights I stayed up talking with him in the basement, but there's too much danger buzzing around us at the moment. We have another escape to make. But we'll have this chance again soon, some place safe where I can fully immerse myself in him, and I don't care who finds out.

I reluctantly break the kiss. "Let's get out of here."

25. Speak Soft

We slink through the quiet halls, constantly surveying our surroundings. With one of his arms draped over my shoulders and my arm around his waist, Nixon leans into me with every clumsy step. As we continue to move, he's able to support himself more and more but still has to rely on me for some support. The wounds on his back make it difficult for him to stand up straight, so he has to slouch forward, making it a challenge to maneuver swiftly through the labyrinth.

He says there's a loading dock similar to TCG's on the bottom level of the facility, where food and medical supplies are brought in. If we can make it down there, we'll sneak into one of the trucks as it finishes loading and we'll be free. When the truck stops again, we'll find our way to one of the few safehouses here in the Red Zone.

When Nixon went over the last-minute plan, I asked if he's been here before since he's so familiar with how everything works. He hasn't, but before he became the Green Zone's leader, he was required to study the layout of this entire facility. It's used for the Elite Auction and the Red Zone's re-education, among other things. As far as Nixon knows, Eli is the only resistance member who works here, masquerading as an Elite with his many different personas—from nurse to soldier and nearly everything in between. Like Nixon, he has forged documents and identification to conceal his true identity and enter nearly any facility and zone without being questioned.

Nixon and I stay close to the wall, prepared to dive into the closest unlocked room if needed. We move as quickly as possible with his injuries, but I wish we could go faster. No matter how much strength he gains in his legs as we walk, it doesn't feel like enough. I'm desperate to get out, for us to be safe again because, for a while, we were.

"There," Nixon says, pointing to the metal door ahead. His fingers are curled around one of the tranqs, prepared to strike if anyone crosses our path. A second one is secured in his pocket, and I'm holding the third, praying I don't actually have to use it. I know it won't kill anyone, but it's close enough to make me uncomfortable. If the moment comes, though, I hope I'm able to do whatever is necessary to protect Nixon and myself.

We push against the silver bar; the heavy door opens, and we enter the dimly lit stairwell. I flinch when the door automatically slams, echoing throughout the endless concrete space. I almost expect someone to come barreling toward us from one of the other levels, weapon ready, but no one does.

I start my descent to the next floor, but Nixon pulls me back.

"Wait," he whispers. Sliding his arm off my shoulders, he passes the syringe to his left hand and grips the paint-chipped railing on the wall. He descends cautiously, motioning for me to stay where I am, and pauses on the fifth step down. Glancing over the opposite side, he checks the platform beneath us. Seeing that it's clear, he reaches out for me behind him, momentarily taking me back to the night of the search at Adam and Lacey's. Stepping down, I grab his hand and he leads the way.

At the bottom of the second set of stairs is a door identical to the one we came through with a faded sign above it. *Level three*. We take each step carefully, hardly putting any weight behind our footfalls.

The heel of my boot scuffs against one of the steps, sending a brief wave of panic over me as the scraping sound penetrates the air.

A man's muffled voice cuts through the silence, followed by static. Through the small window on the door, I make out a guard heading toward the stairwell, completely unaware of our presence. At least ten feet from the door, he's looking around as he talks into his walkie-talkie. Nixon drags me down the remaining couple of steps, pushing my back against the wall and flattening himself beside me. I'm closest to the door, hopefully far enough away it won't crush me if it's opened.

"Now's your chance to help," Nixon whispers, removing the cap from the needle.

"How?" I ask, but I don't get an answer.

The door screeches as the bar is pressed in, and it's pushed open a few inches. The man pauses with one foot in the stairwell, says something about a disturbance on the first floor, and awaits a response from his walkie-talkie. I glance at Nixon, who has his eyes locked on the door, syringe raised and ready. Adrenaline floods my body, pumping furiously as if trying to escape. We can't run. He'll call for backup, and neither Nixon nor I are in any shape to fight off a throng of armed guards.

The voice in the walkie-talkie responds, clearing the guard to continue down to the first level, and the guard pushes the door all the way open, stepping into view. Before I can even think about my next move, I'm against him. With all of my weight, I slam him into the wall beside the door and he yells. One of his hands makes contact with the concrete, preventing his face from slamming into it, and the other instinctively reaches for the gun on his hip. His meaty fingers are fumbling with the holster when Nixon's hand comes into my line of vision, plunging the needle into the man's neck and pulling me back.

The guard lets out another yell and tries to extract the syringe that's still in his neck. Falling forward, his limp body slides to the floor, and Nixon is quick to loot him.

"Good job," he says, standing up and adjusting the volume of the walkie-talkie. He passes it to me, tucks the gun in his waistband,

and removes a pair of handcuffs from the guard's belt. "Help me out."
He grabs one of the guard's arms and motions for me to take the other.

Together, we drag the body to the railing across from the door.

"You trusted me to help you?" I ask, stepping away from the body.

Nixon secures one of the cuffs to the pole and the other around the guard's wrist, making it as tight as possible. "Of course I did."

"I mean, why didn't you tell me what to do? I could've got us caught… or killed."

He pulls the gun back out, scanning the area before we move on. "If I always tell you what to do, you won't learn for yourself. You acted instinctively, which you need to continue to do."

I've never attacked anyone before, much less someone who works for the Society, and while it was probably nothing compared to what those in the resistance have done, it was a big deal for me. I'm not a fighter—Liam received that gene—and I don't want to turn into one either. I want to help and protect those I care about, which now includes Nixon, while holding on to the peaceful nature I've always been praised for.

We continue our descent, listening for any voices or footsteps. My adrenaline rush is still raging and I embrace it, welcoming the burst of energy that comes with it. Nixon must feel it, too, because he isn't leaning as heavily on me or the rail on the stairs and is moving at a quicker pace.

Stopping by the door on the second level, Nixon inconspicuously peeks through the window, checking for any guards or nurses potentially heading for the stairwell. The walkie-talkie has been mostly quiet and whatever does come through isn't of any value to us—guard needed at the front door, patient needs another dose of medication, doctor needed on level six.

"That tracker in your arm," Nixon says, pulling away from the door, "we'll have to get it out as soon as we make it out of here." He starts down the next flight of stairs, gun out in front of him. "They're not activated until you're purchased, but the Society can turn it on at any time if there's an issue."

I run my thumb along the stitches, having completely forgotten about the tracker. The area stings when touched. "Do you think they've turned it on already?"

"Not likely. From the silence on the walkie-talkie, it doesn't sound like they've started the auction yet. Did Eli say anything else to you?"

We're on the platform halfway between the first and second floor, pressed against the wall. Just ten more steps and we'll only be a few feet from the door. Since it's the main level, I suspect there will be increased activity and a plethora of obstacles and enemies for us to avoid. We have a weapon now and two tranqs left, but we'd still be easily overpowered if there was an altercation.

"Not really," I say. "Just that the guards are preoccupied and I had about thirty minutes before they started rounding up prisoners."

Nixon chuckles. "I have a feeling he had something to do with whatever 'disturbance' is down here." Slowly, we take the final flight of stairs. "Stay close and be careful."

Between distracting the guards and giving me the tools needed to rescue Nixon, I realize that Eli's helped tremendously. Even after vaguely admitting to being in the resistance, he didn't directly tell me how to go about escaping or finding Nixon. I guess that, like Nixon, he wanted me to figure it out on my own by trusting my instincts and using whatever tools were at my disposal. At the time, it frustrated me. Vagueness and unanswered questions are what I've been battling since being taken, and all I wanted was a straightforward answer. Now, I appreciate what he did. Hopefully I'll be able to build on it.

One final time, we flatten ourselves against the wall beside the door, Nixon closest to it this time. On the other side of this portal is a short journey to freedom. The loading dock is at the back of the facility, and this entryway should put us somewhere in the middle, bypassing the guards at the very front.

The walkie-talkie crackles and a female voice comes through, saying something about three more escapees making it out the front door and needing all able bodies on the main level. More guards mean we're more likely to be seen. Whatever distraction Eli contributed to better be good enough to hold their attention if we want to make it out of here.

I look to Nixon, wondering if he's thinking the same thing. His eyes are glued to the window, and I can't peer around him to see what he's looking at. Whatever it is, it has his full attention, because he doesn't react to the details from the faceless woman and he's reaching for the second tranq in his pocket. With the gun still clutched in his other hand, he pulls the cap from the needle off with his teeth and spits it onto the ground.

Someone bursts through the door and Nixon reacts without hesitation, sticking the person in the neck. A boy, maybe a couple years younger than me, collapses into the stairwell, and Nixon catches him before he hits the floor. Dragging him to the wall beside the stairs, Nixon sets him down gently while suppressing a laugh.

"What's so funny?" I ask. "And who the hell is that?"

The boy isn't dressed in any sort of uniform, nor does he look remotely old enough to hold any kind of position here. He's wearing sweatpants and a plain black T-shirt, and on the inside of his arm where his sleeve is rolled up there's a string of numbers etched into his skin.

"This is Eli's diversion," Nixon says. "He let out all of the psych patients."

"That's… actually really smart." While guards and nurses are occupied with rounding up their runaway patients, we can slip past them. But looking at the boy on the floor, I feel bad. Naomi is locked up in a place similar to this in the Green Zone, wrongfully accused of being crazy with no discharge date in sight. How many people are facing the same thing here? And how did they threaten the Enlightened Society?

The door swings open again, this time revealing a guard who's likely searching for the now-unconscious boy, and his mouth falls open when he sees us. Nixon raises his gun, but before he can shoot, the guard grabs me by my left arm, positioning me in front of him. Hand trembling, I flick the cap off the last tranq with my thumb. Keeping his gun trained on my attacker, Nixon's gaze briefly settles on the tranq in my hand. His eyes tighten as they quickly meet mine, and I know he's giving me his approval.

"Drop the weapon!" the guard barks, wrenching the walkie-talkie from my hand. Pressing the button on the side, he says, "This is Officer Sh—"

With a deep breath, I swing my right arm down, thrusting the needle into his thigh. He lets out a cry as I jam my thumb against the plunger, dropping the walkie-talkie.

"You bitch!" he slurs, grabbing his leg and crumpling to the floor. His head strikes the concrete, and I instinctively step forward to check if he's okay.

Conflicting thoughts fight their way through my head, but one rings louder than the rest: *I hurt someone.* I know it was to protect us and the outcome is better than if Nixon had fired the gun, but the guilt is a weight I can't lift from my mind. I reach out to the guard, wanting to at least make sure there's no major head injury, but Nixon gently pulls me back by my elbow.

"He'll be fine," he says, stepping in front of me and swiping the gun from the holster. "You did great."

But I feel like I did something wrong. How can Nixon or anyone else in the resistance do this without it eating them up inside?

Nixon shoves the second gun into my shaking hands. "We have to go. There'll be more."

I stare at the weapon, intimidated by its deadly nature. Its only purpose is to kill, and through all of the uncertainty, I know that's the one thing I'm not capable of. "I've… I've never shot one before."

He's at the door, peeping through the window. "Aim at anyone who's a threat and pull the trigger."

"I can't."

"Just try your best. I'll be with you the whole time."

I move toward him, gripping the handle of the gun, pointing it at the floor and keeping my finger off the trigger like I saw Liam do once.

"It looks clear," he says, "but they won't be distracted forever. We're going to run. Stay right behind me, okay?"

"But you're hurt."

"I'll be fine." He looks at me, his eyes serious and face tight. Sweat beads his hairline. "Ready?"

I manage a nod, although I'm the furthest thing from ready. Pushing open the door, he scans the area one more time before we emerge, entering a tiny, dead-end hall with two elevators on the wall across from us. There's yelling and orders being shouted from some other part of the building. No one is in sight, but the voices are close enough to us to heighten the fear of being caught.

We run, or more like jog, taking a right out of the hall. I stay on Nixon's heels, and while keeping my gaze on him brings me some sense of comfort, I force myself to scan my surroundings. Our boots pound against the tiles. My legs are unsteady from the anxiety pumping through me, but I push myself to keep going, willing them to carry me just a little farther.

We take a left, passing through metal double doors. Using my fear as fuel, I know I could probably go faster, but I refuse to leave Nixon behind. He has to be just as terrified as I am—even if he doesn't show it—and his injuries and exhaustion probably don't help. A young nurse pops out of one of the rooms as we approach, and her eyes widen. Nixon spares her a passing glance but doesn't react, and I do the same. She disappears back into the room she came from without speaking a word to us, and I pick up my pace to jog beside Nixon.

"You didn't shoot her," I say between breaths.

"Not a threat," he responds. "But the guards she's about to call will be."

The ammonia-filled air burns my nose as we push ourselves farther. The rooms become a blur and my vision tunnels. Our freedom is the only thing that matters. Nixon stays ahead of me by half a step, and I follow every move he makes, breathe with every breath he takes. My heart is beating so quickly I can hear the blood rushing through my veins, roaring in my ears. The echoes of voices murmur around us, and we race through a maze past murky figures, with only Nixon's memory serving as our map.

Turning a corner, a guard materializes, blocking our path and shouting into his walkie-talkie. Without the slightest bit of hesitation, Nixon raises his gun, aims, and fires. Screams of bystanders are drowned out by the deafening sound, then both are replaced by an overwhelming ringing. The guard clutches his neck, crimson spilling out between his fingers, and drops to his knees. I'm automatically reminded of the murdered men who were originally escorting me to the Red Zone and what the resistance does.

They kill.

I haven't seen Nixon do it firsthand until now, and I'm afraid. Not of him necessarily. Or maybe I am, because it reinforces the fact that I don't truly know what he's capable of. The Enlightened Society kills, too, but unlike them, the resistance does it to protect people. This is all to protect me.

Nixon looks over his shoulder and spins around. One. Two. Three more shots. Then his hand is in mine, jerking me forward, and we run faster. More double doors. More identical hallways. Everything looks the same, and if I didn't trust him completely, I would think we were running in circles.

We make another left, then a right, and are met with four guards perfectly spaced out to block our path. Their weapons are drawn, but they don't shoot and I know they won't. There's too much money in me, and if they wanted to kill Nixon, they would've done it by now.

Nixon comes to a halt, forcing me to stop with him. I squeeze his hand with all of the strength I can manage, thinking a message that I hope he understands through my gesture: *No matter what, I'm not leaving you.*

I glance over my shoulder, spotting two more guards who haven't bothered to pull out their weapons but have their hands on their holsters just in case.

"Drop your weapons and release the girl!" one of the guards in front of us demands.

I tighten my fingers around my own gun without any intention of using it, but not willing to let it go either.

"Ms. Clearson," the guard to the far left says, taking a small step forward, "we're here to help you. Step away from him, and we can get you somewhere safe."

Out of spite, Nixon pulls me closer to him—our hips touching—and raises his gun at the man who stepped forward.

"Drop the gun or we'll shoot!" the angry one shouts.

Nixon chuckles. "No you won't." And he pulls the trigger, sending a bullet straight between the friendlier guard's eyes.

Chaos ensues as the five remaining guards barrel toward us. Hands grab me, ripping me away from Nixon, and somewhere in between being grabbed and Nixon releasing my hand, two shots are fired. One guard goes down. Another curses, instinctively grabbing his bleeding arm but pushing forward.

Able to wriggle from my attacker's grasp just enough to turn and face him, I swing the hand my gun is in with all of my strength. It collides with his temple and I'm free from his hold on me. He stumbles back, and I strike him again in the same spot, sending him to the floor. I don't think about it, I just act. My brain is on autopilot, telling me when to duck, when to hit, when to move. Rhythmic gunshots magnify the feeling of fear and vulnerability. One more blow to the guard on the floor, just to be sure, and I turn around to the pandemonium behind me.

Bullet casings litter the blood-spattered tiles. Out of the six total guards, only one remains conscious. He has Nixon pinned down on his stomach with a knee on his neck, forcing his head down. One of the guard's hands holds Nixon's wrist behind his back as he fumbles with the handcuffs on his belt. With his face toward me, Nixon struggles against the officer's weight, using the hand beneath him in an attempt to push himself up. It only results in the knee digging deeper into his neck, and he winces, letting out a grunt.

Working separately from my own will, my arm slowly rises, pointing the gun at the guard with a trembling hand.

"Let him go," I say, surprised at the steadiness of my voice despite the shaking of my entire body.

The guard instinctively glances at me, not paying me much attention at first, and then does a double-take. Dropping his hand from his belt, he rises to his feet, pressing one of his boots between Nixon's shoulder blades.

"*Fuck!*" Nixon yells, squeezing his eyes shut. Some of the lacerations that had already scabbed over break open, and the guard applies more pressure, smiling as if getting some sort of sick pleasure from hurting him.

"You're not going to use that," the guard sneers. He swipes at the gun, but I back up before he's able to make contact with it. He chuckles, applying more pressure to Nixon's back before stepping off him and slamming his boot against his side. Nixon cries out, rolling over and clutching his ribs.

"Hand it over, little girl," the guard says. "You don't want to get more involved in this than you already have."

He takes a step forward, towering over me. My heart frantically thumps against my chest with every surge of panic. But he's stepped away from Nixon and is focusing on me instead, which is good. He blocks my view of Nixon, and I silently beg him to get up.

"Let us go," I say, "and you won't get hurt."

Bringing my other hand up, I squeeze the handle with all of my might. My index finger barely skims the trigger, and a spark of terror shoots through me.

He laughs again and grabs one of my wrists, bending it back. I yelp, but keep my right hand secure on the weapon. With one long stride, I close the gap between us and press the muzzle into his diaphragm, burying it against the indentation that's already in his body armor.

"I know your kind," he says. "You and I both know you won't pull that trigger." He forces my wrist farther than I thought was possible, causing searing pain to shoot up my arms, and my legs unwillingly collapse beneath me. Landing on my knees, I use my right hand to steady myself, removing my finger from the trigger just before the gun hits the tile. Tears well up in my eyes from the pain that radiates up my arm, but he doesn't let up.

Just as he reaches down to wrench the gun out of my weakened grip, Nixon says, "Hey, asshole."

The guard lets go of me, spinning around to look at the new threat. While he's distracted, I scramble to my feet, stumbling away from the man. I'm only a couple inches away when the first shot is fired, and when I turn to look, a second shot rings.

Cradling the side that was kicked, Nixon lowers his gun. Drops of blood dot his torso, and I can't tell if it's his or not. The guard is on his back with blood spilling from the wounds in his head and chest. I'm frozen in place, my eyes darting back and forth between the two of them, then venturing out to the five other bodies strewn throughout the hall.

My breathing quickens, and no matter how deep I inhale, I feel like I'm not getting enough air. Nixon stumbles toward me. Resting his arm over my shoulders again, he guides me away from the massacred men. We make it down one more hallway before he stops, opening one of the doors absent of a window and pulling me inside a small office with a dented metal desk and two metal folding chairs across from it.

Locking the door behind us, I help him across the room, and with assistance from me and the support of the desk beside him, he lowers himself into one of the chairs.

Grimacing, he wraps an arm around himself, sets the gun aside, and says, "Just give me a minute and we can keep going. We're almost there."

"I'm so sorry," I say through gasping breaths. My voice is recognizable again, though uneven and frightened. "I couldn't do it... I couldn't shoot. I tried."

He entwines his fingers with mine, bringing the back of my hand to his lips. "It's okay. I never want you to have to actually kill someone. It changes you. There's no coming back from it."

The day Nixon saved me—when I hated him with every fiber of my being and hit him with unfair questions and accusations—I didn't understand why he'd killed the Black Hats whose custody I was in. Having just learned that Liam was part of his group, my biggest concern was that Liam was running around killing people, too. But now I know that my brother has never been put in that position, and hopefully never will be. Nixon bears that burden, not only for me, but for all his members whenever possible.

"I'm sorry you had to witness all of that," he says. "I know that's hard enough to process."

"How bad is it?" I ask, nodding at his side.

"Kinda hurts to walk… and breathe."

"Do you have a place in mind for us to get help?"

"Would I be doing all of this if I didn't?" Clutching the edge of the desk, Nixon pulls himself to his feet and picks up the gun. "We'll take a right at the end of this hall. The entrance to the loading dock will be at the very back, but we're close. Five minutes, maybe."

I pull his arm over my shoulders and wrap my arm around his lower back, feeling his drying blood against my skin. I push back my concern for now; there'll be plenty of time to worry soon. We hobble to the door, and Nixon has to put more of his weight on me than he did earlier. I brace myself against him, thankful we don't have much longer to go. I want to do anything I can to help him, but I'm weak myself. The high from the adrenaline is quickly wearing off, and I'm certain I'll crash soon.

In the hall, it's quiet, and I force myself not to stare too long at the bodies and blood that have yet to be cleaned. Once more, our steps are in sync, creeping through the labyrinth. When we take the right like Nixon said, he tells me we have to run. I begin to protest, saying he can't in his condition, but he insists he'll be fine as long as he holds on to me.

So we run. Awkwardly, clumsily, but running nonetheless. The very back wall has a single door with a red and white sign that reads *AUTHORIZED PERSONNEL ONLY*. The finish line is right in front of us, and all we have to do is run. But I feel like I'm in one of those dreams where you run and run as fast as you possibly can, pushing your body to the point of exhaustion, only to be moving at the pace of a snail.

We're getting closer, I know we are, but the space between us and the door isn't shrinking fast enough. Impatience creeps up, probably a byproduct of the impending adrenaline crash. My entire body is sore. Nixon's weight increasingly becomes more difficult to support, but I refuse to let him go.

Ten feet away. What sounds like a vehicle door slams on the other side of this portal to freedom. I can almost smell the exhaust from the trucks.

Five feet. Voices come from the other side of the door. We'll have to be quick jumping into the truck. But we can do it. We'll find Liam and Addison and continue with our exodus from the Northern Unity.

Nixon presses down on the handle, heaving the door open, and my world crumbles around me.

"Going somewhere?" the soldier on the other side asks.

Two more soldiers push their way past him. Nixon and I are grabbed from behind, and handcuffs clinch around our wrists.

"I applaud you for your attempt," the soldier says to Nixon. "I'm genuinely surprised you've made it this far, but you didn't really think you'd get out, did you?" His eyes snap to the guards behind us. "Get them to the auction. We've kept everyone waiting long enough."

We're dragged away, backtracking through the entire facility. Nixon struggles to keep up, and his captor shoves him forward a couple of times, nearly making him lose his footing. I sink my teeth into my tongue until a metallic taste floods my mouth to keep from screaming at the guard.

We're ushered through the halls filled with throngs of onlookers, but I can't tear my eyes from Nixon. Nothing else matters—not these people or this place or what's awaiting us. I'm convinced that as long as I'm looking at him, nothing bad will happen. He's been my safety this entire time. He's always found a way around whatever obstacles we've faced together. This is no different. The stakes are higher, but the amount of faith I have in him is stronger. One way or another, we will get out. He steals a few glances at me, too, but the defeat has settled into his eyes again.

Don't give up, I think. *Not now.*

In a section of the building Nixon and I haven't been through, an armed police officer comes into view, and from the patch on his shoulder, I know he's the Police Chief from the Yellow Zone. At least they selected him to work this auction instead of Addison's dad. The officer steps aside, opening one of the double black doors, and our guards propel us through into the void.

The door slams behind us, and we're locked in a stiflingly hot room without any source of light. Anxious whispers and murmurs buzz in the thick air around us, but I can't tell how many more prisoners are in here. My eyes can't adjust to this level of darkness, but I still squint through it in search of Nixon.

Someone presses against my side and my cuffs clink against another pair as two fingers find their way into my palm.

"I'm here," Nixon whispers.

I squeeze his fingers, searching for the comfort I've come to find in his touch. "How do we get out of here?"

A short pause. "We don't."

"What the hell do you—"

"Ivy, there's no way out of this. I can't save us. I'm sorry."

"Please don't say that." I'm crying, even though I've forced myself to remain as strong as possible for him. I know he can hear it in my words and shaky breaths, but I don't care.

"I'll stay with you as long as I can."

I shake my head, letting the tears flow down my face. My chin quivers like a child and I tighten my hand around his fingers, expecting it to soothe me. This isn't fair. Why us? Why the hell did this have to happen to us?

He promised to keep me safe. Over and over he repeated those words and comforted me when I doubted him, when I was scared. I'm scared now, but it's not just about me anymore. I don't know what's going to happen to him or if I'll ever see him again, and that terrifies me far more than whatever is in store for me. He couldn't keep his promise, but I don't blame him for that. Not in the least bit. He tried his best, and we got so damn far.

"Please don't cry," he begs.

"How can you tell me not to cry?"

"Because that's not how I want to remember you."

A wall across the room dissolves, allowing light to pour in. Two soldiers stand at the newly formed exit and I can see that there are four prisoners aside from Nixon and me—two guys and two girls, wearing the exact same thing as me. Like us, their arms are bound behind them. A couple of them look like they've endured their own beatings, but nothing compared to the degree of Nixon's.

As my eyes adjust to the sudden light, I can see that the wall wasn't a wall at all but a curtain, and a glaring stage has opened up before us. A podium is centered at the front and a crowd invisible to me roars with excitement as a man in a suit enters from the other end of the stage. He beams at the applause, relishing it for a few moments as he takes his place behind the podium. Then he raises his hands to silence them.

"Ladies and gentlemen," his voice booms with enthusiasm as disgusting as his picture-perfect smile, "it is my honor to welcome you to our semi-annual Elite Auction!"

The audience comes to life again, but settles down within seconds.

"We have an exciting evening in store for you and a *very* special guest. For those who are joining us for the first time…"

I rip my eyes away from the speaker and focus on Nixon beside me. He's put on the mask that I worked so hard to get him to remove, but underneath it, I know there's the gentle man I know and trust.

He looks at me, whispering another, "I'm sorry," and, "I wish I could save you."

Then he kisses me. In front of the soldiers. In front of the other *participants*. But I don't give a damn about them, so I turn myself to him as well, giving in to the gravitational pull he has on me. I press myself as close to him as possible, concentrating on our hearts beating in sync with one another and the warmth of his bare skin against my thin shirt.

A soldier finally intervenes, tearing us apart and commanding everyone to get in a single-file line. I end up at the very back with Nixon in front of me, giving me a clear view of the wounds on his back.

"…And for those of you who don't win one of our special prizes this time," the speaker continues, "we encourage you to join us just over a month from now for an extraordinary show in the Green Zone. So, without further ado…" He turns to our little room off the stage. "Men, please bring out the participants!"

The line slowly moves forward, and I make sure to stay right on Nixon's heels. Once we're on the stage, we're instructed to face the crowd and the back of the speaker. More soldiers appear out of nowhere, each of them assuming their positions behind us.

The lights are blinding, beaming down on all of us like a hundred suns. The screaming crowd is a sea of faceless apparitions and their cheers reverberate in my bones.

"Now for our first participant," the man announces. "Noah Burnley, please step forward!"

The boy at the far end of the stage breaks away from our line and stands at the front beside the speaker, fearfully glancing around. The announcer calls out the starting bid—an amount far greater than I could imagine ever spending in my lifetime—and the Elites in the audience shout their offers.

I inch closer to Nixon, our elbows brushing. Blocking out the crowd to the best of my ability, I focus on him in my peripheral vision, memorizing his every detail. From his gentle eyes to the scar across his jaw, I permanently etch him into my mind.

"Promise me you'll be strong, Ivy," he whispers. "No matter what happens."

The boy is escorted off the stage, and one of the girls is called up.

My mind weaves in and out of the past and present. Our last major obstacle was our potential separation when Liam and I were supposed to be escaping the Northern Unity—before he actually made it to Adam and Lacey's. I would give anything to go back to that.

The second girl replaces the first, and the crowd—mostly the men—goes insane when she reaches the front of the stage.

The nights Nixon and I spent under the stars, fully aware that we were breaking the rules, play before my eyes. His laugh that made me smile replays in my head.

"Ivy," Nixon whispers, but I can't answer him. Not yet.

My favorite memory of all pushes its way to the front of my mind and I hold it there as long as possible—the night before Liam and Addison arrived. We held each other under the sheets. His tender touch sent a surge of electricity through my veins, and with his arms protectively wrapped around me, my fears melted away. Then my brother finally showed up with my best friend, and while things were tense at first, we all quickly relaxed. We came up with a new plan—a safer plan—for our escape. What went wrong?

The second boy makes his way to the front, leaving us as the final two.

"Ivy, please," Nixon repeats.

"I promise," I whisper back with tears streaming down my face. The makeup I hate must be smeared all over my face. "But you have to promise me the same thing."

"Friends!" the speaker booms as the last participant is escorted off the stage. "I present to you the most remarkable prize of the evening: Nixon Reed, the Green Zone's lead terrorist!"

"I promise," Nixon says. His beautiful, pained eyes bore into mine. He hesitates for a moment, looking as though he wants to say more, then moves to the front of the stage. And I'm left alone with the soldiers, staring at his back, which he keeps straight with his head held high.

The crowd boos and yells slurs, and the speaker raises his hands to silence them once more.

"Calm down, everyone. You'll have your chance to speak your mind to this heinous man in six weeks. Instead of bidding on this criminal, we'll be doing things a little differently." He takes a dramatic pause that seems to last forever, and with every millisecond, I can feel a new fracture in my heart. "In the heart of the Green Zone, we'll be holding a public execution as a punishment for his crimes."

The animals in the audience roar with excitement, cheering for murder by the hands of the Enlightened Society. And just like that, my heart bursts, shattering like glass into millions of tiny, jagged pieces. My insides cave in and my head is pounding. The speaker says something else about a fee for attending the execution, but I can't focus on what he's saying. The room spins violently and my stomach tightens into thousands of knots when it's announced that the auction has ended.

"*No!*" I scream so loud it feels as though my throat rips open.

Nixon spins around to look at me. I lurch forward, but the soldier behind me jerks me back by my arms.

"*Let me fucking go!*" Swinging my leg back, my foot collides with his groin, and he releases me, doubling over. Two more guards materialize beside me. One grabs me under my arms and the other lifts my feet from the floor, and I'm carried off the stage, watching Nixon for as long as I can.

Just before he disappears from my view, he mouths, "I'm sorry."

26. So Long, Goodbye

I've been sitting in this same chair at the same empty table, staring at the same blank walls for what feels like hours. I'm seated beside the door and have a clear view of it when I turn my head to the right. Goosebumps pop up on my arms as the blast of cold air hits me from every angle. No one has come in since they brought me here after the auction. They've left me with my fragmented thoughts and the events that unfolded earlier. Nixon's expression, full of pain and guilt, is stamped in my mind.

He'll be publicly executed back home, and everyone will gather to witness and to cheer for his murder at the hands of our government. The Green Zone's resistance group will witness their leader taking his last breaths. Piper will lose her brother soon after possibly losing her parents. I doubt I'll be able to attend, but I would give anything to be there. If not to save him, then to be one of the last faces he sees during his final moments.

While sitting in this hideously quiet room, I've tried countless times to find a reason as to why I wasn't called. No bids were cast for me. The whole point of my mother selling me was to participate in the Elite Auction. I fled the Green Zone—and almost the Northern Unity—with Nixon to avoid what had already been arranged for me. I was at the auction, watching everyone else be purchased—or in Nixon's case, given a death sentence—but nothing was decided for me. I'm not sure if I should be grateful or scared.

Grief and anger take the form of a flame, burning as one in the pit of my stomach. It heats my body from the inside out, consuming my entire being. If my hands weren't cuffed behind the back of the chair, I could hit something—the table, the wall, it doesn't matter. Anything to release even a drop of what I'm feeling.

The door opens and a man enters, taking a seat in the office chair diagonal to me. Wearing dark jeans and a button-up shirt, he doesn't look like everyone else I've seen here. He looks young—late twenties if I had to guess, thirty at the most. Leaning back in the chair and plopping a legal pad, pen, and folder on the table, he studies me for a moment, offering what seems like it should be a friendly smile. I narrow my eyes at him in response, imagining the fire inside me wrapping itself around him until he's nothing but ash.

"How are you doing, Olivia?" he asks, rearranging his belongings. The legal pad goes on top of the folder and the pen on top of that. "Or would you rather I call you 'Ivy'?"

"Only my friends call me Ivy," I lie.

"Okay. Well, you're here because I need you to help me figure some things out. Do you think you can do that?"

Rolling my eyes, I shift my gaze to the back wall that I've been staring at since being here. The only help they want involves ratting out other resistance members, and although I only know a few, I refuse to do that. I'll never turn on the people who risked their own lives to save mine, even if the mission was a failure. Liam is in that group, and while I don't know where he is or if he's safe, I don't want to risk him being found out. I want to believe he's safe, lying low until this blows over and he's able to return to his normal life. It hurts to think that he and Addison would leave us in a time of crisis, but I know that when you're in the resistance, your main focus is surviving. Everything else is an afterthought, and it wouldn't have been beneficial if the two of them were captured alongside us.

"Those look uncomfortable," the man says. "Let me take them off for you." Standing, he reaches behind me with a key in hand. The cuffs come off, clanking against the table as he returns to the chair.

Keeping my eyes forward, I cross my arms, attempting to shield myself against the unusually frigid air.

"Tell me about the day you were kidnapped," he says. It's a command, but he says it more like a suggestion.

"You mean by the Enlightened Society?"

"By the terrorist."

I turn to him, forcing an overly sweet smile. "Sorry, I don't recall encountering any terrorists... other than the Black Hats."

He sighs, running his fingers through his curly black hair. Setting the pen down, he rests his hands on the table, palms up. "I'm just trying to help you out here. I know you've been through a lot, and sometimes when you endure an immense amount of stress, you don't think things through clearly. I've seen many people go through what you have—a terrorist kidnaps a pretty girl like yourself, promises to keep you safe from an imaginary danger, maybe even hints at the possibility of a romantic relationship. It's all a manipulation tactic, but we've been able to help many recover. You're lucky our men came when they did."

I nearly laugh. "You're delusional if you honestly believe that. I was safe after I *willingly* went with him." That's mostly true. I wasn't exactly willing at first, but I slowly began to accept what Nixon was telling me. He gave me plenty of chances to leave from the very beginning and I never took them, even when I was still doubtful. As a girl who blindly followed what I was told, part of me was still hungry to know what secrets were buried beneath the foundation of our perfect world.

"Safe how?" he asks, leaning forward.

"I just was."

"Was there an end in sight? He must've told you what was to come of all this. You seem like a smart girl—perfect grades, daughter of the Green Zone's former Police Chief. I find it hard to believe you'd live your life on the run with someone you hardly know."

"He promised I'd be safe from people like you."

Plucking his pen from the table, he jots that down. "Did you have any contact with him or any other terrorists prior to this incident?"

Closing my eyes, I let out a long breath. "No."

They don't know about Liam or the role Addison has played. Good. I refrain from asking about them. As much as I need to know they're okay, I'm not going to offer any information that could incriminate them. If they're safe, that's all that matters. We'll cross paths again one day.

"What possessed you to trust him?" he asks. "Did he threaten you? Your family maybe?"

"No." When I open my eyes, he's angled toward me with one leg resting on top of the other. "I told you, he promised to keep me safe. I already had my own negative feelings toward the Society."

"Did he ever mention your father?"

His question gives me pause, and I run all possible answers through my reeling mind. There's no harm in confirming that Nixon briefly brought up my dad so long as I omit the part about attempting to help Liam find him. But confirming such a thing could paint Nixon as guilty of something they may only have a suspicion of. I don't know how much they know about him, and I'm already dancing around these questions as much as I can.

The speaker at the auction identified Nixon as the lead terrorist of the Green Zone, but as far as I know, they haven't captured any of his members. Surely Eli would have relayed that information to him if it had happened.

I would assume the Society thinks Nixon works alone, but after the incident with Kase, I know that can't be true. Kase must have told them something more than he let on, and turning in his friend and comrade was an easy pass to freedom. I hope Piper gave him what he deserves.

"No," I lie.

The interrogator raises an eyebrow. "Not at all?"

I wipe my palms against my pants. "What does my dad have to do with any of this? He's gone."

Leaning back again, he taps his pen against the pad of paper, fixing his eyes on the few vague notes scribbled between the lines. "I knew your father. We met a few times when he came up here for our semi-annual meetings. He was a good man." As if just remembering a key piece of information, he adds something to his notes. "Did you ever wonder what happened to him?"

"Yes," I say through gritted teeth. The anger overpowers the grief at this point. My dad wasn't the perfect man I always believed him to be, but I don't want him brought into this. I want to preserve what positive memories I have of him. With my hands free, I'm tempted to reach over the corner of the table that separates us and strangle the interrogator. Knowing there are probably guards waiting on the other side of the door in case of an altercation, I clench my fists instead. "But my family and I were never told anything."

He nods slowly. "After the two of you were arrested in the Blue Zone, we dispatched a team to your kidnapper's house. They searched for ties to any other potential terrorists and clues as to what he was planning to do next. There wasn't much, unfortunately—he's good at covering his tracks—but enough for us to make assumptions."

I resist the urge to smile. Nixon's smart and tactical—there's no way he'd leave anything behind for someone to find. Assumptions aren't concrete enough. They need actual evidence.

The two of us were arrested, meaning Liam and Addison got away. But that leaves Adam and Lacey. Neither of them have been mentioned, but I know they were home, and the Black Hats must have torn the place apart.

"Then they got to the basement," the interrogator continues. "A portion of the floor wasn't level with the rest, so they tore it up under the impression there was something underneath." He plants his other foot back on the floor and folds his hands between his legs. "Our team found remains of a body beneath that basement. After running some tests, we were able to confirm that it's Officer Benjamin Clearson."

His words are daggers that slash through my heart. My dad isn't dead. He can't be. I may not know where he went, but this can't be true.

The interrogator pushes the notepad aside and opens the folder. The first page contains generic information about my dad and his career with a picture of him in uniform paperclipped to it. Beside his picture is a side profile of Nixon, and my chest tightens. It was obviously taken without his knowledge. The camera is zoomed in on him from the shoulders up and he's smiling, focusing on something ahead of him. It's an older picture—maybe from a year or two ago. I can tell by the length of his hair, which barely touches the tops of his shoulders. How long have they been watching him?

"The little evidence we were able to find did raise concern." The interrogator pulls a few pages from the center of the pile and sets them in front of me. "These are just some of the documents found in Nixon's home pertaining to your father, dating back to his early days as an officer. We came to the conclusion that he was targeting him before his murder. Whether or not he worked alone, we don't know yet."

With trembling fingers, I flip through the papers. I attempt to skim through the information—some I already know—but am unable to focus. Crisp, black letters merge into one another, forming new words that appear foreign. My stomach churns, threatening to spill what little food I ate earlier.

This can't be happening, I think. *This isn't real. None of this is real.* This room, these files, the auction, being taken from my home—I want to believe it was all imagined. It's a prolonged nightmare that I need to wake up from. If I can just wake up, I'll be home, in bed, with Liam's snoring echoing through the apartment. And I'll sip tea with Mom— the Mom who loves me—in the kitchen that she always keeps immaculate on one of our days off from work. If only I could wake myself up.

But there are parts of this nightmare that are beautiful. Pieces I want to hold on to forever...

"I know this isn't what you wanted to hear," the interrogator says, "but—"

"You're lying!" I say, snapping my eyes to him.

Sympathy flashes in his eyes. Is that authentic, or has he been trained to do that? "I wish I were, but the evidence is all here." He taps a finger against the remaining contents of the folder. "We have photographs from the crime scene, if you want to see for yourself. Although I must warn you, it may be traumatizing to see your father in this state."

The fire inside me is extinguished. Grief overpowers rage now, leaving me empty and cold. It's an emptiness I've never felt before—bottomless, an entity wanting to swallow me whole. It creeps through my veins like a virus, wringing all hope from my spirit with its icy fingers. Pressure builds in my head. I want to cry but my tears have dried up.

Nixon told me he had no idea what happened to my dad. He and Liam looked into his disappearance without any luck. What they did find was that he played a part in the Elite Auction. Nixon wouldn't lie to me. As he said himself, what reason would he have for lying? It took a while, but I finally learned to trust him.

He's not a murderer. In our short time together, I learned more about him than anyone else outside of his family. He's a resistance leader, someone who sees the world for what it truly is and has dedicated his life to fighting it. But he's also gentle and compassionate. Protecting those he's close to is his number one priority. He's not capable of something like this.

Yes, he's killed people, but only when he had to. It was never in cold blood. The guards who cornered us, the Black Hats who took me, and however many others there are who lost their lives to him—they were all corrupt, working for a sinister organization that preys on its people.

My dad was one of them, though. He directly contributed to the auction in some way while running the Green Zone's police department. He was exactly the type of person the resistance targets. And Nixon appeared in the Green Zone just six months before his disappearance.

But Nixon and Liam met on Nixon's third day there and they quickly became friends. Liam hasn't been part of the resistance very long, but he must have told Nixon who our dad was when he was still with us. All else aside, I know how much Nixon cares for my brother. He wouldn't murder our dad, then look into his disappearance for him.

The documents in front of me are dated, but that doesn't tell me when Nixon was able to obtain them. Considering the work my dad did, I assume the Commander wanted Nixon to keep an eye on him as soon as he switched zones, but Nixon made it sound like he dug deeper only after Liam asked for help. I don't know which documents were obtained before his disappearance and which were taken later. If Liam were here, he'd be able to confirm it for me. He'd be able to explain how long Nixon knew about our dad's dark side and how long the resistance was keeping tabs on him.

"Why are you telling me all of this?" I ask. "Why now?"

"Closure," the interrogator says matter-of-factly. "Tying up loose ends from your old life will help you with your transition."

"Transition? I wasn't auctioned."

"No, but you did have a private buyer." He takes the documents from in front of me and flips through the folder until he finds their place.

There was no reason for me to be at the auction, then. I've already been paid for, but they still forced me into that auditorium for no other reason than for me to hear what penalty Nixon would face.

Closing the folder, he places the notepad on top again. "You don't have to defend him. If you let us, we can help you. You'll be going to a nice home with a very wealthy family. Your life can only get better from here. Rest assured, in a few short weeks, that boy won't be able to hurt you again."

"He never hurt me!"

He's about to say something else when there's a light knock on the door. Another man pops his head in and says, "They're ready, sir."

"Perfect," the interrogator says. "We'll be out in a moment."

"Why a private buyer?" I ask when we're alone again. That kind of thing was never mentioned when I learned about the auction. This, along with the trackers and Transitional Adaptation course, is all new to me. It was impossible for me and Nixon to peel back every layer of the Society when our main focus was getting out of the Northern

Unity, but potential private buyers surely should have been something worth mentioning.

"Our VIPs get an early peek at the participants as soon as they're sold to us," the interrogator explains. "You were purchased just an hour after you were listed, which is impressive. Even after your kidnapping, your buyer was persistent on safely retrieving you."

"But why? What does he want with me?"

Clicking the pen, he tucks it in his breast pocket. "We aren't informed of the reasons behind the buyers' purchases, Ms. Clearson. They're ready for you, but if you have any information that can help us, this is your final chance to tell me. Do it for your father."

"I'm not telling you anything."

I don't want to believe my father is dead, let alone that Nixon was the one to kill him. The photos of his body and possibly the crime scene are in the folder an arm's length from me, but I can't bring myself to look at them. Regardless of what he did in his time with the police force, I want to remember him the way I always knew him. Likewise, since he was involved with the sinister side of the Society, I have no desire to avenge his death either.

Chuckling, the man stands and swipes the handcuffs from the table. He moves behind me, jerking me to my feet and forcing my hands behind my back. "I suggest you leave whatever life you thought you had with that terrorist behind," he says, fastening the cuffs on my wrists a little too tight. "I promise, you mean *nothing* to him. Those kinds of people only care about themselves. The sooner you realize that, the better."

With a hand secure on my arm, he guides me out of the interrogation room, through a slightly larger room where three guards are standing by, and the bright hallway opens up to me once more. The facility buzzes with increased activity now that the auction is over. Doctors and nurses bounce from room to room. Guards usher other cuffed prisoners to their own destinations, grumbling orders and shoving those who drag their feet.

As we wind through the halls and rooms that open up for us, I feel as though everyone is staring at me. Eyes look me up and down as I'm escorted. Some are quick, curious glances, but others look longer and harder, dissecting me with their gaze. One prisoner in particular holds my gaze as we approach each other from opposite ends of the hall. Her dark eyes narrow at me, growing fiercer as we get closer, and just as we pass by each other, she mutters something that makes me both angry and sick.

"Traitor."

I've never seen her before, but am automatically inclined to spin around and defend myself against her accusation. In no way am I a traitor, and although I don't know her, she seems to know me—or know *of* me—somehow. She has to be involved with the resistance in some way. That's the only reason someone would consider it traitorous to speak with and be escorted out by an interrogator for the Enlightened Society, and it's only a matter of time until word spreads. Either from other prisoners or through the guards themselves, Nixon will end up knowing. He has to know I'd never do that, though. I'm not Kase. I'm not my mother. I'm confused and torn between what the truth is once again, but I haven't turned on him or the rest of the resistance. After everything I've been through with him and after how much he's helped me, I couldn't.

"I think you'll learn to like your new home," the interrogator says, pushing open one of two glass doors.

Only a handful of stars are visible in the hazy, inky sky. Like in the Green Zone, light pollution prevails here, and I long to be back in the Blue Zone, staring into the brilliantly clear sky with Nixon. A pang of guilt radiates through me. While I'm now someone else's property, I'm at least making it out of this place. Meanwhile, Nixon will be spending the next six weeks here, potentially enduring more torture and interrogations until his execution date. The thought makes me feel sick.

The building we just exited is only one of many in this secluded compound. From where I'm standing, I can make out four identical structures jutting from the ground, all complete with soldiers standing guard at the entrances. An enormous fence topped with spirals of barbed wire lines the perimeter. Two watchtowers are positioned at the front, one at each corner of the fence, their searchlights slicing through the night.

A limousine awaits us, ready to take me away. The interrogator walks me to it, opens the back door, and shoves me inside, pushing my head down with one hand.

"We'll be keeping an eye on you, Ms. Clearson," he says. "You are in no way immune to re-education or any other form of punishment, should your owners decide to go that route. It would be wise of you to behave."

"Fuck you," I growl just as he slams the door and the darkness settles around me.

The vehicle lurches forward, and the facility, along with who I once was, fades behind me.

27. Wrong Side of Heaven

My cuffs are removed, and I'm greeted by a gentleman who looks to be in his early fifties, dressed in black slacks and an untucked white button-up shirt. His sleeves are pushed up to his elbows, flaunting a dazzling gold watch on his left wrist. He moves aside for me to enter and retrieves a wad of cash from his pocket, handing it to the limo driver before shutting the heavy, black wooden door.

The unnecessarily large house is a beast, ready to consume me. The circular entry room has pristine white walls that extend at least thirty feet up with off-set mounted lights making it appear even larger. Two swooping black staircases are on either side of the room, meeting to form a balcony at the top. A round white rug that looks as though it's never been walked across sits in the center of the dark marble floor.

"I'm happy you made it here safely, Olivia," the man says with half-hearted enthusiasm. His graying hair is coming free of the gel that's holding it in place; a single curl dangles at the top of his forehead. "My name is Carson Everett, Level Three member of the Enlightened Society."

Level Three? I was never aware that there were levels to the Enlightened Society. Throughout school, we were always taught that the Society functioned similarly to the government of the United States. The biggest difference is that instead of having a governor or some sort of leader for each 'state', the President and his or her subordinates all guide and control the Northern Unity as a whole. Each zone follows the same rules and regulations and works together as one. It was always understood—by me at least—that those working beneath the President are equals, aiding in keeping the country and its people safe, informed, and in line.

"So, what, did you buy me because you're one of those old guys who fetishizes young girls?" I ask, ignoring his attempt at a handshake. The amount of venom in my voice surprises me, but he doesn't seem to take any offense to it as I hoped he would.

He howls with laughter that rings through the vaulted room and clamps a hand on my shoulder. I try desperately to shake it off. "No, dear, I didn't purchase you for myself. You're for my son. Unfortunately, he's already retired for the night, but I'm sure he'll be pleased to see you tomorrow."

He starts toward the arched doorway on the left side of the entrance, stopping to look back at me. He doesn't speak but lifts a hand, using a single finger to motion for me to follow him. Less than an arm's length from the front door, I have the urge to swing it open and run as far as my legs can carry me. But the property and neighborhood itself are gated, and now that I've reached my destination, I know my tracker will have been activated. My escape would be short-lived at best, even if this man didn't tackle me the second I stepped outside. So I reluctantly follow.

We walk through a dining room, one far larger than Adam and Lacey's, with white marble floors that complement the long dining table, black walls, and vaulted ceiling. I count twelve simple yet elegant teal upholstered chairs surrounding the table that's already set with plates, cutlery, and two vases holding white roses as if expecting guests this late. The next room is an office lit up by a single floor lamp in the far corner. Black bookshelves line every wall, holding labeled binders and thick books embossed with gold lettering. An executive desk faces the French doors on the opposite side of the room.

Opening one of the doors, Carson leads me outside, beneath the pergola with white pillars on either side that attaches the main residence, to a second, more simplistic house. To our right is the winding, wrap-around cobblestone driveway and manicured front lawn, and to the left is a small, curved balcony that looks out into the back yard and a flight of cobblestone steps that descends to the back of the main house. During the short walk to the second house, Carson fishes a keyring from his pocket. He unlocks the single black door and lets me in, flicking the lights on behind me.

While the house is smaller than the main quarters, it isn't any less pretentious—marble floors, vaulted ceilings, chandeliers, and a curved, grand staircase. The living room is fully furnished and decorated, complete with a white leather couch, a flatscreen TV, and a fireplace surrounded by glossy black tiles.

"This will be your temporary home," Carson says, leading me into the kitchen. "It's not how we usually do things around here, but since you were unable to attend Transitional Adaptation, we're forced to take matters into our own hands."

The island in the center of the kitchen boasts a white marble countertop and black base. A ceramic stove rests in the center, and a stainless-steel pot and pan set hangs above it. Full-length windows look out into the lit backyard decorated with sculpted bushes and trimmed trees. From here, I can make out the edge of the sparkling pool behind the main house.

"What's that supposed to mean?" I ask, no less angrily than when I first spoke to him. It's a persona I picked up during my time with the interrogator—bold and angry. I know it's not who I am at my core, but it's what will help me get through this. One way or another, I *will* make it out of here.

"Nothing barbaric, I assure you," he responds with a grin that shows his perfectly straight, sparkling teeth. "You'll be kept here until we're sure you're… *manageable.*"

Control. They want control. They aim to break me down so I won't fight back or lash out. After being on the run with a resistance leader, they more than likely think I've been corrupted. In a way, I have been. But I wouldn't go back and change it for the world. As the Society itself says, *"Safety and knowledge are the powers that hold this country together."*

"As soon as we're sure you're not a threat to our family dynamic," Carson continues, "you'll be allowed to roam the premises as you please. In the meantime, I want to be sure you're as comfortable as possible, so please don't hesitate to ask for anything."

"So let me go."

He laughs. "Within reason, of course."

He continues with the tour of the house. Aside from the living room and kitchen, the bottom level has a sitting room complete with a pool table and its own television, laundry room, and two bedrooms—each with their own full-size bathroom attached. Upstairs, there's another master suite, an office that looks to never have been used, and a personal library.

"Sleep wherever you like," he says when we stop in the upstairs suite. "Clothes have already been folded and put away for you up here. Be sure to clean yourself up, and I'll send a maid out here tomorrow morning to assist you with your makeup."

Then he leaves without any other parting words, and I stand frozen until I hear the front door close. I remain where I am, count to sixty, then bolt downstairs, coming to a sliding stop at the door. Grabbing the handle, I pull as hard as I can. Of course, it's locked from the outside. A burst of anger explodes within me, and I slam my fist against the wood, then scream in pain and clutch at my now throbbing hand.

I roam the house in search of another exit, but there are none. All of the windows are made with what seems to be reinforced glass and permanently sealed shut. The Roman numeral clock in the living room shows that it's well past midnight. Curfew went into effect over four hours ago. If I am able to escape, night-time will be best; on the way here, I only saw one officer on the streets, whereas in the Green Zone I was lucky to not have come face-to-face with one each time I snuck out. But again, I'm stuck with this tracker, and I wouldn't be surprised if there's security patrolling the property until I'm *manageable.*

In the center of the living room, I stand staring out one of the windows that looks out to the front lawn. Reality strikes me like I've just taken a blow to the gut, and my insides coil up in response. The tears don't start until I'm halfway up the staircase. They come as a trickle, silent and steady. My legs mindlessly carry me throughout the second floor.

I'm a ghost, drifting aimlessly with no real destination. In a sense, I'm safe. No longer am I fleeing one place to seek temporary shelter at another. Soldiers and police aren't hunting me, and I'm not dodging bullets or hiding from tracking dogs. For most people, such a shift would be extremely comforting, but I can't take comfort in this. I can't find comfort in the fact that someone who vowed to protect me is about to be killed or that my brother is out there somewhere without any clue as to what has happened to either of us. I'm living with the very people I've grown to hate, having been purchased like cattle without any free will. This isn't safety.

Safety is with Nixon. With Liam and Addison. Safety is anywhere but the Northern Unity.

I'm alone.

Loneliness has never really bothered me. I've always enjoyed periodically shutting out the world, allowing time for myself without catering to others. But this kind of loneliness is insufferable, far worse than I ever felt during my time at TCG. Unlike then, this is permanent.

The spotlights dotting the bathroom ceiling cast a glare on the dark epoxy floor. An elegant white tub is centered in the room in front of a curved wall that matches the floor. On the other side of the half-wall is a full-sized walk-in shower with two entrances across from each other. There's a single vanity on each side of the room, decorated with fake flowers and odd figurines.

I stop at one of the mirrors above the bowl-shaped sink, hardly recognizing myself. My face is streaked with black trails, and the foundation that was caked on so heavily earlier only remains in small patches. My lips are dry, and I peel away a layer of the thick lipstick that's absorbed into my skin. Stray, unruly hairs poke out of my loose ponytail, some matted to the sides of my face and forehead. I'm shocked that Carson didn't mention anything about my appearance—not that I care what he or anyone else here thinks.

Ripping off my clothes, I turn on the massive shower, struggling at first with the multiple knobs that control everything from temperature to water pressure. The panel on the ceiling delivers a gentle rain directly over the square drain. I cross my arms over my bare chest as I step under it, feeling exposed between the two see-through glass doors and the window at the top of the back wall.

For a while, I just stand under the stream, watching the water run down my chest and pour over my folded arms. With it, my hopes and dreams and my very identity are washed away, sucked down the drain and carried to some long-lost place. I'm a shell of who I once was. On the outside, I look the same for the most part, but inside I'm broken—mangled and beaten. My mind has been pushed to its limits and my spirit is weak.

I always trusted the Society. Not once did I question them or speak out against their policies. Then I learned how deep their roots run, and I know I still don't know all of it. The resistance became my temporary safety net, something I could place my new trust in while navigating this web of deception. But today I learned my father's body was found in Nixon's house, buried beneath the basement floor. Someone I saw as a thoroughly good person turned out to be someone totally different.

I still don't want to believe that to be true. There has to be another explanation, and I rack my exhausted brain for it but can't come up with anything. The interrogator was ready to show me the photos, only warning me that it might be difficult to see. Nixon told as much truth as he could about the Elite Auction, but potentially lied to me about my dad.

He referred to Liam as his second-in-command. I wonder if *he* ever knew anything about this. Liam joined the resistance less than a year ago, but he knew that Nixon was the leader before then, and they were friends a couple of years prior. If Nixon told any of his subordinates about what he did, it would be Liam for the sheer fact that he was closest to him. Or would he? If Liam does know, is he okay with it? If it were anyone else who did the kind of work our dad did, I wouldn't give it a second thought, but this is our *father*. No matter what awful things he did, I can't imagine ever wanting him dead.

I clean myself with the soap provided by the dispensers on the wall, glancing at each of the doors periodically. The prickling feeling similar to when I fled the scene of Elizabeth's murder returns. It begins at the nape of my neck and radiates down my spine. I push it away, telling myself it's the fear of being in a new place and the unknown reason behind being purchased.

That's another part of the auction I didn't get a very in-depth answer to. If I'd asked more questions—the right questions—maybe I'd be more prepared right now. Nixon said anything goes after participants are bought, even the darkest things imaginable.

Another, more powerful wave of tears pours from me. I try to focus on the scalding water and the feeling of cleanliness rather than my thoughts of Nixon and what's awaiting me when I meet Carson's son tomorrow. But nothing can distract me. I can't escape my own thoughts, bombarding me without a way to turn them off. I'm drowning in doubt and heartbreak and fear. They threaten to devour me, and I don't know how to fight back against the relentless current.

Mid-shampoo, I think I hear what sounds like a door closing somewhere up here. I freeze, fingers twisted in my drenched, soapy hair, and listen for it again. A few seconds of silence pass, and I continue washing, frantically scrubbing the suds from my scalp. With an unsteady hand, I turn off the water and jerk a towel from the rack as I exit the shower. Wrapping the towel around my body, I tiptoe into the attached bedroom, thankful for it being one of the few carpeted rooms in the house. I pull some clothes from the dresser and get dressed, tossing the towel onto one of the gray armchairs in the room.

Another door closes just as I pull the pants up to my hips, and I'm positive I didn't imagine it this time. At first, I hope it's Nixon or Liam or even Eli here to break me out, but I immediately realize how stupid that is. Even if one—or all—of them were here, I don't know if I could make myself go with them. Not until I got some answers.

I sneak out of the bedroom, heading for the staircase at the other end of the house. I'm cautious at first, but a third and final door—the front door—shuts and I sprint past the stairs and into the library, stopping only when I reach the window that has a view of the side of the main house. Pulling back one of the semi-sheer curtains, I peek out to see a man sauntering to the mansion. It's not Carson; I can tell by the shaggy brown hair and more casual clothes. He pauses half-way to the house, shoves his hands in his pockets, and looks up in my direction. I jump backward, clamping a hand over my mouth to stifle a shriek, but I know he's seen me.

A few moments pass before I have the courage to look out the window again, and when I do, he's gone. Without thinking about it, I run downstairs, checking every single room for intruders. No one's here, and once again, the house is quiet and empty.

I climb the stairs and drift into the bedroom. The tiny bit of adrenaline from seeing the mystery man quickly dissipates, and all I want to do is curl up in bed and allow my sobs to be absorbed by the night.

With the lights out and blankets wrapped around me like a co-coon, I can pretend I'm actually safe. Deep down, I know I'm not, nowhere near it, but the illusion is enough to dry my eyes and ease the grueling sense of failure. But the aching in my heart won't subside. It's a pain I've never felt before, stronger than any grief I've experienced in the past. My heart feels as though a fist is clenched around it, squeez-ing, slowly tightening its grip.

Like my night at TCG, I imagine myself in a happier place at a happier time. The tactic worked before, but this time it feeds the pain. Against my will, my brain conjures up the memories from the Blue Zone. With Nixon. I extend my left arm out, feeling the cold sheets beside me where I wish, more than anything, his body was. I want him to promise me everything will be okay for the hundredth time. I want to melt into his embrace and forget about everything else.

The more I think about it, the more I hurt, but as painful as it is, I can't stop. It's bittersweet but I don't want it to end. Replaying the memories breaks me even more.

One day I'll rebuild myself, using the shards and fragments of who I once was to create someone new. Someone strong and fearless. It won't be today, and maybe not tomorrow, but one day.

With or without help, I'll make it.

28. Fear of Letting Go

Nightmares haunted me each time I dozed off. I woke up too many times to count with the emptiness inside me reminding me of everything that's happened. After each nightmare, I stared into the darkness, waiting for sleep to wrap itself around me again.

I'm already awake when the maid comes, and have been for a while. She lets herself into the house and announces her presence by knocking on my door and saying, "Ms. Clearson?"

Sitting on the bed with the covers pulled over my legs, I tell her to come in, keeping my eyes straight ahead on the window behind the parted curtains. The late morning sun comes in fragments as clouds sail through the blue sky. I don't look at the maid when she enters and give half a shrug when she asks how I slept. She carries a pink box by its handle into the bathroom and only after her back is to me do I pry my eyes from the window. Through the all-glass bathroom door, I watch as she pulls various items from the box—brushes, tubes of mascara, powders, lotions, and more.

My face hasn't fully recovered from the products that coated it yesterday, and I'm dreading the heavy feeling of even more today. But makeup is the least of my problems right now. Soon, I'll be in the same room as Carson's son and learn why they bought me. Part of me hopes that it's to be a maid or something of the sort. That's a little better than the numerous other things that could be done to me. Since Carson specifically stated I'm for his son, though, I know it's worse.

The maid emerges from the bathroom and goes into the walk-in closet to my right. She pulls out a carnation-pink, cashmere cable-knit sweater and high-rise black jeans, laying them neatly atop the wrinkled blankets.

"I'll step into the hall for you to get dressed," she says, clasping her hands together in front of her. She's wearing a simple black dress that reaches her knees and has her platinum blonde hair swept back into a bun. "Is there anything else I can do for you right now?"

I harden my glare at her. I'm still pulling myself out of the haze that hangs over me from hardly sleeping and refusing to accept my grim reality. But she doesn't accept that as a response and waits, matching my gaze.

"No," I mutter. "Get out."

With a stiff nod, she exits the room, but I know she won't wander far—down the hall at the most—in case I get the idea to escape. She looked at me as if I'm a criminal, someone who doesn't deserve to be here. And I don't *want* to be here. But until I figure something out, I'm stuck. At the very least, I can refuse to cooperate, forcing them to keep me locked away in my own separate dwelling.

They can decorate it as elegantly as they want, offer me the finest of things, but none of that changes the fact that this is a prison. Instead of shackles, I have a device in my arm that tracks every move I make, and rather than soldiers with guns, there are maids with pretty things to cover up the true ugliness of this place. Prison or not, though, I'd rather be in here away from the repulsive people who populate the main house and the rest of this zone. I'd rather die of boredom and heartbreak than play their games. I'm not the same person anymore, but I haven't lost my sense of morality.

Pushing the covers off, I drag myself out of the bed, snatching the clothes up on my way to the bathroom. At the sink that's not cluttered with makeup, I splash my face with cold water in an attempt to wake myself up and wash away the intrusive thoughts that plagued me all night. Despite showering last night, I feel dirty. I have a suspicion the sensation won't go away any time soon.

I take my time changing, tossing the clothes I wore to bed on the floor with the ones I arrived in. Usually, I'm very conscious of keeping my space clean, especially in someone else's home. It's respectful—at least that's what Mom always taught Liam and me—but my respect for these people is nonexistent. The jeans fit perfectly, hugging my legs and hips, as does the sweater. The neckline dips down enough to expose the tops of my collarbones, and the sleeves reach my knuckles.

I'm a bit unnerved at the perfectly fitting clothes. I know it's a small detail that I shouldn't give much thought to, but I can't help it. The interrogator told me VIPs get a first glance at auction participants and may purchase prior to the auction if they choose. I was purchased only an hour after being sold by my mother. No one, not even the Elites, would buy something—or in this matter, *someone*—without knowing what they're getting.

The day I came home from Naomi's, after being chased by a police officer and meeting Nixon for the first time, Mom had that envelope with my name on it. When I asked about it, she said it was just stuff for work, and I believed her, despite her obvious frustration at my asking and how quickly she ripped the envelope from my hands when I picked it up for her. Only now do I put together that it was probably information about me that she was submitting for the auction. I was taken over two weeks later. She'd been planning this for a while—I know that from what Nixon told me. Had I succeeded in prying answers from her that day, I wouldn't be here. I would've at least had some time to get away before the Black Hats showed up, and I know Liam would've helped.

Anything could've been in that envelope. Pictures, definitely. Possibly medical records, school transcripts, and more personal details. They potentially know everything about me, and I know absolutely nothing about them. With Carson being part of the Enlightened Society, an entire organization built upon secrecy, I don't imagine I'll have many questions answered, and what answers I do get probably won't be anchored in truth.

"Ms. Clearson?" the maid calls, knocking on the door.

I go into the bedroom, but don't open the door or say anything to her. I sit at the slender black desk beside the front window, pulling the curtains back and positioning myself so I can look out from the swiveling office chair. The maid can wait out there all day for all I care.

Flashy cars zip up and down the road on the other side of the fence with their glaring red license plates. A woman with a cellphone pressed to her ear walks an obnoxiously loud dog on the sidewalk, leading it to the gated mansion across the street. Most of the front yard is covered in the wide, looping cobblestone path. The six sectioned-off chunks of grass house dormant rose bushes, their bare, wooden limbs twisting up out of the ground like spikes.

Another knock on the bedroom door, and the maid calls my name again.

A black van pulls up to the gate and an arm extends from the driver's window, pressing a button on the entry system's keypad. The driver's arm drops to the side of the door and waits a few moments. I lean forward in the chair, squinting against the bright sun to make out who's in the vehicle. The driver gestures with their hand, leaning closer to the window, but I can't make out any features. The arm retreats inside the van, and the gate slides open, allowing the vehicle through.

The bedroom door swings open, and the maid clears her throat in an annoyed manner. I don't turn around. The van stops in front of the mansion's door, but no one gets out immediately. There's no writing or pictures of any kind on the vehicle, and all of the windows are heavily tinted. Something scrapes against the floor behind me, and the maid grunts as the scraping continues into the bathroom.

"This way, please, Ms. Clearson," she says. When I don't move, she lets out a huff. "Now isn't the time to be stubborn. You don't want to keep Mr. Everett and his son waiting."

"Why's that?" I ask.

"Wyatt is a bit… impatient." That must be the son's name. "So if you could let me do my job…"

No one has got out of the van. I don't know who I'm expecting it to be, but seeing them will put my mind at ease. As far as I know, the only people who live here are Carson and Wyatt, and possibly live-in maids and butlers. There hasn't been any mention of Wyatt's mother, but I assume she's here, too.

"Who are they?" I ask, nodding to the window.

The maid approaches, standing to my right, and peers out at the vehicle. "Probably the new landscaping team the Everetts hired."

"In the winter?"

She turns to me, not interested in the visitors. "They plan ahead for the warmer months. Are you ready?"

Rolling my eyes, I stand and follow her to the bathroom, where she's dragged one of the teal armchairs in front of the makeup-packed vanity. When I sit, she plucks a brush from the counter and begins working it through my hair, which I didn't bother brushing after my shower last night. She mutters something under her breath when the bristles get caught in a knot and jerks violently until it's free, pulling my head to the side with it.

When my hair is free of tangles, she squeezes a white substance from a small black tube onto her fingertips and gently works it into my skin. Then she adds an array of other products, drawing lines on my face with different shades then blending it all together. When she does my eye makeup, she keeps telling me to stop flinching, keep my eyes open, and to look up.

"Why are you here?" I ask when she's in the middle of swiping my eyelashes with the curved mascara wand.

"I work here," she says flatly, and switches to the other eye.

"But why?"

"To make money."

I roll my eyes and she tells me to stop moving again.

"So you're here by choice?" I ask.

"Yes."

"And you're okay with what they do?"

She steps back, inspecting me. "What they do is none of my business. You're here because they wanted you, and you're lucky they didn't withdraw after everything."

Leaning in again, she makes some adjustments to my bottom lashes, then turns her back to me.

"So you've heard about me," I say, twisting the sleeve of my sweater around my thumb.

"Everyone has. You were all over the news."

"Is that all you know? What you heard on the news, I mean."

She spins around with a pink compact container and another makeup brush. Tapping the brush against the inside of the container, she dusts the powder along the tops of my cheekbones and the bridge of my nose. "I know you were running around with that terrorist."

"He's not a terrorist," I insist, but I know I'm wasting my breath. Elites will believe whatever they want. Nixon is only a terrorist in their eyes because he's a threat to their perverse activities.

Turning to the counter, she packs up the makeup, slamming the box shut. "I'll let them know you're ready. Wait downstairs." She leaves, not waiting for me to follow, and I wait for the sound of the front door closing before standing up.

My makeup is much more elaborate than it was before the auction. Illuminating powder makes my skin appear brighter. The lines that were drawn and blended onto my face make my features more prominent, and the eyeliner flares out in sharp wings rather than the basic black lines that were drawn on yesterday.

When I went to rescue Nixon, he told me I looked beautiful, and recalling those words brings me both joy and grief. I wonder if he'd find me beautiful now. I wonder if he's thought about me as much as I've thought about him, if he misses me as much as I miss him.

Guilt settles in my gut like a ton of rocks. I feel awful for doubting him after what the interrogator told me. Murderer or not, I don't have any solid proof either way. I've trusted Nixon up to this point, and he's never let me down, so what's wrong with trusting him a little longer? The Society isn't exactly honest. Trusting the person who put his life on the line in an attempt to protect me seems more logical than believing those who kidnap and bid on innocent people. It could be that I'm allowing my emotions to cloud my judgment, but that's something I can worry about after I get answers from him. I *will* see him again.

I make it downstairs just as Carson enters with a man trailing behind him. Carson grins when I reach the last step and says, "Olivia! I hope you slept well. This is my son, Wyatt."

I have a snarky comment prepared for him, but lose the words when I focus on Wyatt, standing off to the side. His shaggy brown hair curls around his ears, brushing the corners of his sharp jaw. He looks older than me, maybe even a couple of years older than Liam and Nixon. He's dressed in ironed khakis and a light blue button-up shirt with the top two buttons undone.

"You," I say. "You were here last night."

His face remains emotionless, careless. Carson follows my gaze to his son, then looks back to me.

"You came in here," I say. "I heard you when I was in the shower. And I saw you walking back to your house."

"I have no idea what you're talking about," he says. His voice comes from deep within his chest and carries no emotion. His callous green eyes snap to his father. "So this is her?"

Carson nods. "What do you think?"

Wyatt walks toward me with his hands folded behind his back, circling me as though I'm his prey. Stopping in front of me, he takes a lock of my hair between two of his fingers, sliding them down to the end then shoving the hand in his pocket.

"She looked prettier in her pictures."

I clench my fists, resisting the urge to punch him in his nose.

"Will she work or not?" Carson asks, hardly masking his irritation. "We don't have much time left."

Wyatt smirks, keeping his eyes trained on me. "She'll work."

"What do you mean I'll 'work'?" I ask. "What am I here for?"

Carson and Wyatt exchange a look, and Carson nods as if answering his son's unspoken question or request.

"You were purchased to be my wife," Wyatt says nonchalantly.

"Excuse me?" I demand.

I'm expected to *marry* this poor excuse of a human? To be a part of this family?

Family is something I have always valued above all else. I may only have one person left from mine, but there's no way I would ever want to be part of the disgusting, immoral, corrupted individuals connected to this person. My skin crawls just at the thought of it. I've been purchased to practically be his slave, no matter how much they try to play it up by sticking the label '*wife*' on it. I'll have no control over what's done to me, and despite Wyatt's remark about my appearance, his eyes linger on my body in a way that makes my skin crawl.

Tears spring to my eyes. This feels like a betrayal to Nixon. It's not my fault, I know that, but it doesn't change the fact that I'm here with another man, one who probably expects all of the physical components of a relationship. Forcing myself to go along with it would kill me, and destroy Nixon, if he were to find out. My heart shatters, imagining that as the last thing on his mind before he's killed.

Not only that, but marrying Wyatt would, by default, make me part of the Enlightened Society in some way, and they'll almost certainly expect me to play a part in their work. I'm used to working in a family business, but selling flowers isn't exactly the same as trafficking humans.

"You're fortunate compared to what happens to others who are purchased," Carson chimes in.

"I am not marrying you," I say. "You can take whatever idea you have and shove it up your entitled ass."

Wyatt's already stiff face hardens even more, and his palm collides with my cheek. The sound rings through the room, and a searing pain explodes in the side of my face. Concentrating all of my rage toward him, toward this moment, I hurl my fist at him, hoping to land a decent punch somewhere on his face. But he catches my wrist mid-swing, twisting my arm. His eyes are wild and hungry.

"I forgot," he snarls, "you're that rebel boy's whore." He releases my arm, shoving me backward, and smiles. "Too bad *he* wasn't for sale. I'd love to bleed him out myself."

"I'd love to see him do the same to you," I spit back. "For someone who's supposed to be a terrorist, *he* never laid a hand on me."

"That's enough, Olivia!" Carson says. "You'll realize we did you a favor by selecting you at some point, and for your sake, I hope you come around sooner rather than later."

The interrogator threatened me with re-education, but since I'm considered the Everetts' property, they can do far worse to me. The Elites are above the law, and they know that. I can't be Wyatt's wife if I'm dead, but I'm sure his father would find him another victim.

"She goes by Ivy," Wyatt says, staring me down. When I open my mouth to ask how he knows that, he cuts me off by adding, "I read your file. Lots of interesting things in there."

"Let's go," Carson says, placing a hand on his son's shoulder. "She needs more time."

Wyatt lingers a moment longer before following his father outside, and I'm locked inside my prison again.

Day two. Depression has made a home in my head. It steals my will to live, and I find myself lying on the couch, staring blankly at the images flashing on the TV screen. Every so often, I switch to the news in hopes of hearing something about Liam or Nixon. I long to see their faces, even if it's just a picture displayed with whatever lies the Society wants to spew about them. But there's nothing. No mention of the execution or whether Liam and Addison have been found.

Liam never mattered to the Society; I knew that from the beginning. Broadcasting his absence was a ploy to get an insight on my whereabouts, and Nixon was essentially a bonus prize that came with my capture. As the day of his death draws closer, they'll probably run a full segment on him, making it out as though the Enlightened Society caught him on their own after retrieving me. There won't be any mention of Nixon saving me and smuggling me into the Blue Zone. That would make the resistance appear organized and powerful, something the Society has spent so long masking. They'll make up something about him being careless, allowing them to catch on. They'll discredit him and everything he and the rest of the resistance have done.

Day three. Grief has stolen my appetite. I've forced myself to eat bits of food here and there, but too much makes me sick. The maid returned to do some light cleaning, acting as though I wasn't here as she glided throughout the house. Other than her, I haven't seen anyone. Neither Carson nor Wyatt have checked on me, and I'm not sure if I should be relieved or bothered by their absence. Their goal is to break me down, to destroy any hope I have of returning to the world outside this gated property. I'm not sure I have any hope left… but there's something inside me, a tiny whisper, that says there's still a chance. There's a chance I can pull myself out of this.

I thought Nixon and I were different in the sense that he was a fighter and I was a survivor—barely. But he was pushed out of his comfort zone long ago, and that forced him to be who he is today. This is my push, although it feels more like I've been forcefully dragged while desperately clinging to my blissful ignorance. Surviving isn't enough anymore. Complacency won't help me. Acting stubborn and bratty isn't getting me anywhere—even though that's exactly what these people deserve. They know that game, and they know I'll eventually crack under their force. It's best to play along, win them over and work from there.

If I can orchestrate some sort of plan to get out of here before Nixon's execution date, there's hope that I can see him again. Part of me knows if I do this, I'm opening myself up to all kinds of abuse by being so close to Wyatt, but I'm willing to endure it if it means I don't have to spend the rest of my life with him—if it means I can be free and be with the person I truly, deeply care for.

So when the maid returns on the fourth day with shopping bags stuffed with new clothes, I tell her I'm ready and want to speak with Wyatt again.

Wyatt doesn't come, though. Not on the fifth or the sixth day either, and I'm tempted to withdraw my offer the next time I see someone.

Day seven. The maid arrives, bursting into my room after my shower with her collection of makeup. I'm clutching the towel around myself when she enters the bathroom. She sets the box on one of the counters and disappears into the walk-in closet, returning with a long-sleeved, pink silk dress with a dark pink belt around the cinched waist. Stepping into the bedroom, she turns her back to the glass door for me to get dressed, then begins on my makeup.

I don't ask questions this time, though I have hundreds burning inside me. She doesn't say anything to me either—other than that she's happy I'm "coming to my senses". When she's finished, I force a smile and thank her for her help in my politest voice. Packing up her belongings, she leads me downstairs and instructs me to wait down here.

Ten minutes pass as I pace the living room, constantly checking the slowly ticking clock on the wall. I run countless things I could say to Wyatt through my head, from introductions to apologies. My prevalent hatred toward him and specifically what he said about Nixon invades my thoughts, stifling the few positive lines I've thought up. Whatever I say, the key is sounding believable, keeping my tone light and optimistic.

The door opens when I'm halfway to the kitchen and I spin around to look at Wyatt, surprised he's not accompanied by his father.

"You wanted to see me?" he asks, seemingly uninterested. For someone who's supposed to be getting married to the girl of his choosing, he doesn't act the least bit excited. His frigid demeanor terrifies me. How am I supposed to do this? I don't know what he's capable of or how far he's willing to go to get what he wants from me.

Nixon may have been cold toward me at first, but he was nowhere near as abrasive or violent. He had real feelings and an authentic personality underneath his hard exterior, whereas Wyatt only has money to throw at people in hopes of getting what he wants.

"I think I'm ready," I say. "I'm sorry for the way I acted a few days ago."

"You realize you'll never see that terrorist again, right? He's getting what he deserves."

My anger takes the form of a flame, crawling up my throat and burning at the tip of my tongue. I can't extinguish it, but swallow it back down, promising myself I'll unleash it and incinerate him when the time is right.

I nod, painting a smile on my face. "He manipulated me. I didn't realize it until now."

Wyatt walks toward me, stopping about five feet away. "This doesn't mean we trust you yet."

"I understand."

"You'll remain here until you can prove yourself to us—mostly me."

"I understand," I repeat, conscious of keeping my body language soft and not defensive.

"Come with me," he says. "My mother wants to begin the wedding planning."

Placing a hand on the small of my back, he guides me outside underneath the pergola, and I drink up the fresh air and warm sun. I've made it out of my prison, even if it's only temporary.

From this moment on, I'll think and act like a member of the resistance, gathering as much information on this family and the Society as possible while getting on their good side. That's the only benefit of being purchased by this family: I'll have all of their secrets at my fingertips.

The truth is ugly. It's a demon with razor-sharp teeth and talons that will shred you to bloody little pieces. Their lies are shrouded in beauty, attractive and believable to the average person. But with time, the people blind to the Society's transgressions will witness that pretty layer being ripped away, revealing the demon that's coming for them, too.

29 Nixon: The End Is Where We Begin

I've been beaten, tortured, and isolated for over a month. These four stone walls have become my home. I've forgotten how it feels to have the sun warm my skin or the wind whip against my face. Fresh air and human interaction are distant memories. The only time I've been released from solitary was when I endured grueling interrogations and the torture that followed from my lack of cooperation.

Aside from interrogators and soldiers, Eli is the only person I've seen, and his visits are sparse. It's a damn miracle he hasn't been found out yet. He's been doing this for over a decade, but this is the largest setback to the resistance since he's joined. The Society is monitoring everyone closely—more than usual—and Eli isn't immune to it.

He and Piper have split the responsibility of leading my group in the Green Zone, communicating mostly by radio and sometimes sending scouts from their own groups to check in. They're all safe, including Liam and Addison, who made it back home after the ambush. Liam did exactly what I always told him to do in a situation such as that one, and for that, I'm genuinely proud. As my former second-in-command, he should be stepping up to fill my position, but Eli doesn't think he's ready since he's never been out in the field, in the middle of action. I argued that Liam has the brains to pull it off, but Eli refused to hear me out.

For now, my group is lying low until this blows over. No missions have been carried out since my capture, and missions that were active at the time were abandoned. That leaves the largest resistance group in the country dormant, and I know the Commander probably isn't happy with that. Eli never told me how the Commander responded to my failed mission and our capture, but I can guess that it was similar to—if not worse than—when I had to tell him my group lost Liam.

After the auction, rumors spread of Ivy turning me in, along with everyone she's met in the resistance. A guard was the first to inform me of the rumors, saying she was seen by multiple people walking out of the facility with an interrogator after being questioned. I didn't want to believe it. It wouldn't be the first time someone I'd grown close to turned on me, but I had faith in Ivy. When I asked Eli about it, he said she *was* escorted out by her interrogator, but could neither confirm nor deny whether she sold us out. If she had, though, Eli wouldn't be here anymore, or he'd be locked up like I am. So I let the soldiers and interrogators spew all the bullshit they wanted. I know the truth.

If this had been a few weeks ago, I wouldn't be surprised if Ivy turned us all in. She was so naïve, happy to live her lie and kiss the Society's ass, but that's not who she is anymore. Watching her grow in such a short period of time was amazing. The more she opened up to me, the more she learned to trust me, and I let myself trust her, too. It started out just as me sharing little pieces of myself to make her more comfortable, but it escalated as I realized how easy she was to talk to. She listened to my every word, absorbed every piece of information I shared. Not because she *had* to, like my members, but because she wanted to. She offered comfort when I didn't even realize I needed it. I was the one offering comfort, reassurance, and safety in the beginning, and she reciprocated in a different but genuine way.

I trusted and cared for her in a way I've never felt for anyone else before, and I don't regret that for a second. What I do regret is not being able to keep my promise to her. After everything, we still got caught, and I have this powerful intuition telling me it was because of Kase.

It doesn't help that no one can get in contact with Ivy. No one in the resistance knows where she was taken or how she's holding up after all of this. All we know is that she had already been claimed by a private buyer before she was taken to TCG. Even if we had a location, it's not like a squad could storm the place. Our hands are tied after a victim is purchased and taken to their permanent destination. Not only is it dangerous to those who would be carrying out the operation—more so than what we usually do—but it could potentially bring down the entire resistance if the Society were able to trace them back to their leader or the Commander. Like me, Ivy is trapped. At the very least, I want someone to let her know that I'm sorry.

The metal door screeches open, and Eli enters with a defeated look on his face.

"Already?" I ask, standing from my cot.

He nods, walking farther into the tiny cell, and glances over his shoulder before saying in a hushed tone, "I have a plan in place. We are not letting you die today."

"I'm afraid this is out of your control."

"Don't doubt me, Nixon. You're forgetting I have the most skilled group in the Northern Unity and the most influence over the Commander. Your group is aware as well."

"Don't drag them into this. They have enough to deal with."

The military invaded the Green Zone after Ivy and I were captured and will remain there following my execution in case there's an uprising. Public execution only happens in the Yellow Zone, and a while back, President Hoffman promised we weren't going to adopt their form of punishment. So far, there hasn't been any sort of protest that Eli has heard of, but the Society is taking whatever precautions they feel are necessary.

"You're their leader," he says, "and they care about you just as much as you care about them. They need you."

"Liam should've already stepped up."

"Liam is not ready!" He looks over his shoulder again, checking for any passing guards. "Even if he were, it wouldn't matter, because we're not letting them kill you."

"Any word on Ivy?"

"We still don't have a location—and may never get one—but word is she'll be marrying her buyer's son in a couple of weeks."

"God damn it." Eli doesn't know anything about what happened between Ivy and me. I'm sure he heard about our kiss before the auction and her outburst after my execution was announced, but I never confirmed any of it with him and he never asked. One great thing about Eli is that he's not one to pry. "You have to get her out of there."

"You know we can't—"

"Just *try*." I hate that she's there. I hate myself for not being able to protect her. I can't imagine how scared she must be right now, trapped somewhere as someone's property, let alone being forced to marry a pawn within the Society. The thought of someone else kissing her, touching her, calling her his wife… it sickens me. No one deserves that, but especially not Ivy. I don't know exactly what there is between us, but I know I want to be the one doing all of that with her. "Please. She doesn't deserve to be there."

"I'll see what I can do, but I can't promise you anything." He pulls me into a quick hug, mindful of the wounds all over me that have just begun to heal.

"It's been great working with you, Eli," I say.

"And I'm excited to continue working with you," he says.

I don't argue. He can believe whatever he wants if that helps soften the blow of reality. I'm not going to take that away from him. He's the most optimistic out of all of the resistance leaders. Maybe it's because he works so closely with the Commander and feels he can achieve anything with the extra help… but being too optimistic gets you into trouble.

"They're finishing their preparations for your trip to the Green Zone," he says. "Someone will be in soon to retrieve you."

I nod. "Thank you for everything."

He turns and walks toward the door, holding himself with confidence. "See you on the other side, my friend. Good luck."

The door screeches shut, and I collapse onto my cot and wait for my angel of death to come for me. The single lightbulb dangling from the moldy ceiling casts eerie shadows throughout the cell. After six weeks here, my eyes still haven't grown accustomed to the pockets of darkness. They've played tricks on me, showing me things that aren't there. My past hides in them, revealing itself as ghostly fragments during my days of sleep-deprivation and starvation. My memories have played out before my eyes, from childhood up to the present. It's mainly the bad stuff that haunts me.

The door opens again, and two soldiers storm the cell, jerking me up by my arms. One shoves me against the wall, binding my hands behind my back. Then, a soldier on either side of me—hands gripping my arms—I'm propelled out of my cell and through the halls. The eyes of all the other guards outside my cell are on me as I'm ushered through the building. Hushed voices circulate around me, and I'm able to pick up on a few of their words.

"*Terrorist… He deserves to die… Murderer…*"

Just before we reach the back exit of the building, I catch Eli talking to another nurse a few feet away. His eyes lock with mine, and he gives me a small nod before I'm hauled through the double doors.

A helicopter awaits on the landing pad at the rear of the compound. Its blades whip furiously, slicing through the air, ready to take me back to the Green Zone. My group will be there, I'm sure of that. They're the most loyal people I've met, and as much as it will wound them watching my life be taken, I know they won't allow me to endure it alone. That's comforting in a way, but also humiliating. What kind of leader am I if I couldn't save myself? How did they ever trust me to protect them?

None of that matters now. I can pity myself and my group all I want, but that doesn't change what's happening. I accepted my fate the second it was announced at the auction. I've made friends with death, and I know it will welcome me with open arms.

I just hope my sister isn't there. Watching me die will destroy Piper. As far as I know, our parents are gone. Their whereabouts have been kept hidden, and if Eli knows anything about them, he hasn't told me. Piper and I were close before Adam and Lacey took me in. She was always like a sister to me and she always considered me her brother. If Adam and Lacey are dead, I'm all she has left, and soon I'll be taken away from her, too.

The whipping of the blades is deafening as I'm loaded into the helicopter and strapped in. A hollow pit opens in my stomach. This is it. I'm returning home to die.

The one thing I can take pride in is that I didn't tell the Society a damn thing. Unlike Kase, I didn't break under their torture. My group and every other resistance member is safe, both inside and outside of the Northern Unity. Ivy was right. I'm stronger than I give myself credit for.

The downtown streets are crowded with hundreds of onlookers. They yell and cheer when I exit the helicopter, escorted by the two soldiers. But they're not cheers of adoration or support. They're hungry for my blood. Barricades have been set up to block off the execution site and keep the crowd at bay, making a clear path for me to walk. People wave flags, and banners with the Enlightened Society's emblem—an owl surrounded by a circle of thirteen white stars—are draped over the front of the barricades.

At the end of the makeshift aisle, where the city opens up to a more rural area, a wooden stake juts from the ground with a base constructed of straw and planks of wood. Another soldier waits beside it, rope in hand and eyes of stone focused on me, and a small gang of Elites is positioned behind him, far enough away not to be injured during my execution. They've chosen to burn me at the stake, a barbaric form of execution once used in the Old World to punish those found guilty of heresy, blasphemy, and treason. But the truth isn't treason, and I can only hope that one day these ignorant citizens will see that.

I keep my gaze forward, ignoring the slurs being yelled at me and the spit that coats my skin every few feet. Along the way, I spot a few of my members. Sebastien and Isaac are pressed against one of the barricades halfway up the aisle. I can make out Jonah's fiery red hair toward the front, and the more I search, the more of my men I see. The only one I can't find is Liam, but I don't blame him for not being here.

When I reach the end, one of the soldiers removes my shoes and socks and shoves me forward, forcing me against the stake. He turns me around, pressing my back against the splintery wood, and the soldier with the rope moves behind me, removing my cuffs. One strand of rope is pulled tight around my chest and biceps, another around my calves, and a final piece is fastened around my wrists behind me.

The soldiers grab the two blue five-gallon containers that are off to the side. Twisting off the black caps, they begin circling me, dousing my clothes and the materials beneath my feet with what smells like kerosene. The potent odor burns my eyes and nose, and I try not to squirm at the chemicals eating into my wounds. When the soldiers have thoroughly soaked me and my immediate surroundings, they take their place in front of the mob over fifty feet away.

President Hoffman emerges from the group of Elites and stands in front of me with a microphone in her hand. The crowd erupts with excitement when they see her, waving their flags and shouting words of praise. Once they calm down, she starts off by welcoming them and thanking them for their generous contributions in order to attend this *eventful day*.

"This is a difficult day for the Green Zone," she says, and I can hear the feigned sympathy in her shrill voice. "These criminals only care about one thing: Destroying. They want to destroy everything you and the Enlightened Society have worked for. None of us wanted an execution to take place here today, but let it be known that traitors like this will be prosecuted to the fullest extent of the law."

I roll my eyes, and can't help but smile at her bullshit. The crowd cheers, but a few of my members at the front remain poised.

"I assure you," she says, "that we are searching diligently for anyone else who may be tied to this despicable terrorist behind me, and they, too, will be brought to justice. We will not rest until every single one of them is captured and has faced the same fate. Until then, raids will continue at random, and anyone suspected to have connections with any terrorist organizations will be detained. Again, I want to thank you—not only for gathering out here today, but for showing your undying support for the Enlightened Society."

The crowd roars, shouting words of love and support for the snake as she returns to her group of Elites. From the other end of the aisle, two men dressed in all white start toward me—one in front of the other, the man at the back carrying a rod with a wick at the top. The crowd falls silent, everyone's attention on the executioner making his way toward me. I've never heard this city so quiet, like everyone is collectively holding their breath. The only ones who keep their eyes trained on me are my members, unmoving and seemingly unfazed.

On the inside, I'm fucking terrified—not of death itself, but of the method that's been chosen for me. But on the outside, I force myself to appear strong, as I always have for my team. Holding my head high, I scan the crowd, making eye contact with every single member I spot. Some keep their expressions solid and unreadable, but others offer a remnant of a smile or a nod. The ones closer to the front mouth something I can't read.

The men stop at the empty space between the crowd and me, and the one in front turns around, lighting the wick of the torch before retreating. The executioner moves forward with slow, calculated steps. I train my glare on him and death flashes in his eyes, mocking me. Ten feet from me, he stops, raising the torch from the ground, and extends his arm, preparing to drop the flame onto the kerosene-soaked base.

I suck in one final breath, locking my eyes on him and saying my silent apologies to my group, my parents, my sister… and Ivy. Even though I won't be able to witness it, I hope Eli keeps his promise and tries to get her out of that hellhole.

A crack rips through the blanket of tense silence. Everyone freezes, including the executioner, who turns to face the crowd, pulling the torch away with him. Heads whip in every direction in search for the source of the sound. There's a second crack, and a hole splits open in the executioner's chest. He drops the torch, clutching his injury as he crumples to the ground.

Three. Four. Five.

Screams pierce the air, and waves of people break past the barricades like a tsunami. Soldiers have their weapons drawn but hold their fire as they push their way into the frenzy of people, unsure of where the continuous gunshots are coming from and not wanting to shoot at innocent bystanders.

The torch has fallen just a few feet diagonal from my pedestal, but the flame reaches out, desperate to make contact with me. I struggle against my restraints as something pulls on them behind me. A blade cuts into the heel of my hand before the rope falls from my wrists.

I can't see any of my members now. Bodies and faces morph into one giant wall of panic.

The rope comes away from my chest and legs, and I'm yanked from the flammable materials and the stake. Looking up, I expect to come face-to-face with a soldier who's taking me away until they get a handle on this situation, but instead I'm greeted by a familiar, smiling face that I've never been so thankful to see before.

"You really thought we were going to let you die?" Liam asks as we push our way through the bodies trying to seek safety from the ongoing gunshots. He tosses me a jacket that I quickly pull on, stuffing my hair inside the hood as we run. I don't know where we're going or what his plan is, but I trust him no matter what.

The Elites have fled. Not a single one of the cowards are in sight.

"Jesus fucking Christ, I love you guys," I say between gasps, breathing in the kerosene that weighs down my clothes.

I had come to terms with my fate. Today I was supposed to be a martyr, a symbol for the rest of the resistance—but martyrs must die.

And I am very much alive.

End of Book One

Counter Ops: Book 2
Coming 2021

Acknowledgments

To my husband, Martin: Thank you for believing in me and relentlessly encouraging me to follow my dreams. Thank you for not allowing me to give up when I wrongly told myself I couldn't do it. I can't express how grateful I am for your help when I asked for it and the many nights you stayed up reading my drafts and talking about everything *Pretty Lies* for hours on end. Thank you for being my alpha reader, cover artist, formatter, web designer, and my number one fan. I love you so much, and this book would not exist without constant love and support.

To my editor, Emma: Thank you for taking on my manuscript and helping me fine-tune my story and voice. You have made the entire editing process much less daunting than I feared it would be. Not only are you a phenomenal editor, but you're an amazing friend! You're sweet, selfless, talented, and absolutely hilarious. I am so thankful to have you in my life, and I can't wait to work with you on *Counter Ops*!

To my critique partner, Riley: Thank you for all of your insight, suggestions, outstanding feedback, and critical eye during my rewrites! Your perspective and creativity helped me take this story to a whole new level and fill in all of the gaps. Thank you for taking the time to read over my entire imperfect manuscript and rereading sections after I had made even more changes. I've absolutely loved working with you on each other's stories and I'm excited to have you on board with book two!

To all of the talented members of Written By Wolves: Thank you for creating music. So many of your songs played a role in shaping this plot, and without hearing your song, "Pretty Lies," I may have never picked up this manuscript again. And from the bottom of my heart, thank you for being so incredibly generous and giving me permission to use your lyrics at the beginning of this novel.

To my mother-in-law, Margi: Like your son, thank you for pushing me to follow my dreams and encouraging me throughout the entire writing and publishing process, and thank you for supporting me and treating me as if I'm your own. You read *Pretty Lies* when it was a rough draft that was riddled with errors, but you saw my potential and didn't let me give up! And thank you so much for being such an incredible artist and bringing my characters to life with their portraits! I love you!

To my readers: Thank you for supporting me by reading this book. Parts of this novel are raw pieces of myself that I'm happy to be sharing with you, and I'm so thankful that you've decided to follow me on this journey! Reading (and writing) was always an escape for me, a way for me to block out whatever chaos was surrounding me. I hope that my stories, whether they're in the *Pretty Lies* universe or not, can be an escape for you, too.